Killed in the Act

By William L. DeAndrea

KILLED IN THE ACT
THE LUNATIC FRINGE
THE HOG MURDERS
KILLED IN THE RATINGS

Killed in the Act

WILLIAM L. DeANDREA

PUBLISHED FOR THE CRIME CLUB BY

DOUBLEDAY & COMPANY, INC.

GARDEN CITY, NEW YORK

1981

All of the characters in this book
are fictitious, and any resemblance
to actual persons, living or dead,
is purely coincidental.

Library of Congress Cataloging in Publication Data

DeAndrea, William L.
Killed in the act.
I. Title.
PS3554.E174K5   813'.54
ISBN 0-385-17824-7   AACR2

First Edition

Library of Congress Catalog Card Number 81-43259

*For Christine and Steve Teter, without whom
it wouldn't have been.*

I don't expect you to believe any of this. I lived through it, and I had trouble believing it myself. It was a long time before I even let DeAndrea see it; he says it's silly to expect anyone to believe it—it's all too ridiculous. And he's right, it is ridiculous. Maybe that's why it hurt so much.

—Matt Cobb

Killed in the Act

CHAPTER 1

"Live! From New York!"

—CHEVY CHASE, "NBC SATURDAY NIGHT," NBC

When I walked into the commissary for lunch that day, I thought the only thing I had left to do with the Network's fiftieth anniversary celebration was sit back and watch it happen. "Sight, Sound, & Celebration" was going to be a weekend-long extravaganza featuring half a century of American pop culture, as shown by the Network's radio and television programming. There would be two full days of old shows being presented, appreciated, and discussed in depth. Then, to top it off, the Network was devoting six hours of Sunday night prime time to a super-sized birthday party, presented live from Studio J in this very building.

"SS&C" was to feature "more superstars than one could imagine in one place at one time"—unquote, Salvatore Ritafio, Vice-president, Public Relations. I'd seen the guest list, and it looked as though this might be one show that actually lived up to its hype.

There had been a time when I might have been one of the small army of people trying to see that it did, but not any more. My work for the Network wasn't done in studios any more. All I had on my agenda was lunch.

Which wasn't something to be rushed into. The fourth-floor commissary is such a dingy, noisy little place, it's hard to believe it's stuck in the heart of the Network's modernistic skyscraper. Furthermore, the food is terrible. The meat loaf tastes like it was fabricated from something they swept from the floor, and the roast pork is better left undiscussed.

There's no obvious reason for the food to be so bad, it just is. What makes it worse is the knowledge that down in the lobby is one of New York's finest restaurants (also owned by the Network).

Still, the Accounting department can show you just how big a profit this den of dyspepsia rakes in during your average year. It's peanuts to the Network, of course, but for a cafeteria, it's astronomical.

It prospers because they bring the tourists to it. The tourists, having shelled out three seventy-five for a tour of the building, are willing to put up with a mystery-meat sandwich and lukewarm Coke for the chance to eat near a Real Live Actor. The actors, being actors, are glad to oblige.

The only trouble is, there are fewer actors around all the time. Except for a couple of soap operas and game shows, everything is being produced out in California these days. Network sages viewed the fact that "SS&C" was being done here in the Big Apple as nothing short of a miracle. Rumor had it that the mayor himself had pleaded with Tom Falzet, president of the Network, to do the show here to bring the town some much-needed positive publicity. Whatever the reason, Falzet, who usually wrote turgid memos to complain about the excessive use of toilet paper in the washrooms, had authorized the expenditure of large sums of money to fly that unimaginable quantity of talent to New York from their Los Angeles poolsides.

It happened that a Los Angeles poolside was the subject of a lot of the lunch-time conversation I overheard as I slid my tray past what was laughingly called "food."

Three different sets of people were talking about the murder of Jim Bevic. The conversations weren't exactly loaded with facts—all any of us in New York knew was that he'd been found three days ago floating in somebody's pool, and that the police there called it murder. Nothing else had been released to the panting public, or if it had, it hadn't worked its way East yet. No doubt the LAPD was saving details for its own reasons.

People made do, though, despite the lack of facts. Two secretaries from Accounting were telling each other what a tragedy it was. One said, how terrible, such a good writer, and only thirty years old. The other said, don't be silly, he had to be thirty-three if he was a day, but at least it was lucky he wasn't married.

It usually makes me a little uneasy to hear about people roughly the same age as I am dying violent deaths. I had the feeling this time, too, but it was mixed with puzzlement over why an unmarried murder victim was luckier than a married one.

I was still thinking about it when I was distracted by the weatherman from Channel 10 News. Channel 10, a local station, is owned and operated by the Network, and has its studios in NetHQ (short for Network International Headquarters, the building's official name). The weatherman, who had pretensions to Science, was speculating on the condition the body must have been in when it was found Sunday after having marinated in chlorinated water overnight. Then he started speculating on the condition the body would have been in if it hadn't been found until today, Wednesday.

For the first time, I was happy I was eating at the commissary. Anywhere else, talk like that would have dampened my enthusiasm for a meal. Here, it didn't much matter.

A few tables farther down, the producer of a Sunday afternoon public affairs interview show was sitting up very tall and declaiming, ostensibly to his assistant, but really to the room at large, that Jim Bevic's book, *Fellow Travelers*, had been the absolute final word on McCarthyism, witch hunts, and especially the broadcasting blacklist, of the fifties, the one that had effectively, but unofficially, barred anyone from working in the industry unless he could prove lifelong revulsion with everything Russian, from dancing bears to salad dressing.

I had read *Fellow Travelers*—more than once—and I agreed it was a terrific book, but I felt obliged to point out to the guy that it was obviously not the last word, since he himself seemed to have plenty left. He made indignant noises, but some of the tourists at neighboring tables applauded me, so he gave up.

I paid a bored, just-short-of-surly register girl for my meal, such as it was, then scanned the room for Llona's dark, glossy head.

She was sitting in the far corner, doing her best by a plate of limp lettuce some optimist in the kitchen had called a salad. Llona was a vegetarian. She waved a slender hand to me, and I went over to join her.

"What was that all about?" she asked.

I told her. She grinned, and shook a fork with two bent tines at me. "I've been warned about you, Matt Cobb. I know all about your English-teacher mentality. But if you start correcting my press releases, I'll beat you to death with your own dictionary."

"Look," I said, "don't get the wrong impression. I'm not a Mad Grammarian, lopping off heads for split infinitives—I've been known to occasionally be guilty of that myself." She caught the joke and smiled. I went on. "To quote Kin Hubbard: 'It ain't ignorance that's the problem, it's folks knowing so many things that ain't so.' That's my gripe. I get peeved at people, especially people who are supposed to be in the communications business, who make stupid mistakes in the attempt to convince people they're important."

"My," she breathed, "you sound *important*." She had a low, full-throated laugh. She sounded good.

"You're evil, Llona," I told her.

She batted her eyelashes. "I try," she said. She didn't look bad, either. Llona Hall was occasionally taken for an actress by some of the tourists, but what she was was a middle-level executive in the Public Relations department. She had the same kind of aura a lot of stars have: all ambition and dedication, with just a *touch* of ruthlessness. For her, her status today was just something she had to put up with till tomorrow.

Llona had shiny black hair, worn shoulder length and curled under. She had long bangs, parted in the middle, and curving back along her forehead like a curtain going up, to show her big chocolate-brown eyes with their long black lashes.

Her nose was small and slightly pugged; not nearly enough to be unattractive. Her skin was clear and healthy; beautiful, like snow and roses. If she wore any makeup besides bright red lipstick on her wide mouth, it wasn't discernible. She had regular white teeth, and she dealt with the lettuce in a way that was far from dainty, but still ladylike.

Llona wasn't a big girl; she was about a foot shorter than I was, making her five-two or -three. She was wearing a green turtleneck blouse, with a gold medallion on a chain, a flaring plaid skirt, and practical two-inch wedge shoes. The outfit was modest and sexy at the same time. The skirt accentuated the way her hips swelled from a narrow waist, and the turtleneck followed the curve of breasts that a purist would probably have said were too large for her frame.

I, however, was not a purist, and it seemed to me if anything could make a success of a lunch of one salty hot dog on a soggy bun with watery mustard and relish, having someone like Llona across the table to look at was it.

She waited until I had bitten off a piece of hot dog, chewed and swallowed, before her impatience showed.

"Well? How did you make out?"

I was working on a second bite. I showed her a polite palm while I finished it. "She doesn't like it," I said when my mouth was empty, "but she'll do it."

Llona was happy. "*That's* a relief. You know she wouldn't even talk to me on the *phone*? It would have looked pretty strange not to have the founder's only surviving relative on the dais."

Llona was in charge of lining up the guests for the big black-tie banquet scheduled for Friday night. It was to be a huge media event, Public Relations' big play to the other media for coverage and plugs for the money-making portions of the anniversary program.

The banquet had a couple of other purposes. For the talent, it would be a chance to unwind after dress rehearsal Friday afternoon. For the Network brass (not including me—I was a *very* junior vice-president), it was a chance to blow the speeches out of their systems. The speeches would be taped, and the highlights shown on the televised party Sunday night. That was a smart idea on the part of Porter Reigels, who was producing and directing. On an occasion like this, you *have* to have the big shots, but you don't want to put them on the air live, where they can come down with an attack of camera fright, or worse, "flaming," also known as "diarrhea of the mouth."

Llona had had no trouble getting the important executives to appear on the show. The Network has more hams than Iowa. But with Roxanne Schick, granddaughter of the founder of the Network, daughter of his successor as president, largest single stockholder in the company, and at nineteen, one of the fifteen or twenty richest women in the world, it was a different story. She had given both Llona and Ritafio flat refusals when they sought her out for the dinner. For a lot of reasons, Rox and I had become very special friends, so the Department of Public Relations called in the Department of Special Projects, and asked me to help.

Roxanne took no joy in any close association with the Network, and I couldn't say I blamed her. A Network power struggle had ended in the crippling (and last month, the death) of her father, and the suicide of her grandfather; though to the rest of the world, *that* had been an accident at sea. Roxanne's mother escaped being tried for murder by committing her own kind of suicide, inside her head. She was in a private institution, but most people thought of her as dead, the way Llona apparently did.

Still, you can't escape who you are, and I finally managed to convince Rox that a trip down from college and an appearance at the banquet wouldn't hurt her.

"However," I told Llona, "Miss Schick has set a few conditions."

A wary look came into the chocolate eyes. Llona said, "Oh?"

"She wants her introduction and her speech to total forty-five seconds or less."

Llona was smiling again. "Is that all? Relax, this is PR speaking, remember? You people in Special Projects specialize in handling disasters, but *we* specialize in ignoring them. *We* don't want to hype the Schick name; not after the ARGUS scandal." She looked pensive. "Think we'll ever know the truth about that?"

"No," I said. At least, she wouldn't if I could help it. With hard work and luck, I'd managed to make that mess seem a lot smaller than it really was, and I wasn't about to blow that success just to satisfy someone's curiosity, no matter how cute she was.

"Well," she said, "it doesn't matter. How are things in Special Projects?"

"Quiet," I said. It wasn't often I could say that. "Special Projects" is a deliberate euphemism—what we really do can't be summed up in one of those pithy phrases the Network likes to paint on doors. "Trouble Shooting" would be close, but we also try to anticipate and avoid trouble if we can. It entails a lot of sneaking around, a lot of Machiavellian manipulations. I try to keep it as clean as possible.

"I wish *I* could say things were quiet." For just a second, Llona let her smile slip, to show me how tired she was. For just a second, while she proved her point. Then, cool and lovely as ever, she said, "I am going crazy. Never deal with TV people more than three at a time."

"That bad, huh?"

"Someday," she said, "I'm going to buy myself a little island, and just lie in the sun all day." She was smiling, but she sounded as though she meant it. "I'm going to be overjoyed when Sunday is over, and we're through with this."

"I have a few people upstairs just sitting around reading magazines. Anything Special Projects can do?"

She shook her head. "Not unless you feel like smoothing a couple hundred ruffled egos. Some of them have murder on their minds."

I jump to conclusions. It's a bad habit, especially in my job, and I try to minimize it. My brain, though, has a tendency to make decisions and take action without letting my conscious self in on it. That's handy when I'm under pressure—I don't have a chance to get nervous, for one thing—but it can lead to severe social embarrassment, as it did this time. I heard Llona say "murder," and making the too-quick association said, "I didn't think the show-biz types would be taking much notice of Jim Bevic."

Llona looked surprised. "Jim Bevic?" she said. "What about him?"

I shook my head. "That's the murder that seems to be on most minds around here," I said.

"Oh no," Llona said, "it's not about Jim. I was just using a figure of speech."

I raised an eyebrow. Llona didn't strike me as a name dropper. "You knew him?"

"We went to high school together. I dated him a few times."

"I didn't know," I began. I was all set to be sympathetic, but Llona waved it aside.

"It wasn't a romance or anything, we were more like pals—he was editor of the school paper, and I was his assistant. I used to kid him about winning the Pulitzer Prize someday. I phoned him after he actually did win it. That was the last time I talked to him."

"You kept in touch, then."

She shrugged. "Sporadically. He was a nice guy." She sighed. "Still, I'd like to go back home and pay my respects at the funeral, but with the way they've got me jumping around here, I'll never get the chance. I tried to call Alex—Jim's brother—but he was out of town."

I returned to Network business. "What's the problem?" I asked. "Complaints?"

"You guessed it."

"What are they complaining about? Isn't the Network putting them up like royalty across the street in the Brant? Aren't some of the old-timers from radio about to get their first checks since V-J Day?"

"The ones *that* old aren't the problem," she told me. "The big problem is Melanie Marliss. That . . . that *taco* cook she brought along has her all worked up, and then *she* gets everyone else going."

I could see that. Melanie Marliss had been getting people worked up for years—primarily male movie-goers. She was a tried and true Network alumna, though. She got her start as card girl and sketch extra on the "Shelby and Green Program," then graduated to the enormously successful "Harriet Gunner" series, a sort of mid-sixties "Charlie's Angels." One honey-haired, long-legged, amply endowed Melanie Marliss had been plenty for girl-watchers in those days.

After "Harriet Gunner" folded, Melanie went right into pictures, and today, if you wanted financial backing for a picture that featured a woman in the major role, you went to a money man and said "Streisand," or you said "Marliss," or you said good-bye.

"What's her complaint?" I asked.

"Shelby and Green," Llona told me.

"What's the matter? They remind her of her humble beginnings?"

"It's not that," Llona said. "They're just not here yet. Melanie says, or rather, this Lorenzo Baker says, that Melanie is a superstar—that's the word he used—but unlike other superstars who are coming for 'SS&C,' Melanie has come to be in actual sketches, and of course, her production number, instead of just being interviewed by the Anchorman on the show. He says the Network needs Melanie more than Melanie needs the Network. He says if Shelby and Green were allowed to show up five days late, Melanie Marliss could have been allowed to also. She could have been devoting the time to pre-production on her new picture."

"According to *Variety*, he's producing her next picture," I said.

Llona was suddenly angry. "That's another thing. Who the hell does he think he is? Who says he can produce? I've been in the TV business over five years, and they wouldn't let *me* produce a station identification slide." She took it out on her last piece of lettuce, then said, "So who is he? *'Lorenzo's Tacos'!* And you know what I found out?"

"What?"

"He's from *Ohio!* His name is really Larry Baker, and he's about as Mexican as . . . as that hot dog!"

I shrugged. "It's happened before. In the old days, if you wanted to be an actress, you had to sleep with the producer. Now, if you want to be a producer, you have to sleep with the actress."

Her face was a lovely shade of red. I wasn't trying to calm her down, because I recognized her symptoms. PR people have to be nice all the time, no matter what, and it really gets to them if they can't blow off steam occasionally.

"Oh, right," she said with heavy sarcasm. "I suppose if I slept with Burt Reynolds, I could produce *his* next picture?"

"You could try."

"Don't tempt me," she said. Then she laughed. "Okay, Matt, tantrum over. Thanks."

"Any time," I said. "But what's the matter with Shelby and Green?" I found it hard to believe they didn't have a good reason for not showing up. I've spent a lot of time talking to Millie Heywood in Network Operations—she's been with the Network a long time, and likes to talk about the old days. According to her, there never was a more professional act than Shelby and Green. They were never unprepared, they were never late, and they always kept the convenience of the crew in mind. Millie had, in fact, been present when short, redheaded Lenny Green and tall, bespectacled Ken Shelby first met. It had been in the old studios on Thirty-fifth Street—Shelby was a staff director with the Network then, and Green was a comedy-magician.

"We don't *know* what the matter is," Llona whined. "Ritafio sends them telegrams, Porter Reigels sends them telegrams; all they'll say is 'Unavoidably detained.' Reigels is furious—he's talking about dropping them from the show. Which would be a shame," she went on. "Do you remember them, Matt? They were something."

They certainly were. Saturday night was Shelby and Green night in the Cobb household while I was growing up. They had that telepathic timing that a comedy team must have, and they had their respective characters worked out perfectly. Green was like a frisky puppy, cute, but given to indiscretions. He was highly skilled at sleight of hand, and used the skill in outrageous ways. Shelby was like the puppy's embarrassed master, always trying to laugh off the damage.

I was surprised to realize how much I had been looking forward to seeing them together again. I told Llona so.

"But Porter won't drop them, now," Llona said, showing me her crossed fingers. "They're *supposed* to be arriving at Kennedy Airport a little after two. Along with Shelby's wife, of course. Alice Brockway."

I smiled. "My first love," I said.

"Huh?"

"She used to play the big sister on 'Home and Mother,' remember? When I was about seven, I developed a monumental crush on her. Lasted for years."

Llona giggled. "But she was so *wholesome.*"

"I *like* wholesome."

"That's a shame," Llona said, with mock sadness.

"However," I said, "I don't like 100 *percent* wholesome."

She grinned, and looked me over. "I didn't think so." She glanced at her watch. "Well, time to get back to work."

She rose to go. I did, too. "Llona," I said, "let's go to a show or a ball game sometime, all right?"

"That would be nice. As soon as this nightmare is over, okay?"

"It's a date," I told her.

CHAPTER 2

"Okay, Chief, I'll get on it right away."
—EVERETT SLOANE, "THE DICK TRACY SHOW," SYNDICATED

Special Projects was nearly deserted. The only person there was my secretary, Jasmyn Santiago. If Castro had known how cute and efficient little Jasmyn was going to turn out to be, he would never have chased her family out of Cuba.

"Did I miss something?" I asked.

"Oh, hi, Matt," she said. We're very informal in Special Projects. "What do you mean?"

"Where is everybody?"

"Well, Shirley is out on the actress hunt, and Ragusa and Kolaski are following up the nut letters, to see if we should call in the police."

"Good," I said. "I approve." This was an easy outfit to be boss of.

"Harris called from Indiana," Jazz said. "He's planning to offer that bribe sometime over the weekend. He wants to know if he should go ahead."

"Sure, the sooner the better. Standards has been chewing the carpet over this." Standards is the department of the Network most people think of as the censor, but that's not really fair. A big part of their job is to try to keep the Network from being used to rip off the viewers. To do that, they try to check the accuracy of all the commercials we run. Often, Standards will commission an independent testing outfit to check advertisers' claims. There had been rumors, though, that one particular outfit could be reached by an advertiser eager to have his product pass.

Harris Brophy, a genial, handsome cynic, and my star operative, was in the field trying to get the truth. Once he had it, we'd turn it over to Standards and let them take it from there. Probably wouldn't amount to much—they'd tell the Feds, and the Feds would make the testing firm sign a consent order: "I never did anything wrong, but I promise to stop," that sort of thing.

With Smith on vacation, and St. John coming in for the graveyard shift, all the East Coast personnel of the department were accounted for. I laughed as I went into my office—Brophy, Arnstein, Ragusa, Kolaski, Santiago, Smith, and St. John—the place always reminded me of a 1942 Hollywood war movie.

I sat at my desk, opened a package of Sugar Babies, and read a few reports. Tried to read them, anyway. Instead, I found myself thinking about Alice Brockway—not the way she was today, middle-aged, but still pretty and vivacious, showing up in an occasional guest shot on a situation comedy, or giving money away on a game show—but the way she used to be when she played the big sister (also named Alice) on "Home and Mother."

The show had already been canceled and sent into syndication before I discovered it. I used to run home from school to watch the reruns. Alice Brockway on that show was the cleanest and nicest person in a *world* of clean and nice people. She was my idea of female perfection. She lived in a town where everyone owned his own house, with grass around it that dogs never messed on.

That was exotic to me. I grew up in a neighborhood that would have been a slum, if the people who'd lived there had let it. In that kind of place, you are taught at an early age how to deal with criminals and perverts, the way a kid in Kansas is taught to deal with tornadoes and locusts.

But the town of "Home and Mother" didn't have criminals, perverts, tornadoes, *or* locusts. Alice's TV father made plenty of money, and was never grouchy when he came home from work.

That was the place for me, all right. I used to be on my best behavior, trying to be worthy of Alice. If they would only keep those reruns going, I used to tell myself, I could catch up to her in a few more years, and she and I could go steady, and I could take her to the prom, whatever that was.

I ate another Sugar Baby and laughed at myself about the whole business. I wasn't stupid enough to expect a flesh-and-blood Alice Brockway to live up to my boyhood fantasies, but I was human enough to hope she would.

The phone buzzed. "What is it, Jazz?"

"It's Shirley, Matt. She says she's done it."

"Terrific. Put her on." The line clicked. "Shirley?"

"Hello, Matt." She sounded pleased with herself, so I could tell she'd managed to track down the long-running star of our equally long-running soap opera.

Shirley Arnstein was a workaholic, a pleasantly plain girl, who (before she came to the Network), used to do a lot of the work a certain member of the House of Representatives was supposed to be doing but wasn't. She was like a mama-tiger when she was protecting the interests of the Network, but extremely shy otherwise. Her biggest complaint was that I didn't give her enough to do.

"Congratulations," I told her, "this is the fastest Doreen has ever been found. Where was she this time?"

"In a convent up in Duchess County. She was going to become a Sister of Saint—"

"Never mind. How in the world did you get her out of there?" I didn't even want to *ask* how Shirley figured out Doreen was there in the first place.

"I had to join up, myself," Shirley said. "Or, rather, I had to tell them I wanted to."

"Oh," I said. *Who says the TV industry never offers anything different?* I thought. Now we had Jewish nuns. Then it occurred to me that might not be so funny. "You didn't sign anything, did you?"

"I would have," she said, "but black looks lousy on me."

"You've been hanging around Harris too much, wise mouth," I said, laughing. Then I sighed. "Okay, I'm ready. Let me talk to Doreen."

So, as I must do three or four times a year, I talked with Doreen. It was the same old story; she couldn't stand her character any more. Doreen played a character that every soap has one of—the Normal One. For twenty years (Doreen told me), she had had to listen to all the other actresses talk about their affairs, their abortions, their murder trials, and tell them everything would be all right, and pour them another cup of coffee. "If I have to pat *one more shoulder,*" she told me through bitter tears, "I'll go *insane!*"

We worked it out. While I kept Doreen talking about her accursed happiness, I had Jazz calling all over the city, trying to find the show's producer and head writer. When she had, we set up a conference call. The producer and writer promised on their mothers' souls that within the next month her character would fall in love with a transsexual pro-football player, who was dying of an incurable disease.

Doreen sniffed back tears. "That's all I ask," she said. Fade to black. Another mission accomplished for Cobb's Commandos.

I had to laugh. By the time they were ready to start taping the new plot, Doreen would have decided that her image was too important; that her public didn't want to see her that way. Then, in a few months, she'd run away again.

Thinking about it made me tired. I looked at my watch, saw that it was close to five o'clock, said, "To hell with it," to no one in particular, and left the office.

I intended to head home to my borrowed apartment, but as I stepped into the stainless steel elevator (it always reminded me of the inside of a cigar tube) I was overcome by a strong sense of *noblesse oblige.* Executives taking off before quitting time used to be one of my pet peeves when I had been punching a clock.

I decided to go down to Studio J and check in on the preparations for the Big Show. I momentarily forgot what button I wanted to push. NetHQ is a confusing place, especially around the production floors. Unlike CBS and ABC, who have studios in separate buildings in various parts of town, NBC and the Network have production facilities in the same skyscrapers that house their offices. It must have been an interesting problem for the Network's architect to make it all come out even—Studio B, for example, where Channel 10 News originates, is one-and-one-third stories high.

Studio J, though the biggest room in the building, wasn't as much of a problem—it takes up most of the seventh and eighth floors; a two-story rectangle-within-a-rectangle, surrounded by corridors that open out onto dressing rooms and rehearsal rooms on both floors.

The entrance to the studio proper, I finally remembered, was on the seventh floor. The eighth floor offered access to the control room, which overlooked the studio, and that was about it. That, and the catwalk. They still build TV studios with catwalks above the lighting grids, but they're very rarely used any more, at least in our studios. Now, when a technician wants to get at the lights, he gets lifted up to them in a portable hydraulic elevator, or has the light mounted on a pantograph, which is an accordian-like gadget that lets you pull the light down to the floor and adjust it there.

There was a tiny ceremony going on in the seventh-floor hall when I got there. A guy from Building Services was hanging a sign on a door. It could have been the door to just another conference room, complete with low, suspended-tile ceiling with built-in fluorescent lighting, black linoleum floor, and blank white cinderblock walls. Every conference room in the building is that way. I guess they don't want their creative geniuses distracted by the decor.

But *this* (former) conference room was now the J. V. Hewlen Kinescope Library. Young Jerry de Loon, the librarian, was out in the hall superintending the hanging of the sign.

I joined him. "Very impressive," I said.

He grinned. "Yes, indeed, Mr. Cobb. I'm glad they got around to it before I was finished and gone."

"How's the work coming?"

"Too darn well. I'm into the fifties already."

The J. V. Hewlen Kinescope Library was only a few weeks old. A small warehouse in Passaic, New Jersey, had been condemned to make way for a municipal parking lot or something, and, to everyone's surprise, it turned out the Network owned it. The place had been full of forgotten kinescopes, sixteen-millimeter movies of TV shows, taken right off the screen. That's the only way shows could be preserved before videotape became practical in the late fifties. Since kines of many old shows are rare, and some are actually valuable—the Art of today is frequently the Crap of yesterday—the Network fixed up the conference room with a bunch of shelves, a viewer, and a pad and pencil, and hired Jerry to find out exactly what the Network had rediscovered, and to put it in some kind of order. When that was finished, so was Jerry's job.

"Don't be so damned conscientious," I told him. "They don't expect you to get it all done in a month."

Jerry was a big kid, but not tough. With his round, florid face, and platinum blond hair, he looked like an apprentice Santa Claus.

He scratched his head. "Hell," he said. "I just get so involved in watching the shows, I forget to go home."

"So watch them twice," I told him, and he laughed. I said, "Congratulations on your sign," and left him.

I've always thought the Network could generate a lot more revenue from Studio J if they stopped doing shows from there (they only used about one fifteenth of the floor space for the game show that was the regular tenant) and remodeled it for racquetball. They could get quite a few courts in.

The place was so vast it was hard to remember I was indoors. When I looked above the top of the standing set, past the light grid and the catwalk, I could see a wide, black ceiling that looked as big as a night sky. There were even twinkling red stars in it—the electric eyes of the smoke detector-sprinkler system. *That* was relatively new; Falzet had only decided to have the Network spring for it when he saw the news tapes of a high-rise office building fire. The sight of people jumping off the building, choosing death on the pavement when they realized they were cut off above the fire, had made him think. His office is the thirty-seventh-floor penthouse of NetHQ.

A side effect of the new system was the angry red SMOKING POSITIVELY PROHIBITED signs that had been posted in conspicuous places around the studio. Those smoke detectors were extremely sensitive. One cigarette wouldn't set the sprinkler off, the firm that installed it had said, but fifteen or twenty would, and nobody was interested in checking the claim.

I wandered around the studio, watching them put the finishing touches on the set. There was to be no studio audience for "Sight, Sound, & Celebration," or rather, the performers themselves were to be the audience. The whole studio had been converted into a kind of rolling, multilevel stage, with stars clustered in informal groups, according to their era. Each cluster was centered around a big TV monitor, so the celebrities wouldn't have to strain their eyes to see something that was going on at the other end of the room. Acts would be performed in several different areas, eliminating the need to have the stage crew rush like crazy to change sets.

My ultimate destination was the far wall of the studio, which had been changed into a mini-museum of TV and radio memorabilia—the Golden Baritone's throat spray, Captain Justice's mask and ultra stun gun—things like that. I was in no hurry to get there, though. There was a lot to see on the way over.

Flats had been erected around three walls of the set, each decorated with a picture representing some Great Moment in Network History, starting with a blowup of a three-hundred-fifty-pound woman in a horned hat and fur vest, screaming into a microphone the size of a pie plate. A performance of *Die Walküre,* sung in New York and transmitted by telephone line to radio stations in Philadelphia and Schenectady, had been the first thing ever broadcast by the Network. This had never been an outfit to do things in a small way.

Not too far away was a picture I could have re-created from memory. Just seeing it again made me start to laugh. It had happened on the "Shelby and Green Program"—you've probably seen the tape of it yourself, or at least the still. The picture shows a very famous, very pompous movie actor, standing with his trousers at half mast, revealing loudly striped boxer shorts. To his right stands Ken Shelby, wearing his patented look of dignified horror. To Ken's right stands the lovely Melanie Marliss, in her abbreviated (for those days) card-girl outfit. Her uncontrollable laughter threatens to bounce her right out of it. Standing to everyone's left, *behind* the dignified personage, who is still oblivious to the situation, Lenny Green, with a look of fiendish glee on his face, is holding the actor's belt aloft.

The dignified actor was never quite the same after that, but then neither was I. It would be good to see Shelby and Green together again. I looked at the picture, and remembered and laughed, and hoped their plane had arrived safely.

When I finally turned away from the picture, I was surprised to find the entire cast of the "Shelby and Green Program" walking right toward me.

CHAPTER 3

"One of these days, Alice. One of these days . . ."

—JACKIE GLEASON, "THE HONEYMOONERS," CBS

They walked right by me, up to the seats and monitor.

Shelby and Green were there, of course, looking very much as they had when they'd broken up more than ten years ago. And Melanie Marliss. Whatever anger she'd felt about Shelby and Green's late arrival had apparently vanished. She was smiling and nodding as she listened to Porter Reigels talk about the show.

"Now, the Anchorman will talk to Melanie first, then I'll run the Harriet Gunner tape, then, we'll go live to you two."

Reigels was a tall, rugged Texan, with a whispery drawl and a deeply lined face. He was legendary in the fields of movies and television because he never swore—the language you usually hear in a studio when the camera's off could make a longshoreman blush.

Nobody seemed to mind my listening in. It's my face. People have told me I look like I know what I'm doing, even during those extended and frequent periods when I don't. So I listened as Reigels went on. "After the chitchat, Ken and Lenny and Melanie, you go over to that area in the corner, there, for your sketch. Now, I *wanted* to talk this over with you, but since you weren't here, I put the 'Reluctant Magician' in the run sheet. Okay?"

Shelby said, "Fine," and looked at Green. Green shrugged and said, "Okay by me. I'm not about to go learning new material at this stage. Not with the money *this* chicken outfit pays."

I smiled. As usual, it was the delivery that made it funny—that, and Ken Shelby's painfully embarrassed reaction-take. They might never have broken up.

"It'll be fine, Porter—" Shelby began, but a haggard-looking woman in dark glasses cut him off. "Why that sketch?" she snapped.

My God, I thought, *that's Alice Brockway.* I hadn't even recognized her; I'd thought she was Reigels's production assistant or something.

"What's the problem?" asked a specimen with shiny black hair and an equally shiny black mustache who had a proprietary hold on

Melanie Marliss's elbow. It was Lorenzo Baker, the taco tycoon, whose face was as familiar as that of Colonel Sanders. He could pass for a Mexican, as long as he kept his mouth and eyes shut. The midwestern twang and baby blues were too obviously north-of-the-border for his deception to be successful anywhere outside his printed taco wrappers.

Though the Golden Goddess he was hanging onto topped him in both height and weight, Baker was going to be everybody's big brother —just give the problem to him, and everything would be hunky-dory. People like that get on my nerves. I distrust anybody who doesn't think he has enough problems of his own.

Evidently, Alice Brockway thought the same way. "*Shut up!*" she told him. She turned to Reigels. "Everybody is sick of that routine," she told the director.

Ken Shelby smiled, but his teeth didn't move when he talked. "Now, dear," he said, "that's hardly possible. Considering the act broke up twelve years ago."

I was troubled and confused by all this. It had the look of something that could get out of hand and make trouble, and I don't like trouble. It occurred to me to wonder where Llona was.

"Well," Porter Reigels drawled, "it'd be kind of a shame to change it, seein' as how that's what we lit the set and rehearsed the camera angles for. You folks, as you might recollect, weren't here."

Shelby and Green had the good grace to look embarrassed. Lorenzo Baker was about to make a remark, but after a noise of fury from Alice Brockway that made human speech seem inadequate by comparison, he shut up.

Alice turned on Lenny Green. The little comedian almost jumped when he saw her face.

"What's the matter with you, Len?" she hissed. Green had his back to me, giving me a perfect view of Alice's face. I was happy she was wearing the dark glasses—judging from the rest of her features, her eyes might have turned me to stone.

"Hey, Alice," he said in his pleasantly hoarse voice. "Calm down, all right? People *like* the Reluctant Magician, it's one of our best bits."

"Sure," she said. "You go into a box, and disappear from view, while my *beloved* stays outside and mugs at the audience. Don't think that if you go along with him on this, he'll get the act back together. This is a one-time thing, Len, and you're going to let him get all the camera time!"

"But *I* get all the laughs," Green said.

Alice's calm was deadly now. "How long are you going to go on listening to him?"

Green laughed. "If I *had* listened to you, Ken," he said to his ex-partner, "maybe I'd be as rich as you are now, right?"

"He's an egomaniac!"

Her husband spoke. "I'm an egomaniac. I suppose that's why I quit show business and went into real estate?"

"You went into real estate because you love money even more than attention!"

I should break this up, I told myself, but I was too involved in the conversation. It was all those veiled references to the mining scandal that was widely rumored to have been the cause of Shelby and Green's breakup. They, and a whole lot of other famous entertainers, actors, and even government officials (who, theoretically, should have known better), were big news in the late sixties, when they entrusted extraordinary sums of cash to a man named Ollie McHarg for shares in an outfit called Utopia Uranium. They found themselves holding an extremely empty bag when McHarg took off with the cash and left them the proud owners of nonexistent nuclear material processing plants. No one had told them that "Utopia" means "no place."

As it turned out I didn't have to break anything up, because Llona came bustling into the studio. She gave me a little wave, then looked at the group of stars. Undoubtedly, she noticed that all was not exactly roses and lollipops, but she followed that first principle of PR: "Trouble does not exist until it is acknowledged," and chose not to acknowledge it.

"I'm back," she announced, cheerfully and unnecessarily. "The hotel has your rooms all ready, so when you're through here—"

"I'm through," Alice Brockway said. "I'm going to lie down. You're a fool, Len. Excuse *me.*"

That last was addressed to me; the first words the girl of my dreams had ever said to me. She had crashed into me while building up a head of steam on her way to the door. I said, "Clumsy of me," as I stepped aside, and she actually gave me a tentative smile as she strode on.

No one said anything until the echo of her last high-heel click was gone from the studio. Then Llona, in a kind of desperate attempt to change the subject, lit on me.

"I—I want you all to meet Matt Cobb. He's one of the vice-presidents here at the Network."

"My God," Lenny Green said, feigning shock. "Vice-president of what? Diaper-changing?"

"I know what you mean, Lenny," Melanie Marliss cooed. She looked from Llona to me and back. "It *used* to be, the entertainers could count on being the best-looking people in the Network, but look at these two."

"They just wanted to make you feel at home, darling," Lorenzo Baker crooned. His voice was not suited for crooning.

It had raised my self-image a few points to hear that Hollywood's reigning sex symbol thought I was good-looking, but I could see that Llona, in some feminine way, was taking it as a mild insult.

"I'm pleased to meet all of you," I said. I told Shelby, Green, and Marliss, truthfully, that I was a big fan of theirs.

"Since you were a child, right?" Green said, and everybody laughed. Melanie insisted that everyone get on a first-name basis; then Llona made the rare (for her) gaffe of bringing up my boyhood crush on Shelby's wife. Not only did that prove I *had* been a fan since I was a child, it also violated the tacit agreement to forget about Alice's conduct that afternoon.

Ken Shelby felt obliged to do something about the situation. He was still wearing his smile, but by now, it looked more like *rictus sardonicus* than any human emotion.

"You'll . . . ah . . . you'll have to make allowances for my wife," he said, adjusting his horn-rims. "If there are two things that put Alice in a bad mood, they're getting up early and jet lag, and today, she's had to put up with both."

Porter Reigels shrugged it off, saying, "Well, it don't really matter for this afternoon. I hope she's feeling better by tonight, though. I want to have a read-through, tonight about—what time was it you said you could make it, Mel?"

Melanie, in turn, looked at Baker, who said, "About eight o'clock. Melanie and I will have an early dinner." He was being gracious.

The whole setup seemed wrong. It was unsettling to fall in with a bunch of big stars, then listen as they exhibited marital flare-ups and social embarrassment like any civilians from Scarsdale would.

Lenny Green said, "Hey, Porter, if you expect the Reluctant Magician sketch, you better make sure they've got two trap doors in this set."

"They're there," the Texan assured him. "You sent me the goldang specifications in your letter, didn't you? I c'n *read*, y'know."

"What about the vanishing cabinet? Did you go to the magic shop I mentioned?"

Reigels sighed. "Yes, I did, and I think you're getting a kickback on it, too. Cost us an arm and a leg. Got it in the prop room."

"Good," Green said. "But I better take a look at it, anyway, if I'm supposed to disappear from it."

Reigels said it would be a heck of a note if he *couldn't* disappear from it, and said to come along. Ken Shelby said he'd better go with them, and they strode off. I noticed Green was limping slightly. Llona waved me a hasty good-bye, and took off after them. "They still don't know what rooms they have in the Brant," she explained.

Melanie said that reminded her of something. "Lorenzo dear, please go back to the hotel and see if that telegram from Paramount has come yet."

"Not necessary to go back right away, Melanie. It's too late to do anything about it today, anyway."

"Nonsense," she told him. "You know it's three hours later out here. I'll be right along, I promise. I just want to say hello to my old wardrobe girl. I understand she's still working here. Please go, Lorenzo. For me?"

He said, "Of course," and obeyed. He didn't make it from taco king to movie producer by defying his meal ticket, that was for sure.

That left me alone with Melanie Marliss, with only about thirty-five carpenters for chaperones. I was just as glad to have them. The woman had something that in the right circumstances could make a gentleman forget to be gentle. But I don't have to tell you that—millions of people have sat in movie theaters memorizing every inch of Melanie Marliss's face and body. I can only add that she was just as beautiful in three dimensions as in two. She had some laugh lines at the corners of her eyes that don't show up on camera (she was no spring chicken, after all), but God (or Clairol) had given her hair a warm honey glow no film could ever capture, and that made up for it.

"I never did find out what you're the vice-president of," she said.

"Special Projects," I told her.

She looked surprised. "Oh, the Network snooper. Whatever happened to McFeeley?"

"He had hip trouble and retired."

"Oh. Remind me to have you give me his address. He got me out of some . . . embarrassing spots when I was with the Network. You must be very smart to replace him so young."

"I'm not smart," I told her with a smile, "just dedicated. Smart people *avoid* trouble."

"Is it trouble that brings you around here?" Her voice took on an edge of wariness, under its usual velvet.

"No, no trouble for a change. I'm just a hopeless TV fan. I came down here to look around. I was especially interested," I said, pointing to the Shelby-Green picture, "in *that.*"

"Oh," she laughed. "That was really something. That was the last show the Network let us do live. Lenny is crazy in front of an audience."

"Well," I said, "I'd like to know how he did it, myself. I mean, it's obvious that Green got the belt off the guy when he shook hands with him . . ."

"Yes?"

"Oh," I said, "sorry." It had occurred to me, somewhat belatedly, that this was a hell of a topic to discuss with her, especially since it was probably the first and last chance I'd ever have to speak to Melanie Marliss.

"But," I went on resignedly, "Green was off on the other side of the stage for two or three minutes before the guy's pants fell down. How'd he do that?"

"I can't tell you that," she grinned. "I made a promise. You know Lenny started in the business as a magician's assistant? Well, not revealing secrets is one thing he's serious about, even if the tricks are played more for laughs than anything else."

I could understand that, and told her so.

"I can tell you this, though," she said. "It's really very simple. If you're as smart as Hugh McFeeley, you'll be able to figure it out.

"Oh, and I want to warn you—Lenny has been hinting about a surprise ending to the sketch, but he won't tell anyone what it is. Not even Ken, and that's rare. I think someone ought to warn Porter before Lenny launches his surprise on the air live, don't you?"

She didn't give me a chance to reply, but said instead, "I've really enjoyed meeting you—Matt? It's so nice to have a chance to talk to someone for five minutes without autographs or money being mentioned."

"The pleasure was all mine."

"How sweet." She put out her hand, and I took it. It was a friendly grip she gave me. "Will I see you again?" she asked.

"I'll be at the banquet."

"Wonderful."

I said I thought so, too. She asked where the wardrobe room was, I told her, she took her hand back, and left.

I took a few minutes to look around the rest of the studio—that's what I'd come down for in the first place, remember—but before I finished, the carpenters and stagehands started to pack up their tools, and that told me it was time to go home.

CHAPTER 4

"And now, for something completely different."
—JOHN CLEESE, "MONTY PYTHON'S FLYING CIRCUS," BBC & PBS

Naturally, I had just stepped out of the shower when the phone rang. I stayed in the bathroom drying off, but opened the door so I could hear what was going on as the phone-answering thing took the call.

"Hello," I heard myself say, "this is the pre-recorded voice of Matt Cobb. Due to circumstances beyond my control, I am unable to bring you my living self at this time. Please leave a message when you hear the thousand-cycle tone, and I'll get back to you as soon as I can. Thank you."

As usual, when he heard my voice coming from somewhere, and saw my body somewhere else, Spot, the purebred Samoyed whose house guest I was, dashed back and forth between the phone and me, giving me a dirty look each time he reached the bathroom. I was watching Spot, and his luxury Central Park West apartment, for Rick and Jane Sloan, a couple of friends of mine with more money than they knew what to do with. They decided to send some of the excess to Thailand in the form of an archaeological expedition, and then, at the last minute, decided to follow it.

After the beep, I heard the agitated voice of Llona Hall say, "Oh, *damn!*"

Fainter, but still clear, as though he was sharing the receiver with her, Sal Ritafio's voice said, "What's the matter? He's there, isn't he?"

Instantly, my heart started to bleed for him. That was the secret of Ritafio's success. His face (which resembles two chocolate chips pressed into a matzoh ball) and his voice (a tremulous tenor) were so piteous, nobody could refuse the guy for fear he would pine away and die. He always looked harried, like a man trying to feed seven hungry lions with six pieces of meat.

Now I had to go pick up the phone. I wrapped the towel around myself. It's silly to do that when the only one who's going to see you naked is a dog, but I do it anyway. When the towel was secure, I had to dash across the big white shag rug to get to the phone before Llona decided to hang up.

"Hello?" I said breathlessly.

"Matt?"

"Yeah. What's up? You sound troubled."

"I'll say. We've been ripped off."

"Oh, boy," I said.

A television camera, *one* television camera, costs anywhere from fifty-five thousand dollars up. Add in the cost of the lens and the pedestal, and it's *way* up. The nightmare was that some night some nut would back a truck up to the loading dock and make off with about three million bucks in hardware. It would have to be a nut, because the stuff would be almost impossible to fence, but he could hold it for ransom or something. The real worry was the possibility it would get damaged in transit. One scratch, and good-bye twelve-thousand-dollar lens.

"What did they get?" I braced myself as I asked the question.

"You're not going to believe this . . ." Llona said. She sounded grim.

That's a conversational gambit that never fails to set my teeth on edge. "I'll believe it, I swear," I assured her. "What did they steal, for Christ's sake, the Anchorman's denture?"

"Oh, my God," I heard Ritafio breathe. "Don't even *think* that!"

"Well," I demanded, "what was it?"

"The bowling ball," Llona said.

I was dripping on Jane Sloan's carpet. A cool October breeze was blowing in through the window and giving me chilblains. I had a frisky white dog with a silly grin on his face trying to make a game out of snatching the towel off me.

"The bowling ball?" I tried very hard to keep my voice from cracking, the way it often does in times of stress. "*The* bowling ball?"

"Yup," she said sadly.

Llona was a beautiful girl, but enough was enough. "*What the hell are you talking about?*" I yelled.

"Melanie Marliss's bowling ball, Matt!" There was a note of impatience in her voice, as though she thought I should have realized it all along. She was probably right.

"Oh," I said. "*That* one." I looked at my wrist, called myself an idiot for expecting to see my watch there after I had just come out of the shower, then looked at the wall clock. "I'll be there in ten minutes."

"Hurry, Matt."

"Yeah, good-bye."

"Wait, Matt! I forgot to tell you. They also stole 1952."

"What?"

"Have to go now, I think the ambulance is here."

"*What?*"

She hung up on me. That girl certainly knew how to pique my interest. I rushed to get dressed.

What had been stolen (along, I reminded myself through tight lips, with 1952) was more than just your average bowling ball. It was nothing less than a show-business legend.

"Harriet Gunner" hadn't been too big a success its first season on the air—in fact, it was just barely renewed. For the following season, it was decided to make some changes to round out the character. They gave Harriet a hobby. Making that hobby bowling had been Melanie's own idea. Not only did it pick up a lot of viewers in places like Buffalo and Cleveland, where bowling is the national sport, it gave the producers an excuse to have Melanie hang those incredible legs out of one of those short skirts women bowlers wear, and show them to the drooling public.

The rest, as they say, is history. "Harriet Gunner"'s ratings went through the roof, and Melanie Marliss became the Big Star she is today.

Melanie never forgot what (she felt) that maroon sphere had done for her. It became her good luck charm, her talisman. You couldn't read a story about her that didn't mention it. She hauled it with her all over the world, even on location in places they'd never even *heard* of bowling. It had been loaned (with great publicity) to the Network to join the throat spray and stun gun on the wall of relics I mentioned before.

Given Melanie's devotion to the thing, and her famous tantrums, this had the earmarks of a real migraine for all concerned, especially me.

I put on my jacket, checked to see if my fly was up. I had decided to skip the vest and tie in the interest of speed. "Come on, Spot," I said.

The Samoyed pricked up his pointy ears and looked at me as though he wondered if I really meant it.

"No kidding," I told him. "Come on, this is going to be a real treat."

The quickest way from Rick and Jane's apartment to the Network is to cut the southwest corner off Central Park, coming out at the top of Sixth Avenue, then dashing down a block or so to the Tower of Babble. But I wasn't *about* to go dashing through the park alone at nine-thirty at night, not even if somebody had made off with Tom Falzet's truss.

So I brought Spot with me for protection. Spot is a friendly little cuss, and his natural inclination would be to prance up to you and lick your face. He has been trained, however, at a word from me (or Rick, or Jane), to jump on you and rip out your throat.

He likes to run, too, and living in a big city high-rise, he doesn't get enough of that to suit him. He was making up for it now, though. I just held the leash and ran along behind.

When we got to NetHQ, I paused in the lobby for a few seconds to catch my breath. It doesn't look right to respond to an emergency looking like a man who has just missed drowning.

Lenny Green came into the lobby. "What's going on, Matt?" he asked.

"I was about to ask you the same thing," I told him. "Where are you coming from? I thought you'd still be rehearsing."

"Broke up about thirty minutes ago," he said. "I walked Alice back to the hotel, and I'm going to meet Ken in there for a drink." He pointed vaguely in the direction of the Network Lounge, the classy restaurant in the lobby.

I figured he might be a witness to whatever it was that had gone on up there, so I asked him to come up with me. He didn't ask why; just shrugged and smiled, and said sure, but he ought to tell Ken, since he, Lenny, was late already. A quick check of the Lounge, though, showed us Shelby wasn't there, so we went to the elevator bank, where, conveniently, a car was waiting for us.

A few seconds after the elevator had started, Green said, "Look at that!" and pointed to the floor-indicator lights over the door. Without thinking, I looked, but I didn't see anything surprising. I did, however, feel something in the region of my right hip pocket. I shot my right hand around my back, and caught him by the wrist.

I turned to see the famous boyish grin. "Reflexes like *lightning*," he said. "I once got away with picking J. Edgar Hoover's pocket on national TV, you know. This is one of the few times I've ever been caught."

I felt pleased with myself. The old basketball reflexes were still good —good enough for me to catch the man who had made a fine performing art (as had Harpo Marx before him) of picking pockets.

I told Lenny Green that I had been watching the night he lifted J. Edgar's wallet, and we talked about it. Then, just before the elevator stopped on the seventh floor, he said, "Here, Matt."

"What's this?" I asked him. He had something in his hand.

He opened the hand to show me my own watch. "I took it off your other wrist when I let you catch me in your pocket," he chuckled. "Sorry, I just can't help myself."

I was embarrassed, but I didn't get a chance to get as embarrassed as I might have, because the elevator stopped, and the doors opened on madness.

Broadcasting is, as anyone who works in it can tell you, a crazy business, but we generally don't pay much attention to that part of it—we get used to it, the same way, I suppose, a fish doesn't pay much attention to the fact that water is wet. Sometimes, though, like during a tidal wave, for instance, the water that surrounds him is brought forcibly to the fish's attention.

There was a tidal wave of craziness sweeping down the hallway toward me.

The first wave was the stretcher. Two guys in white suits, no doubt the crew of the ambulance Llona had mentioned, were scooting a wheeled stretcher down the corridor as though they were warming up for the Indy 500 time trials. Lenny Green and I had to jump out of the way to avoid becoming statistics ourselves, though I admit the guy in front of the stretcher *was* mumbling, "'Scuse me, 'scuse me, 'scuse me," as they barreled along.

Then, when they were in the elevator, just before the doors closed, the patient sat up on the stretcher. It was Jerry de Loon. He had a bandage on his head, and a worried look on his face. "I'm sorry, Mr. Cobb," he said, with great sincerity. The door closed before I could ask him what for.

Next, Llona came running down the hall, saying, "It's all a mistake!" until she saw who it was. "Oh, Matt," she said, "thank God it's you! I was afraid it was the fire department!"

That set Lenny Green off. "There's a fire here? What are you, crazy?" He raised his hoarse voice to a bellow. *"Evacuate the building!"*

"No, no, no!" Llona screamed. "There's no fire, it's all a mistake! Go see for yourself." Llona let out an enormous gust of air that blew one of her bangs askew, and she brushed it back into place with her hand. "Honest. Colonel Coyle is there, he'll tell you there's no fire." Coyle was the man in charge of Building Security.

"Yeah, well, I'd like to see for myself," the comedian said, and off he went.

"This is *impossible*," Llona said.

I wasn't about to argue the question. I didn't even know what it *was* yet, but it looked impossible to me, too. Carefully, I formulated a series of simple questions, and much to my surprise, got a series of intelligible answers that enabled me to get an idea of what had happened.

"Okay," I said, and Spot cocked his head to listen. "Let me see if I've gotten this straight. Porter Reigels had a bunch of people here, doing read-throughs for some of the sketches for Sunday's show—the Shelby-Green people and who else?"

"Some real old-timers from the radio days took a separate room to rehearse the re-enactment they're doing of 'The Theodore Farnsworth Show.'"

"Right. Now, the Shelby and Green thing broke up at nine o'clock or shortly after, and everybody went home, right? Or to the bar downstairs, or whatever."

"Right, except Porter Reigels went to his office upstairs."

"Yeah," I said in disgust, "but it's not going to be a whole lot of help, since according to you, everybody has gravitated back up here."

"You know how news shoots through this place," she said.

"I know. It's just that this is going to be an alibi-busting exercise. Even if it was someone from outside, not connected with the Network, the police are going to have to ask everybody in the building where they were, and who saw them, and all that crap. Or I'll have to do it." I sighed. This was going to be a mess. "Tell me about the actual robbery again, Llona."

She told me. "Somebody came into the Kinescope Library, knocked Jerry out, or something, and made off with all the kines from 1952. I don't even know if Jerry knows what's happened. He was in a lot of pain.

"Anyway, when he came to, just a few minutes later, apparently, he staggered out into the hallway, and rang the fire alarm to get help."

The alarm had brought Coyle to the scene, of course, from his office in the basement. When he discovered the theft of the film, he immediately summoned more guards, for a quick check on what else might be missing—that was when Melanie's ball was discovered to be gone.

It occurred to me that the Network was blessed with dedicated employees—Jerry, Llona, and Colonel Coyle, all working late.

Anyway, in all the excitement, everyone had forgotten that the alarms in this building were also on a direct line to the firehouse.

"Now that we remember," I said as calmly as I could, "why don't we call them on the phone and tell them they don't have to bother?"

Llona looked thoughtful. "Good idea. I'll do it right away."

"Yeah," I said, "do that." She nodded briskly, then took off for the nearest phone.

She was just about to disappear around the bend, when a blood-curdling scream of *"I'll kill the son-of-a-bitch who's responsible for this!"* came from the other direction, and froze her in her tracks.

My brain chose that moment to remind me that a noted movie critic had described the owner of that voice as "the epitome of gentle, yet healthy feminine radiance."

"Melanie just found out, I take it," I said to Llona.

"I suppose so. Coyle had one of the guards go to the Brant to get her."

"Wonderful. Are you sure there's nothing else you haven't told me? We're not under attack by the FALN or anything?"

Llona had a small smile for me. "Not yet."

By now, Spot, who hates to be left out, was pulling at his leash in an attempt to see what all the shouting was about. "Okay, boy, let's go," I said. He shook his head to make his silver collar jingle, then, hanging his tongue jauntily from the side of his snout, he led me down the hall to Melanie.

For the second time that day, I came within touching distance of Melanie Marliss. If anything, she was even more beautiful than she had been before. Her face was hot and flushed, her delicate nostrils flared, her sensuous lips parted, her green eyes flashing. Her honey-colored hair was in disarray, and her chest under her tight sweater was heaving with passion, which was no inconsiderable heave, believe me.

My luck, it was the wrong kind of passion. She brought the world's most photographed face two inches from mine, and said, *"Are you in charge here, Cobb?"*

My luck again, I had to tell her I was.

"Aha!" You would have thought she'd proven some great point. "This guy Coyle tells me *you're* the one that's going to get my bowling ball back!"

Thanks a heap, Coyle, I thought. *They steal it from under your nose, then you set me up to take the rap.* Nice.

"I'll do what I can," I told Melanie.

"You'd just better find that bastard, fast!" said the epitome of gentle, yet healthy feminine radiance. "Or I'll sue this Network for everything it's got! How can you be so *stupid!* This is an inside job, I swear it! I—"

"Calm down, Melanie," Lorenzo Baker said, stroking her shoulder. "You don't want to say anything that would prejudice your case do you?"

I hadn't even noticed he was there—Melanie Marliss's primal fury had drowned him right out. Still, I was glad to see him. I wasn't too crazy about the sentiment, but his words *did* seem to be having a calming effect on her. America's sex symbol had left off slander, and was now contenting herself with describing what she would do when she got her hands on the thief. If the Marquis de Sade had been around, he would have been jotting down notes.

Then, out of a knot of people huddled a few dozen yards down the corridor that included a whole bunch of former radio and TV greats (including Shelby and Green, but not, I noticed, Alice Brockway), trouble came striding in the form of Colonel Jasper Coyle.

Coyle was a ramrod-straight retired army man. As a soldier, it was his first instinct to meet force with force. I didn't especially need somebody to come and yell at Melanie Marliss and set her off again.

Spot came to the rescue. Melanie was saying, ". . . and another thing, *eeee!* What the *hell* . . . ?"

The Samoyed was licking on one of the famous knees. She looked down at him. Spot looked back, in that cute little insouciant way of his. Perfect beauty (woman) gazed on perfect beauty (canine). Melanie

was almost as famous as an animal lover as she was as an actress. Spot
was an easy animal to love. Immediately, she squatted and hugged the
dog's fluffy neck.

"Hel-*lo*, poochie," she cooed. "Did Mellie scare you with her yelling?
I'm *sor*-ree."

What a trooper that mutt was. Normally, that kind of fawning made
him as sick as it did me, but he stood there and took it, even taking an
occasional slurp at Melanie's face for good measure.

She gave me a long hard squint. Obviously, if I owned such a terrific
dog, I couldn't be such a louse. "This your dog?" she demanded.

"We live together."

"What's his name?"

Here we go again, I thought. "Spot."

"Spot?" She was obviously puzzled.

"Yes," I said wearily. It got tiresome explaining Rick Sloan's little
joke all the time. "He's named for the gigantic white spot that covers
his entire body."

"That's cute," Melanie said, and kissed him on the muzzle.

So Spot had achieved a détente before the Army even arrived.
"Hello, Colonel," I said.

"Hello, Cobb," he said coldly. It should have been *Mister* Cobb,
since I was a vice-president, in charge of my own department, and he
was merely a supervisor, answering to the Director of Building Services,
and the vice-president in charge of Network Operations, but I didn't
make a point of it. It would only upset him. He couldn't get over the
idea that a man who had been a colonel in the MP's should "mister"
someone who had been a mere sergeant.

"Have you met Miss Marliss and Mr. Baker?"

"I have just recently had that pleasure," he said, and bowed to
Melanie. The old fossil had style, anyway. Melanie appeared to like it.

He turned to me. "It was bound to happen, you know," he grumbled. "Wouldn't have if they'd listened to me. Told them the place was
vulnerable." If Coyle had his way, we'd broadcast from a cave.

Not wanting to give Melanie a chance to gather more ammunition
for that lawsuit, I suggested she go have a seat somewhere until the
police came. It was a pleasant surprise when she actually did.

"Well, Colonel," I said when she and Baker had left, "how, specifi-
cally, is this module of the Tower susceptible to infiltration?"

I was kidding him, but only partly. Coyle didn't think you meant it
until you gave it to him in his native tongue: Pompous Bullshit.

"It's possible someone could have gained entrance as part of a tour
group, then broke ranks and concealed himself in the latrine. Then he
could have breeched Studio J—the entrance to which is *not* locked, de-

spite my recommendations—stolen the material, and escaped down the fire stairs."

"Isn't the opening of one of the outside doors of the fire stairs supposed to set off the alarm system?"

He gave me a superior smile. "The alarm," he oozed, "had already been activated. Remember? I'll know more about the situation after I debrief the de Lune boy."

"That's pronounced de *Loan*," I corrected him irritably, "and *I'll* do the debriefing around here. You call the police."

"Do we need the police?" Another superior smile was on Coyle's face, but the tone of his voice would have gone better with a contemptuous sneer.

My patience snapped. "Why is Jerry in the hospital, Colonel? He came down with a sudden attack of aggravated assault, right? That is a crime, no? Now, I realize it would be swell for the glory of the outfit if we could solve this all by ourselves, but we have a catch-22 in civilian life, too, Colonel: If you don't tell the police about a crime, that is *also* a crime. So call them."

His teeth were clenched, and his fists were, too. His face got very red, but all he said was, "As you say, sir." He stalked off.

Llona came back. "I called the fire department," she said.

"And?"

"They didn't believe me."

It figured. The NYFD answers more false alarms than any other fire department in the world. They've come to expect them. Naturally, when somebody calls to tell them they're *not* needed, they're going to be suspicious.

"That's all right," I told Llona. "They think you've invented a new kind of crime, the false non-alarm." I shook my head. "What hospital did they take Jerry to?"

She told me, and I said that's where I was going if someone needed to reach me.

"I'll ride down with you," she said. "I'll meet the firemen in the lobby and try to convince them there."

It was total insanity, I reflected on the way down. Here I was, a reasonably mature human being (at least, I thought I was), starting out on a desperate hunt for a bowling ball that had been stolen from a woman who made millions of dollars from people paying to see moving pictures of her with little or no clothing on.

I looked up at a sudden noise. Llona was banging her palms against the stainless steel wall of the elevator, making a sound like native drums in a cheap jungle picture. She was usually so cool and in control; I had to look at her in surprise. She turned around, met my eyes, then took two quick steps toward me.

I was fatalistic about it. After an attack on the (for all I knew) perfectly harmless Jerry de Loon, and the theft of a bowling ball and the entire year of 1952, it only figured that *I* would be attacked by a pint-sized female public relations specialist.

Luckily, it wasn't violence she had on her mind.

Before I could do anything about it, assuming I *wanted* to do anything about it, she had her hands clasped behind my neck and was pulling my face down to hers.

We kissed each other quite thoroughly. When we broke apart, I said, "What was that, a new PR technique? I mean, this time was fine, but I think it would make me think twice about getting on an elevator with Ritafio."

"I . . . I had to do something to . . . well, it was a way to break the tension," she said at last, a little defiantly. "I've been under a *lot* of pressure, and tonight . . ."

"Hey," I said softly, "it's better than beating on the walls, right?"

She smiled at me. "Much better," she said.

The doors opened on the lobby, and sure enough, the firemen were there. Coward that I am, I left Llona to deal with them.

CHAPTER 5

"Surpraz, surpraz, sur-praz!"

—JIM NABORS, "GOMER PYLE—USMC," CBS

"Spot, stay!" I told the Samoyed on the hospital steps. Like the obedient pooch he was, he lay down on the concrete to wait for me. Dognapers would try to move him at their own risk.

At the desk, I found out (after the unavoidable bureaucratic confusion) that Mr. de Loon had just been admitted, should they check to see if he was out of x-ray? He was, and they told me his room number.

When I came into the place, I'd been prepared to bluff and/or cajole my way to seeing Jerry—assuming, of course, that he was healthy enough. I'm sneaky, but I'm not callous.

It didn't prove necessary. Jerry had been asking for me since they'd brought him in. He'd managed to give them the impression I was next of kin or something, so I got sent right up.

It turned out I had to wait awhile, anyway, because there was another test they wanted to do. When it was finished, and they wheeled him into his room, he seemed chipper enough, considering he'd caught a hard one in the head.

A man in a white coat, Kindly Old Doc, right out of Central Casting, complete with silvery hair and wire-frame half-glasses, joined me for a brief conversation in the hall.

"How is he?" I asked.

"That's hard to say, before I've seen the x-rays," the doctor told me. "Nothing alarming in the EEG, which is encouraging."

"He doesn't seem too bad, from what I've seen of him," I said.

"Head injuries are tricky," he said. "Not like you people show on TV, you know. Makes me mad. 'Mannix' was the worst. That one of yours?"

"No." Something in the way he looked at me from the corner of his eye made me glad I could say that.

"The damn show was a menace. Every week, Mannix got clubbed into oblivion, woke up in two minutes, felt the back of his head, and said, 'Just a bump on the head.' That's what your friend told me, 'Just a bump on the head.' Stupidity. He tells me some girl named Mona or something called for an ambulance over his objections. *That* was smart."

"Can I talk to him now?"

"Yes, but not for too long. It's getting late, and if he wasn't so bound and determined to see you, I'd make you wait." He looked at his watch. "In a case like this, we check his reflexes and lucidity every fifteen minutes. I just did it when we brought him in—you can stay until the nurse comes around to do it again."

I thanked him and went in. Jerry was lying quietly on the bed, one bare foot sticking out where he had apparently kicked the sheet free. He had a fresh bandage on his head, and bruises on his throat.

"Hello, Jerry."

"Hello, Mr. Cobb." Despite all the talk about his wanting to see me, it was obvious that Jerry, at the moment, was afraid of me. I do not especially enjoy being feared.

"I'm sorry, Mr. Cobb, honest. It wasn't my fault. I—I'll make it up to the Network somehow."

Oh, for Christ's sake, I thought in exasperation. "Jerry," I said, "relax, will you? Nobody's mad at you, I just want to ask you some questions."

"Yes, sir." His hands shook on the crisp white sheet. "It's just that it took me *so long* to finally break into the industry, and when I get my chance, I *blow* it—"

It didn't look like this was going to be a very fruitful interview, unless I could get Jerry to stop apologizing to me for something I wasn't mad at him about in the first place.

"Jerry," I said ominously, "the questions, remember?"

He swallowed, and got ready for Torquemada Cobb, Master of the Third Degree. "I—okay," he said at last.

"Who was the star of 'Pete Kelly's Blues'?" I demanded.

That did the trick. Surprised, he forgot to be scared. "Jack Webb," he shot back. Trivia, he didn't have to think about.

"Not the movie," I said, "the TV series."

"Why . . . ?" He looked at me for a second, decided I must be crazy, then said, "Oh, okay—it was William Reynolds."

"Congratulations. You passed."

"Passed?"

"How could I let them fire the only other person left in New York that even *remembers* there was a series called 'Pete Kelly's Blues'?"

Jerry laughed, then winced, then laughed some more, burning off some of the tension and fear. "Thanks, Mr. Cobb," he said when he was finished. "I really made a jerk out of myself, didn't I?"

"Not at all," I said. "That business with the fire alarm was fast thinking." That pleased him. "Now, I want you to tell me what happened tonight."

"All right, but I don't think it's going to help much in catching him."

"Are you sure it's a man?" I asked. First things first.

He was going to shake his head, but decided it hurt too much. "No. I never saw the person."

I sighed. "Well, tell me what you remember, anyway."

"Well, like I told you this afternoon, I've finished up '49, and I've been working on 1950."

"That's why you were there late?"

"I thought I'd at least finish that year tonight. You see, the first thing I did when I came on the job was run through all the canisters just to see what the actual shows were—*this* time through, I was getting the credits, running the actors down, checking for exact air dates, and like that."

"Go on."

"Tonight—I don't know what time, I lose track—I was in the library. I had the door closed, I didn't want to disturb the rehearsals—do you know about the rehearsals?" I nodded. Jerry went on.

"Anyway, I was watching an old Ann Garson show—wasn't she a great singer?"

"Not a bad comedienne, either," I conceded. "Then what?"

He shrugged. "Somebody knocked on the door. I figured it was one of the people who usually drop in when I work late—from News, or Ops, or Special Projects, you know, on their coffee break. But I . . ."

"Yes?"

"Well, I also sort of hoped it would be one of the stars, you know? Like, while I was running the 'Ann Garson Show,' if Ann Garson *herself* would knock on the door." Just the contemplation of it brought a smile to his face. "Like Shelby and Green did this afternoon.

"But even if it wasn't a star or anything, I didn't mind. I like when people come around. It makes me feel—well, more like a real part of the Network."

"So you opened the door," I said.

"Right. And nobody was there. So I stuck my head out to take a look, and he—somebody grabbed my throat."

"Stick with 'he,' it'll make it easier to talk. You didn't see him at all, huh?"

"Nope. He was on the right side of the door, and he had me, right away. He pushed my head back—or rather, I pulled it back, trying to get away, and he kept pushing, then after a couple of seconds, my eyes went all red—I remember thinking I was dying. Then he let me go, but before I could see again, or even breathe, he got around behind me, and hit me on the head. It happened so fast, I didn't have a chance!" Jerry said. "I'm sorry."

"Will you for God's sake stop being sorry?" I snapped. "Believe it or not, Jerry, even though the Network is a big, cold corporation, we haven't come to the point of expecting employees to lay down their lives in the line of duty."

"Their *lives?*"

"Who knows? If you had a chance to struggle, he might have increased the pressure on your throat, and then what? It's just as well you *didn't* fight him."

I gave him a chance to get the idea that the Network doesn't expect kinescope librarians to be two-fisted death, while I ruminated on Jerry's story, what there was of it.

From the mechanics of the thing, you could see the thief was right-handed. Or ambidextrous, after I thought about it a second. Or a lefty who thought swinging a sap more intricate a task than grabbing an Adam's apple. So to hell with that flight into deductive reasoning.

The attacker's attitude seemed to have been that, while he had no great regard for Jerry's well-being, he would let the boy live if he couldn't identify him. Maybe. Or else he just beat on him to minimize interference with the theft. Or for kicks. The police were going to love this case.

"Now," I said, "you noticed the cans from 1952 had been stolen as soon as you came to?"

"I set off the fire alarm as soon as I came to," the librarian said. "I didn't know anything was stolen, until just now. He took 1952?" I nodded. "Why?"

"I was about to ask you the same question. What was there somebody would want to take?"

"You got me," he said in wonder. "All I knew at the time was that he'd trashed the place but good. Nineteen fifty-two, huh? There wasn't nearly as much there as there was from other years."

"How much?"

"Only fourteen one-hour cans."

Fourteen cans, I thought, *my God.* Fourteen hour-long cans of sixteen-millimeter movie film would weigh a ton, and make a stack several feet high. Not impossible to carry, maybe, but not exactly a bag of feathers, either. With Melanie Marliss's bowling ball balanced on top, it would make one hell of an awkward package, especially if you expected to slip surreptitiously down seven flights of fire stairs. You couldn't bank on Jerry setting off the alarm to mask your exit for you, either.

"What was on the film, Jerry?"

"Bunch of Saturday morning stuff. 'Coony Island,' the puppet show; 'Dr. Wonder'—he used to do science experiments and explain—"

"I remember it. Anything else?"

"There was a cooking show called 'Gone to Pot.' One episode. I never heard of it before; nobody else I talked to did either. I finally had to go to Traffic and dig up the old logs to find out what year it belonged to. I think that was it.

"Oh, and there was a kine of 'Be Still My Heart.'"

"Hmmm," I said. That was interesting. It represented the first inkling for a possible motive for the theft of the films. It wasn't *much* of a possible motive, and it said nothing at all about the bowling ball, but it was something to think about.

I thought about it. "Be Still My Heart" was one of the classic live dramas from the so-called Golden Age of Television. I say "so-called" because it is a well-documented, if little-acknowledged, fact that a large percentage of the programming then was flat-out terrible. For every play like Reginald Rose's "Twelve Angry Men," Rod Serling's "Requiem for a Heavyweight," or Paddy Chayefsky's "Marty," there were *dozens* of episodes of "The Continental" or "Strike It Rich"—shows, incidentally, that far outdistanced the live dramas in audience appeal—another little-acknowledged fact.

The illusion of the Golden Age exists because people compare the best of the past with the worst of now. Sure, any era that didn't have "Real People" on the air is going to look good in retrospect, but compare "Queen for a Day" with "M*A*S*H," or "Lou Grant," or any of a number of equally fine shows, and it wouldn't be so hard to believe the Golden Age is now.

But I digress. Roger Shazenick's "Be Still My Heart" had been a great show, and would have been in any era. It was also an immediate critical success when it first aired in the fall of 1952, so the Network had a lot of prints of the original kinescope made up. A lot of those prints made their way into museums and colleges (that was where I first saw the show), as well as into some private collections.

Could it be, I asked myself, that some fanatical collector wanted a copy of "Be Still My Heart" so badly he'd steal one? It didn't seem likely, but hardly anything does any more.

There was something else about that show I was about to remember, but I was distracted by Jerry. It wasn't anything he was doing—he wasn't doing anything. He wasn't, in fact, moving at all.

I picked up the white button from the bed, and started pressing it, over and over. But that didn't seem like enough, so I started yelling, "*Nurse!*"

In practically no time, the nurse was there, along with the doctor, whose name I never did find out. With a professionalism it was a joy to see, they pushed me the hell out of the way, and tried to do something for Jerry. All I could do was watch, and pray a little.

CHAPTER 6

". . . And don't you forget to tell the truth!"
—CLAYTON (BUD) COLLYER, "TO TELL THE TRUTH," CBS

When I finally woke up, Thursday, my mouth felt like the Ayatollah had washed his beard in it. It was much later than my usual wake-up time—I'd go to the office when I was ready to face it, if I went at all. Falzet had called a meeting for late that afternoon, but the way I felt, I needed a meeting with him the way I needed the heartbreak of psoriasis.

I was determined to act as if trouble was something I read about in a book once. I got dressed, gave Spot clean water, patted his head for his morning dose of affection, then took him for a walk. I picked up the papers on the way. I read the funnies and sports in the *News,* then turned to the *Times* for the classified. I read the Apartment for Rent ads grimly. It's a rule of life in New York that all kinds of places are available except one that would suit you. It was still a couple of months before Rick and Jane were due to come back, but I thought I'd better start looking. The trouble was, I'd gotten spoiled living in their plush eagle's nest.

It occurred to me in one of my brilliant flashes of social insight that the recent sharp increase in pre-marital cohabitation might have been contributed to by the housing shortage—"Love, shmove. You gonna let this apartment go to *waste?"*

And that broke the spell. Jerry de Loon, as it turned out, had been a cohabitator. I'd been to his apartment in Queens last night, to tell his girlfriend, Hildy, what happened. Hildy was a very plain girl, with buck teeth. She wore her hair in a brown braid that reached below her waist. She was extremely pregnant.

I was with a policeman, a detective from the Eighteenth Precinct. He was mad at life in general, and took it out on me by forcing me to tell her. "You're in the word business," he said.

Words. I gave her the doctor's words. Jerry suffered a trauma. That means somebody hit him. He developed a hematoma. That means a blood clot. The hematoma broke loose and traveled until it became an embolus. That means it blocked off a blood vessel—in Jerry's case, an important one in his brain. He expired. That means he died.

Hildy had words, too, but they were screamed, or sobbed, or confused. Most of them were to convince the detective and me that we were wrong. Couldn't we see she was going to have a *baby*, for Christ's sake?

"Jerry's *happy*," she had maintained. "We're going to get *married*. He told me before he wouldn't until he proved he was worth something. I always *told* him I didn't care if he swept out buildings at night so he could try to get a job at one of the networks, I knew he could do it, after college and all.

"But he said, 'What if I never get a chance?' He was mad when he found out I was . . . was gonna have a baby—well, not mad, worried.

"*But it's all right now!*" she insisted. "Jerry's got a chance, and I know he's doing a good job. He says the Network changed our luck, after two years of tough times.

"You're Mr. Cobb? Jerry looks up to you, he talks about you all the time. Why are you lying about him? Why? *Why?*"

It had gone on for hours, and Hildy's voice kept yelling *why?* in my sleep. I didn't know, and I still don't. One smack on the head, and he died—no warning, no anything. According to the doctor, the way Jerry had died was "rare, but not unprecedented."

I said a vulgar word, with feeling, and picked up the papers again. Jerry got two lines in each of the accounts. The *Times* article devolved into a discussion of the seminal effect of the "Harriet Gunner" series on the Women's Movement, and the *News* devoted better than a quarter of a page to an old cheesecake photo of Melanie Marliss.

I said another vulgar word and pitched the papers away from me again. This could have gone on all day, but I was interrupted by the building intercom buzzer, which meant the doorman had something to say to me.

"What do you want?" I snapped.

"There's ah . . . a policeman down here, Mr. Cobb," the doorman said.

The doorman's mild Spanish accent was replaced with a gruff Brooklynese. "Just tell him it's Rivetz, willya?"

"Send him up," I said.

"Yes, Mr. Cobb." He clicked off. I had to wonder what Rivetz wanted. Horace A. Rivetz was a hard-boiled little detective with spikes of iron-gray hair sticking up from his head, and a face like a clenched fist. He and I had first met in a cheap Times Square hotel room, with the freshly killed body of a man named Vincent Carlson on the floor between us. He spent most of his effort on that case trying very hard to pin a murder rap on me. He was man enough to admit he was wrong, however, and since then, relations had been cordial.

I was a little surprised to see him—I'd figured the death of a nobody (I made fists) like Jerry de Loon would be handled on a lower level than Headquarters, which is where Rivetz operated from.

Rivetz rang the bell, and I invited him in. "Nice place you got here, Cobb," he said.

"Thanks. What can I do for you?"

"You can take a little ride with me."

I had an uncomfortable flash of *déjà vu*, and said so. Rivetz grinned. "Relax, Cobb, I'm not even on duty, officially. I'm doing the lieutenant a favor."

"Lieutenant Martin wants to see me? What about? That's from Hammacher-Schlemmer."

Rivetz gave a little guilty start, and put down the lamp he'd been looking at the bottom of. He asked me how much it cost. After I told him, he whistled and said, "My wife is just gonna have to live without one, then." He whistled again. "All that money for something to hold a light bulb, for God's sake.

"Anyway, I don't know what the lieutenant wants, although he did get a complaint from one of the precinct boys about you talking to the de Loon kid before they had a chance to."

That made me mad. "What did they think? Jerry died sooner because I showed up? What a lot of crap. Listen, if *I* didn't talk to him, no one would have *ever* talked with him."

"We'll find out when we get to Headquarters," Rivetz said. "Of course, you don't *have* to come . . ."

"I'm coming, don't worry." I told Spot to behave himself while I was gone.

Nobody but my parents has known me as long as Detective Lieutenant Cornelius U. Martin, Jr., has—he and his family integrated our neighborhood when I was six years old, and Mr. M. was still pounding a beat. I got to be best friends with his son, Cornelius U. Martin III, and Corny and I divided our time pretty evenly between my place, his place, and the basketball court.

Corny was living out in Wisconsin now, coaching at a small college, but I still saw his father pretty frequently.

The lieutenant's office was a cubbyhole on the third floor of Headquarters and the lieutenant himself filled it up pretty well. He was big and powerful-looking, but just recently he'd started to show signs of slowing up a step, as though his body had finally decided to believe that snow-white hair on his head. His big, round face was kind, but not kindly—there was too much shrewdness in it for it to look kindly.

Besides the lieutenant's desk, there was one cracked leather armchair in the office. As the guest, I got to sit in it. Rivetz sat on the window sill.

After the hellos had been taken care of, the lieutenant said, "What have you got planned for today, Matty?"

"Nothing much," I told him. "I have a meeting at the Tower at three o'clock."

"What about?"

"What do you think?" I asked.

"In other words, it's about the murder," he said.

"That'll be touched on," I said, "but the main event will be what to do when Melanie Marliss sues the Network for negligence for losing her bowling ball."

"Oh, come on," the lieutenant said.

"Well, last night, or rather this morning, when the festivities broke up, the taco king delivered the message on behalf of the star, who was not speaking to any of us. Remember Groucho Marx in *Duck Soup*? 'Of course you realize, this means *war!*'? That's how Lorenzo Baker was last night. He's very protective of his little Melanie's interests, you know. The fact that a lawsuit against the Network would be monumental publicity for the picture he's producing is just gravy."

"How much could she get?" Rivetz asked. "I paid sixty bucks for my bowling ball. To me, that's a lot of money, but to a movie star, it ought to be peanuts."

"Actually, the ball didn't cost her anything—it was the thanks of a grateful Network. What Melanie wants to be recompensed for is mental anguish and things like that." I grinned. "And guess who's in charge of getting it back?"

"You, right?"

I nodded grimly. "It's not going to be easy, maybe, but I don't mind, because when I find the guy with the bowling ball, I'll have Jerry's killer."

"Yeah," the lieutenant said. "Just you don't forget the police are going to have something to say about it, too."

"Of course."

"Don't 'of course' me," he said. "I know you. Obstructing justice seems to be a hobby of yours."

I denied that. Once I knew it was justice, and not just spadework, I was obstructing, I always stepped aside. "There's nothing for the Network to hide, this time," I told him.

"Good. Maybe we can all help each other out."

Rivetz, who had been perusing a folder of reports, snorted. "We're all gonna need help, too. According to this, everybody was somewhere else. A few even have alibis—woman named Hall, man named Ritafio, together in an office. Bunch of people rehearsing a re-enactment of the

Theodore Farnsworth radio variety show—that ought to be good. What a voice that guy had." Rivetz broke into song, a surprisingly good impression of Theodore Farnsworth doing "Song of Romance." He stopped just as abruptly as he started.

"Anyway," he went on, ignoring a look from Lieutenant Martin, "they all alibi each other, as do, let's see, Lenny Green and Alice Brockway, who say they were across the street. Other people claim they were in their office, alone, or they went to the bathroom and the bar downstairs, alone, or they went home, also alone."

"Why shouldn't they?" I asked. This was the second time around for me. The precinct detective with whom I had gone to Queens, had had me alongside him when he interviewed every single person who'd been in the building at the time, and the results weren't going to change.

"No reason," Rivetz said. "I was *about* to say it looks from this like an outside job, maybe two or three people to carry all that stuff."

"It was an inside job," Lieutenant Martin said flatly.

"Oh," Rivetz said. I didn't say anything; the lieutenant would get to the point soon enough.

"Matty," he said, eying me closely, "in that way you have of doing things, you and your Network have landed smack dab in the middle of another one."

"What do you mean, Mr. M.?"

"I mean I want you to tell me, without evasions, lies, or English-teacher tricks, everything you know about Jim Bevic."

I had to admit, it threw me for a loss for a few seconds. Then the dawn broke. "Don't tell me," I said. "You're looking into this for the LAPD."

"Sort of semi-officially," he said. "I'm doing a favor for Bob Matsuko."

"Who's he?" Rivetz wanted to know.

"Homicide lieutenant," Mr. M. explained. "I met him that time I went out to the Coast to bring that embezzler back a few years ago. Japanese guy. Good cop.

"So he's got a homicide out there that leads to New York, but for a lot of reasons, he doesn't want to ruffle any feathers, so he asks me to keep an eye on it. I told him I'd do what I could, but that we were going fifteen-, sixteen-hour shifts just on our own stuff. He'll be happy to know that thanks to last night his murder is tied right *in* with our own stuff. Do you follow me, Matty?"

"Sure," I said. "You're saying the murder of Jerry de Loon and the theft of the bowling ball and film tie in with the murder of Jim Bevic in some way." I told myself to relax. Someday, this was going to make sense.

"*'In some way,'*" he mocked. "You're no fool, Matty, you know as well as *I* do in what way."

"Yeah?"

"Yeah," he said. "So tell me what you know about Jim Bevic. All of it."

I couldn't see what he was driving at, but I decided to play along and tell him what I knew about the reporter. I didn't know much.

"He was a writer," I said. "A good one. He was somewhere in his early thirties when he died. He used to work for some newspaper in Ohio or somewhere—"

"Pennsylvania," the lieutenant corrected. He sounded ominous.

"Okay, Pennsylvania," I conceded. "According to the dust jacket on his book, he quit that, and took up driving a cab by night, and writing and researching by day, until he came out with a book called *Fellow Travelers,* about the Red Scare in the forties and fifties. Good book, made the best seller list. I bought one three-four years ago when it came out. He was going bald—"

"That all you can tell me?" the lieutenant snapped.

I thought about it. "That's about it. The obituary in the paper could tell you as much."

"I *know* that. Don't fool with me, Matty, I'm warning you."

"What do you want me to say, for God's sake?"

"What was he working on when he died? What was he doing in Costa Rica just before he went to Los Angeles?"

I sputtered at him. "How the hell am I supposed to know?"

"You published him, didn't you?"

"Oh, for crying out loud," I said.

"You can't hold out on me this time, Matty. I looked it up. Since the year before Bevic's book came out, the publishing company, Austin, Stoddard & Trapp, has been a wholly owned subsidiary of the Network!"

I shook my head at him. "Mr. M.," I said, "the Network also has a wholly owned subsidiary in Altoona, Pennsylvania, that makes paper boxes. That doesn't mean I'm up on all the latest dirt from the corrugation machine."

"I know how you and your Special Projects people get around."

"Austin, Stoddard & Trapp isn't even in the Tower—they have their own building on the East Side. You think Bevic was working on a book when he was killed? Why don't you ask his editor? *He* ought to know."

"I already did. They don't know anything. *They* say. All they know is he was working on a new book. He was very secretive about that kind of thing, they tell me.

"*All* you people who work for the Network are secretive." He ran a hand over his head. "All right. I thought you'd know—you seem to know everything that goes on in the Network. You say you don't, and maybe you don't, but *I'd* still like to find out. In fact, there's a *bunch* of things I'd like to find out.

"I'd like to know what Jim Bevic was doing in Costa Rica. I'd like to know why he went from there to L.A. I'd like to know how it turned out that Lenny Green found him floating in Ken Shelby's swimming pool . . .

"And I'd *really* like to know why on the very day they're finally allowed to leave L.A., they're in or near a building that houses the corporation that owns Jim Bevic's publisher while a man is being killed!"

CHAPTER 7

"Extremism in the defense of Liberty is no vice. Moderation in the pursuit of Justice is no virtue."

—BARRY M. GOLDWATER, 1964 REPUBLICAN NATIONAL
CONVENTION, ALL NETWORKS

"It makes me mad to have to say this," I admitted, "but I don't think Jerry's death was part of a plan. I think as far as our bowling ball pilferer is concerned, his death was an unfortunate complication."

"How do you know?" the lieutenant asked.

"Well, say he *did* for some reason have it in for Jerry. He did a pretty sloppy job, didn't he? Especially after the efficient way Jim Bevic was taken care of. I mean, it was a big surprise that Jerry died at all."

"Where does it say a killer can't screw up the same as everybody else, Matty? Hell, if they didn't screw up, we'd never catch them."

"How do you explain the bowling ball and the kinescopes?" I asked quietly.

"I don't explain anything," he said irritably. "At least not yet. Maybe the killer wanted to leave a false trail or something. All I know is, Jerry de Loon was murdered, and I'd be a dope if I didn't look for someone with a reason to kill him."

I sighed. "I suppose so, but I doubt you'll find anything. You might want to check out his girlfriend's parents."

"I know how to do my job, Matty," he assured me.

He was right, of course, and I knew how to do mine. "The Network would appreciate it," I said, "if you would keep publicity about Shelby and Green in this case to a minimum."

"This is the first you're hearing about it, right? Hell, it's even the first time Rivetz has heard about it. Don't worry, L.A. and New York both want to keep this as quiet as possible until something solid turns up. Let the reporters latch on to a show-business angle, and it's nuthouse time. You'll notice it hasn't even come out yet where the body was found."

"Yeah," Rivetz said, "I been wondering about that. How did Green come to find the body in Shelby's pool?"

"I'm going to fill you in on that now," the lieutenant said. He took a manila folder out of his desk, and put on a pair of reading glasses—another recent concession to age.

"You understand," he began, "officially, Green and Alice Brockway are witnesses, not suspects. Shelby, supposedly, was out in Arizona, working on a real estate development he's in on. Bob Matsuko kept them in L.A. with sweet talk as long as he could, but there was no evidence to hold *anybody* on, let alone three prominent citizens like them, so when they absolutely insisted they had to come to New York for that bash at the Network, he had to let them go. He asked me to keep an eye on them."

I rubbed my forehead. Public Relations was going to love this. I could see Llona's face now, and hear Ritafio's whine.

"What happened?" I asked.

"Well, according to Matsuko, Green says he was driving around the neighborhood—Beverly Hills, some neighborhood—and drove up to Shelby's house on the chance he might be home. He wanted to talk about the letter they'd gotten from Porter Reigels, finalizing what sketch they were going to do on the show. They hadn't had much of a chance to go over it in person, because Green was getting over a broken leg at a friend's ranch out in the desert somewhere. Hurt it in some kind of freak accident, but it's pretty well healed by now."

"He still limps a little," I said.

"Anyway," the lieutenant went on, ignoring me, "he drove up to the house, and rang the bell. He wasn't surprised to get no answer, because, though the Shelbys have servants, they often let them take the afternoon off, especially if Mrs. Shelby is the only one home.

"Green decided, he says, that as long as he was there, he might as well exercise his leg, and walk around the house to see if they were in their pool—built-in job away from the house."

"And he went there and found the body? One of the few details that *has* gotten out is that the body'd been floating for at least twenty-four hours. Nobody discovered it in all that time?"

"It's not that hard to believe. The servants don't go down to the pool unless it's to bring the Shelbys a drink or something. Shelby himself was out of town, and his wife, at the time the murder must have been committed, was heading out to a taping of 'Hollywood Secrets,' which I find out, isn't done in Hollywood at all—"

"Burbank," I put in.

"Yeah. Anyway, since the way they do these things is to tape five shows in one evening, one right after another—"

"You know how they lift a fingerprint?" I said. "They brush or blow this very fine powder, light for dark surfaces, dark for light ones . . ."

Don't ever let anyone ever tell you black people can't blush. The lieutenant's face went from brown to cordovan, and he said, "Okay, Matty, you got me that time. I don't have to tell you your job either. From now on I'll skip the technical TV stuff. What I was driving at was that it would have been dark by the time she got home.

"There's also a twelve-foot-high wooden fence around the pool. It would be hard for someone just casually passing by to see a body floating in the water.

"Green, though, says he opened the gate and went inside the fence. There was no phone handy to call the police when he found the body, so he went back to his car, drove around Beverly Hills until he found a patrol car, and led it back to the house.

"By the time they got there, Alice Brockway was home. Since, *as you know*"—he shot me a challenging look—"they do two weeks' worth of 'Hollywood Secrets' at a time, ten shows, she was supposed to be at the NBC studio Sunday evening, as well, but—and this is confirmed—she came down with a migraine and had to go home. Needless to say, when the cops told her she had a corpse in her pool, she nearly passed out."

"Completely needless," I said. "I've seen some of Alice's emotions in action. What has the investigation turned up since?"

The lieutenant shrugged. "The autopsy made it murder—Bevic died of drowning, actually—he was alive when he went into the pool—but he'd been knocked unconscious first."

"It couldn't have been an accident?" I asked.

"Not according to this. He was hit with something more or less rounded, like a sock full of sand. If he'd hit his head on the edge of the pool, the characteristics of the wound would have been much different."

I could see how that lent credence to the lieutenant's position the two deaths were connected. Bopping heads isn't a rare *modus operandi,* or anything, but it was an indication.

"I didn't need this, you know," I said. "I have enough trouble coping with life when everything is going right."

Lieutenant Martin snorted. "How do you think I feel? I'm stuck with a homicide that looks like all the answers to it are out in California. Or Matsuko. *He's* got a case where his four top suspects—excuse me, witnesses, take off for New York like a flock of homing pigeons."

"Four?" I said, surprised. "Shelby, Brockway, Green, and who else?"

"Wilma Bascombe," he said. "She's a tricky one. As long as L.A. wants it all kept unofficial, we've got no leverage to get in to see her." I asked him if they'd tried; with a disgusted look, he assured me they had.

Meanwhile, I was thinking, Wilma Bascombe, of course, why didn't *you* think of her, jerk, but I said, "How about if I give it a try?"

The lieutenant grinned. "I was hoping you'd say that, Matty, but all you might get out of it is a ride in the country. I've got to warn you. I've been out there once, and she doesn't make it easy for people to come visit her."

Which was understandable. Throughout the forties, Wilma Bascombe was a Star (capital "S") of stage and film, as much a sex symbol, in her day, as Melanie Marliss was now. Different type, though. Where Melanie was "gentle, yet healthy feminine radiance," Wilma was regal, enigmatic; an ice sculpture with a cold, unearthly beauty. She had won one of the first Tony's, and a best-actress Oscar for her performance in *The Empress and the Vagabond*.

At the start of the fifties, at the height of her fame, she announced she was "tired" of acting, and quit to join the faculty of a college in New York City, making its drama department even more famous than it already was. Occasionally, she could be prevailed upon to appear in a television play, because, she said, she felt she should learn the new medium in order to teach it.

In 1952, people started to hear rumors that the Empress had socialistic leanings, and that sort of thing was just not tolerated. Wilma Bascombe was summoned to appear at yet another of those congressional committees.

A lot of entertainers testified before those committees. Some admitted the error of their ways, said they were very sorry, and were told to go and sin no more—after they provided to the committee a list of their erstwhile friends, so that *they* could come to Washington and apologize, too. Some stood mute. And some went out of their way to martyr themselves. They were the ones who had trouble finding work for a long time afterward.

A very few, including Wilma Bascombe, told the committee what to do with itself. One of my earliest memories is watching that hearing on my family's first TV, a seven-inch screen in a five-foot high cabinet. I remember it because I was scared—I didn't know what was going on, but those men must have done something really bad to deserve the cold loathing and the measured contempt the pretty lady was treating them with. A radio commentator said it was Wilma Bascombe's greatest performance, with what accuracy he never knew, because he committed suicide three months later rather than testify before that committee himself.

The committee was so shocked at the verbal flogging Wilma Bascombe had given them, they let her get out of the hearing room before they could remember they wanted to hold her in contempt. She was added to the blacklist of course, but the college, like the great institution it was, stood by her. Wilma went on to chair protest meetings. She wrote books. To some people, she was a heroine, and to many, she was a traitor.

As the years went by, and the witch-hunt days began to seem more and more like the crazy nightmare they truly had been, Wilma Bascombe became respected, almost revered, though she had stopped being active in any kind of political movement even before the fifties ended.

Then *Fellow Travelers* came out. Jim Bevic, in researching for his book, had somehow come across papers signed by some important officials that provided indisputable proof that Wilma Bascombe was a fraud. They showed, in fact, that she *did* give her greatest performance in front of that committee. She was then, and always had been, a true-blue American. Her testimony, and later her speeches and books, had been ghosted for her to give her credibility with the left; for years, she had been funneling names and information directly to certain offices in Washington, D.C.

The effect of the book was astounding. All of a sudden Wilma Bascombe became a non-person as non as any Soviet had ever been. She was an embarrassment to *everybody,* right *or* left. It was ironic that the university, which had stood so nobly by her when it was thought she was out to overthrow the government of the United States, dropped her like a used tampon when it was revealed she was working *for* that same government.

When the scandal broke, any potential protectors Wilma might have had in Washington were either dead, discredited, or too busy trying to save their own hides to worry about her.

Wilma had simply disappeared into the Long Island mansion she'd bought with the royalties from her ghosted books—disappeared so thoroughly that I had to hear her name mentioned before I could remember that if there was one person in the world who could hate Jim Bevic enough to want him dead, Wilma Bascombe was probably that person. And now, the lieutenant was telling me, she'd been seen on the Coast about the time Bevic was murdered.

I remembered something else, too; it had eluded me last night.

"Mr. M.," I said, "do you have a list of the kinescopes that were stolen?"

He shuffled through the folder a second, then said, "Yeah, right here."

"Do you remember the play 'Be Still My Heart'?"

"I've heard about it."

"Do you know who the star was?"

"Sure, that blonde, the one that married what's-his-name."

"Right. But I bet you didn't know she was a last minute replacement who did the show with only four days of rehearsal."

He raised a white eyebrow. "You mean she filled in for . . ."

"Wilma Bascombe. It's a big part of Network lore—'Kid, you're going out there a dancing pack of Chesterfields, but you're coming back a Star!' And she did, too. People don't usually mention the star she replaced, or why she had to replace her, but it's no big secret."

"I'll be a son-of-a-bitch," Rivetz said. "But what about the bowling ball?"

Good old Rivetz. Always there to make things difficult.

"I think I'll be on my way," I said. I left the policemen to their work and went back to the Network to check out a car.

CHAPTER 8

*"Chr-r-r-is, this mon can r-r-really dr-r-r-ive
an automobile!"*

—JACKIE STEWART, "ABC'S WIDE WORLD OF SPORTS," ABC

Long Island isn't named after anybody—it really is a long island, an
overgrown sand bar that sticks a hundred twenty miles out into the At-
lantic. Llona and I had driven to potato-farm country before I turned
off the highway and pointed the car north.

Llona was playing hooky from her job. Back at NetHQ, I'd popped
into her office to find her chin-deep in paperwork, surrounded by insistent telephones. She looked at me and said, "Wherever you're going, I'm
coming with you. If I don't get out of here, I'll scream!"

The shape of Long Island has led to a unique road-building philosophy. There are straight, modern highways you can take if you want to
travel the island lengthwise (east-west), but if you want to go north or
south across its width, you have to be happy with narrow, twisting
roads that always remind me of paved-over Indian trails, which some of
them probably are.

Llona and I were on one of them now, with a rocky hill for a wall on
either side, and the trees above making an autumn leaf canopy so thick,
it was hard to remember the sun was out.

Llona and I were making small talk, or just listening to birds singing
or the Network car's motor humming. I was enjoying it. It was nice to
be out in the country with a pretty girl, and on company time, too.

Then Llona gave me something to think about. She turned to me
and said, "Matt, do you mind if I ask you a personal question?"

"Not if you don't mind my reserving the right not to answer it."

She laughed. "That's fair. I just wanted to know if you ever hear
from Monica Teobaldi any more."

My initial impulse was to say, "What's it to you?" but I stifled it. I'm
very touchy on the subject of Monica Teobaldi. Monica was an actress
over whom I had made a total idiot of myself. Twice. She treated my
heart the way Spot would treat a pound of fresh liver. The worst of it

was my suspicion that any time she decided to come back to New York and get me alone for five minutes, I'd let her do it again.

I looked at the road. "I get a postcard from her sometimes," I said. "I didn't know the gossip was still fresh."

"You know how it is, Matt. Talk goes on about anybody who's single. People are probably gathered around the water fountain right now, talking about us."

"You're probably right," I told her. Just what we needed. "But why do you want to know about Monica?"

"Oh, just wondering."

"Oh," I said. I was wondering too. Llona didn't strike me as a big one for idle curiosity.

I didn't press the issue, because just then the car emerged from the woods into bright sunshine, and I could see, across an expanse of dirt road, the sprawling brick mansion that was Wilma Bascombe's retreat. It had ivy on the walls, and gables on the roof.

There were lots of gables. I was about to count them, but a beam of reflected glare bounced off the rearview mirror and stabbed me in the right eye. I winced, keeping the car on the road by memory.

After a second or so, the angles changed, and I could see into the mirror. A blue Cadillac was on the road behind us.

"Looks like we're not the only visitors Wilma has today," I said.

Llona turned around for a look. "That's interesting," she said. "Maybe she's not as isolated as you think."

Neither were we. The Cadillac had accelerated from the twenty miles per hour that made sense on this road to about ninety-eight, gaining on us as if it wanted to wrap its grinning grill around the rear bumper of the Network car.

"Matt! Are they *insane?*" Llona's voice told me she was afraid.

I couldn't blame her. This road wasn't the donkey trail it had been in the woods, but it wasn't the Bonneville Salt Flats, either. A car forced off that dirt road would have all sorts of complications to contend with—chuckholes, bushes, tree stumps, even some boulders. And there was no doubt they were trying to force us off the road.

I was standing on the accelerator to stay ahead of them, but I was just barely doing it. It was obvious the Cadillac had more under the hood than it had left Detroit with.

Llona had turned backwards on the car seat, looking at them. I yelled at her: "Don't look at them, look at the road. Try to find a place we can turn off."

"What?"

"I said look for a place we can get off the road without cracking up!" She looked, and so did I, but no luck.

Now the boys had a new game. Honking the horn (*"Shave and a haircut—two bits!"*), they'd edge the Caddy forward and give the rear of the car a playful nudge. Bump. Bump-BUMP. Like that.

There were two young men in the Cadillac. I could see them quite clearly in the mirror. There was only a trunk, a hood, and a few inches of clearance between us, after all. What I could see best was the insides of their mouths. They were laughing. The passenger slapped the driver on the back. They laughed some more. They had the ugliest uvulas I had ever seen.

One of them, the driver, had red hair, a pug nose, and freckles; the other had a head that looked like he had shaved it three days ago. They reminded me of someone—a comedy team. Not Shelby and Green—not intelligent enough. And these guys were both the same size: big.

Finally, I got it. They reminded me of Jerry Mahoney and Knucklehead Smiff, only these dummies were flesh and blood, unlike Paul Winchell's wooden creations.

We'd covered a lot of ground by now. The big brick house took up most of the horizon. I calculated that at the speed we were going, we'd probably whiz right up the limestone steps and through the living room and the kitchen before coming to a stop in the pantry. If we lived.

There was a jolt, a big one. My head hit the ceiling; my teeth clacked together. "What the hell was *that?*" I demanded.

"The road is paved again," Llona said. "Matt, do something!"

I ignored the command, tore my eyes away from the mirror, and saw that Llona was right. The road we were currently traveling at one hundred six miles per hour was, in fact, the best stretch of pavement we'd seen since we left the Long Island Expressway. It was wide enough for our playmates to pass us, and they did so.

Once by, they *really* opened that engine up, gaining about a hundred yards on us. I let go about nineteen cubic feet of air, and eased my foot off the accelerator.

That undoubtedly saved our lives from the next trick those two idiots pulled. The Caddy's brake lights went on. Llona sobbed, "Oh, my dear God." I took it as a last prayer, and added a quick amen.

Old Jerry Mahoney was a skillful driver, even in fear for my life I had to admit that. After he hit the brakes, he put his car through a beautiful two-hundred-seventy-degree counterclockwise spin, then skidded sideways down the road for another few dozen yards.

I can only lay claim to luck. I stomped on the brakes, and the nose of the Network car dipped so much, I could have sworn we were going downhill. We did the Caddy ninety degrees better and made a complete circle, coming to a smoking stop exactly three inches from the passenger side of the blue car. The two cars made a "T" on the road.

This position dictated what must have happened next. With my car in the way, the only way out of the Cadillac would be from the driver's side, and since the car had bucket seats, the passenger (Knucklehead), would be delayed by the necessity to wiggle over everything in following the driver out of the car.

I didn't see any of this. I had my eyes closed thanking God for not letting me die in such a stupid way. I opened them at a sound from Llona, who was crying softly into her hands. She looked at me in the same instant, and we said, "Are you all right?" simultaneously, and started to laugh.

I was too busy laughing to notice the redhead until he darkened the window.

I started to open the door. I had a few words I wanted to say to this clown. I wanted to give him a piece of my mind. A big piece, as much as I could spare.

I never got the chance. He was opening the door with one hand, while the other one, heavy as twenty-six dollars' worth of chuck steak, grabbed me by the back of the neck and dragged me from the car. I landed heavily on the blacktop, tearing my jacket.

My assailant looked at me in righteous anger and said, "You bedda get outta heah, *aw relse!*"

Despite his Long Island (pronounced Lun-GUYland) accent, it was easy to see Jerry Mahoney here was a Country Boy. A lot of people not familiar with the New York Metropolitan Area (and some who are) are surprised to learn this, but past a certain point, Long Island is chock-a-block with Country Boys.

He tipped off his origins by standing over me in a belligerent pose, waiting for me to stand up so the real fighting could get started. A City Boy (like me, for instance) would never have done that.

They have a lot of neat things in the Country. I mean it. They have Fresh Air, and Pure Water, and Natural Bran Fiber, which helps them grow big and strong. They have hard work to do, and they get a lot of sleep, which keeps them rested and in trim.

In the City, all we have is Streets. A Street is a rotten place to grow up, but it is educational. One thing you learn is that violence is a force of nature, and nature does not follow rules. In the Streets, the good guys try to avoid situations where violence will be involved; but, when you must inflict pain, you do it fast, well, and with the least possible risk to yourself.

I'm a Bachelor of Arts, and I wear a tie every day, and I meet famous people, but the Street is still with me. I assessed the situation. In a "fair" fight with this freckle-faced creep, I would probably have been killed. I had the height on him, and maybe the reach, but this guy walked like a panther, and he was built like one of the statues out at Rockefeller Center.

"Come on, get up," he urged. He had big fists.

"Sure," I said. I pulled back my leg, as though to comply, then pistoned it heel first into his kneecap. He looked at me in surprise. That lasted until the pain got to whatever he used for a brain. Then he clutched at the knee and fell down.

I turned and got ready for Knucklehead, who was rushing toward me. He had mercy on his mind, though, instead of mayhem. He knelt by his fallen comrade and shouted at me, "What's the matter with you, are you crazy?"

Llona came out of the car and stood by my side. "Are *we* crazy? We could have been *killed*. I'd like to go kick him in the other knee."

"You'd better not," Knucklehead said. Jerry groaned and rubbed himself. I felt guilt starting to replace anger, and I went over and checked him out myself. "It isn't broken—it will be okay."

I stood up again. "Now, what the hell is going on here?"

Silence.

"Would you rather tell the judge?"

"Are you cops?"

"No, but I'm on a first-name basis with several. Come on, before I get angry."

I was surprised when that worked. I must have looked more formidable than I felt. They started by telling me their names. Jerry Mahoney was Sam Nelson; Knucklehead Smiff was Robert Murphy. Sammy and Murph. It was nice to have that sorted out.

Murph, the brains of the outfit, was petulant. "Nobody would have been hurt, you know. Sammy knows what he's doing. He used to be a stunt driver."

Llona snorted. I said, "That's nice. What was he doing, aside from reckless endangerment, and a close brush with vehicular homicide?"

"Getting ahead of you. To cut you off before you reached the house."

"That was worth risking four lives?"

"It's our *job*," Murph said, and Sammy nodded soberly. "We're Wilma's bodyguards," the redhead told us.

"I won't touch her body," I promised, "but I'm going to talk to her. Move."

I expected more of an argument than I got. Apparently these two were like the Corsican Brothers—the kick I'd given Sammy had taken the fight out of Murph as well. Or maybe the boy with the shaven head was the non-violent type.

We walked back to the house. Sammy was limping, but otherwise okay.

At the top of a flight of wide stone steps, I rang the doorbell. Murph made a noise. I asked him what was wrong.

"We—well, we aren't supposed to go in through this door."

"You won't have to go in."

I rang the bell again, then started when a hard-faced female person opened the door and asked me what I wanted. Since she was wearing a black dress with a white apron and cap, I figured she was the maid, though what she looked like was an early makeup test for *Star Wars*.

"Good afternoon," I told her as cheerily as I could manage. "May I speak to the lady of the house?"

The illusion that the maid's face was a fright mask was reinforced by the fact that it never moved, not even her eyes. When she was sizing the situation up, she moved her whole head, as though her eye sockets were hard to see out of. First she looked at Sammy, then Murph, then Llona, then me. Then she said, "What?"

I made it simpler this time. "We want to see Miss Bascombe," I said.

Again, the maid swiveled her head around the scenic route before looking at me. "What for?"

I tried to think of an explanation this creature would buy, but while I was working on it, the maid stepped aside, and I found myself looking into the famous face of Wilma Bascombe.

CHAPTER 9

"Any reproduction . . . of any descriptions or accounts . . . without . . . express, written consent . . . is prohibited."

—STANDARD DISCLAIMER FOR TELEVISED SPORTING EVENTS

Some people soften and sag when they age. Some tighten up, and take on a sharper appearance. Wilma Bascombe belonged to the second group. The bone structure of her face, classic though it was, was too easily discernible under her skin. Her dark blue eyes were as intense as ever, but in their new environment, they looked feverish, even unhealthy. Two taut cords marred the delicate long throat. She seemed to have become all angles and edges. Only softly curling hair that had gone snow-white broke the pattern—that, and the heavy silk brocade house gown she was wearing.

I don't want to give the wrong impression. She was still a very handsome woman. It just came as a surprise that she had aged so much since she had commanded the public eye, though of course, it shouldn't have. I watch too many movies on the Late Show.

"Yes?" she said.

"My name is Matt Cobb," I said, "and this is Llona Hall. We work for the Network."

"I'm sorry, I don't talk to reporters."

"We're not reporters," Llona said. "But we would like to ask you some questions."

"I don't answer questions, either."

I raised an eyebrow. "Not even about a murder?"

Wilma Bascombe turned up the corners of her unpainted mouth. She seemed to notice Sammy and Murph for the first time, though they'd been standing there looking miserable all along. "Do you suspect my employees of murder?"

"No, ma'am," I said. At my side, I heard Llona make a skeptical little grunt. I told the former movie star that we'd have to do some talking about them, too. When Wilma Bascombe asked what I meant, Llona piped right up and told her.

She directed a cold look at her employees, and they seemed to feel it strongly enough to shiver. She told them to get back to work. "I promise they'll be available, Miss Hall, if you wish to take legal action."

She opened the door wide to let us in. "I've been called a number of names in my life," she said over her shoulder as she led us through an oak-paneled hall. "Can I add murderess to the list?"

"No one is calling you a murderess," I said.

Wilma Bascombe smiled a lovely smile, but said nothing. After some seconds had gone by, she said, "Well?"

"Well what?"

"'*Yet,*'" she said. "Robert Taylor said that line to me in a movie: 'No one is calling you a murderess—*yet.*' You resemble him, has anyone ever told you that? You are larger, of course, but there's the same quality—"

Miss Bascombe stopped abruptly and changed the subject. "Of course," she said, as though that was what she had been talking about all along, "I want to apologize for Sammy and Murph." We entered a big, dark drawing room.

"For their existence, or only their conduct?" Llona asked.

"I'm not responsible for their existence, thank God," Wilma Bascombe said. "They were students in my last class at the university before . . . before I stopped teaching. They were terrible actors; they are a little better as handymen. And they'll work for me. A lot of people won't. Would you like some tea?"

"No, thank you," I said. She pointed to some chairs by the fireplace.

She turned her attention fully to me, and it felt like an honor. I couldn't help thinking that if Wilma Bascombe hadn't been born in a country that has nothing but commoners, she never would have been used by the government, she would have *been* the government.

"You say you are not reporters, then, Mr. Cobb. Are you actors?"

"Not unless it's necessary," I said.

"Some of us are lucky," she said. "You will have to excuse me. I don't follow the news any more, for reasons you probably understand. Who has been murdered, and how am I concerned?"

I answered both Miss Bascombe's questions at once by saying, "Jim Bevic. His books were published by a company the Network owns."

Silence. She crossed her hands in her lap.

"Reactions, Miss Bascombe?"

"Well, Mr. Cobb, I hardly know what I should say. I only met the man once . . . Of course it's terrible, but . . ."

"It doesn't arouse any emotion in you? Fear? Happiness? Sorrow? Shock?"

She shrugged. "Well, surprise, certainly."

I shook my head. "The police don't think so."

She didn't go to pieces over it, or anything. She simply said, "I beg your pardon?"

"The police claim you've known about Jim Bevic's murder since the day it happened."

Actually, that statement was slanderous. Wilma Bascombe may have been in California when the body was found, but since Bevic wasn't found until twenty-four hours after he died, the only one who knew he was murdered the day it happened was the killer.

Miss Bascombe's face showed disappointment; whether at me, herself, or life in general was hard to say. With a ladylike sigh, she said, "All right, Mr. Cobb, I admit it. Deceit is a tactic that has never rewarded me. I trust you can appreciate my desire not to be involved in this."

"Yes, ma'am," I said, "I sure can. Especially since that was your first trip to California since when? Nineteen seventy-two, right? Especially since you flew back to New York right after word got out the body had been discovered. Police get suspicious about things like that. Especially about reports that you were traveling in disguise."

"I was visiting my son," she said. "My son is an artist; he lives in Los Angeles."

"The police out there talked to him," I said.

"Of course." She was looking intently into the palms of her hands, as though she expected to read her own future in them.

"Why *did* you leave Los Angeles immediately after the murder was discovered, Miss Bascombe?" I asked. "If you don't mind telling me."

"Why do you think? You know how my name is associated in the public mind with Bevic's. People suppose I hated him, though I . . . I didn't."

Suddenly, she smashed a delicate fist into the arm of her chair, and turned on Llona and me the cold, contemptuous fury she had counterfeited so well in front of the Senate committee. "I didn't want to answer *questions!*" she hissed. "My life has been ruined by questions, and I'm sick of them!"

Llona could no longer hold herself in. She leaned forward. "But, Miss Bascombe, there are always questions. They only get worse if you run away." Llona sounded exasperated.

Wilma Bascombe laughed, very bitterly. "I didn't want to embarrass my son, Miss Hall, that's the extent of it. In the circles in which my son travels, being related to *me* is a distinct drawback. I'll have you know that I wore a wig and dark glasses—you may call that a disguise if you like—when I flew *to* California, as well as when I came back."

Llona wasn't satisfied. "But why did you run away? If you're innocent, you should have stayed and fought."

"Aren't you aware of who I am?" she asked in mock surprise. "I'm
the woman who lived a lie for nearly thirty years; the spy; the traitor. I
tried to escape the questions, because I know how unlikely it is anyone
would believe me about *anything*. Just as I know you aren't going to
believe me when I tell you this: I had no reason to hate Jim Bevic—
that in fact, I rather liked him."

"If it weren't for Bevic's book," I said, "you wouldn't be known as
any of those things. That sounds like a reason to me."

"Don't be a fool," she said.

"Then enlighten me," I told her. "The way it seems to me, the only
person you might hate more than Jim Bevic would be the person who
gave him those documents."

She laughed at that, a loud humorless laugh that seemed to dance on
the edge of hysteria. Finally, she took control of herself enough to say,
"Excuse me, please. You can't appreciate how really funny that is."

She wiped a tear from a dark blue eye. "You see, *I* gave him the documents."

Well, Cobb, I said to myself, *didn't expect that one, did you? Life
sure is educational, ain't it?* I could feel my eyes open wide in surprise.
I probably looked as stupefied as I felt. I asked her to explain.

"Yes," she said. "Yes. Explanations. Questions and explanations, always." She stood up and walked to a window, where she lifted the curtain aside to let in a wedge of bright autumn sunshine. Then she
dropped the curtain and the light disappeared.

"I was going to marry a man," she said. "It was only after I'd fallen
in love with him that I realized I'd gotten to be nearly forty years old
without ever loving anyone. Oh, my son, of course, but that's different.

"I was weary of my career, and it was no sacrifice to give it up. Then
the war—excuse me, the 'Police Action' broke out in Korea, and he had
to go—wanted to. He was a pilot. After a few months he was shot down
and captured.

"He died under torture at the hands of the Communist Chinese.

"I had taken the position at the university to pass the time until he
got back. When I learned I had nothing to wait for, I stayed on.

"One day, a young man came to my office. He was from Washington. He offered me," she said with great precision, "a chance to serve
my country."

She came away from the dark window. I was startled to see how soft
and vulnerable she looked all of a sudden. It was as though that one
blast of sunlight had melted the ice Empress.

"The young man from Washington told me," she went on, "that
there were communists all around us—that the people who had hurt

my . . ." She groped for a word, didn't find it, gave up. ". . . hurt him over and over until he died, were planning to take over the country he had died for. They were all through the entertainment business. They were all through the academic community. If I were only to gain their confidence, I would be in a perfect position to aid the government in the struggle against them—to report on their actions.

"And don't think for one second there weren't actions to report," she said, suddenly stern. "There were, and still are, people who want to hurt this country in any way they can. The idea that I was some kind of—of heroine to these people made me sick, but I did it because it was important.

"At least I thought so at first. But as the months went by, I was asked for information on people who just *disagreed* with the government—they weren't out to destroy it.

"So I gave less and less information all the time, but I could never stop completely, or they would have revealed me. I didn't want that. I had come to love teaching young actors, helping them find their talent, and use it. But then—"

I was beginning to get the drift of where she was going. "But then there was Watergate," I said.

"Exactly, Mr. Cobb. Watergate. Everything was cut out from under me. Mr. Hoover died. That young man from Washington, no longer young—well, you know what happened to him. Every day, there were new revelations. Secrets going back years, decades, were raked up. There were 'leaks.'

"I've never been so afraid of anything as I became afraid of leaks. I knew it was inevitable that one night, some smirking reporter would turn up to reveal what I'd been doing all those years, getting other people's dirt all over me."

Then, Wilma Bascombe told us, Jim Bevic asked to interview her for his book. She put him off at first, but he was persistent, and she finally agreed to talk to him.

"We talked," she said, "in the same office where I'd spoken to the young man from Washington." She swallowed, then went on. "Jim Bevic told me what he had in mind, showed me his notes. He expected me to be angry, because he planned to do an honest job of it for once."

I told her I knew what she meant, there. A lot of facts tend to get ignored these days when the Red Scare is discussed. Jim Bevic hadn't ignored them. He didn't try to say the witch-hunting mentality was anything but a disgrace ("I have higher standards for my own country than I have for any dictatorship," he wrote); he hadn't hesitated to remind the smug that while some citizens of the United States were being "martyred" with forced unemployment, unforgivable as that was, the Stalin government a lot of them admired so much had devoured

half of Europe, and was systematically *murdering* its political oppo-
nents by millions, or even tens of millions.

"I thought people might understand, if it came out in that context,"
Wilma Bascombe said. "Maybe the country *did* go mad with fear, but
there *was* something to fear. Bevic planned to point that out. I thought
that way the truth could come out without my being seen as some kind
of monster. I—I was wrong."

Her naïveté astounded me. In the communications industry, we
know better. People love scandal. Let a juicy fact become public, and
people will pick it up and repeat it who have no inkling of the *existence* of a context, let alone what it is or what it means. Let somebody
come up tomorrow with incontrovertible proof that Franklin D. Roosevelt was a closet transvestite, or something, and the phrase "New Deal"
will never be heard again—people will be too busy telling each other
(a) they never even *suspected* it, or (b) they knew it all along, or (c)
their brother-in-law is the same way.

Wilma had been a symbol of refusal to succumb to the pervasive paranoia of her era. When it was revealed that she had in fact been one of
the chief victims of it, the shock drowned out everything else.

"Why didn't you make the papers public yourself?" I asked. "Why
didn't you tell your own story, instead of letting Bevic do it for you?"

She shook her head angrily. "I won't beg for *anything,* Mr. Cobb, especially forgiveness. I'd like to be understood, but I won't tolerate being
forgiven. I'm not ashamed of what I did. The *communists* understood
that." She laughed bitterly. "They didn't degrade themselves the way
the young man from Washington and all his cronies did. That's why I
made Bevic promise he wouldn't reveal where he learned the truth
about me. I wanted to find out what the public would think."

Well, I thought, she certainly found out. I said nothing.

After a while, Wilma Bascombe said, "You think I'm lying."

"I don't know," I admitted. "I'll tell you one thing—if it is true, you
owe it to yourself and to history to come out with it."

"*If* it's true," Miss Bascombe said. Her voice was very cold.

"It would be nice to see a little evidence."

"Wait here," she commanded, and swept from the room.

When the door had closed behind her, Llona said, "What's she up to
now?"

I shrugged. "Getting evidence. I don't know what it could be, but if
it holds up, scratch one suspect. What did you think of her, Llona?"

Llona let out a breath and blew her bangs askew. "She makes me furious. She has this image of queenliness, and she lets men use her like a
dishrag. Why didn't she *fight?* For her good name? Or at least for her
good intentions? She was an incredible fool."

Llona got up and leaned against the mantelpiece, looking at Wilma's

Oscar. When she turned back to me, her brown eyes were very soft. "But I feel sorry for her, too," she said. "Look at all she had. I used to watch her movies; my mother used to worship her. Lots of women did, I bet. Men probably dreamed about her. Now she has to hide here, with Sammy, Murph, and that Charles Addams maid. I don't think she deserves anyth—"

Llona stopped because Wilma had rejoined us. I didn't know how much of it she had heard.

Without a word, she handed me a piece of once-white paper. It was a receipt, handwritten in gray felt-tip pen. It was signed "James M. Bevic," and it enumerated certain documents. Wilma Bascombe had given him these documents (the receipt said) on the condition that he not reveal where he had gotten them without written permission from Wilma Bascombe.

"I could have this authenticated for you," I said.

"How do I know you won't destroy it?"

Llona looked like she wanted to cheer. Wilma Bascombe was finally wising up.

"That's an excellent point, Miss Bascombe. I'll tell the police, and they'll send a man for it." She hesitated. "It would establish your innocence, or help to," I said.

"My innocence," Wilma Bascombe said wistfully. "Very well, Mr. Cobb. You have a policeman sent to get this receipt."

"I will. And make sure *you* get one too, when you give this to him."

She said she would. Now came one last hard part. I had to ask her where she was the night before.

"Last night?" She was surprised. "What happened last night?"

"A friend of mine was killed in a robbery at the Network building last night, Miss Bascombe."

"I—I'm sorry to hear that, but what does it have to do with me?"

I scratched my head. "Well, among other things, the thief got away with a kinescope of 'Be Still My Heart'?" I was hating this.

"So?"

"Well, the police have to look at things from all angles, Miss Bascombe. Two people have been murdered. In both cases, you happened to be in or near the city where it took place. Of course, you live near New York, but your being in Los Angeles attracts attention—you realized that yourself when you tried to slip away."

"Go on," she said. The ice was back, harder than ever.

"It has to be noticed, too," I said, "that something connected with each murder, Bevic in the first case and that kine in the second, is tied in with something you might understandably be bitter about."

"I have explained why I had no reason to be bitter toward Jim Bevic."

"Pending the outcome of the test on this receipt," I reminded her.

"Can you please tell us where you were last night?" I asked. "I'm going to have to make a report on this. I'm just trying to be thorough."

"I was *here*." She sighed. "I'm always here. Don't say it, Mr. Cobb, except when I'm in California, yes. I don't expect you to believe me." The world had turned its back on her, but she was bravely resigned to it.

"I don't suppose you can account for the Rover Boys?" I said.

"They were here, too. Would you like to ask them?"

"No, thank you," I said, rising. "That'll be all for now, Miss Bascombe."

She closed her eyes for a few seconds, as though she were gathering strength, then stood up slowly, suddenly a very old woman.

"Yes," she said. "For now. I'm sure you'll be back, won't you?"

"I'd like to bring your receipt back, when the police are done with it, if that's all right with you."

Wilma Bascombe shuddered, but like a good hostess, showed us to the door.

der for

smoke and grass

Barbie and Ken

of an open boat

between a

and a hard place

not a monster

of a chance

Wed Dec 28 13:53:10 CST 2016

Updated: 12-28-2016   Created: 05-13:

Date	05-29-2009	Bib Code 3 -
Level	mMONOGRAPH	Country	nyUNe
rial Type	jMusic CD	

####Ka 4500

ocn318929605
090529s2009   nyucn   e
886974871224
2 88697487122|bRCA Records
ROCK/DAVE
Dave Matthews Band.
0 Big whiskey and the groogrux king|h
Matthews Band.
New York :|bRCA Records,|cp2009.
1 sound disc :|bdigital ;|c4 3/4 in
Lyrics in container.
0 Grux|g(1:11) -- Shake me like a monk
is|g(4:28) -- Lying in the hands of
am|g(3:53) -- Dive in|g(4:26) -- Spe
Squirm|g(5:32) -- Alligator pie|g(3:

CHAPTER 10

"Why? Because we like you!"
—JIMMIE DODD, "THE MICKEY MOUSE CLUB," ABC

I was late for the meeting in the penthouse of the Tower of Babble. I blamed it all on Sammy and Murph. First, I had to take Llona back to the Network. Next, I had to go home to change my suit, which had been ripped when Sammy threw me to the ground. Then, as long as I was home, I figured I'd give Spot a break, so I arranged for him to go to the park with the Rhode children from downstairs, and their nanny, Miss Featherstone (pronounced "Fearson"—don't ask me to explain British pronunciations). Spot likes kids. I made a note to remind Rick and Jane of that when they got back.

Despite all this, it was only eighteen minutes after three when I made it up to the president's building-wide office on the thirty-seventh floor. They'd made a lot of progress in eighteen minutes—ties were loosened, ashtrays full.

Theoretically, this was a production meeting. The production meeting is a very important part of the creative process in television. That's where the people who have conceived a show trade ideas with the people who will have to put it to work. At its best, a production meeting can provide an almost artistic satisfaction, like choral singing. Everyone contributes his own little note, and the result is something more than anyone could have come up with on his own.

That's at its best. This particular production meeting was far from that. For one thing, the cast was wrong. I mean, you'd expect Porter Reigels to be there, as producer-director of the show. Tom Falzet, president of the Network, had named himself executive producer (to get his name in all the publicity material), so he belonged there. Sal Ritafio's presence was fine, too. Publicity is such an important part of a project like "Sight, Sound, & Celebration" that the constant presence of a PR person is almost a must.

But then there were the rest of us. Me, for starters. Special Projects has about as much to do with producing TV shows as Joe DiMaggio has to do with producing coffee. The same went for Colonel Coyle, of

Security, and for Wilberforce, a little barracuda in rimless eyeglasses who was the head of the Legal Department.

They were sitting at a huge table in the mathematical center of Falzet's office. Numerous assistants and flunkies were there, too.

Reigels was talking as I came in. "I think it's a *good* idea," he said. He was using the Texas whisper, the same tone of voice Lyndon Johnson would use so often when he wanted to sound sincere. "If we can get Melanie to believe finding that bowling ball is important to us, she'll play along. You know—"

Falzet interrupted him. "Well, I see you could finally join us, Cobb. It's nice you can make time for things of such trivial unimportance like this."

Falzet was in his fifties, slightly horse-faced, but still handsome. He was one of those people I had complained to Llona about—he liked to fill his mouth up with syllables to hear himself talk longer. He was always making himself ridiculous by saying things like "trivial unimportance." As opposed to what, vital unimportance?

"Yeah," I said. "Sorry I'm late. Bomb threat."

A murmur of consternation went around the table.

"Relax," I said. "It's all taken care of." I paused before adding, "I think." Then, happy in the knowledge that I had done my bit to ensure the meeting would be as brief as possible, I said, "What have I missed?"

Reigels said, "Well, we were just discussing a suggestion by Sal, here"—he slapped Ritafio on the back, hard—"that we tell the press old Matt Cobb is devoting all his energies to getting that bowling ball back."

"It's always effective PR," Ritafio said meekly. "You know, 'We've put our best man on it.'"

I had to laugh.

Falzet barked, "Dammit, Cobb, this isn't funny!" He doesn't like it when I laugh at something he doesn't get.

I straightened my face. "No, sir," I said.

"Anyway," Reigels continued, "I was about to say I think it's a fine idea. I know all the wrong ways to deal with Melanie—all that's left is the one I wouldn't try." He grinned. About five years ago, Reigels had directed Melanie in her only box office catastrophe. During the filming, the gossip columnists had a field day, because Reigels and Melanie fought the whole time. Reigels came out the winner (at least in the press) because his cuss-free insults were printable. Unfortunately for him, it had been a Pyrrhic victory. The movie stank, and worse than that, it lost money. Reigels hadn't worked a whole lot since, and it was no secret he was broke. The rumor was that Falzet had tabbed Reigels for "SS&C" because he would work cheap for the chance to be a winner again.

"I should have learned earlier," the director said, still grinning, "that that blond mustang just don't understand it when you say 'no,' but you can lead her a mile if you tell her, 'I'll try.'"

Wilberforce talked quietly, too. While he spoke, his hands constantly tormented a paper clip. I wondered why it didn't snap. "I don't like the plan," he said. "It's only a gesture to Marliss's ego. There's no guarantee she won't sue, anyway."

"We could at least delay it until after the dang show has aired."

Wilberforce nodded. "That's fine for you, Mr. Reigels. After the show airs, you are through with it. But what if Mr. Cobb fails to find this . . . *toy*? Not only would Marliss still be free to bring suit, Mr. Ritafio's 'gesture' could be interpreted as an admission of responsibility." If Wilberforce had ever in his life been frightened, or excited, or in love, or done *anything* remotely human, the experience had left no trace in his voice.

"She won't do that," Reigels insisted. "Melanie is—well, believe it or not, she likes to think she's 'jes' folks,' but that the public sought her out and made her be a star."

I could see that. It was a crock, of course, but I could see where it would appeal to Melanie Marliss. It would be a nice rationalization for all the privileges of celebrity she enjoyed—the public forced them upon her. It made an interesting contrast, I thought, with Wilma Bascombe, whose hang-up was she didn't want the public to know she was human enough to care *what* they thought.

"It may be you're right," Wilberforce purred, "but there is also Lorenzo Baker."

Reigels snorted. "Melanie's current lap dog."

"Lap dogs have teeth, and have been known to use them. From what Mr. Ritafio tells us, Baker is very quick to assert Marliss's status."

"But the publicity value *alone*," Ritafio piped up.

The discussion showed signs of becoming a free-for-all, and I hate those. Without consulting my mind, my mouth said, "Does anyone care what I think?"

Instantly, they all shut up. Falzet said, "Yes, Cobb. What do you think?" And he folded his hands like a kid waiting for a treat.

All right, I asked for it. Now I had to think something. There were a lot of things wrong with Ritafio's plan. As far as I could see, all of Wilberforce's objections were valid. Besides that, it would make Special Projects, and especially Matt Cobb, highly visible. If I fell on my face, it might give Falzet enough ammunition to get rid of me, no matter *how* friendly I was with Roxanne Schick.

But there was one thing very right about Ritafio's plan. If it was publicized Network policy to find that stupid bowling ball, then no one could complain when I devoted the whole department to it—and to finding the bastard who took it.

"Jerry de Loon," I said.

"What?" Falzet looked puzzled.

"Jerry de Loon," I said again. "It just occurred to me that it would be nice if somebody mentioned his name."

"Oh. Yes. But what do you think of Ritafio's plan, Cobb?"

"I'll do it."

Ritafio got as close to a smile as he ever did. Reigels said, "That's a boy!" Falzet nodded judiciously. Wilberforce shook his head. The various flunkies copied their bosses.

"*However,*" I went on, "I have some comments about how we should go about it." Translation: I'll do the dirty work, but I'll pick the guy who hands me the shovel.

Falzet caught on, realized he no longer had a choice, and signaled me to continue.

"First," I said, "if the Network is going to make a gesture, let's make it a real gesture. I think Melanie would be most impressed if the message came directly from the president of the Network, don't you?"

Coyle spoke for the first time. "I have to agree with Cobb, sir. Only the commander can speak for the entire company."

It had been a mistake for the colonel to remind Falzet he was there. Falzet asked him what he had done to prevent future thefts.

Coyle replied with the military equivalent of a squirm—the humble bluster. "Well—ah—we have—ah—beefed up patrols by guards—and stationed men—ah—at fire exit doors . . ."

"Locking the barn door after the cow is gone," Falzet said, dismissing him. Another thing that irked me about our president was that he could never get a cliché right.

"One thing I *don't* want," I said, "is reporters all over my back. Special Projects is the smallest department in the corporation, and I can't spare a person just to say 'no comment' on the phone."

Ritafio was about to cry. "But the whole *idea* is to generate a good press—"

"Then *give* me somebody, for crying out loud. Can you spare anyone?"

Ritafio's face lightened a little. "That's even better!" Maybe this was a production meeting after all. "This way, we can have a professional dealing with the media!" He thought it over for a few seconds. "How about Llona Hall? She's my best, and she's free after the banquet tomorrow night."

"Llona will be fine," I said.

"I'll brief her right away," Ritafio promised.

Porter Reigels beamed. "Terrific, terrific. I'll go with you, Falzet, when you talk to Melanie. I can apologize to her again for that stupid movie—that always seems to put her in a good mood."

"She has forgiven you, then?" Wilberforce wanted to know. I decided he was asking because forgiveness was a concept with which he was not familiar.

"*Dozens* of times," Reigels drawled. "We get along just fine, now."

"Then it's all decided and settled," Falzet intoned. "But what do you plan to do, Cobb, while Reigels and myself are approaching Miss Marliss?"

"Myself will be working on neutralizing Lorenzo Baker," I told him. "In fact, I better get started. If you'll excuse myself?" I beat it before he could tell me how bad my grammar was.

I took the stairs down the two flights to my office, said hello to Jazz, went into my office, and sat down. I looked in my desk for my purple jelly beans, took a handful, then walked over to the brown-glass window. I stood close to it, and looked down on the people scurrying around on Sixth Avenue below. When you work in a tower, every now and then it helps if you take an occasional peek into the real world.

I went back to my desk. The first thing to do was to figure out what I was up against. I had two parallel ambitions: Find Melanie's toy (for the Network); and find the person who killed Jerry (for me, or maybe for him, or his girl). That much was simple enough, but then the complications set in. What could anyone want the bowling ball for? To bowl? To hold for ransom? Did they plan to make John F. Kennedy's campaign joke come true, and collect a bunch of bowling balls to make a rosary for the Statue of Liberty? Or was the motive simply to make trouble for the Network? Or was it to bother Melanie Marliss?

A real headache, and I hadn't even started speculating about the stolen kinescopes, yet. Kids' shows and "Be Still My Heart." What for? First I thought the kines could have been a blind for the theft of the bowling ball, then I turned it around and said the bowling ball was taken to obscure the motive for taking the films. Then, as unlikely as it seemed, I considered the possibility that both had been stolen as a blind for the murder of Jerry de Loon.

And as long as I was thinking grim thoughts, I finally let an idea that had been gnawing quietly at the bottom of my brain all day into my conscious thoughts. Maybe Jerry was in on the thefts. I could see it as a variation on the prison-escape scene that's been in thousands of bad movies and TV shows. Jerry is in cahoots with someone in a plot to despoil the Network of its treasures. Jerry lets his confederate (who has hidden out somewhere in the building) into the library. They load the kines, along with the bowling ball, into some oversized knapsack or something—or even better—(I was really getting started now)—the kines are already long gone. Jerry (in this theory) has been stealing them, one a night, from the library, slipping them under his coat. That's why he works late so often—he doesn't want anyone to back into him on a crowded elevator and come up against a concealed can of film.

Anyway, whatever the cohort plans to get away with, he has it, and is ready to go, when Jerry says, "Let's make this look *real* good, like on the bad movies and TV shows. Hit me on the head."

So his friend hits him. Just a friendly tap, he thinks, but he doesn't know anything about hematomas, emboli, and the like. The friend goes down the fire stairs, and waits for Jerry to get over his wooziness enough to pull the fire alarm and mask the confederate's exit from the building.

"Aah, *shit*," I said in disgust, but I couldn't fool myself into thinking that wasn't the best theory yet. Not that it was a great theory by any means, but it did explain why the bowling ball and the kines were apparently taken on the same night—they weren't, but the bowling ball had been taken to create that very illusion, and set the police on the trail of a Mr. Universe who could carry that much film at one time.

Unfortunately, it didn't explain what Jerry, or his helper, or Mr. and Mrs. America and All the Ships at Sea, for that matter, wanted with kinescopes. Nostalgia? Jerry could have looked at those kines whenever he wanted to, even after he left the Network. The plan was to open the library, by appointment, to anyone who wanted to use it. The Network would get a tax credit that way. Maybe he was planning to start a fire somewhere—some old film stock burns like crazy. But if a fire was what the thief had in mind, gasoline would be easier to get, surer to use, and harder to trace. The only other possible reason I could come up with was that the thief planned to carve them up into triangles and corner the market on guitar picks.

I was depressed; not only because I liked Jerry and hated to think of him as a crook, but because a careful survey of all my speculation failed to show the first hint of a lead, or even a question to ask that one could check the answer to.

Unless, of course, the bizarre bowling ball business really *was* connected with the murder of Jim Bevic five days ago. Then there were leads enough to retire on. There was the question of what Bevic had been doing in Costa Rica; what he was doing after that in Los Angeles; what (if anything) Shelby, Green, and Brockway had to do with Bevic's death (besides providing the premises and finding the corpse); and finally: did Wilma Bascombe have anything to do with it at all? It was heartening to realize two great American police forces were eagerly pursuing all these questions.

The trouble was, I was a New York Boy, and this looked like a California crime. Except for Jerry de Loon, every important figure in this case, down to and including Melanie Marliss's bowling ball, either resided in Los Angeles (Melanie, Lorenzo Baker, Porter Reigels); was in Los Angeles at the time Bevic was murdered (Wilma, or Bevic himself); or possibly both (Shelby, Green, Brockway). But *whatever* the category, they had all left the land of Sun and Fun for the city of Hustle and Bustle.

And, I had to keep reminding myself, there was no guarantee there was any connection at all.

Still, it couldn't hurt to get a few facts. I swallowed a last gooey morsel of jelly bean, sighed, and buzzed my secretary on the intercom.

"Yes, Matt," she said promptly.

"Jazz, put a call through to the Coast and get me Shorty Stack, okay?"

She hesitated. "You mean it?"

"Desperate times," I told her, "call for desperate measures."

"Right," she said. "I'll place the call right away."

CHAPTER 11

"Strange visitor from another planet . . ."
—WILLARD KENNEDY, "THE ADVENTURES OF SUPERMAN," ABC

Any conversation with Shorty Stack was an experience. Shorty, on the Network organization chart, was listed as Assistant Vice-president—Special Projects, West Coast, but he'd been at this sort of thing a lot longer than I had. By rights, he should have gotten my job when the position opened up, but he turned it down because he didn't want to come to New York. Shorty once told me he found no difference between New York and downtown purgatory. He said he wouldn't fit in.

I'd never met the man—all our conversations were over the phone—but from what I heard, even present-day Los Angeles wasn't his natural habitat. He'd been intended for Hollywood circa 1932, but had been misplaced in time.

Jazz buzzed me back. "He's not at Network Village, Matt," she said, naming our West Coast headquarters.

Jazz suggested that she try his home, and I told her to go ahead.

"Oh," she said, "Shirley's in her office. She wants to see you when you have a minute."

"Okay, send her in."

Shirley had a big grin on her face when she came into my office, but I couldn't ask her what it was about right away, because Jazz had put the call through.

"This'll only take a couple of minutes," I told Shirley. "Sit down." I picked up the phone to talk to Shorty.

"Matt, baby," he said in a jolly, piping voice. "Good to hear from you. What's doing?"

I promised myself that someday I would go take a look at this guy and find out if he was for real. Meanwhile, it was fun to picture him the way I imagined him, sitting in a director's chair at poolside, wearing dark glasses and a beret, with an ascot around his neck, and smoking a cigarette in a long holder.

"Shorty," I said, "you know everything, right?"

"Hey, that's what the job is, right, sweetheart? What do you want to know?"

"I suppose you heard about the bowling ball fiasco?" I asked.

"Natch," he said.

This was too much. Natch. "Come on, Shorty, you're putting me on, right?"

"Matt, baby, the bowling ball bit was in all the papers, of *course*, I heard about it. Like I said, it's the job. Now, how can I help you?"

"I want to know about Melanie Marliss's boyfriend."

"Heh, heh. Now *you're* putting old *Shorty* on, am I right?"

"Not a bit."

He sounded disappointed in me. "Sweetheart!" he said. "You're talking about the female that gets more ink than anyone in the *world*, outside of maybe Jackie. Melanie and the taco tycoon have been all over every rag and scandal sheet in the country."

"I know. I'm looking for something they didn't get."

"Hell, they don't *get* anything; they make it up. It's common knowledge out here Melanie Marliss is Miss Squeaky Clean. No booze for her, and as for dope, forget it. No pot puffer, pill popper, or coke snorter ever works on one of Her Majesty's pictures. She takes her men one at a time, three-four years each. Besides, sex is no sin in this business, it's a spectator sport, know what I mean?"

"Yeah," I said. "Like soccer. Look, Shorty, what I'm really interested in is something about Lorenzo Baker."

"Something about him, sweetheart, or something on him?"

"On him," I admitted. "He may be a pest." I told him about the prospective lawsuit.

"There must be something in the air in New York makes people paranoid," Shorty said. "That phony bastard doesn't care the sweat off his balls for Melanie's maroon marble, he just wants his name in the papers."

"That's what I figured, but it doesn't make any difference. The Network is going to look pretty stupid if this gets to court."

"Can't let that happen, can we? Okay, I'll look into it personally, and if I can't find anything, I'll get something rigged up, *then* find it."

"No, Shorty," I said flatly.

"What was that I heard, sweetheart, a scruple? You've been working Special Projects over three years and you still got scruples? How the hell can you stand it?"

I would have told him, if I'd known myself.

Meanwhile, Shirley, the workaholic, unable to bear just sitting and not doing anything for five minutes, came over and started to straighten out the things on my desk. I didn't mind; that was probably the only way it ever would have gotten straightened.

On the phone, Shorty said, "Okay, Boy Scout, I'll get you the whole truth and nothing but. Anything else?"

"Well, yeah. There's a chance—a small one, but still a chance—that the Jim Bevic murder is tied in with this. I'm pretty well up on the mechanics of the case, and I've talked with Wilma Bascombe, but maybe you can give me some background on Shelby, and his wife, and Lenny Green."

"Hey, file a report on your talk with Bascombe, all right?" I said I would, and there was silence for a few seconds.

"Shorty?"

"I'm thinking, sweetheart. I have to sort things out, you know. I'm carrying thirteen generations of Hollywood gossip in my noodle."

"Your *noodle?*" I couldn't stand it any more. "Shorty, you don't really talk like this all the time, do you?"

"*Nah,*" he said in disgust. "In the office, I wear the suit, and when the corporation robots come out from New York, I have to talk perfect English to them—the whole bullshit treatment. I'll tell you, sweetheart, it's a pleasure to talk to a guy like you, a friend. Then I can relax, and be my real self. It's a pleasure. I mean that sincerely."

I looked at the phone. *Give it up, Cobb,* I told myself. Real or fake, Shorty Stack was beyond my comprehension.

So, for that matter, was Shirley Arnstein. After she'd finished my desk, she straightened all my pictures. Now she was wiping the smudges from my window.

Shorty thought things over for a few more seconds. Finally, he said, "Well, I'll tell you. There's not much to say about Alice Brockway. She's got a temper, but what the hell, she was a child star, and they all get spoiled rotten. She used to be part of Lenny Green's harem—"

"Green's? When?"

"Oh, years ago, when the team of Shelby and Green first made it big, they both had to comb women out of their hair. Green, especially. The girls called him the Wand, and not because of magic he did in the act, either. Still do, as far as I know. Only thing back then was, he had a sick wife, so all the women knew it was a temporary thing. Of course, the wife is dead now."

"You mean Alice Brockway met Shelby because of Green?"

"Yeah, apparently Green fixed them up. Very adult, you know? Green was best man at the wedding and all that."

"What about when they broke up the act?"

"Well, that was the Uranium thing. Green cost them this money he and Shelby had set aside to invest—something like a million bucks—and Shelby was understandably miffed. Brockway, by the way, was against the split-up."

I pulled my lip. That provoked some interesting speculation. That scene yesterday in Studio J made it obvious that my boyhood dream girl was still fond of Lenny Green, maybe platonically, maybe not. Could it be that Green and Brockway had a little tryst planned last Sunday, and Bevic stumbled in on them? But even if that were true, what the hell difference did it make? That wasn't something to *kill* a person over, certainly. Hollywood adulteries were as far off his journalistic beat as it was possible to get.

"This sounds like old news, Shorty," I said. "Anything more recent?"

"Well, Matt, baby, they haven't exactly been in the public eye the way they used to, you know? The only thing that's happened was there were rumors about Shelby's land deal in Arizona—a bunch of enterprising Italian-American boys was supposed to have a black hand in it. It looked like something solid for a while. Arizona real estate's been known for that kind of thing, lately. But nothing ever came of it. You know rumors. We Network Bigs should know them if anybody does, am I right?"

"You are right," I said. "Get back to me on Baker, okay?"

"You got it, sweetheart."

"Then everything's copacetic." If you can't beat them, I decided, join them.

"Bye, now," Shorty said. "Give my sympathy to all your fellow inmates of the Big Apple."

"And you pass mine along to the smog-breathers of Tinseltown," I told him, and hung up.

I asked Shirley what was on her mind.

"I finally heard from Harris," she said, taking a seat. "He offered that bribe."

It took me a moment to remember the possibly crooked independent testing laboratory. "What happened?" I asked eventually. Life would be a lot simpler if we only had to worry about one thing at a time.

Shirley was fighting a smile. "Well," she said, "not only did they turn out to be honest, they were downright militant about it. He's in jail."

The smile was in full blossom now. I smiled too. Usually, things seemed to go much too smoothly for Harris Brophy.

"He sounded very indignant on the phone," Shirley said. "Just as he handed over the money, the person he thought was the crooked employee pulled out a badge and arrested him. Come to find out, they had spotted the crooked employee on their own, months ago, and planted a cop in his place to weed out their crooked clients. Harris walked right into the trap."

"He may never get over it," I said. "Still, kind of restores your faith in human nature, doesn't it?"

"Why?"

"To investigate somebody who actually turns out to be honest?"

"I never thought of it that way, but I suppose so." I should have realized it would be a new idea for her—I'm sure nothing like that had ever happened when she was working for the Congress.

"Anyway," she said, "I suppose I ought to get started, and go out there and rescue him."

"No," I said.

"Come on, Matt, fun is fun, but we can't leave him out there to *rot!*" Her concern was real. Shirley was carrying a very bright torch for Harris; a fact *he* only noticed when it was convenient. One day, it was going to make trouble in the department.

I asked Shirley if she didn't think "rot" was a little too strong a word. "I doubt the State of Indiana has him chained to a dungeon wall," I told her. "Besides, I didn't mean, 'No, we won't get him out of there,' I meant, 'No, you're not the one who's going to do it.'"

"Why not?" she protested. "I want to see his *face.*"

I grinned. "That would be something to see, all right. Knowing Harris, I wouldn't be surprised if he's spending all his time slumped in a corner, playing the harmonica." For a second, I was tempted to let her go, but I hardened my heart and said, "No, we'll send St. John. He's a rookie, and it'll be good experience for him.

"You," I told her, "I need here, especially with Harris out of action for a while. I've got something important for you to do."

That perked her up right away. "What is it?" she asked eagerly.

"I want to know everything about Jerry de Loon. I don't think the cops are checking too deeply into his background, but if you run across them, efface yourself, you know what I mean?"

"They'll never know I'm there," she said.

"Good." If it turned out Jerry *was* involved in the kinescope caper, and Shirley turned something up, I'd have to tell the police. But if he wasn't, I wasn't about to go spreading my theory around. I didn't want Jerry's memory to suffer just because I have a soiled mind.

Shirley said she'd get right to it, and left. The intercom buzzed. I gave Shorty mental congratulations for fast work.

"Yes, Jazz," I said.

"Llona Hall on the phone, Matt."

I took the congratulations back. "Okay, Jazz."

Llona wasted no time on hellos. "Give me three reasons I shouldn't be furious with you," she said. Her voice said she was half-mad already, and she was giving me a chance to cajole her out of it.

I was willing to try. "Because of my innocent charm and youthful good looks?"

"Ha!"

"Mmm," I said, thinking. "Because we both have double letters in both our first and last names?"

"What kind of a reason is that?"

"Mystical," I said. "What's your sign?"

"Never mind. You've got one more chance."

"The Network needs you. Special Projects needs you. I need you."

"You would mention that. Okay, Matt. I was going to take a few days off and get away to the country after tomorrow night, but okay."

"I'll make it up to you," I promised.

"How?" She sounded skeptical.

"Buy you a pretzel?"

She laughed. "Trying to impress me with your wealth, ay?"

"You said it, kid. What the hell, I'll even spring for an Italian ice."

"Wow," she breathed, "you don't even give a girl a chance! Okay, but I have to be at the Brant at quarter after five."

I looked at my watch. "Plenty of time. Meet you by the fountain in two minutes."

I told Jazz to arrange for someone to take a message if Shorty called, and left the office to go meet Llona.

CHAPTER 12

"Ahh, there's good news tonight!"

—GABRIEL HEATTER, MBS

"How do you like your pretzel?" I asked Llona.

"Not bad," she said around a mouthful. "It could use some mustard."

"Philadelphians adulterate innocent hot pretzels that way. We just don't do that in New York."

"I went to college in Philadelphia." We were sitting on the broad edge of the Plaza fountain, watching the rush hour develop. Llona said, "Wish I were going home."

"Don't stay late on my account," I told her. "I was just going to drop by your office for a couple of minutes tomorrow."

"Tomorrow will probably be even worse. I have a nightmare that some bus boy at the Brant will put the cards in the wrong places, and two women wearing the same dress will wind up at the same table, and the press will all be there to take pictures of a hair-pulling match."

"Is that why you're going there now?" I pointed across the street. "Are you planning to give the help an IQ test?"

"No, it's too late for that. Actually, I'm going over because Alice Brockway called up and asked especially for me. And like a good little PR girl, I promised I'd be there." She made a face.

"Mind if I tag along?" I asked.

Llona grinned at me. "Still looking for a chance to talk to your boyhood crush?"

"Yup." It was true. I did want to talk to Alice. I wanted to talk to all three of the late arrivals from California, and this looked like a heaven-sent opportunity.

"Okay," Llona said. "You might as well tag along. You can carry me when my feet give out." She had slipped her shoes off, and was rubbing her feet. "I'd like to scream whenever I hear somebody describe Public Relations as a desk job."

Llona stretched her very nice legs, pointed her toes, and scissored them up and down. "Damn pantyhose, anyway," she said.

"You lost me," I told her.

"What I'd like to do most in the world at this moment is soak my feet in this fountain, but you can't take pantyhose off in public the way you can stockings. Where can you buy garter belts these days, I wonder."

"I wouldn't know. I haven't bought one in years. Do you always discuss underwear with strange men?"

The dark brown eyes widened. "Are you strange? Really?"

"Positively eerie," I said. I checked my watch. "Only fifteen minutes until you've got to see Alice Brockway, so if I'm going to fill you in, I'd better get started."

Llona was all business while I brought her up to date. I didn't give her every thought and fraction of thought I'd entertained, but I gave her a pretty good idea of the areas Special Projects would be looking into. She had to know, because each possibility presented a different PR problem, and she had to be ready. If, I reminded her, any of them was really the truth.

"So *that's* why you want to come along with me," Llona said. "You want to talk to them about Jim." She shook her head. She said she doubted her high school friend's death could have anything to do with the Great Bowling Ball Caper.

"I *still* want to talk to Alice Brockway, bowling ball or not."

She put her shoes on, stood up, and turned a mock frown on me. "Well, all right. Just don't go around accusing anyone of murder."

Llona was very versatile. She could jay-walk and outline PR tactics at the same time. I lost a few words of the plan when she scooted ahead of me and let a smelly city bus get between us, but from what I heard of it, it was a good plan. The idea was to make Melanie happy, so Llona would stress the Network's opinion that everything had happened and was continuing to happen because people loved Melanie, from a souvenir-hunting bowling ball thief to a dedicated Network investigator.

"We'll get her where she lives," Llona said, as we landed on the far curb, "right in that big, fat ego."

The Brant Hotel is a huge cube of a place, fairly new. Outside, it's hard to tell any difference between the Brant or any of the other steel and glass office buildings along Sixth Avenue. They try to make up for it on the inside, with lush carpets, crystal chandeliers, and shiny green draperies. The elegance carries over to the staff, too. I knew from previous visits that the men's room attendants here wore uniforms that looked as though they'd been designed for the palace guard of some country out of Victor Herbert. The bellboys looked like space cadets.

"Miss Brockway wanted me to call upstairs when I got here," Llona told me. "Shall I tell her you're with me, or do you want to be a surprise?"

"Tell her," I said. I figured it would be just as well to keep people happy for as long as possible. I could start barging in where I wasn't wanted any time.

The house phones were by the registration desk, across the lobby; in other words, somewhere between here and Cleveland. To pass the time on the walk, Llona and I counted autograph hunters. They were everywhere—lurking behind closet doors, furniture, and potted plants. They were mostly female, anywhere from nine to ninety.

We stopped counting at thirty-five. I was surprised a tony place like the Brant allowed them to hang around, but Llona explained it was the Network's idea.

"The Brant is getting four promotional consideration announcements during the six-hour program," she said. "So when Sal tells them the Network wants the fans to have a reasonable amount of access to the stars, the hotel management listens."

"That makes sense," I said. The Network was probably giving the Brant something in the way of cash, but the main remittance was to be made in the most precious thing the Network has: air time. Those four plugs, totaling about forty seconds, would have cost the hotel something over a hundred thousand dollars, if it had bought them as commercial time. When you watch a game show and hear the phrase "Prizes and Promotional Consideration furnished by . . ." you know the same kind of deal has been made, only on a much smaller scale.

Llona went to make her phone call. I walked to a stand by the desk, and amused myself by comparing credit card applications. Places like the Brant not only honor credit cards, they love and obey them, too. It makes the process of parting with your money less painful if you don't have to hold it in your hand before you say good-bye to it.

A giggle drew my attention to a group of leather chairs. Four young girls, say, twelve to fifteen, were sitting there. One of them spotted me, and there was a lot of whispering behind cupped hands. They got off the chairs, and came toward me, kind of shy and tentative. Finally, though, they reached me. They surrounded me, and started to study my face. It wasn't the first time that kind of thing had happened; there are about five different actors I just miss looking like.

The leader of the girls, a little olive-skinned gypsy, finally said, "Excuse me, sir, but are you anybody?"

That wasn't an easy question. The metaphysical implications alone were staggering. So, I did what I try to do with most difficult questions —I ducked it.

"Do I *look* like anybody?"

Now, the intellectual pressure was on her, and I had to admit, she handled it well. She sized me up for a while, then said, "Nah. Sorry we bothered you, mister." She led her pals back to the chairs.

Llona rejoined me. "What was that all about?" she asked. She tilted her head in the direction of the girls.

"I've been weighed in the balance," I said, shaking my head, "and been found wanting."

Llona smiled. "I know the feeling. It may be some consolation to learn that they love you upstairs."

"Alice doesn't mind if I tag along, then?"

"Said she'd never forgive me if I didn't bring you."

I could hardly wait. We took a wood-paneled elevator to the twelfth floor.

A Brant Hotel space cadet was knocking on the door of the Shelby suite when Llona and I arrived. On his cart was a silver ice bucket with a green bottle in it, and four crystal glasses.

"Looks like good news," I told Llona. "They've ordered champagne."

"A magnum, no less," she said, impressed.

We were right behind room service when Ken Shelby opened the door for him. "Right on time," he said when he saw us. He smiled happily. Shelby said, "Hi, folks," and Alice Brockway rushed across yards of luxurious Brant sitting room to take our hands and engulf us with warmth.

It was hard to believe she was the same woman who had stalked angrily from Studio J the day before. The dark glasses were gone, and I could see happy little sparkles in her eyes. She seemed younger, and even slimmer than she had yesterday, though that part of it could have been an illusion caused by her general air of happiness. As one who had loved her, I was glad to see it. It occurred to me that today, Alice looked like she had spent her whole life in the trouble-free town she'd lived in on "Home and Mother." She looked great.

Ken Shelby, meanwhile, was about to tip the bellboy but had a thought with his wallet in mid-air.

"I'm sorry, son, but another friend has arrived, so you'll have to get us another glass."

"It's not necessary," I said. I usually stay away from alcohol while the sun is out.

Shelby wouldn't hear of it. "Nonsense, Matt," he said.

Lenny Green said, "Damn right! We're celebrating, and you're going to join us!"

"In that case, sure," I said. It was easier to drink champagne than argue.

"What are we celebrating?" Llona wanted to know.

"Something the world—and I—have been waiting for for over ten years." Lenny Green was being serious. That was a sight very few people had ever seen. He wiped his eyes with the side of a finger, and didn't quite sniffle. He got up and walked over to his former partner and put his arm around his shoulders.

"Ken and I are getting the act together again."

"That's great!" Llona said. "And you want me to arrange for the announcement? You want the Network PR department to handle it?"

"We didn't want to impose on you," Alice began.

"Impose? This is fantastic. My boss might even smile! This will get a lot of coverage."

"'NETWORK REUNITES COMEDY GREATS.'" I set the headline in the air with my hand.

"Exactly," Llona said. "Can I use your phone?"

"You have to ask?" Lenny Green made a noise. "The Network's paying for it, right?"

Llona looked at her watch. "Damn, past five-thirty. Too late for the six o'clock news. I'll shoot to break the story in time for the elevens, then set you up with interviews tomorrow."

"Reigels is going to love that," I said. "Dress rehearsal is tomorrow."

She dismissed that with a wave of her hand. "He can work around it," she said. That was the unofficial motto of all Public Relations departments everywhere.

Just then, the bellboy returned with my champagne glass. He brought it on the cart, untouched by human hands. This hotel was ridiculous.

Shelby picked up the glass, handed it to me, and told Green to open the champagne. Then he reached for his pocket to give the boy his delayed tip, and Green started to laugh.

We all looked at him, to see him holding a wallet aloft. It was official. Shelby and Green were back in business.

"Didn't waste a second, did you, Len?" Shelby said. Everyone laughed. The wallet was restored to its owner, the bellboy was taken care of, the champagne was poured, and we drank to success and happiness.

After that, Llona reached into her purse for her little black book, and picked up the phone to spread the good news, first to Ritafio, then to the various media. No one had to remind her to tell Network News, Channel 10, and our two radio stations first. That was basic.

While she was doing that, I grilled Alice Brockway and the newly reunited comedy team. I got about the same results as I would have had grilling an ice cube—no special results, just a dwindling of the material I was working on.

I did manage to learn that Lieutenant Martin had stopped by earlier in the day. Mr. M. had made a wonderful impression on them, but I didn't think they had made such a great one on him; at least, if they gave him the same answers they gave me, they hadn't.

Not that it couldn't be true, just that it was so goddam depressing. They just added to all the negatives the L.A. police had gotten during the initial Jim Bevic investigation. They professed total ignorance about Jerry de Loon; they'd only met him once. About possible motives for an attack on him or for the theft of the bowling ball or the kines—and about any connection between any of those things and the death of Jim Bevic—they claimed complete bafflement.

"The police told me about your connection with the case," I told them. "Why you were late coming here."

Alice was irritated. "Awfully nice of them," she said sarcastically.

"They were doing the Network a favor—or, rather, they were doing one for me. Lieutenant Martin is an old friend of mine. He knows the Network doesn't want that kind of publicity for you any more than you do, and he knows I have more leverage in the industry to keep things quiet than he does."

Shelby scratched his head. "I have to agree with my wife. The fewer people who know about it, the better."

Green sighed. "Well, what are we gonna do? Sew up his mouth? He knows. We'll just have to go along with him. Jerry seemed like a good kid when we met him."

Husband and wife supposed he was right, but their faces said they hoped they could trust me. I was glad they didn't ask me straight out, because I wouldn't have known what to tell them. As far as priorities went, it was a dead heat between the Network and the law, with the human race third.

"There's something I ought to tell you, before someone thinks of it and comes to arrest me," Shelby said. He was very urbane, very civilized. We could have been at the Club, discussing the rules of a squash tournament.

"What's that?" I said.

"Do you have a list of the stolen shows?"

I gave it to him from memory. "Episodes of 'Coony Island,' 'Saturday Afternoon Sundae,' 'Dr. Wonder,' 'Horsin' Around,' and 'The Dandy Donny Daniels Show'; one half-hour of a cooking show called 'Gone to Pot'; and one complete copy of 'Be Still My Heart.' All from 1952. I can't give you exact air dates, or casts and crews, because Jerry hadn't gotten around to cataloguing that stuff before he died."

"Well," Ken Shelby said, "I directed all those shows, one time or another, except for 'Coony Island'—that was Gene Kassos's baby all the way—and, of course, 'Be Still My Heart.' The only thing I ever directed in prime time was game shows. I was the regular director for 'Dr. Wonder,' and 'Dandy Donny Daniels.' "

"Have you told that to the police?"

"Not in so many words."

"What's that mean?"

His handsome face took on just the slightest tinge of pink. "It means it doesn't mean a damn thing! That I directed these shows, I mean. I was a staff director for the Network, of *course* I directed the Saturday afternoon schlock! I directed 'Day on Trial' and the 'Endless Road' soap opera, too. One week I directed fifty-nine-and-a-half hours of programming. There was a flu epidemic."

Lenny Green said, "Jesus, when we met up and took the act on the road, it must have been like a prison break for you."

"A vacation, at least," Shelby said. He turned back to me. "The point I was trying to make is that the whole *staff* of us was switching around from show to show. Ask Porter Reigels. He was with the Network then. He was the regular director for 'Horsin' Around,' but I'll bet he did most of the other shows, too. I know he took over 'Dr. Wonder' when I left to form the act with Lenny."

I didn't say anything, but I found that little tidbit of information very interesting, too. I'd have to have a talk with the Texan as soon as I got a chance.

I changed the subject. "Did any of you know that Wilma Bascombe was in California when Jim Bevic was killed?"

From across the room, I saw Llona look away from the phone at me, with her mouth pursed and her eyebrows raised. She wasn't missing a word.

"Did she have anything to do with anything?" Green asked.

"I don't know," I admitted. "Did the police ask you about her?"

The police hadn't. *Smooth move, Cobb,* I told myself. The lieutenant was going to have remarks to make about my letting them in on this.

Oh well, too late to worry about it now. I pressed on. "Can any of you tell me anything that would help us be sure about her one way or the other?"

It was back to blank stares again. Alice Brockway admitted after I had repeated the question a few times that one of her first jobs as a child actress had been a bit part as a third-grade student in *Miss Teasdale's Romance,* a Wilma Bascombe vehicle of the mid-forties.

"Okay," I said. "Thank you for your patience. If you think of something, the Network (meaning me) would appreciate it if you'd let me know."

I suppressed a sigh as I took a mental inventory of the conversation. Two new facts—one and a half. Somewhere in the back of my mind, I had probably known that Porter Reigels had been a Network staff director. Alice's work in that movie, I hadn't known. It was tempting to think one or both of these facts would mean something, but I resisted the temptation.

Broadcasting is a very inbred industry. Four networks, working primarily in just two cities. A handful of motion picture companies are also centered in the same two cities, heavily involved in TV production. People change jobs often. That makes for a situation in which everybody knows everybody, especially everybody that does the same kind of work. In this business, the only surprising reaction to the mention of a name is "Never heard of him."

Llona had finished her phone calls, and came back to join our cozy little group. "I don't want to do anything more until I talk to your agent," she told Shelby and Green.

"That's the point," Shelby said. "We don't have an agent. It's something we have to talk about."

"Why don't you call your old agent?" I asked.

"We *never* had an agent," Green told me. "Ken handled all that stuff. The boy was a genius." Shelby gave him a curious look.

"I can't do that kind of thing any more," the tall man with the glasses said. "Not only is show business more complicated these days, but now I have my real estate to look after."

"Don't *you* have an agent, Len?" I asked the redhead.

He made a noise. "I *had* one, the same one Alice uses. We fired each other after I broke my leg. He was a thief anyway, although Alice seems happy enough with him."

"I don't ask much of him," Alice said. She sounded almost apologetic.

"What's the big deal?" Green said, walking to the phone. "We get somebody new. I'll call William Morris. I like guys who'll look up to me."

Green made the call, and had some late-working flesh-peddler interested within seven minutes. ". . . No, I'm not kidding. Yeah. Right. We'll hop a cab and be there in no time." Grinning, he faced the rest of us.

"First crack out of the box, huh, partner? They want to talk to us right away."

Shelby smiled. "Well, what are we waiting for, partner?"

Shelby got his coat from the closet while Green went down the hall to get his.

"Want to come along, dear?" Shelby asked his wife. "You've been looking forward to this as much as Len has."

"No, I'd be useless at a business discussion. I'll wait here."

"I think *I'd* better go along, though," Llona said. "I'll fill them in on publicity so far." She turned to me. "See you tomorrow, Matt."

"*The elevator's here!*" Lenny Green's voice came in a bellow from down the hall. Raise it a couple of octaves, and it could have been a kid calling to the other neighborhood kids that the Good Humor Man had arrived—a sound of combined joy and urgency. There was no doubt how *he* felt about the reunion.

Llona and Ken Shelby exchanged grins. Shelby kissed his wife's cheek, and he and Llona rushed to join Green before the elevator got away.

"This is nice for the Network," I told Alice Brockway. "Nice for all their fans, too, including me. I'm glad I was able to be here, and I'm glad I finally got a chance to meet all of you. I'll probably see you tomorrow at the dress rehearsal . . ." I was making polite noises on my way to the door, but just as I was about to reach for the knob, I heard, "Please don't go, Matt," and I turned around to see Alice Brockway smiling coquettishly at me.

CHAPTER 13

"The facts, ma'am, just the facts."

—JACK WEBB, "DRAGNET," NBC

I have a hard time thinking of myself as irresistible, so I wondered what Alice was up to. Then I decided I was flattering myself. I had merely been fooled by the contrast between yesterday's Alice and to-day's. After yesterday's fire-breathing act, any sort of smile would seem like a special favor, and common friendliness would look like bait.

I had to admit, though, that she didn't make it seem any less of a come-on when she sat on the crushed brown velvet of the sofa and patted the cushion next to her. "I want to talk to you," she said.

I was wary. "What about?"

"A lot of things. Come on, Matt, I don't bite."

I decided to take her word for it, and sat down by her.

"What can I do for you, Alice?" I asked. Her smile got broader, and I decided it had been a poor choice of words. I tried again. "What do you want to talk about?"

"Well," she began, "do you remember the terrible way I carried on at the Network building yesterday."

"Vaguely," I said.

She tossed her yellow hair and laughed like little bubbles. I'd always loved the way she did that. Alice Brockway said, "Anyone who can lie that well should be a producer. Such a straight face, too."

"I get a lot of practice," I told her.

Alice poured us some more champagne.

"Well, it's certainly been effective. Of course, you *do* remember, and so does everyone else, to my everlasting shame. I want to apologize."

"Jet lag," I said. "A tense week with the police after having found a body in your swimming pool. It's understandable you'd be a little out of sorts."

"You're very kind, but there's more to it than that. I blew up because yesterday, I despaired of Ken and Len getting the act together again. Ken has been putting Lenny off for *years*, but when he agreed to appear on this show, I thought he'd give in, at least enough to do a college concert tour; Len would have settled for that."

"But why all the fireworks?" I asked. "Your husband is doing very well in real estate, and Lenny Green was always working, in Las Vegas or somewhere else."

She shook her head. "You don't understand how *important* it was for them to get back together. You can't really appreciate how wonderful today is.

"Separately, both of them are fine at what they do, but together, they're the best. Don't you agree?"

"They're among them," I conceded.

"Ken *loves* show business," she went on. "I called him an egomaniac yesterday—I suppose it's true. He's a brilliant man, you know. If you can get Lenny serious for a moment, he'll tell you Ken is a comedy genius in the tradition of Chaplin, Keaton, and Laurel. The only trouble is, Ken isn't *funny*—he's too serious-looking, too handsome. That's why the public and press gave most of the credit to Lenny.

"Lenny *is* funny—he's a natural clown, and a great interpreter of material. He spotted Ken's genius the minute he laid eyes on him. At least that's what he says. It didn't take him long to see it, in any case."

"This happened when Ken was working as a director for the Network?"

"Yes, it did. Did you know that before he met Len, Ken had never even been out of New York? Lenny was born in Chicago, but of course in vaudeville he'd been all over. I met him on the Coast.

"He talked Ken into forming the act. It's never been widely publicized, but it was *Ken* who developed the characters in the act—Lenny as the magical imp, and Ken flustered and embarrassed. Ken created most of the bits, too. Lenny loved doing them on stage.

"Of course, Lenny was responsible for the magic. That's how he started in the business. Ken was a fast learner though. He still has the quickest mind of anyone I know. So besides a great comedy team, they were a great magic team."

"Aha!" I said.

"What's the matter?" Alice asked anxiously.

"Excuse me for interrupting, but I think I just fulfilled a challenge. That night the Great Man's drawers fell down, it was *Ken* that did it, right? Lenny got the belt and walked away, but Ken had learned enough light-fingered technique to get the fly open and give the waist a little tug while engaging the Great Man in conversation. Then Lenny holds up the belt on the other side of the stage, and everyone wonders how *he* did it. Terrific."

Alice smiled again, and agreed with me. "They really were. That's the reason, you know, that they never said anything to contradict the idea that the stage image was the way things were in real life—it made the comedy better if people thought Ken was really as horrified as he acted, and it made the magic easier, too; everyone, as you said, was watching Len, while Ken made the trick work."

"I'm going to look over some of their old shows again," I said. I was rather pleased with myself. I'd have to tell Melanie Marliss I was as smart as she thought I was.

The feeling lasted about three seconds. Determining the cause of the descent of someone's trousers was a pretty piddling thing to be proud of when Jerry de Loon's murderer was still running around. I took a sip of champagne, and told myself to concentrate on business.

"Still," I said, "all good things come to an end. Why was it so important they get back together?"

Alice took something more than a sip, and said, "For one thing, Matt, Lenny Green is an old and dear friend of mine, and I'd hate to have his suicide on my conscience."

"Are you telling me that's why your husband gave in? Green threatened to kill himself?"

"No, no!" she snapped. "Lenny wouldn't do anything like that! But he talked about killing himself—not to Ken, or me, but to other people.

"Lenny is broke, Matt. That Utopia Uranium thing wasn't his last bad investment, not by quite a few. He's one of the legendary soft touches for friends, and, like a lot of entertainers in Las Vegas find, a good part of the money they pay him never gets past the casino."

"Declaring bankruptcy is not the disgrace it once was, Alice," I told her. "And it's a lot less permanent than suicide."

She took my hand with both of hers. It took will power not to pull away. This situation was getting out of control. Her hands were very warm. "I guess you can't understand unless you've been there, but I'll try to explain. Lenny can't stand not being a star any more. With Ken, he was one of the biggest. Now, he does old jokes and magic tricks, and not even in the main room, either. They still call him a star, but there's a definite caste system involved—you know that yourself—and Lenny is now strictly second class.

"When he broke his leg, it seemed to be the last straw. He was laid up for months, lost what work he did have. And he thought too much. And you know, Matt, his heart isn't too strong. He had a mild heart attack while he was in the hospital with his leg. He was brooding all the time.

"I could see the only one who could help him was Ken."

"And Ken didn't want to," I said.

"That's just the point—he *did* want to. That's what used to make me so furious. Ken is so *proud!* After they had that fight about the money, and that Ollie McHarg ran away, totally ruining the plans for the movie, Ken said he'd never work with Lenny again. In fact—"

"Hold it," I said. "What movie are you talking about?"

Alice looked surprised. "Oh," she said. "I'd forgotten you didn't know. There's something about you that makes a person feel you know all about them. Of course, I have to explain about the movie." She gave my hand a little squeeze.

"In addition to everything else, Ken, as you found out tonight, worked as business manager and agent for the team. He had a natural talent for business just as he had a natural talent for comedy.

"Ken was very jealous of the act. He wanted it to be just the two of them in control of their career. Lenny wanted to make a movie. I mean, the television show was going well, but Lenny wanted to make a movie. He wanted to direct. He always had ideas going for it.

"Ken suggested, and Lenny agreed—at first—that they'd produce the picture themselves, to retain complete control. Ken set up a fund, and for several years, they put a portion of all the act's earnings in it. Ken's plan was to have two million dollars put aside. He didn't plan to *use* it, but when he went to money men to put together the package for the movie, he knew that massive a cash reserve would *force* them to take him seriously."

"But it was taking too long, right?" I suggested. "Lenny got impatient."

Alice nodded sadly. "The fund was about halfway there, and Ken figured they'd be able to make the movie in another three or four years. Then Lenny came in contact with McHarg. Lenny is a child, really, and he believed McHarg's ridiculous promise to double his money in a year with an investment in uranium."

"Who brought them in contact?" I asked.

"Some cheap, bovine, little tramp that Lenny was seeing at the time."

"You sound bitter," I said.

She let go of my hand momentarily and had some more champagne. "I am, a little. Indirectly, she was responsible for breaking them up, after all. Lenny's judgment is so bad, I can't really hold him responsible."

I made encouraging noises, but her words and voice seemed to me to be inspired by a warmer emotion than just concern for a friend. I asked Alice what happened next.

"It was silly," she said, shaking her head. "The whole thing was silly. Lenny told Ken about McHarg's promises, how excited he was about them. Ken shouldn't have laughed at him, but he did. After that . . ."

After that, it followed a pattern familiar to anyone who's ever gone overboard in an argument. Alice lined it out for me. Lenny said he was trying to help get the picture started before he was too old and too blind to see it. Ken said that if all Lenny's ideas were as bad as investing in uranium, it probably wouldn't be worth *making* the picture. Lenny, hurt, had said, "Well, let me invest *my* share of the money." Now Ken was hurt. To him, there were no shares—it had always been *our* money. "I thought we were a team," he said. Lenny said he had always thought so too, but now that it had crossed his mind, wasn't Shelby hogging all the comedy writing, and making all the business decisions as if he were a single act?

After that, it degenerated rapidly. They swapped accusations of wanting to break up the act. They insulted each other.

"They . . . I mean, Ken even threw it up to Lenny about me and him—before I met Ken, when Len's wife was sick. I took a long time to forgive him for that." Alice finished her drink, and poured another.

"That was the climax, naturally," she said. I was surprised to see her smiling quite beautifully at me. "Lenny was going to storm from the house, but Ken got very dramatic.

"He issued a challenge. He said to Lenny, 'I'll play it your way. Tomorrow, I'll get that money, and give it to McHarg, and at the end of a year, if we even break *even*, I'll apologize on the air. But if we lose even a *penny*, we split whatever's left, and you and I are through. Is that agreeable?'

"And Lenny said, 'You're damn right it's agreeable!' I tried to talk them out of it, but I couldn't."

Alice looked soulfully at me. She may have been talking about Shelby and Green, but the messages from her eyes were just for me. *Dammit,* I thought, *why couldn't this have happened when I was fourteen?*

"Of course you know the end of the story," Alice went on. "The TV show was on summer hiatus, and Ken and Lenny were booked for a month of state fairs. It only lasted two weeks, because two weeks after Ken handed over the money, the scandal broke, and McHarg was gone, with all the money—Lenny's and Ken's, and everyone else's."

She put her glass down. "So Ken, with all his pride, held to the bargain, and walked out right in the middle of the tour.

"He's never said so, but he's regretted it ever since. That act was his creation, but he couldn't do it alone—not even an inferior act, the way Lenny was able to do—he couldn't sing, he had no interest in straight acting, and he wouldn't *hear* of working with a new partner."

"So he went into real estate," I said.

"Yes, he did." She picked up the glass, and started swirling it around again. "Made a success of it, too. But he misses show business so much. Ken has to have the spotlight. He misses the excitement of being in front of an audience. Even if somebody else gets the acclaim, Ken has to be in something that will . . . well, that will dazzle people.

"He tries to do it in real estate, you know. He's always working on these big, spectacular deals for vast developments, but it's not the same for him.

"These two men, Matt, have wasted ten years—more than that. That's why I have to ask you what I'm going to ask you."

"What's that?" I asked.

"I want you to stop asking about that reporter."

CHAPTER 14

"There's always room for one more!"
—THEME SONG, "ROOM FOR ONE MORE," ABC

I looked at her. Her eyes were very clear, very sincere. "You do, huh?" I asked.

"Yes."

"Is this just a whim of yours? Or do you have a reason?"

"I *told* you the reason."

"I must be slow. Tell me again."

Her face said she was vulnerable and helpless. I hated myself.

"Matt," she said, "when Ken finally relented enough to agree to appear on 'Sight, Sound, & Celebration,' I was almost deliriously happy. I thought if everything went well, Shelby and Green would be back together. Then, when we found the body in the pool, everything started to go wrong. Ken was interrupted at an important point in his business in Arizona, and he stayed angry during the entire time the police kept after us.

"Now, in spite of everything, he's made up with Lenny, and possibly saved both their lives—"

"Isn't that a bit of an exaggeration?" I asked.

"I don't think so," she said soberly. "They're like brothers, really. That's why their feud lasted so long. It was more a family thing than anything else. You've never seen them apart. It was awful.

"In any case, now that they're back together, I don't think it's a good idea for you to jeopardize everything by continuing to plague us with questions about something that's only an unfortunate coincidence!"

I finished my champagne. I did not feel lightheaded at all. I looked at Alice.

"Ma-att," she chided gently, "don't just stare at me."

"Sorry," I said. My voice sounded funny. It was coming home to me that this woman next to me with her legs folded under her, with her hand resting innocently on my thigh, was my lifelong fantasy, the one that had shaped my ideas of everything that was worth wanting in a woman.

"Sorry," I said again. "But did it ever occur to you that the body's being found in your pool wasn't a coincidence?"

Alice's eyes opened wide. "Matt!" she breathed. "You're not accusing . . ."

"No, that's not what I meant at all. It just occurred to me that it was in all the papers and on the air that Shelby and Green were getting back together for this show. Maybe someone put the body in the pool hoping that when it was discovered the publicity, or maybe the police would keep that from happening."

Alice shook her head. "Who . . . who would want to do that?"

"I don't know. You'd know who your enemies are better than I would. I mean, Lenny Green's enemies. Your husband's enemies."

"We don't *have* any enemies." She snuggled up to me. "You're frightening me, Matt."

I swallowed. "Yeah. Well, maybe it was a silly idea anyhow,"

Alice said, "Not silly," and leaned over and kissed me, for real.

I am not proud of what happened during the next several minutes, but by God, I don't regret it either. Apparently somewhere along the line, Alice had managed to plug into a few of my other fantasies. And even while I *knew* how stupid this all was, I was feeling things that made me think I was going to catch fire, or maybe melt.

It was a suitable place for an adolescent fantasy—in the equivalent of the family parlor, on a sofa. I was fourteen again, and Alice was Alice, *but we both knew what we were doing.*

Alice pulled me down on top of her, according to the script. I knew it was time for me to be gallant. "What about your husband?" I said.

She looked at me through half-closed eyes, raised her head, and bit my nose. "He doesn't mind," she said.

That's when I got a look at myself and woke up. I sighed and cursed, got up and started adjusting my clothes.

"What's the matter?" Alice wanted to know.

"I'm sorry, Alice." An understatement. "But I guess I do mind."

She laughed. More bubbles. "Don't be so *juvenile,*" she said. "Ken *understands.*"

"I'm sorry," I said again. I felt guilty; this was the friendliest I had ever gotten with a married woman still living with her husband. I felt horny, frustrated; it was easy to see Alice would have been *very* good. I felt betrayed; there hadn't been any husbands lurking around in my fantasies, whether they minded or not. I felt square; it looked like I cared more about Mr. and Mrs. Shelby's marriage than they did. And I felt totally and irredeemably stupid for letting it go so far in the first place.

Alice couldn't believe it. "Where did you get these *ideas?*" She was still laughing when I left her.

I walked home—I needed the air.

While my supper was getting ready, Spot and I played fetch. He had the game down pat, except for one little thing. He'd sit patiently at my feet, like a little white altar boy, waiting for me to throw the tennis ball. After I threw it, he'd yip happily, and chase it around the apartment, then bring it back. What I hadn't been able to get through to him was after he did that, he was supposed to let *go* of it. It made a whole different game of it when, each time, I had to reach into his mouth and fight him for a soggy, disgusting tennis ball. Knowing him, it was probably his favorite part of the game.

After supper, I took Spot for his evening walk, came back home and watched TV for a while, read for a while, then went to bed. Tomorrow was going to be a long day. I tried not to worry about what would happen the next time I saw Alice.

It also turned out to be a short night. At 5 A.M., Shorty Stack called. "Matt, baby, did I wake you up?"

I'd like to be able to say I gave that question the kind of answer it deserved, but what I said was more like, "Mmrf pfrx."

It didn't faze Shorty. "You won't mind when you hear what I've got to tell you," he said. I expressed skepticism, but after he told me, I was forced to admit he was right.

"Not bad for ten hours' work, huh, kid?" he demanded. "Worth calling you at home, right?"

"Absolutely," I said around a yawn. "I think this ought to take care of Lorenzo Baker. Thanks, Shorty."

"Piece of cake. Old friend in the Treasury Department," he said. Shorty's old friends tended to be people he has embarrassing photographs of.

I said good night and hung up, but I couldn't go back to sleep. After a while, I said to hell with it, got up and sang the National Anthem with the sign-on show, then had my soul uplifted by "Sermonette," and my brain improved by two segments of "Sunrise Semester." This country probably has the best-educated insomniacs in the world.

Finally, halfway through the morning news, I decided it was late enough to go to work. I dropped my coat off in the office, and just wandered around the building a little. The place seemed deserted, even forsaken, but that was an illusion. It was only the executive and production floors that were empty. For the News Department, it was one of the busiest times of the day, and the local TV and radio stations would be going full steam.

On a whim, I went down to the seventh floor, and took a walk to the J. V. Hewlen Kinescope Library. I tried to go in, but the door was locked. By God, nobody else was going to get killed in that converted conference room; not if Colonel Jasper Coyle had anything to say about it.

Not having anything better to do, I decided to see if the barn-door philosophy extended to the door of Studio J as well, even though the rest of the artifacts from the relic wall were now locked in Coyle's safe in the Security office.

It did. The big door to the studio was locked. I jiggled the knob a little, and was just about to walk away, when the door swung open, and tall, hard-eyed Porter Reigels poked a shiny chrome six-shooter in my face.

"Hey," I protested, "I'm one of the good guys!" I think my voice cracked. I mean, I knew Reigels didn't swear, but no one had ever said he didn't shoot.

"Oh, it's you," the Texan drawled. "Here kinda early, aren't you?" He put the gun up. Now that I wasn't looking straight into it, I could see it was a pretty puny gun, especially for a Texan. Still, I felt a lot more comfortable when he slipped the gun into his pocket.

"You're here early yourself," I told him, "unless you're bedding down in the studio to guard the place."

"Nah," he said, grinning and inviting me in. "I just got here—couldn't sleep, so I left the hotel, let myself into the studio with my key. The dress rehearsal is today; I've been going over things in my mind."

"Why the pistol?" I asked.

"Hmph," he said. "Listen, Cobb, I don't know anything about this bowling ball stuff, and I don't really care a drop of sow sweat. But, it may have reached you, this show is going to be almighty important to my career; it's going to decide if I'm still going to *have* a career.

"So when I hear someone catfooting around the hall, and trying the door, I feel obliged to check and see if it's not this same troublemaker coming around to mess up *my show!*"

Reigels said "my show" with the same far-seeing gaze that Lorne Greene used to use when he said, "My land." I mentioned to the director that some of his previous shows, like "Horsin' Around" had been made off with in the great kinescope heist.

"So?"

"Nothing. Just that you might have mentioned it."

"Shoot. Don't I have enough to worry about already? Look, Cobb, I'm about to have a dress rehearsal for a six-hour live program. Not only that, I've got to have it done in time for every lady to get dolled up, and every man to put on a monkey suit, and go across to that hotel there, and *dance*." He kicked at the floor. "Well," he went on, "thank heaven for this Sylvanus fellow. He promises me the lighting is all set; says he'll need only about twenty minutes for adjustments."

I could understand his relief. Lighting is the most intricate and time-consuming part of pre-production in the TV studio. One of the most important, too—if there's not enough light, or not the right balance of light from front and back, all of a sudden you've got a very expensive radio program.

"I don't mind your hanging around," Porter Reigels told me, "but you've got to let me keep my mind on the show, you understand?"

I nodded.

Reigels wanted to go upstairs to the control room, but a big metal bin, a square about eight feet on a side, was blocking the door. "Dern carpenters," Reigels muttered. "They bring it into the studio to hold scrap wood and sawdust and trash, that's fine, keeps the place clean. But why the Pete do they have to put it right in front of the door to the control room stairs?"

"Guess we'll have to use the elevator," I said, and Reigels said, "Suppose so." You'll notice neither one of us even *thought* about pushing the thing out of the way. The way the various unions in the broadcasting industry protect their territory (i.e., viciously), one quickly learns never to do anything that someone else might conceivably be paid for doing.

I tested Reigels's reaction to the news of Shelby and Green's getting back together. He said he thought it was wonderful. They were both nice guys, and the news had to help the ratings for "SS&C." It didn't necessarily mean anything. He'd had plenty of time since the news broke to pick a reaction and practice it.

It was nearly nine o'clock, so I told Reigels I'd take a rain check on the control room visit. I wanted to be the first one in my office, for once.

It was a vain hope. When I went into the inner office, I found Harris Brophy waiting there, smiling at me. "I came early so I wouldn't have to be chewed out in front of everybody else," he said.

I took a reassuring peek at Sixth Avenue through the brown-glass window, then sat at my desk. "Hello, Harris," I said. "Only a conceited bastard like you would expect to be chewed out for something no one could expect him to be able to control."

"I was hoping you'd feel that way," he said, still smiling. There had to be something Harris didn't find ironic or satiric or amusing, but I've never found out what it was.

He handed a manila folder across the desk to me. "Shirley asked me to give you this. She was so busy working on it, she couldn't spare any time to welcome the prisoner home." He clicked his tongue.

"Not even a yellow ribbon, huh?"

I leafed through the folder. It was a twenty-one-page report on Shirley's investigation of Jerry de Loon. I was spared the necessity of reading details of all the inquiries she had made (since yesterday afternoon!) because she had included a neat little précis of the report. The upshot of it was, as far as Shirley could tell, Jerry de Loon had been nearly as innocent as his own unborn child.

I greeted the news with mixed emotions. I was happy Jerry was in the clear, but that left just that one feeble lead, Jim Bevic. "Lots of activity," I sighed, "but precious little progress."

Harris laughed. "Hell, Matt, that's what life is all about."

"Time to go to work, Harris," I told him. "Get the file on the nut letters, and run them down. And while you're at it, find out if anyone has a vested interest in seeing that Shelby and Green don't get back together again. Call Shorty Stack out on the Coast for help, if you have to."

"I thought I wasn't being punished." He grinned.

"Shut up and get back to work."

As the door closed behind him, the intercom buzzed, meaning my secretary was on the job. "Good morning, Jazz," I said.

"Good morning, Mr. Cobb." That meant someone was in the office. "A *Miss* Hildegarde Bjoerling would like to see you."

"Who?"

"*Miss* Hildegarde Bjoerling. She doesn't have an appointment. What?" There were some murmurings on the other end, then Jazz came back. "She *says* you might know her as 'Hildy.' "

"Oh, right." Now what the hell could *she* want, I wondered. "Send her in, Jazz." A pregnant girl introducing herself as "Miss" anybody would account for Jazz's disapproval too. Despite flashy clothes and flashier cosmetics, Jazz adheres to the principles she learned from her strict Catholic parents.

Hildy walked in, her pregnancy preceding her, and that braid bouncing along behind. I got up to help her sit.

She leaned back, and clasped her hands at the top of her stomach, but not before I got a look at how they were shaking. The poor kid was scared, and the Spanish Inquisition she'd gotten from Jazz hadn't helped.

"I have to apologize for my secretary," I said. "She's under orders to protect me from paternity suits."

Hildy blushed, then showed me a small smile. "Thanks, Mr. Cobb," she said.

"I haven't done anything. How can I help you, Hildy?"

"Well," she began, then hesitated. She scraped her protruding front teeth over her lower lip, and began again. "Well, I—I don't know who to turn to with this, and—and I figured you were Jerry's friend. Right?" She looked at me.

"Yes, I was his friend, Hildy."

"Then, I think you ought to know that someone has been spreading *lies* about him. Some woman has been going around, asking sneaky questions about him; did he ever do anything dishonest; did he use drugs, or gamble, or anything like that, and he *didn't,* and nobody but a liar can say he *did,* but I don't know how to *stop* it!" She was gripping the arms of her chair now, and leaning forward in it as far as she was able.

I felt like a louse. Worse than that. Sure, Shirley had been as discreet as she could be, and sure, the Network had to *know* about Jerry's honesty, one way or the other, but how could I have explained that to Hildy?

I didn't try. Instead, I said, "I'll make it stop, Hildy. I promise. And I'll get the truth out, too."

"What will you do to the person who's responsible?" she wanted to know. "How are you even going to find her?"

"She won't be hard to find," I said. "And the person who put her up to it will suffer for it." He already was suffering.

He suffered even more when Hildy started to cry, tears of gratitude this time. "Oh, thank you, Mr. Cobb, thank you," she sobbed. "The—the baby isn't going to have Jerry, b-but it's going to have Jerry's name, and I want it to be a *good* name. I was so afraid . . . alone . . . thank you."

And the big slimy hypocrite behind my desk said, "It was nothing, Hildy, honest. Look, is there anything else I can do? Anything I can get you?"

"Well, *snf*"—I gave her a tissue to wipe her eyes—"I was thinking . . . Jerry was . . . he died before he got paid that week, and . . . well, I've got to pay the rent next week, and . . . well not *exactly,* but I kind of *am* his w-widow, and . . . Well, do you think they'd give his pay to me?"

The correct answer to that question was "The state of New York does not recognize common-law marriages, so legally you are nothing, and never in a hundred years would the Payroll Department give his pay to you."

Instead, I told her, "Wait here, I'll go talk to them." Hildy's face lit up. I gave her a reassuring pat on the shoulder on the way out.

I went to the men's room down the hall, and stood around for a few minutes, thinking. It always cracks me up when people who live together put down a marriage license as "just a piece of paper." Pieces of paper are very important. The Constitution of the United States is a piece of paper. So is a dollar bill, or a death warrant.

Without that marriage license, Hildy was about to be pitched into the street, not that it was much of a step down from the dump she was currently living in, but winter was closing in, and any roof was better than no roof. And Hildy didn't strike me as the type who'd enjoy bringing up a kid on Welfare.

So the program (in addition to all my *other* programs) was to secure the rent on the current place, or, find her a better place, and, line her up a job for after the baby came. One was easy, and I had a glimmer of a way to accomplish two. Three, I could worry about later. I went back to the office.

I told Hildy it was all set with Payroll, but it would take a while, so she would take my personal check in the meantime, and pay me back when Jerry's check finally came through. It took some convincing, but she finally agreed. I might be able to get the money back, I might not. It didn't matter—I owed her.

I invited Hildy to the commissary for a cup of coffee.

"I really shouldn't have coffee," she said, patting her stomach.

"Orange juice, then. The orange juice at the commissary is pretty good, especially if you don't like it cold."

The commissary was where I started the second phase of my plan. Millie Heywood, whom I have mentioned before, was the head technician for Network Operations. She was loud, vulgar, and aggressive—on the outside. It was a carry-over from the years (a whole lot of them) when she had been the only female techy not only at the Network, but in the whole broadcasting industry. She had been kind of a one-woman Liberation movement back in the forties, and she'd made it stick.

I happened to know, however, that she had a heart like a marshmallow, soft and sweet. I'd figured correctly that it was about time for Millie's coffee break. Hildy and I joined her at her table.

"Go away, Cobb, goddammit," Millie said, "let a person relax once, can't you?"

"Thank you, Millie," I smiled, "it *is* a lovely morning." That was the only way to handle her. I introduced Hildy. Millie, when she heard that Hildy had been Jerry's girl, apologized for being rude, a first.

Millie asked me what I wanted. To Hildy, she added, "This bas— guy, always wants *something* from me."

I pleaded innocent, said all I wanted was to bask in the presence of a Network pioneer. Before she could say anything, I asked her how the technical end of "Sight, Sound, & Celebration" was coming along.

She shrugged. "Not so bad, yet. Still, there's twelve cameras involved here, and we got to make sure the colors match on every damn one of them. Usually, we only use that many cameras for the goddam Super Bowl, and outdoors, we got the sun for lighting, so it's not so bad."

Hildy crinkled her eyebrows, and asked Millie to explain what she was talking about, and Millie was flattered. She really went into it, doing diagrams and equations in orange juice on the table top.

I wished everything I planned turned out as well as that did. After a couple of minutes, Millie looked at Hildy and said, "You like cats?" Millie had adopted, and nursed back to health, about a hundred cats. Hildy said she *loved* cats. Millie smiled, and went on talking about color temperatures, and light diffusion, but after another two minutes, she said she could use some help taking care of the cats she currently had, and invited Hildy to move in with her, at least till the baby came.

Then Millie snapped at me. "What the hell are you grinning at, Cobb? Don't you have something to do?"

"It just so happens I do," I said. My elation died at the age of two and a half seconds. "I have a lot to do." I left Hildy with Millie, and went back upstairs.

CHAPTER 15

"Will it be a hit [bong!] *or a miss* [clunk!]?"
—PETER POTTER, "JUKEBOX JURY," ABC

It wound up with Harris, Shirley, Stan Kolaski, and I going over the
nut letters. A nut letter is different from a hate letter. A hate letter is
dissatisfied ("Why do you perverts always show Negroes kissing white
women?") while a nut letter promises to do something drastic about it
(". . . or I'll come there with my shotgun and kill you all!!"). You
might not be surprised at how many of these we get, but you *would* be
astounded at how many are actually signed, and have return addresses.
We follow up any hate or nut letter that has 40 percent or more of the
words spelled right. It's the smart ones who are dangerous.

We were looking for a letter from someone with a peeve against
Melanie Marliss, bowling, bowling balls, old kinescopes, the Network
in general (very few of those—most people who write these things are
mad at individual shows), or the Network's fiftieth anniversary festivities in particular.

It killed the morning, and was good for a few laughs, but it didn't accomplish much. There were a few possible-but-unlikely missives.
Harris, Shirley, and Stan took one apiece, and followed them up. I
would hold down the Tower.

By now, it was lunch time. I decided to splurge, so I went to the
Brant and ate there. On the way back, I checked in the Crystal Room
to see how preparations for the banquet were going, and I ran into
Llona. She had the situation well in hand, so I gave her a quick hello
and good-bye and left.

Then I cashed that rain check to visit Porter Reigels in the control
room. I got off the elevator on the eighth floor.

Theoretically, the director of a show has absolute power in his control room, the same way a captain has absolute power over his ship at
sea. In reality, though, the director is responsible for a lot of ego-strok-
ing—sometimes he has to be not only the director, but a performer for
the sponsors or politicians or other big shots who join him in the control room.

The setup of Studio J accentuated the idea of the control room as a show in itself. Behind the people at the console (director, assistant director, technical director, projectionist, and audio man) there were three rows of plush theater seats.

There were no guests, at the moment. I supposed the VIP's were waiting until the actual show Sunday night, or maybe practicing their speeches for tonight's banquet.

This was a dress rehearsal for a six-hour show, but it would take less than four hours to do. Reigels had chosen not to rehearse any of the chitchat with the hundreds of celebrities who'd be milling around that set. That was a calculated risk, based on his confidence in the Anchorman's unparalleled skill as an interviewer. Sure, an ad libbed conversation is fresher than a canned one, but only if the interviewee has something to say and sufficient talent to make sentences out of it. Some very famous people couldn't ad lib a request for directions to the bathroom.

I let the door close quietly behind me, and took a seat in the back row. Judging by the time, Reigels should be in the home stretch of rehearsing the sketches and production numbers, and a glance at the fourteen black and white monitors (one for each camera, one for slides and graphics, and one for the video tape machines) and two color ones (special effects preview and the one that showed what was going over the air) bore that out. Sparkle and Brad, our Network's early seventies answer to Sonny and Cher, were finishing up the rehearsal of a medley of their hits.

"Thank you, darlin's," Porter Reigels said when they had finished. There was no window from the control room into the studio. Most studios are set up that way. There's no need for a window. The only reality the people in the control room need concern themselves with is what shows up on the monitors. In TV, what you see is all that exists. Think about it. How do you know Walter Cronkite ever wore pants? For all you know, he was naked behind that desk. The point is, it doesn't make any difference.

I didn't need a window, though, to visualize what Sparkle and Brad and everyone else on the floor of Studio J were doing as Porter Reigels spoke over the public address system. They were standing still, with their heads tilted back at forty-five-degree angles, listening to the disembodied voice in the same attitude Moses probably assumed while he was listening to God.

"Real nice," Reigels went on, and now that some of the cameramen were moving for their next shots, I could see on the monitors I had been right.

"Just make like an audience for a while. We've got the Reluctant

Magician and the finale to do, then we can go get pretty for the party."
An open mike in the studio picked up some scattered applause.

Reigels switched from the PA mike to his headset, which tied him in
with all the other members of the crew. He asked the stage director if
Shelby and Green were ready, and if the cabinet had been set up. He
apparently got yesses to both, because he nodded. He spoke to Millie in
Master Control.

"Ready to roll and record," he said. Reigels was taping the dress rehearsal, and would have all day Saturday to go over the tape and decide
if he wanted to do anything differently. That is, that was the way it
was supposed to happen.

When everyone was in place, Reigels told Master to roll the tape,
and when he was informed it was up to speed, he started directing.

"Okay, we're coming up on camera six. Ready, announcer. Up on
six, announce."

The technical director and audio man pushed the buttons that would
make it happen. It's not as easy as it sounds. With the huge electronic
console they're working, they look like Sulu and Chekov at the bridge
of the Starship *Enterprise*.

Meanwhile, the announcer, who had his own private booth, wrapped
his deep, rich voice around his line: "And now, the Great Bomboni!"

Nothing. Camera six took a picture of the magic cabinet on an otherwise empty stage.

"Announce," Porter Reigels said again, smiling already. The announcer repeated, "The Great Bomboni!"

More nothing, for six interminable seconds. Then Ken Shelby edged
sheepishly onto the stage, in the character of the Great Bomboni's manager. He looked at the camera, and said, "I . . . I'm afraid the Great
Bomboni is still . . . ah . . . still attuning himself with the infinite."

Lenny Green's voice, off-camera: "I don't *care* what you're paying
me for, I'm not getting into that undersized outhouse for anybody!"

Shelby smiles, raises a hand to ask the audience's indulgence. He
walks off-camera, and returns dragging Lenny Green by the elbow.
Green is wearing a magnificent black cape with scarlet lining over a
rumpled brown suit. He doesn't walk too steadily. In a stage whisper,
he says, "I'm not the Great Bomboni. I'm not the Great Bomboni. This
is a fake. They promised me a bottle of—"

He can't finish, because Shelby has clamped his hand over the
smaller man's mouth. In a supposed aside, through gritted teeth, Shelby
says, *"The real Bomboni disappeared."*

Green, also through gritted teeth, says, *"Well, he's supposed to, ain't
he?"*

"I mean he disappeared with the gate receipts!"

"*Oh,*" Green says, nodding. "*I'll go look for him.*" He starts to walk off, but Shelby has him by the belt.

"*You can't go,*" Shelby says, "*you're the only one the magic turban fits!*" Shelby ignores Green's quizzical look, and plays to the audience. "And now, Allura, the Great Bomboni's trusted assistant, will bring the secret of Bomboni's power: the Magic Turban of Mysta Maru!"

Green says, "Give Mister Maru his turban back, I'm going." He starts to leave. Shelby tries the belt trick again, but Green's pants come away, showing yellow-and-green striped shorts. (Shelby and Green really liked underwear gags.) He gets about halfway off the set, with the camera following him, when he walks right into Melanie Marliss, wearing a few wisps of chiffon and a sequin or two. Green decides to stay.

Usually at a rehearsal, nobody laughs, but about that time, people in Studio J, professionals all, were caught up by the Reluctant Magician. Maybe a hundred people were watching the act, either firsthand or on a studio monitor, and laughing their heads off. We were laughing in the control room, too.

Shelby, Green, and Marliss picked up on the laughter, and it showed in the act. The lines got crisper, and their faces even funnier. Green went into a little impromptu Sally Rand bit with his cape, not quite revealing his hairy legs. It almost broke Melanie up.

Shelby brought them back to the script. He explained how the Great Bomboni was going to go into the cabinet, and how his assistant was going to be locked in the trunk, and how they would magically trade places.

The Great Bomboni managed to misconstrue this to mean that he would be locked in the cabinet with Melanie's pulchritude, and he was suddenly eager to do the trick. After two minutes or so of double entendres, the Great Bomboni said, "Let's get in the box," with a leer and a pant that satirized every lecher who ever lived.

He capped this with a look of surprise mixed with confidence when the door of the cabinet opened of its own accord. His face seemed to say, maybe I *am* magic.

His assistant pointed the way in, and Bomboni entered. Shelby closed the door behind him.

"*Hey!*" the voice came from inside the cabinet. "*Hey! Let me out!*"

"The Great Bomboni is calling on his friends in the spirit world to help him out of this worldly prison!" Shelby yelled, trying to drown out the cries of the man in the box.

"I'll call on my friends in the Police Department and put you *in* prison," the Great Bomboni yelled. "Let me *out!*"

The audience's laughter got even stronger when the cabinet started to vibrate as the sides rattled to resounding thumps. The yelling never stopped, and neither did the laughter.

Meanwhile, Shelby had assisted Melanie into the trunk and locked her in. The camera draws back and music swells dramatically over the sound of Lenny Green's voice yelling dire threats if he isn't released this minute.

Then, with the yelling still going on, the door of the cabinet swings silently open, and Melanie walks out, holding a tape recorder that yells, in Lenny Green's voice, "Boy, you can't trust *anybody* these days, can you?"

Thunderous applause. Shelby returns, opens the trunk, and the Great Bomboni is not there! "Where did he go?" Melanie breathes. "I went to the corner for a drink. I got sick of waiting for you guys. Meet me there," says the tape recorder.

Shelby and Melanie look at each other, shrug, and leave the stage arm in arm. More applause, and laughter (even applause in the control room, which is practically unheard of).

"Okay," Porter Reigels said. I was aware of his direction again. "Music up, talent out for a bow, Anchorman goes to greet them, on camera twelve. *Now!*"

The Anchorman, Melanie, Shelby, and Green were cued accordingly, and assembled on their marks for the bows. Camera twelve, mounted on a boom, put their smiling faces up on the monitor.

Then things started to happen.

Camera twelve's picture began to look like a painting someone had tried to do on boiling oatmeal. It got lumpy, and ran. Porter Reigels saw it, and from behind him, I could see his head swivel, scanning the other monitors for a shot he could switch to. No dice. All the pictures looked like that.

Over the audio monitor, we could hear the sounds of Studio J; loud shouts, and surprised little screams. There was also a crackling noise, like bacon frying.

Porter Reigels grabbed his headset and yelled, "Somebody tell me what's going on down there!" When he heard the answer, Reigels said, "Oh no!" and his head sunk to the desk.

I got the information from the technical director, though I had to shake him out of a shocked stupor to get it. "Fire in the carpenter's bin," he said. "Sprinklers cut in."

Just then, the mikes in the studio, which to my surprise had not yet shorted out, picked up a noise that sounded like the end of the world, a roaring, splintering crash that I swear I could have heard even without the microphones.

"*What the hell was that?*" I demanded, but I guess I didn't expect an answer, because I was already running from the control room.

I sprinted to the corner of the building, where the stairs were. As I ran down the hall, it occurred to me that we'd have another visit from the fire department, because the sprinklers were tied in with the alarm system.

Since bells were already ringing, and buzzers already buzzing, it didn't make much difference if I set off another switch by opening the door to the stairs. Just as I hit the landing that marked the halfway point between the eighth and seventh floors, I heard the seventh-floor fire door bang open. I figured I was going to see a mad rush by panic-stricken celebrities, but only one figure came through the door, a less-than-medium-sized fellow, with soaking wet black hair, and soaking wet high-fashion men's clothes.

He looked disheveled, furtive, and just plain scared, and it took me a few seconds to recognize him. It was the taco king himself, Lorenzo Baker. I had been meaning to talk to him about Shorty's call, and now that he was running away the way he was, I wanted to talk to him even more.

I called his name, and chased him down the stairs. He looked at me over his shoulder as though I were a harpy or something. His feet never slowed for a second.

The chase was on for real, now. I was determined to catch him if I had to chase him all the way back to Los Angeles. I mean, it could have been he was just rushing back to the Brant to change into some dry clothes, but I doubted it. I didn't want him to get away.

Baker's mind was working in one direction—straight down. He could have left the stairwell at any floor and had a good chance of losing me in the corridors, but he stuck to his original plan of heading for the bottom of the building and out.

I had longer legs, but he had a half-story head start, and he was fast. I gained on him, but only a step or two at a time. I didn't catch him until the landing of the second floor, the headquarters of Channel 10.

I reached out and grabbed a handful of wet Botany 500. It spun Baker around, and I edged past him, positioning myself so that I could defend the door to the building or the stairs to the ground floor.

If Baker wanted to, he could have turned and headed back up the stairs, but I doubted he would. In fact, I prayed he wouldn't. I was breathing like a steam calliope, and my legs were lead. Baker looked better, but not much.

I was still trying to collect air enough to speak when Baker, seeing I had cut off his path, got a cold look in his eye.

I braced myself for a rush, but got a scream instead. "Hai-*ya!*" Baker had dropped into a crouch, and was waving open hands at me. One panicky corner of my mind made a note of the fact that Baker was wearing a black belt. That was just stupid, and I told myself so. Karate black belts are not used to hold up pants.

Actually, the whole thing was academic. Baker could hold a *paisley* belt and still be trouble. Street fighting and army judo don't exactly add up to a Martial Art.

Baker waved a hand to indicate I should get out of his path, and yelled "Wa!" I wondered if it was impossible to do karate and speak English at the same time.

I waited too long for Baker's taste. He decided to move me himself. Recognizing me for a pigeon, he didn't bother with faking or feinting. He aimed a vicious swipe at me with the edge of his hand. I managed to block it with my left forearm, but the impact left my arm numb. It fell, and I couldn't lift it.

He tried a kick this time. With fear-quickened reflexes, I dodged clear, and the kick hit the door to Channel 10 like the proverbial ton of bricks.

I resolved to start kicking at him. What the hell, I figured, I might get lucky. As it turned out, I got luckier than I had any right to hope.

Baker launched what was supposed to be the *coup de grâce,* a flying kick at my head. It was lovely to see, and I saw it in a kind of psychic slow motion. David Carradine would have been proud of it. If it had connected, my head was good for a fifty-yard flight.

But the kick never reached home. Instead, the door to the corridor leading to Channel 10 opened up, and the mild-mannered host of "Rise and Shine, New York," a local talk show, asked what all the noise was about.

Baker's sidewinding leg smacked the edge of the opening door, changing the direction of the force of the kick, and knocking him off balance.

Baker went flying ass-over-teakettle, as my grandmother used to say. He landed hard on his back on the stairs. The wind was knocked out of him, and he was going to have an interesting, parallel set of bruises, but he was okay.

The talk show host seemed puzzled by my gratitude, but not so much that he didn't accept my offer to buy him a steak at the earliest opportunity.

He went on his way. I put out a hand to help Baker up, being careful to stay out of kicking range. He looked at the hand as though he was trying to decide whether to take it or snatch a pebble from it. He took it. I pulled him to his feet, whipped him around so I was behind him, and got his arm in the come-along hold, a useful little trick they teach to the MP's. He could try the karate to his heart's content, now, because any strenuous effort on his part was going to break his arm.

Baker must have known intuitively that it would be much wiser of him to keep his mouth shut, and he did. I marched him down the hall to the elevator. A couple of Channel 10 employees asked what we were doing. I told them Baker's back had come out and I was helping him get it back in.

I was deliberately *not* thinking of what we were going to find on the seventh floor. I was especially not thinking about that splintering crash. On a radio show called "Lights Out," they once did a sound effect of a man being turned inside out by twisting a belt so it creaked, and crushing strawberry boxes. The sound I'd heard had been like that, only louder.

I thought of trivial things instead. I thought of how Shelby and Green had worked that trick—Green and Marliss switching boxes by way of the trap doors. The oldest gimmick in the book, really. What made it go was the illusion that Green was still in the box. The deception was manufactured by Green's voice on the tape recorder, and a motor-driven weight that made the thumps and shaking. The comedy helped, of course. It's hard to laugh and figure at the same time.

I thought of how pleased I was to have the power to spike Baker's romance with Melanie. Especially now. Lorenzo Baker would do a little dancing today, to any tune I cared to whistle.

I thought of how my arm hurt, but that made it feel worse. I wondered how Shorty had forgotten to tell me about Baker's karate.

I thought of Llona, then asked myself how *she* got in there.

As always, the anticipation of what I'd find on the seventh floor seemed to have been worse than the fact. Of course, I didn't know what the fact was yet, but that was how it seemed. Building Services had the sprinkler off, and Colonel Coyle and the Security boys were dealing with crowd control. They had their guns on, today. Coyle wasn't fooling around.

The colonel was supervising as a couple of his men took names from the hundred or so wet, miserable-looking people who were lined up all the way down the hall. There's only one reason to do that.

"Called the police, eh, Colonel?" I asked.

"I have."

"Good move," I said. "I caught this one trying to run away. Ah, thanks." A couple of uniformed guards took Baker off my hands. "Watch him," I said, "he's a black belt."

One guard, a black guy who must have stood six-six and weighed two-ninety said, "Me too." That was the end of my worries about Baker. I told the taco tycoon we'd talk to him later, or the police would.

"Have you been inside?" I asked Coyle. I suddenly noticed that while I had seen Alice Brockway (she'd been in the line outside the studio), I *hadn't* seen Ken Shelby, Lenny Green, or Melanie Marliss. I felt just a little sick.

"I have," Coyle said again. "That's why I summoned the police. I bleeve"—Coyle was from the Midwest—"I bleeve we've got an attempted homicide. It all comes from *amateurs* dictating policy, *especially* when it comes to Security. Why—"

I'm sure there was more, but by then I was opening the door to Studio J to see for myself.

I climbed up to the set, and felt the rug squish under my feet. The whole place felt like a swamp. Spraying water had peeled all those beautiful big pictures off the walls.

Far across the room, standing almost where they had been when I'd last seen them smiling for camera twelve, were Ken Shelby and Lenny Green and Melanie Marliss. Even from a distance, I could see they were stunned.

They weren't standing *exactly* where they'd been before, because the magical cabinet was there. It was lying on its side, but at a funny angle. Something was wrong with the floor, but I didn't think the water had done it.

I was right. When I got there, I found out the water hadn't done anything to the floor. The cabinet was the way it was because it had not quite fallen through a big jagged hole in the wooden floor of the set.

"Coyle told us to wait here," Lenny Green said tonelessly. He still had the turban on. It was unraveling. He still wore no pants.

"Somebody tried to *kill* us," Melanie said. She had a tone of wonder in her voice, as though she were a child, or trying to impress a child. Ken Shelby was comforting her, and she needed it. She was trembling. She was also, I noticed in spite of myself, almost unbearably sexy. Her costume hadn't stood up to the water very well, and what was left was transparent where it touched her, and translucent where it didn't. I had to remind myself to get back to work.

Shelby was plenty shook up himself, but he seemed to be in the best shape. I loaned him my handkerchief to wipe his glasses, then put the question to him. "Somebody dropped something from the catwalk on you?"

He pushed wet gray hair from his forehead. "It *would* have been on us—right on our marks. Thank *God* that fire started."

Green was nodding like a bobbing-head doll. "Uh huh. We ran for cover when the sprinkler started, and *Bam!*"

"I'm interested," I said quietly, "to see just what it was he dropped on you. Help me lift the cabinet out of the way, all right?"

They looked at me. Even in an emergency, they thought of Network protocol.

"Look, I'll pay union dues for us, all right?"

That did it. We lifted up the cabinet, and looked into the hole.

I knew what was going to be there. I'm not clairvoyant, or anything —my life is just like that. I live bad jokes.

That's why, before we even moved that magic cabinet, I knew that in the middle of the broken plywood, gleaming like a dull ruby in the navel of some belly-dancing giantess, would be Melanie Marliss's bowling ball.

And so it was.

CHAPTER 16

"I'm so confused!"

—JOHN TRAVOLTA, "WELCOME BACK, KOTTER," ABC

A little while later, Lieutenant Martin leaned over that same hole to look at the bowling ball. "Well, Matty," he said, "that solves *your* case."

That called for sardonic laughter, and I gave him some. "Oh, right. Sure, the lawsuit is off, but I'd still like to know who killed Jerry. And took the kinescopes. And tried to use the bowling ball like a pile driver on three of our stars."

The lieutenant grunted. "Me too," he said.

Rivetz joined us by the hole. "Okay, Lieutenant, we got their stories and sent them home or to the hotel to dry off. I told them that detectives might be calling on them."

That was good to hear. By the time the cops had arrived, the crowd had been making ominous rumblings.

"Where are the three who were onstage?" the lieutenant asked.

"I sent them to their dressing rooms. They'll meet us in the Marliss babe's dressing room. God, is she a piece. Even better than in the movies. Oh, I almost forgot. Alice Brockway is with them—wanted to stay with her husband."

"That's okay with me," the lieutenant said. "Where's Baker?"

"He's with Marliss. He won't be going anywhere. If he does, it's his ass, and I told him so."

"Mmm." Martin scratched his chin. "Even so, go keep them company, Rivetz." He went. To me, the lieutenant said, "Anybody check the catwalk yet?"

"No, I was saving that for you."

He feigned surprise. "I don't believe it! Matt Cobb saving police work for the police!"

I ignored him. "Do you want to go up there now? I got the key from Coyle."

"Yeah, let's go. Where is Coyle, by the way?"

"He's reporting to Falzet," I said. They deserved each other.

"This is a tough break for that Reigels," the lieutenant said.

"Tough break for the whole Network. 'Sight, Sound, & Celebration' may turn out to be the Anchorman showing home movies."

We went up to the eighth floor, to the door of the catwalk near the stairwell I'd chased Lorenzo Baker down. The lieutenant paused outside the door.

"How many ways are there to get out on that thing?"

"Two—no, three. There's a staircase from the studio itself, like the one to the control room, and there's a door into the corridor on either end. I only brought us to this one because it's closer to the spot the ball must have dropped from."

"It doesn't make any difference, I just thought we'd get a break once. Either for the person coming in or for when he was going out, but forget it. These locks are shiny and nice-looking, but you can pick them with a Q-Tip."

"Coyle has mentioned that."

"Yeah? Why didn't you listen to him?" I told the lieutenant to ask Falzet, and he went on. "Anyway, that covers getting in. He could pick the lock from the hallway, or he could have come up from the studio. Nobody would be watching a door behind the walls of the set while the show was on, right? As for leaving, all he had to do was dash back down to the studio by one of the three ways—"

"Not this way," I said, pointing behind me. "If he'd come out this door, I'd have seen him."

"Okay, one of the other two ways. All he had to do was join the crowd again. In the confusion, it would be easy."

I nodded. "How does Baker sound to you?"

"Why should he want to smash his own woman?"

"There's more to Baker than you might know."

Naturally, the lieutenant wanted to know what I was talking about, but I put him off by unlocking the door. There was a small platform, then the catwalk itself.

"Watch your step," I told him, "and don't look down more than you have to."

"Yeah," he said, with a little more breath than necessary. When you're standing *on* something, it always seems a lot higher than it does when you're looking *up* at it, and the catwalk had seemed plenty high even then. If you *did* look down, everything below seemed tiny, but very hard.

As I stepped out onto the catwalk, I could understand why lighting men used it as little as possible. It was solid enough—the lieutenant and I are a couple of good-sized guys, and the catwalk didn't wobble under our combined weight—but it *seemed* like such a wispy, flimsy thing. There wasn't enough of it to look at, if you know what I mean. The floor of the thing was metal grillwork, with a rim of maybe a half-inch projecting above it. The hand rails, which I held onto for dear life, were pencil-thin steel rods, and they were only about two and a half feet above the grill, so we either had to stoop or bow our legs to use it. Between the grillwork and the railing there was a gap easily big enough for a man's body to fall through if his foot slipped.

I concentrated on the placement of my feet, because the catwalk was wet, and it was a little slippery. I had a grudging admiration for a man who could scoot across this thing to the other door, the whole width of the studio, with sprinklers pouring water in his eyes, even if his purpose *was* murder.

"Son of a gun," the lieutenant said.

"What is it?"

"He left something. Look."

"Where?"

"Right where we're heading. Don't you see something white?"

"Well," I said, looking, "let's hope it's a monogrammed handkerchief so we'll know who it was that left it." Then I saw it, and it was too big and too stiff to be cloth.

Cautiously, we made our way to the spot. I let go of the railing to bend down and pick the thing up. I got a superfluous admonition to be careful from Lieutenant Martin. The white thing was a piece of cardboard, just a little thicker than shirt cardboard, but the same kind of material. It had been folded many times to make a tight little wedge, but because it was wet now, it had expanded and come loose to a great degree. There seemed to be something written on it, but instead of unfolding it there, which would have taken both my hands off the railing, I stuck it in my pocket. We could look at it later.

There was nothing else to be found up there, but the lieutenant asked me to orient him to the studio.

"Okay," I said. "Directly below us, on this side, is—was, I mean, the place on the floor of the set where the marks were for Shelby, Green, and Marliss to take their bows."

"Marks?"

"Yeah, T-marks or crosses made with tape for the performer to stand on. Then the cameraman knows where the person is going to be, and he can line up his shot before he gets there. Otherwise, he'd always have to be focusing on the air. It wouldn't look good."

He was going to scratch his head, but changed his mind, kept his hands on the railing, and nodded instead. "Convenient. Convenient for Mr. Bowling Ball, too. He can line up *his* shot before the person he wants to hit is on the scene."

"Which raises another interesting question: Whom, exactly, did he want to hit? I mean, those marks were pretty close together, and from this height, they must have looked even closer. How could he pick one with any accuracy? Did he bring a Norden bombsight with him? Or was he looking to get all three of them?"

"Maybe he didn't care," the lieutenant suggested.

"Sure, a nut. That would fit, I suppose. The whole thing is nutty. And since a falling object accelerates at the rate of thirty-two feet per second per second—"

"Hold it, hold it. What are you talking about?"

"The law of falling bodies. Any object, regardless of weight, increases its velocity at a rate of thirty-two feet per second for every second it falls."

He shook his head and grinned. "Where do you *get* this stuff?"

I grinned back. "I was a faithful watcher of 'Dr. Wonder' when I was a kid. TV is very educational, you know."

"Yeah. Maybe I ought to get rid of you and bring in this Dr. Wonder."

"You can't, he's dead. All I was trying to say was that that ball was traveling pretty damn fast by the time it hit that wood. A nut would like that. Whoever was hit would be smashed to jelly."

"Hell, I could have told you that," he said. "Those people are damn lucky that fire broke out, Matty. Damn lucky."

I nodded. "Fire broke out just over there." I risked taking an arm from its hold to point to the bin, not far from the place where the three performers had left the stage just before returning for their bows. "Must have been a big surprise for the killer—or rather, the dropper. No, goddammit, the *killer!*" I cursed myself for forgetting Jerry. "The killer is all ready to cut loose with the ball, when all of a sudden, it's raining inside, and they run right out from under it."

"Could be frustrating," the lieutenant agreed. "Come on. If we can get off these damn monkey bars without falling, I want to see what's written on that cardboard."

We both breathed a lot more freely outside. "I just found out I'm afraid of heights," the lieutenant said. We laughed, burning off nerves.

With great anticipation, I took the soggy cardboard out of my pocket and unfolded it. It was a rectangle about two feet by two and three-quarters feet. There was writing on it, in pencil, big block letters and numbers: "2×4 72PCS L16FT."

"Oh, for Christ's sake," I said. What a disappointment.

"What is it?"

"It's a label. The bundles of wood the carpenters got to build the set were labeled with cardboard like this. This was off a bundle of seventy-two pieces of sixteen-foot-long two-by-fours."

"Shit," the lieutenant said. "I was hoping it was a code. I haven't come across a good code since I was with Narco division." He took the label from me, looked it over for a while. "Hey, how did this get up on the catwalk? It's too high to throw up there. From these creases, this thing wasn't folded into any paper airplane and flown up."

He was right. Someone had to have brought it up there, and to me it looked like the killer was the only choice. I said so to Mr. M., and he said that was how it looked to him, too.

"I just wish I could think of a *reason*," I said.

"All we can do is ask," he said reasonably. "Come on, Matty."

The caption on the scene in Melanie's dressing room could have been, "The bigger they are, the *nicer* they are." Everyone was being pleasant. Melanie Marliss was blow-drying Alice Brockway's hair in front of the lighted mirror. Alice greeted me cheerfully. Apparently, there were no hard feelings. Lenny Green, dressed now, was lighting Rivetz's cigarette. As he puffed, the detective listened while Lorenzo Baker told Ken Shelby about our little encounter on the stairs. ". . . I suppose you can't really blame Cobb. It must have looked suspicious—"

"What looked suspicious, Mr. Baker?" the lieutenant asked. He reminded them of his name, and said he was happy they'd all had a chance to change into dry clothes. "What looked suspicious?" he repeated.

Baker smiled the charming smile that was immortalized on the taco bags. "Why, my dashing down the stairs that way."

"It looked suspicious, all right," I said, rubbing my arm. "Why did you run?"

"I was just telling Ken. I was in the studio, watching the act, just as I've watched the rehearsals all week, you know—I never get tired of that sketch. Have you ever seen it, Lieutenant?"

"Long ago. It's funny. How about getting on with your story?"

"Ah . . . of course." There was a worried gleam in the non-Mexican eyes. "When the sprinkler started, I headed for the exit, like everyone else, but I thought I saw the other door, the one Mr. Cobb saw me come out of, opened by someone sneaking out. As I told Mr. Rivetz, I thought it might have been the person who dropped the bowling ball. So I chased him."

The hair drying by the mirror was finished. "That was very brave of you, Lorenzo," Melanie said.

"Lieutenant," Lenny Green said, after exchanging a significant glance with his partner. "I don't want to sound big-headed or anything, but there was a lot of publicity last night and this morning about Shelby and Green getting back together . . ."

"No!" Alice Brockway said. "Matt said the same thing last night, but I won't believe it! Ken and Lenny don't have an enemy in the world. And I don't think Melanie does, either."

Marliss smiled at the other woman. "None that would want to turn me into a pancake, at least."

"We've been looking into it, up at Special Projects. Nothing so far," I said.

"We'll check too," Lieutenant Martin promised. "But right now, I'm talking to Mr. Baker. Rivetz, did you walk through Mr. Baker's story with him?"

"I sure did."

"And?"

"He's lying his head off."

Baker resented that, and wasn't shy about saying so.

"Come off it," Rivetz sneered, doing his job. "From where you say you were standing, you can barely see the hinges. *Maybe* you could see the door open, but I doubt it, especially the way everybody tells me that water was falling."

Baker was eloquent. He didn't say he actually *saw* anything, he said he *thought* he saw something. "Besides," he stroked his mustache, "I certainly couldn't have dropped the bowling ball. People saw me down in the studio at the time."

"That's true," Alice Brockway said. She sounded reluctant. She probably didn't like Baker any better than I did. "I was standing near him, and I heard some of the other witnesses tell the sergeant—"

"Detective First Grade," Rivetz was quick to correct. A Detective First makes more money than a sergeant.

"Tell him . . . ah . . . that they saw Mr. Baker, too."

I still didn't like it. "Didn't it occur to you, Lorenzo, when I caught up with you, to *tell* me you were chasing somebody, instead of unleashing the amazing power of oriental Martial Arts?"

I had made a point with the lieutenant. "I think maybe you just better come downtown and tell us some more about it," he said.

Melanie was irate; Baker soothed her. Then, making a determined face, he said, "Lieutenant, can I talk to you in private for a few seconds? There's something I want to tell you."

"In a minute," Martin said. He was letting Baker stew for a while. He turned to Shelby, Green, and Marliss. "Now," he said, "you three were directly under whoever it was that dropped that ball. Didn't any of you see anything? Hear anything?"

Shelby shook his head and looked grim. "I wish I could say I knew there was someone up there, but I can't. Did either of you?"

Neither Green nor Marliss had.

"We had a lot to do," Shelby went on. "We wanted to hit our m—that is pieces of tape we're supposed—"

"Your marks," Mr. M. said, as though he'd known it all his life.

"Right. You can't hit your mark and be looking straight up."

The lieutenant supposed he was right. Actually, if for some reason they *had* been looking up, there was still no guarantee they could have seen a person on the catwalk. The lights would be in the way, for one thing.

"What puzzles me, though," Shelby said, "is how someone got out on the catwalk carrying the bowling ball without being seen. You'd think a person carrying a big red object like that would be noticed."

"When can I have my bowling ball back, Lieutenant?" Melanie asked.

The lieutenant narrowed his eyes at her, trying to decide if she was kidding. "Not for a while, I'm afraid," he said. "It's evidence." Melanie wasn't happy about that. She gave the impression she'd give up her jewels to get it back. Green told her to relax, at least the ball was safe with the police.

The lieutenant wasn't through yet. "You sure you didn't notice anything?"

They were sure. Shelby said, "Even after the sprinklers started, I was too busy trying to pull my partner out of the rain. It's a good thing I did, eh?" He patted Green on the back.

"Didn't you want to go, Lenny?" I asked.

"I've got a slow-motion brain, Matt. I realized that when I broke my leg." It occurred to me it might be interesting to find out just how he *had* broken his leg, but he went on before I could ask. "When the water came down, I just didn't know what was going on—I was still being the Great Bomboni . . . or not being. You know what I mean. The Great Bomboni never had to run away before."

Alice Brockway smiled warmly. "A method actor." Everybody but Lorenzo Baker laughed.

Lieutenant Martin said, "We can have that talk you wanted now, Baker."

"Wait a minute!" Green broke in. "What about the fire? I'd like to thank the person who started it. Can you find out?"

"We're looking," the lieutenant said. "Though I'm sure it was an accident—garbage emptied into the bin with a cigarette not quite out, something like that. I doubt it was deliberate."

"It would be one hell of a coincidence," I said, "if someone were deliberately setting a fire at the very moment someone else was getting ready to drop a bowling ball fifty-odd feet on people."

"Well, it was still lucky," Green said.

The lieutenant signaled to Baker. Melanie gave her lover a curious look, but he smiled and told her not to worry. Rivetz, Baker, Martin, and I left. Marliss, Brockway, Shelby, and Green stayed behind.

Out in the hall, Baker pointed at me and said, "*He's* not a policeman. I said private. You gave your word."

Baker was right. If he'd insisted, the lieutenant would have had to run me. I wanted to be in on it.

"You want me to be there, Baker," I said.

"I do not."

"Yes you do. I know why you're in the taco business, you know. If I can't join the lieutenant in talking to you about it, I'll talk to Melanie about it. Then where will your movie be?"

"You bastard!" Baker looked as if he wanted to go into the karate bit again, but the presence of two cops changed his mind.

"What are you talking about, Matty?" the lieutenant asked.

"Let's talk in my office," I said. "For Baker's sake I don't want any more people than necessary to hear about this."

I told Jazz to hold all calls, sat at my desk, got my guests seated (Rivetz took a window sill again—he liked sitting on window sills), and got started.

"All right, Baker. I think the lieutenant should know about you."

"How do *you* know about me?"

"The Network is everywhere," I told him. The lieutenant's face said get on with it, so I did. "It's no great secret," I began, "that before you were Lorenzo Baker, you were Larry Baker, from Canton, Ohio. You went to Hollywood in . . . ah . . . sixty-four, right?" Mentally, I was kicking myself for not having taken notes when Shorty Stack called. Notes always look impressive. Baker had no reaction to the date, so I figured I could trust my memory.

"You were going to be an actor, but you weren't too successful. You got some work as an extra, but not enough to live on. To supplement, you started dealing in grass. Nothing much, at first.

"But you had a talent. You were a natural businessman. They tell me, for a while, you were one of the top young marijuana wholesalers in Southern California. Then you branched out. Cocaine. Smack. Mescaline."

Lieutenant Martin was mad. "Matsuko didn't tell me anything about this."

"He didn't know anything about it," I said. "The Feds caught Larry one day. He talked, in exchange for immunity. Right, Larry? They let you go, let you keep the money you made. You took it, whipped up a batch of the taco sauce recipe you probably picked up in Mexico along with the cash crop, and went into business with Lorenzo's Tacos."

Rivetz was grumbling. "All right, they gave him immunity, so he's got it, right?" Rivetz hated immunity. "So what's the difference what he did before? We can't bust him for it."

"The difference is," I said, "that Melanie Marliss is staunchly anti-drug. If this got out, she'd be a laughingstock—letting an ex-pot pusher produce her next movie. So if she hears about Lorenzo's past . . ."

"Gotcha," Rivetz said with glee. "Instead of using those fantastic boobs for a pillow, he'd have to go buy a magazine if he even wanted to *see* them. Like the rest of us."

Baker swallowed, opened his mouth, closed it, swallowed again. "You don't plan to tell her, do you?"

"I don't think the police will tell if the Feds want it quiet," I said, "and speaking for the Network, as long as the Network is happy, we want everybody else happy. Do you follow me?" *Ahh, blackmail,* I thought, *it's wonderful.*

Baker seemed to take it as par for the course. "I follow you," he said. "Melanie won't sue."

That was nice to know. Took a little of the pressure off.

"Thank God you found out," Baker said, surprising me. "Now I can tell you why I ran from you, Cobb."

"Why?" Mr. M. asked.

Baker looked up at him. "I thought he was trying to kill me."

I made a noise. "All right," the taco king protested, "now I know I was wrong. But I've been getting threats on my life. Three so far. I couldn't do anything but keep them a secret. You see that, don't you?"

"Sure," I said. "If you went to the police, Melanie might somehow find out about your past, and if you told Melanie, she'd insist you go to the police." Like Jack Benny, Baker faced the question, "your money or your life," and was having trouble deciding. He'd squealed on the narcotics sellers, and they play rough, but if he lost Melanie, he lost his dream of success in show business.

"How did these threats come?" the lieutenant asked.

"Phone. At the hotel."

"When was the first one?"

"Thursday morning." Right after Jerry's death.

"What did they say? Man or woman?"

"It was whispers, like someone had laryngitis—I couldn't say. The words were always the same: *'Baker, the second you look the wrong way, you're going to die.'*

"That's why I ran when everything started happening in Studio J. I was afraid someone would come up to me in the confusion, and stab me or something."

"So you lied when you said you saw someone running from the studio."

"Yes. The only person I saw was Cobb, and from the way he chased me, I thought he was the one."

"I never stab people in the confusion," I said. "They take too long to die." I turned to the lieutenant. "What are you going to do?"

"I don't know. Give Baker a quiet little bodyguard, I guess. I sure don't want anyone else getting killed on me. What else can I do? Work the routine." He waved a hand at Baker. "You can go. I may want to talk to you later."

Baker rose, looking like a man who has gotten off far better than he ever dreamed he would.

"See you at the banquet," he said, jauntily.

CHAPTER 17

"Tension, pressure, pain! Tension, pressure, pain!"

—ANACIN COMMERCIAL

I passed a relatively calm half-hour. By that I mean I didn't have to
fight anybody, at least with anything more lethal than words, and I
didn't have to engage in any extortion. All I had to do was fight off
phone calls. Reporters from all over town—all over the *country*—were
calling up the Network, and getting Ritafio's patented double talk. A
lot of them weren't happy with that, and called Special Projects for the
truth, which I more or less gave them. I considered it an investment. It
was silly to think the Network could be saved from embarrassment
now, and any time I talked to a reporter, it was a favor that could be
collected at a later date.

After a half-hour of that, though, things started to jump. The door of
my office burst open, and Llona flew in, close to tears. *"I quit!"* she
said. "I don't have to take this! I can't run a banquet in the middle of—
of *chaos!"*

"Think of how Porter Reigels must feel," I said quietly. "If he didn't
swear this afternoon, he never will."

"That's different," she said. "He's in charge! He's responsible to himself; he gets paid for doing the one job. He doesn't owe his *soul* to the
Network! He doesn't get calls from Falzet's second secretary telling him
to stop everything he's doing and wait! I won't take it! I quit!"

"Okay," I said. "But why quit to me?"

"You'll do, you're a vice-president. I won't wait around here long
enough to speak to Ritafio. Do you know nobody has said anything to
me about the show *or* the banquet? I don't know if they're on or off."
She clapped her hands to the sides of her face and slid them down, pulling her lovely features into something that looked like a reflection in a
fun-house mirror. She was also leaving ink smudges from her fingers.

"Stop it," I told her. "You're making your face all blue."

She looked at her hands and made a furious, frustrated noise back in
her throat. "I'm going to run away to an island somewhere, I swear it!"
I remembered she'd said that to me before.

"Come here," I said. I got a Kleenex, wrapped it around my finger, had Llona lick it, and started scrubbing the ink off her. She took it meekly, like a kitten having its face washed.

"You'll have to put your makeup back on," I told her. "But you can stop worrying about whether the banquet is still on. And the show. If you just thought about it for a second before you decided to quit, you'd have realized that."

"You mean, 'The Show Must Go On'?"

"Not only that. Look at all this free publicity, Llona. God almighty, this will be the highest-rated show of all time! People will tune in just to see what happens next. If they call this off, they're nuts!"

She was wavering. "Well, maybe, but after all the months I've worked on this to have something happen today . . . I just can't stand thinking about it."

I smiled at her. "You're just tense. Care to bang my wall? No? Oh, that's right, there's a better way."

Llona and I were about an eighth of an inch away from working off our tensions when Lenny Green came in.

"Is it okay, Matt? Your secretary was away from her desk—*oops!* Heh, heh, heh." He started to go back out.

"No, come in, Len," Llona said, without even a blush. "I was just getting back to work." She patted her hair back into place and left.

"Nice girl," Green said when she was gone. "Sorry if I broke anything up. Sure beats a coffee break, doesn't it?"

"What's on your mind, Len?" I asked.

"Well," he began, "I don't really know if I should be telling you this . . . Ken told me not to . . ."

I raised an eyebrow. "Oh?"

"Yeah, he thinks I'm blowing it out my ass about this, but I don't. Matt, I think that ball was supposed to hit Ken. Did you see the crack in the floor? His tape there is practically 'X marks the spot.'"

"Why Ken?" I asked. "Why should someone try to crush *his* head?"

"I don't know. If it was me, maybe, but Ken I don't know." He rubbed his hair. "Look, Matt, Ken is my ticket back to the top, there's no doubt about that. He was my ticket to the top the first time around. I don't want anything to happen to him for that reason, sure, but I owe him one, a big one. I wrecked the team before, and that was just wrong. I like the guy as a friend."

I told him how hard I thought it would be to drop anything from that catwalk on a target, but it didn't impress him.

"All I know is this," he said. "One of those people running around the studio today tried to smash somebody with Melanie's bowling ball, and the person it would have been was Ken. Even if it *wasn't* Ken, it would have been Melanie or me. I'm not too crazy about that idea, either."

I shrugged. When a person has latched on to an idea that strongly, all you can do is change the subject. "You know, I thought at first the fire-and-water bit was the surprise ending of yours I've been hearing so much about."

That cracked him up. I've noticed comedians really like to laugh. "Oh no, my boy, oh no! The last surprise I had like that broke my leg!"

I'd been looking forward to finding out about that. "Look, Len, just how did you break your leg? Is it possible that was an attempt on you that failed?"

"You never heard the story of the exploding toilet bowl?" He was aghast. "And I've known you what? Two whole days? I'm slipping. No, Matt. No attack on me. Just my own stupidity.

"I was in a hotel in Palm Springs. Me and—well, me and a soft bumpy person had slipped away for a weekend of bliss . . ." It was a story masterfully told, in great detail, and with embellishments like impressions of an Italian waiter and a gay bellboy. The main part of the story took place in the suite Lenny and his companion had taken.

They embraced, he was stroking her hair, and didn't like the way it felt. The lady was trying a new hair spray. He said her hair was beautiful as Nature had made it, and to get rid of the spray immediately.

"So she did. What I *didn't* know was that she was going to get rid of it by spraying the can into the toilet bowl until it was empty.

"So my love returned to me, and after we shared the bliss I mentioned earlier, I lit cigarettes for us. Romantic, like Paul Henreid, you know? Unfortunately, before the after-love smoke was finished, I had to take a leak."

"Oh no!" I said. I could see what was coming.

"Bright boy," he said, "you catch on fast. I finished the cigarette, and nonchalantly flipped it into the toilet, whereupon—"

"Whereupon the hair spray and propellent caught fire . . ." I was laughing too hard to go on.

"Caught fire my ass! It exploded like Hiroshima! Blew my poor naked body across the room!"

"And broke your leg?"

"I'm not finished yet. Broke my rib. The leg was my own stupid fault. I made the lady friend run away, because I needed an ambulance, and I didn't want her to get in the papers. I—I didn't want to get her in trouble with her husband." His smile vanished for a split second, then returned.

"Anyway, I finally convince her to go, and there I am, lying naked on the linoleum when the ambulance guys show up. They're very efficient and businesslike and all that, but when we're going down the stairs, them carrying me on the stretcher, they ask me what happened.

"I've told you I've got a slow-motion brain, Matt. Like a dope, I *told* them. They were just like you, no compassion for a fellow human being. They laughed so hard, they dropped the stretcher, and *that's* when I broke my leg.

"That's why I split up with my agent, you see. He wanted me to sue the ambulance company. I told him he had to be crazy, if he thought a comedian would sue somebody for laughing when he told a story, no matter *what* happened. Then he wanted me to sue the hospital when my foot got infected under the cast. I still have to soak that sucker in this potassium permanganate—nasty purple stuff—twice a day.

"So don't worry, my surprise ending is something a whole lot less spectacular than that. Safe, practically boring."

"Promise?"

"Promise. Well, I'll let you get back to work now, find out if there's still a show Sunday. Keep an eye on Ken for me, okay? Just don't let him know."

I told him I'd do my best, and he thanked me profusely and left. I was still smiling. I reflected that if Lenny's lady friend had been a regular viewer of "Dr. Wonder" (directed by Ken Shelby), it never would have happened. She would have known the explosive properties of aerosol products.

Reports came in from Harris, Shirley, and the others about their various wild goose chases. I dealt with more reporters. About four o'clock, the official word came down that the Network would never let a little thing like total destruction of sets or costumes stand in its way. "Sight, Sound, & Celebration" would air Sunday night, as scheduled. I felt proud.

I decided to pass the word to Police Headquarters, figuring they'd like to know. I got Rivetz on the phone, and told him the good news. His reaction was to say, "Hurrah, hurrah," in a bored voice. He was equally impressed by the news of the follow-ups to the nut letters.

"Oh, by the way, the lab got back to us on that fire, if you're interested."

"I'm interested."

"Everything in that bin with the exception of a little glass tube—part of an eye dropper they figure—was combustible. You had wood shavings, sawdust, paper, some really volatile floor-cleaning compound, and stuff like that. Also, the remains of seventeen cigarettes, any one of which could have done the job. Hell, there were even traces of glycerin on the inside of the eye dropper. What do you people use glycerin for?"

"Tears."

"What?"

"On the soap operas. For actresses that can't cry on cue, glycerin looks just like tears, but lasts longer."

"Oh. Thought we had something there for a second." I started to say good-bye, but Rivetz had something else to tell me. "That receipt was genuine, by the way."

"Receipt?"

He was impatient with me. "Yeah, the receipt we got from Wilma Bascombe. You're the one who told us about it."

"Oh, right," I said. I had forgotten the ice Empress completely. "I guess we can forget about her, then," I said.

"I don't know, that reporter is still dead, Cobb." He hung up.

I thought about that for a few seconds. Not only was Bevic still dead, but Lenny Green had talked about his and his partner's troubles without once mentioning the fact that Bevic was found in Shelby's pool by none other than Green himself.

It wasn't so much he hadn't mentioned it—I could see where he might like to keep the subject from coming up—it was that I hadn't noticed it. Maybe Lenny Green wasn't the only one around with a slow-motion mind.

I strolled around the building for a while, looking at all the busy people. Now that the bowling ball was back, Special Projects was off the hook for a while—as always, out of sync with the rest of the Network.

There was a kind of London-blitz mentality floating around the Tower of Babble. Everyone I saw, from six-figure-per-annum executives, to ninety-five-dollar-a-week gophers, went about his job with either a cheerful or grim intensity that seemed to say, "Let the bastards do their worst!"

I roamed the Tower. I wandered from the penthouse (where I was turned away from a high-level conference between Falzet and Reigels) to the basement, where I found Colonel Coyle positively joyful. It seems that he had finally garnered some concessions from the Brass on the Security matters he'd been harping on.

When I walked in, the colonel was poring over a lock catalogue, and at the same time working out plans with the Chief of Hotel Security (aka the Head House Dick) at the Brant to protect the banquet. From what Coyle was planning, along with what I knew and guessed the NYPD would be doing, I figured there'd be more guys with guns at the banquet than at a Mafia funeral. I felt so safe I couldn't stand it.

Eventually, I killed enough time so I could go home. I took Spot for his walk, played Frisbee with him. He catches really well, but he can't throw worth a damn—no thumbs. Back at the apartment, I opened a can for Spot's supper, got him fresh water, and talked the case over with him while he ate.

I discussed my latest theory. "What if Jim Bevic told somebody something? Like if he found something new about Wilma Bascombe, for instance . . ." I took a few seconds to think of something that could possibly be new about Wilma Bascombe. She was a triple agent, loyal all the time to the left? Let's don't be foolish, Matthew.

"To hell with it," I said cheerfully. "Jim Bevic was an investigative reporter. He found something out. Let's say, he found out Melanie Marliss is really a man. How does that strike you, Spot?"

"Woof!" he said. Spot's talents as a conversationalist are as limited as his talents as a Frisbee player.

"Okay, we'll assume that's the case. Now—suppose Bevic, checking the story, tells Shelby or Green about it before Melanie kills him. No! Better yet, she's only afraid he might have told them. That would explain the attack on Shelby and Green, and nominally her. She stole her own bowling ball, and had Baker drop it when she was there to divert suspicion from herself, though knowing when the ball was coming down, she could have easily ducked out of the way."

Spot didn't even bother to say "woof." He knew how stupid that theory was. For one thing, as any movie-goer could tell you, Melanie was not a man, and if she ever had been, the doctor that had done the hypothetical job was an artist to rival Da Vinci. For another, there was the fact that she and Baker had been in New York when Bevic had been killed.

Of course, it was possible Bevic had found out about Baker's drug business. I assumed they grew some pot in Costa Rica, and Bevic had been there. But Baker had an alibi for the time the bowling ball was dropped. And in this version, Baker has every reason *not* to risk Melanie's lovely neck.

But the big thing wrong, I told myself again, was that it still gave no reason on God's battered earth for using that stupid bowling ball in the first place. If you wanted to murder somebody, why couldn't you just take him by surprise and beat him over the head with a baseball bat? After all, that was a close approximation of what had happened to Jim Bevic and Jerry de Loon.

If Bevic was connected with this at all. I caught myself making fist marks in Jane Sloan's six-thousand-dollar white leather sofa. I made myself stop. Then I asked myself, *And why were those kines taken, Cobb?* and I wanted to scream.

I decided it was time to get ready for the banquet. There was an hour and a half to go, but I still had to shave and shower, and it takes me a long time to get my bow tie right.

CHAPTER 18

"Put a little fun in your life . . ."

—KATHRYN MURRAY, "THE ARTHUR MURRAY PARTY," NBC

That banquet was a mistake; at least that's what hindsight tells me. Not that any new catastrophe took place. The consensus of the press was that the Network was bearing adversity with style.

Style isn't everything. I was there, and though it might have been my imagination, I perceived a mind-poisoning atmosphere in the ballroom that hung on the gold-lamé drapes and dripped off the ridiculous square crystal chandeliers.

Too many people there Friday night had seen what happened Friday afternoon. They kept looking at the chandeliers, I guess for falling bowling balls. They (and I, I suppose) kept looking over their shoulders, unconsciously watching for the Phantom of the Network.

Outwardly, the men were suave, and the women charming. Fashions were probably being set. One paper printed that every gown in the place was an original. Melanie Marliss wore something in fire-engine red that was half sequins and half see-through. Only she could have gotten away with it. There were slits and plunges and pants and turbans and hats and things I don't even know the words for.

Roxanne Schick, who winked at me when I came in, was all in white, very demure, very pretty. Llona was in purple velvet. It whispered when she walked, and must have weighed a ton, but somehow, it took her out of competition with the other women, and made her the hostess. The whole weight of the dress was suspended by a velvet ribbon tied behind her neck. There was no back to the dress. Llona stood very straight, as though the weight of the material were a penance.

Network executives were there, and the press, and the celebrities, and politicians, and waiters and musicians, and the grim-faced security guards. The only thing this opening of the big fiftieth birthday celebration lacked was a lexicographer to give us words for the new emotions that were loose in the room.

Lorenzo Baker, for example, never took his eyes off me, and I could never tell if it was hate or fear or respect, or what. I got the feeling he was thinking of me as someone who had the power to destroy him, and no real reason not to.

That, in turn, depressed me. I've never wanted to be dangerous. I've never wanted people to brood about how much better their lives would be if I weren't around.

Melanie Marliss was a little afraid herself. Baker was too busy guarding his flank from me to be the constant shower of approval to Melanie he usually was. Melanie didn't want to lose the upper hand, but it was easy to see she was excited by the prospect of a Lorenzo who was less of a yes-man and more of a man.

Porter Reigels was sitting at the head table, not taking part in the general pre-dinner mingling. A teetotaler as well as a non-swearer, he was knocking back ginger ales like a man drinking whiskey as though it were water, if you follow me. When I talked to him, it was almost like he was getting drunk on them.

"It's a comfort, Cobb, that's what it is, a comfort." His Texas drawl was a lot more noticeable than usual.

"What's a comfort?"

"Knowin' when it's gonna happen. My whole life comes down to Sunday. Monday, I go back to Hollywood, or back to Texas. Mebbe shoulda never left Texas." He killed the bottle of ginger ale.

"Listen, are you still carrying the gun?"

"Dern right." He patted his hip. I tried to talk him into giving it to me, but he narrowed his eyes and said anyone who wanted to leave him unprotected with a lunatic around would have to fight him for the gun—he called it "Mah ahrn."

Shelby and Green talked about the act. They talked all through dinner, all through the speeches, and would have talked all through the dancing, if there was a way they could have danced with each other. As it was, whenever one got dragged away to dance, the other would wait impatiently for him to return. From what I overheard, their main concern was how badly, if at all, the water had damaged the mechanism of the Great Bomboni's magic cabinet. They'd check it out tomorrow.

Alice Brockway was the hardest to figure of all. She sat on a chair between Shelby and Green like a queen on a throne. She was in a dress of a color somewhere between yellow and amber and she made it glow like the sun. As a boy, I'd wanted to catch up with her in age, but it looked as though she was catching down with me. She smiled at everybody. The two men talked across her. She never said a word. She was very beautiful and happy.

All these little private vibrations were being picked up subconsciously by everyone else; condensed and amplified like radio signals, and put back into the atmosphere for the process to start again. It got so there was an almost audible whine of emotional feedback behind the standard party sound track of talk and music and clinking glasses.

None of this interfered with anyone's enjoyment of the meal itself, at least not that I could tell. The chefs of the Brant did their all to give the Network full value for the prime time plugs that were coming Sunday. The food had started out as veal and carrots and ice cream, but by the time the culinary artists got through with it, it took four pages of fancy French calligraphy to describe it.

Llona had placed me at a relatively calm table, with Theodore Farnsworth and my congressman and his wife, among others.

The cameras and video tape recording stuff were set up while the lights went out for the chef to set fire to the ice cream.

The speeches followed the food.

To my surprise, Falzet gave the best speech. I'm sure he didn't write it himself, but I was still impressed. He did full justice to the long and eventful history of the Network, and he showed a confidence in the future that was very becoming to a Leader of Persons. He touched on the current problems without belaboring them. He was pompous and humorless (a trademark), but he also came across as sincere (a rarity) and even literate (a miracle).

A few heavyweight VP's came next, followed by Roxanne Schick. She lied prettily about how happy she was to be there, and how proud she was to represent the family of Mr. Hewlen at such an auspicious moment. The whole thing took forty seconds, well under her limit.

Porter Reigels drawled thank-yous to everybody for everything, then said he had to go back across the street to whip the show into shape. If I ever got applause like that for leaving a party, I'd start to get insecure.

It was all very corny, but nice. The Network *had* done a lot of good things over fifty years—it had brought the nation and the world closer together; it had made practically everyone an eyewitness to history; it had exposed corruption; and most important, it had diverted and entertained millions.

Then the orchestra took over. Roxanne deliberately didn't hear Falzet's request for the first dance. Instead, she swept off the dais and swooped down on me. "Dance with me, Cobb," she said. "You won't see me in a dress again until Graduation Day."

I told her her dignity was slipping.

"No time for dignity," she said. "I have an exam Monday, and right after this song, I'm hopping in my car and going right back to school."

So I danced with her. I made small talk, asked how school was, and all that, but inside I was thinking that this was the third time I had her in my arms, the first time she wasn't thrashing. The first time I held her, she was a fifteen-year-old mainlining junkie too long without a hit, and I held her to keep her from shaking herself apart. The second time had been just a few months ago . . .

"You're feeling guilty, aren't you, Cobb?"

It was scary that she should know me so well. "Of course not," I said.

She shook her head in time to the music. "You know you can't lie to me, Cobb. Don't try. Or feel guilty, either. There's no reason to."

"My, how times have changed. Isn't that my lecture?"

"Not any more," she said. "You're the one who's being stupid now. Look," she said, suddenly very serious, even solemn, "that night was a nightmare. Hell. We'd both been knocked silly, and we both needed someone—someone we could trust not to hurt us. That's who you are to me, Cobb." The music stopped and the spell was broken. The flip defenses were back up in case the world at large might be listening in. "So don't blow it now, Cobb, got it?"

I smiled back at her. "Yes, boss."

"That's another thing," she said, as we walked to the check room to get her coat. "I'm giving you a direct order as principal owner of this Network."

"Well, let's hear it, Rox."

"I don't know what's going on around here," she said. "After—well, after what happened this summer—I'm afraid to even think what it might be. And I'm not going to. I've got to think of something to say about George Bernard Shaw that he didn't already say about himself for that test Monday.

"But whatever it is, Cobb, I want you to promise me that if it comes down to a choice between the Network and you, you will choose *you,* even if it bankrupts me, and I have to *earn* a living like a normal person. Okay?"

"Sure." I nodded.

"Promise?"

"I promise."

"Good," she said. We got her coat, went outside, and waited for her car to be brought around. Then this elegant lady grabbed me by the ears and kissed me, hopped into a battered Volkswagen, and sped away to the waiting arms of GBS.

I went back to the party.

I'm not a good dancer. I can't seem to move my feet to any rhythm but that of a bouncing basketball. My card was pretty well filled despite that, though. I managed not to step on anybody's feet, not even my own.

Every now and then, I'd catch a glimpse of Llona, standing just out of the lights in some corner of the room, scanning for trouble the way an owl in a treetop scans for mice. She wasn't dancing or drinking or anything; she was working. In odd moments, I'd have a few words with her. In one odd moment, it was arranged that after the ball was over, I'd see her home.

Her vigil was largely wasted. Nobody got so drunk that he passed out, and no one made any passes at anyone else's spouse. At least, if passes were made, they weren't noisily resented.

At the end of the night, the band took no chances on generation gaps. They played "Good Night, Ladies," and "The Party's Over," *and* "Good Night, My Love." If people stayed after that, they deserved to turn into pumpkins.

In the cab on the way to Llona's apartment, which was down in Greenwich Village, she sat with her head back and her eyes closed. A little pulse jumped in a hollow at the base of her throat, just above the edge of the purple velvet.

"It really went well," I told her. "You did a terrific job, Llona."

"Ritafio will get all the credit," she said without opening her eyes. "You'd think he could have at least mentioned my *name*. How was the food?"

"It was terrific, didn't you taste it?"

"I'm a vegetarian," she said dolefully. There was more conversation, but you get the idea. I recognized her mood for what it was—the letdown after the completion of a big project. Llona felt drained, felt weak, wondered if it was worth it.

She showed signs of bouncing back before the ride was over. I pointed out to her she'd been spared the burden of PR for the bowling ball hunt, and that perked her up a little.

When we got to her address, she asked me if I wanted to come up for a drink. I didn't have anywhere else to go.

Llona's apartment was a sort of modified loft, one big room, with the windows near the ceiling. The windows were many and large, and let in, at artistic angles, rays of soft white light that were coming either from the moon or from mercury vapor lamps out in the street.

The room looked even bigger than it was because there wasn't much in it. A sofa, which probably converted to a bed; a chest of drawers; a bookcase; a refrigerator; a hot plate; a couple of wooden chairs; and over where I judged the best light would fall in the daytime was a sewing machine. No stereo. No TV.

Because of the size of the windows, I could take this all in even before Llona turned on the light. "Welcome," she said when she hit the switch. "It's not much, but I'm not going to be here forever. Will you get the drinks? White wine for me, in the refrigerator. Liquor is behind the couch."

I said white wine sounded fine, and headed for the refrigerator. "Where are the glasses?"

"In the cabinet under the hot plate."

I found them, good no-nonsense glasses, and poured the wine, good, no-nonsense wine. Llona was sitting on the sofa, kicking her legs the way she had yesterday afternoon at the fountain in the plaza. Her feet were bare, and she was holding a stocking in each hand.

"I see you managed to turn up a garter belt," I said.

"Mmm hmm," she said, around a sip of wine. "Found it yesterday at the lingerie shop in the Brant. I was going to try Forty-second Street if they didn't have it there."

I raised my glass. "To the rich and the kinky," I said. She laughed. My eye was drawn to the sewing machine. It bothered me, didn't seem to fit. Then I saw the scraps of purple on the work surface and the floor.

"I must congratulate you on your gown, madame," I said, "especially since it appears you made it yourself."

"Thank you," she said, smiling and dimpling. "I'm glad you like how it looks, because the damn thing is like a millstone around my neck. No more velvet—it's hard to sew, and it weighs a ton."

"Do you make all your own clothes?"

She finger-combed her dark hair. "Let me read your mind," she said. "You're thinking, 'Why does a woman who is reasonably well paid—though not well enough, of course—live in a place furnished slightly better than a nun's cloister, and make all her own clothes?' That's what you're wondering, right?"

"None of my business. You're happy here—"

"I hate it here! I grew up in a room like this, only smaller, and I watched my mother go nearly *blind* over a sewing machine, making her clothes, my clothes, and clothes for other women who could afford a seamstress. I can't wait to get out!"

I apologized, though God alone knew what for, and Llona gave a conciliatory murmur. The conversation lapsed. I was going to finish my wine and go.

Llona drank the rest of hers first and asked for more. I poured.

"I saw you with Roxanne Schick tonight, Matt," she said.

I laughed. "I wasn't hiding," I said.

"That's not what I meant. Why don't you marry her?"

"Just like that, huh?"

"I saw how she looked at you. You could have her in a second. She's rich, she's pretty, she's young—"

"Too young," I said. "Besides, Roxanne and I are much closer as friends than we ever could be as lovers. Can you understand that?"

Llona cocked her head and rolled her tongue around the inside of her mouth while she considered it. "I think I can," she said at last. "You believe in love, don't you, Matt?"

"How do you mean that? The way I believe in Santa Claus, or the way I believe in the Free Market Economy?"

"I don't know what *you* mean."

"Are you asking me if I think love exists, or if I think it's a good idea?"

She shrugged. "Both, I guess."

I got the feeling the answer was very important to her. I was learning a lot about Llona, just from sitting in this room. It proved she'd go through a lot for her dream, whatever the dream happened to be.

"Well, it definitely exists," I told her. "It hurts too much to be an illusion. I mean, you can't be stabbed with a rubber knife."

"What about the other part?"

"Is it a good idea? I don't know. I'm not the right person to ask. You should ask winners how they like a game."

"That's just it," she said. She stood up, started walking around the room. In the places where the lamp didn't reach, she'd walk in and out of the shafts of light from the windows.

"Just what?" I wanted to know.

"Winners," she said. "Losers. Love is a trap, whether it's real or not."

"That's a little severe, isn't it?"

"*I* don't think so. It trapped my mother. She worked as a waitress in a hash-house for years, when I was a little girl, putting my father through medical school. Then, as soon as he was successful, he left us, and married an administrator from the hospital. He found her more 'intellectually compatible.' *She* was a winner.

"It killed my mother—made a fool of her, don't you see? There was the alimony, but then my father and his—that woman—died in a plane crash, and there was no money at all. Mother had to sew, because she wouldn't go on Welfare, and she'd dropped out of school to work. Do you mind if I turn off the lamp? It hurts my eyes, and we don't really need it."

"Go ahead." I got the impression this was something Llona had thought a hundred times, but never said. She kept walking around the room, coming in and out of the light like a purple ghost. Every once in a while, she'd swing her round arms and rustle her dress like a little girl does.

"That's what *love* does, Matt. It makes you put yourself in a position where you can be used and thrown away after." She was standing near the sewing machine, drawing her index finger over it.

"Look, Llona," I said, "granted, your father was a hard core louse—"

"It's not only *us*," she corrected me. Now that she wasn't talking about herself, she was crisp and businesslike again. "Just look at the women we've met over the past couple of days. Why does Alice Brockway act so crazy? Because she's a mental bigamist!"

"Polyandrist," I corrected automatically. "Do you really think so?"

"Of *course.*" Llona was scornful. "Couldn't you see her beam to-night, now that they're together, the three of them? She wants them both, and now she'll be able to handle it more easily."

"*More* easily? She's been doing it all along?"

"It seems obvious. She acts much more married to Green than to her real husband."

That was something to think about. Llona's hang-up could be serving her as a lens, letting her see things like this in sharper focus.

"Now, Melanie Marliss is different altogether. She loves herself. She's loved herself right into the position of Goddess of Love, and now the only men who'll come near her are the ones that want something, like Lorenzo Baker. Other men are intimidated. And what's worse, she knows it."

I nodded grimly. On target again. "And what's worse than that," I said, "she encourages it." I could remember her flirting with me over that poster.

"That's right," Llona said. She thought we were arguing, and she thought she was winning. She picked up momentum in her speech and in her walking. "And, Matt, look at Wilma Bascombe, and what happened to her—and the man she loved wasn't even *alive.* It's a trap. No way out."

"And what if it is?"

"It's not going to catch me," she said sternly. "I'm going to depend on *me.* Nobody else. I'll pay my own way—*that's* why I live like this. I'm going to get enough money, sooner or later, to do exactly what I want. And as soon as I want to do it, that's even more important. And no one is going to take it away from me, or use me, or change my mind or slow me down."

I finished my wine. "It sounds," I said slowly, "like a very lonely life."

"It doesn't have to be!" she blurted. "People can be friends! I—I overheard what Roxanne Schick said to you. A friend is someone you can trust not to hurt you. Men and women can be friends. They can share, without *owning* each other's *lives.*"

I stood up.

"Matt," she said, "it shouldn't be a big deal if, some night, two people happen to want each other. Should it?"

I joined her in the white light. That pulse was still jumping, or was jumping again, where her throat joined her pale shoulder. I kissed it gently. "No big deal," I said.

We embraced and kissed and parted. I reached behind Llona's neck, pulled a loose end of the ribbon, and the velvet slithered to the floor with a low whisper. It revealed Llona and a garter belt and nothing else. Her body caught the light and gave it back in a way that made it seem the light was coming from her. I held her again.

Llona was soft breasts and strong legs, gentle hands and sharp teeth. All the while, my mind remembered and respected what the woman had said, but when it was over, and she smiled at me, and I saw the glitter in her chocolate eyes, I couldn't help thinking that whatever it was, it was at least something that *felt* like love.

CHAPTER 19

". . . Whose fatal death did so much to bring his life to an end."

—ORSON WELLES, "THE MARTY FELDMAN COMEDY
MACHINE," ABC

You have to make allowances when you share a bed with someone. You have to expect an occasional jostle or sound interrupting your sleep. I knew that, but I wasn't making allowances for the right things.

For one thing, Llona slept holding on to me, and I wasn't used to that. For another thing, when I finally did drop off, I didn't expect to be awakened by a loud wet crunch about six inches from my ear.

It scared me to death. My eyes jumped open, and I registered, without thinking, that the sun was up. I sat up and spun my head around wildly. Llona was looking at me like she thought I was crazy. She was eating an apple.

I wiped my brow, shook my head, and waited for my heart to slow down. "I thought somebody was coming through the wall or something," I told Llona.

"I can't help it," she protested. "I always wake up hungry after." She brushed hair out of her eyes, then held the apple out to me. "Want a bite?" I held her wrist, to steady the apple, and bit.

"What happens now?" I asked. "The landlord comes to throw us out?"

She laughed, and gestured around at her belongings. "Yes, you've yielded, and we must leave this glorious paradise. Either that, or we go to sleep for a hundred years."

"Actually," I said, "the way things have been going, that sounds pretty attractive."

"Not if it's just sleep," Llona said, and I admitted she had a point.

Then she stopped smiling. "Matt," she said, "I want to thank you for last night."

"Hey," I said, "if you didn't have to say please last night, you don't have to say thank you now."

"I'm not talking about that," she said.

"Oh." I felt like a jerk.

"I mean putting up with me when I went into my autobiography. I was tired. You were very sweet."

I was puzzled. "Because you wanted to talk and I wanted to listen?"

"Nobody wants to listen to other people's troubles. Other people's troubles are boring. Even my own troubles are boring."

"It wasn't only your troubles you talked about," I told her, touching her nose. "You had something to tell me, and you put it on the record, that's all. You sounded like you meant it."

She hadn't *acted* like she'd meant it, though.

"Still," she said, "I appreciate your listening, and the way you accepted what I said."

I saw her eyebrows go up a little, and knew that last part of it was a question. "Sure," I lied, then changed the subject. "Llona, is there anything you have to do today?"

"No," she said happily. "And thank God! I thought I'd never live to see the day!"

"Like to help me out with something?"

She looked at me quizzically for a few seconds, then laughed, and put her arms around my neck. "You," she said, "are a louse. How could I say no now? What do you have in mind?"

"Well, if I remember what I read in the paper correctly, Jim Bevic's funeral is today, up in your home town. I want to go."

"Why?"

"Crazy reasons. Stupid reasons. A hunch. His murder doesn't fit in—it's too normal. Jerry's death and that business in the studio yesterday seem like a plot by Mel Brooks in collaboration with Rube Goldberg."

"Okay, but why go to the funeral? I mean, there's no real reason to say Jim's death is connected at all, from what I've heard."

"It's *got* to be connected." I was surprised to learn how totally convinced I was of that. My brain was making decisions without consulting me again. "It's like that fire in the studio starting the same time as the dropping of the bowling ball." She asked me what I meant, and I explained that the coincidence of an accidental fire upsetting the mischief of the ball-dropper was a lot easier to swallow than the coincidence of *two* mischief makers striking at precisely the same moment and upsetting each other.

"The same way I find it easier to believe Bevic was in that pool and Shelby and/or Green almost got crushed for one comprehensive reason than I do two completely separate murderers are picking on Shelby and Green. Do you follow me?"

"I think so. But what can Jim's funeral tell you?"

"I have no idea. Maybe if I can talk to his friends and family, I could get to know him better. That's where you can help; you can tell me about Jim from your own knowledge, and you can point me to the right people to talk to. What do you think?"

She thought it over for a few seconds. "I think," she said at last, "that this is the stupidest conversation I've ever had with my arms around a naked man."

And, of course, once she had pointed that out, it was obvious that she was right.

When (eventually) we got up, there was still plenty of time to make it to the services. We took a cab to my place, where I put on my black suit to go with Llona's dark gray dress, then to the Network to check out a car. We brought Spot with us. He loves to ride in cars, and besides, if I'd gone without him, he probably would have called a lawyer and sued Llona for alienation of affection.

It was a nice drive. The morning sun shone over our shoulders and made designs with the shadow of the George Washington Bridge on the rippled surface of the Hudson. Later, we enjoyed the leaves across northern New Jersey and northeastern Pennsylvania.

Actually, in the world of TV, we never left New York. Television can't be bothered with political boundaries. The country is broken up into something over two hundred Areas of Dominant Influence, or roughly how far the signal from a given market penetrates into the countryside before it overlaps another signal. The New York ADI is the largest one in the country, taking in twelve counties in New Jersey, fifteen in New York, and one each in Connecticut and Pennsylvania.

Pike County is the one in Pennsylvania, and that's where Llona's home town was. It was a one-industry town, a mill town, and after the bright October leaves of the surrounding country, it seemed to be even grimmer and grayer than it was. The overwhelming impression was of squat limestone buildings garnished with soot in front of the four smoking chimneys that towered over the mill on the edge of town.

"Charming, isn't it?" Llona said. "This is a good place to be *from,* if you know what I mean. That's the grade school I went to."

She pointed to a building that looked no different from any of the factories.

The church was at the end of the town's main street. It was gray limestone, too; but inside were blue skies, and fluffy white clouds, and pink cherubs; serene Virgin Marys and radiant Christs. The statues of gold or marble had been covered with purple cloth, for mourning, but even so, it seemed as if all the color and beauty of the town had been gathered up and stored in the church, maybe for safekeeping.

Llona and I were a little late, so we slipped quietly into the last pew. Spot was in the car. During the service, which was in English, I was astonished to find my old altar-boy Latin complete and intact in my brain.

The priest was young, no older than Bevic had been, probably. He said all the right things: Jim Bevic had exposed corruption, and brought honor to his parents, and was a good Catholic and all that.

By the size of the crowd, and by their reactions, it was easy to tell that these people felt a real loss. The town had been proud of Jim Bevic, the Local Boy Who Made Good.

The priest gave the coffin a few last sprinkles of holy water, and gave the congregation a few last whiffs of incense, and the service was over, except for the procession out front to the hearse. The cross, the walnut and bronze coffin, the priest, then two old people, crying copiously, obviously the bereaved parents.

Walking behind the parents was a bigger, younger version of the old man. Llona whispered to me that that was Alex Bevic, Jim's older brother, the one we should talk to.

We didn't get to talk to him until after more of the same at the cemetery. Llona, Spot, and I got an unexpected honor when the funeral director waved the big, black Network car into the cortege right behind the flower truck.

Whenever I got the chance, I'd exchange a few words about Bevic with a fellow mourner. The only thing I learned was that I was kind of sorry I never got to meet the fellow. The impression I got was that he was a good person, but not too good to be true. Everyone thought enough of Jim to tell the truth without censoring himself for speaking ill of the dead.

Llona steered me to people to talk to, like the editor he had worked for at the local paper, an old girlfriend of Bevic's, and the retired principal of the high school they'd attended.

I was still trying to find a tactful way to approach Alex Bevic when he solved the problem by approaching us.

"Llona?" he said, and smiled. Llona had told me that Alex Bevic kept the mill in business practically singlehanded. He was their globe-hopping salesman. He had the right tools for the job. He had a warm voice, and the same honest features his father had brought over from Eastern Europe. "It was nice of you to come."

Llona said, "Hello, Alex. Sorry that this has to be the reason I'm seeing you again. Where's Julie?"

"In Chicago," Bevic said. "With her new husband."

Llona said, "Oh," and flushed.

There's nothing like a bit of foot-in-mouth to get a conversation rolling along. First, Llona apologized for bringing the whole thing up, then Alex apologized for being so blunt. Then I said my name and stuck out my hand for Alex to shake, whereupon Llona apologized for not introducing me, and Alex apologized for not introducing himself.

"I guess I must still be in shock, a little," he said. "I only just got back to the States from Upper Volta two days ago. That's when I first heard about Jim."

"What were you doing in Upper Volta?" A stupid question, but it was out of my mouth before I realized it.

"Selling them insulators for a power plant," he said. "I haven't even been back to my own place yet—Mom and Pop are pretty broken up, and I've been staying with them."

I liked him, and saw there was no need to try to finesse information from him. I told him about the Network, and why I was there.

He had his face tight in a grimace when I finished. "That's pretty hard to believe," he said.

"I know."

"Well, sure, I'll help you all I can, of course. The bastard killed my brother, right?"

I held up a hand. "That's only what I think," I cautioned him. "I've been known to make a mistake." The understatement of the decade.

"I know. That part's all right, I just don't think I know anything that will help. The last time I spoke to Jim, he was thinking about going down to Costa Rica."

"He went," I said. "In fact, he went straight from there to L.A. You don't happen to know," I said, not hopefully, *"why* he went down there, do you?"

Sometimes, I get lucky.

"Sure I do. I was the one who gave him the idea as a matter of fact."

I wanted to grab him by the lapels and yell at him to tell me, but I exercised restraint. I swallowed and said, "Why, Alex? What idea did you give him?"

Llona was as worked up as I was; I could hear her heavy breathing.

Alex said, "For years, Jim wanted to do a book about that guy that ripped all the stars off with the uranium scandal—"

"Ollie McHarg," I said.

"That's right, McHarg. And I happened to find out, when I was down there a few months ago, that that's where McHarg is."

No jumping to conclusions, Cobb! Facts first. "How did you find out?" I asked.

"No big deal, really. I got friendly with someone in the government, you know, and one night we went out for a few, and he got to complaining how his country was getting to be a dumping ground for fugitives from American justice. I said he was exaggerating; the only one I could think of was Vesco."

But challenged, Alex went on to tell us, the government official told of a few others who were taking advantage of the fact that these two friendly American neighbors, Costa Rica and the United States, happened not to have an extradition treaty. McHarg, though, took no chances. He maintained a strict incognito, and backed that up with liberal portions of bribe money.

Llona shook her head. "I can't believe that the U. S. Government didn't even know he was *there*," she said.

"Llona, they knew he was there," I told her. "But since they couldn't touch him anyway, why reveal it and embarrass themselves?" She shook her head again. I turned to Alex. "Didn't you tell this to the police? This is important."

"What police? I haven't even *seen* any police."

That seemed unbelievable until I thought it over for a second. The police have a lot of work to do, so they have to work to a routine or they'd never be able to handle it all. One of the first steps in that routine is Talking to the Relatives, and Alex had been out of the country while they were doing it. They would have gotten to him eventually—one of the later steps in the routine is Go Back to Start of Routine.

"Okay," I said, "you will. If you don't mind, I'm going to tell a policeman friend of mine about this as soon as I get back to New York."

Alex glanced at his watch, then over his shoulder to where his parents were still being consoled by the young priest.

"They—uh—wouldn't have had to wait too long to find out, in any case," Alex said. He took another glance. I asked him what he meant. "The only reason my government friend found out about all this is because *his* brother is a journalist, too. It seems that McHarg was too big a ham and a con man to enjoy being out of the public eye, so he approached my friend's brother about collaborating on a book about the swindle. That's why I told Jim . . . he'd . . . better hurry . . ." Alex caught his face as it was about to break, and turned tears into a kind of half-baked sneeze. I wanted to tell him to go ahead and cry, but he probably wouldn't have taken it too well.

"Listen," he said, "I've got to get back to my folks—"

"I've got to know *more*," I snapped. "Did he call you? Write?"

"I don't know, I was out of the country! You'd better ease up, Cobb, this is no place for this kind of thing."

I apologized, he accepted. "But look, you haven't been home long, have you? Haven't gotten your mail?"

"No, I haven't. He may have written. Now that I think of it, he may have told my folks something. Look, I'm sorry about before, I said I'd co-operate—"

An old sales trick, apologizing for something the other person did.

"—so here's what we can do. I've got to stick with my folks, you understand that, right? So one of you come with me, and maybe we can talk to them a few minutes, if we don't upset them, and the other one can go to my apartment, and check the mail."

"I'll go to your place," Llona said. "Do you still live on Rumson?" Alex said he did.

"All right," I said. "Anything from Jim, anything from the West Coast, anything from Latin America, okay, Llona?"

"Sure, Matt," she said.

"And I'll go with you, Alex. And thanks."

"Forget it, it's for Jim." He took out a key case, removed a key. "This will let you in, Llona," he said, giving it to her. "And, while you're there, bring me a couple of clean shirts, will you? Top left-hand drawer in the bedroom. This is going to be a long weekend."

We followed the limousine in the Network car to the house of Alex's parents, then Llona dropped me off and left for Alex's.

I learned a lot talking with the old folks. Not about the case—Jim's death was just Fate catching up to them, the way they saw it—but about the people themselves.

Alex had to translate, because little, withered Mrs. Bevic had no English, and gnarled, twisted Mr. Bevic had just enough to get him through a day at the mill, and he was retired from all that.

They had no idea why their son was killed. To them, the idea that a person could be killed over something he wrote in a book was not tenable in America. They couldn't read their son's book, but he had been honored and respected for it, even though it said something bad about the government. That was what they had come to America for, they said.

I thanked them, and went out to the porch to wait for Llona.

Llona was gone longer than I expected, but eventually she returned to report no progress. She seemed very upset over it. For the first time since I met her she seemed hesitant and indecisive. I grinned at her, and gave her a playful punch on the chin, to cheer her up. "I never said it was going to be easy," I told her.

She gave me a weary grin in return. "Well, you were right."

We knocked on the door to deliver the shirts, then got in the car and headed home.

CHAPTER 20

"Meanwhile, back at the ranch . . ."

—COMMERCIAL TRANSITION, "HOPALONG CASSIDY,"
SYNDICATED

Llona had gasped when she first saw where I lived. "How can you afford such a magnificent *place?*" she'd breathed. I told her it wasn't what I had, it was who I knew who had it.

Now I told her to make herself at home, and called Lieutenant Martin.

"I'm probably a fool for asking this," he said as he picked up the phone, "but what can I do for you, Matty?"

After I told him what had happened that morning, he said, "I knew it. I knew it. Sometimes I think you were put on earth to make trouble for me."

"Come on, Mr. M., this is an important piece of the puzzle."

"Maybe," he said.

"At the very *least,* it explains Jim Bevic's trip to California. If he was starting a book on McHarg, it's only natural he'd go talk to some of the victims of the swindle, right? Shelby and Green were among the more prominent victims, remember?" Then I got another idea.

"But it could even be more than that. Something about that old scandal could be the cause of Bevic's murder or the attempt on Shelby and Green. Or both. Maybe Bevic found out something from our pal Ollie, and the killer is afraid he told one of the boys." The lieutenant grunted. "Well," I said, "it's something to look into, isn't it?"

"You think you've practically solved the case for me, don't you, Matty?"

"I wouldn't go that far," I began.

"You damn well better *not* go that far. According to you, all I've got to do is find a bowling ball dropping maniac who was in Los Angeles last week and New York this week, and who was tied in with this Utopia Uranium racket over ten years ago. Did I leave anything out? Oh yeah. He's got to have a hot line to Costa Rica. Either that or a crystal ball, because according to you, he knows what happened at a conversation *we* can't even say for sure took place!"

He knew I was aware of all that, he was just complaining about the work it would take to check it out. But we both knew it would have to be checked out, so I didn't bother to defend myself. Instead, I said, "Don't yell at me, I'm only an idea man."

"Swell," the lieutenant said. "Any ideas on how I should go about this?"

"Well, for one thing, you should talk to everyone who was fleeced in the UU scandal . . ."

"Right," he said.

". . . And you should try to have a few words with Ollie McHarg down in Costa Rica, and find out if Bevic talked to him, and what was said if he did."

"I was afraid you were going to say that," Mr. M. sighed.

"What's wrong with it?"

"Nothing, Matty, nothing; it's the thing to do all right. Just that I've been through this kind of thing once already, trying to find out why Bevic was down there in the first place. Jesus, I don't know whether a foreign country or our own State Department is the bigger pain in the ass to work with. This could take months."

"Maybe not," I said thoughtfully.

"Matty, you scare me with that tone of voice, you know that? What are you up to?"

"Look, the Network doesn't have treaties with anybody. We can't violate protocol, right?"

"Matty, I'm warning you!"

I knew he was, that's why I hung up.

"I've got to go down to the Tower for a little while," I told Llona. "You can stay here, if you want. Spot seems to think you're okay, so that's good enough for me."

She was playing with him, laughing like a little girl. "Thank you," she said. Her face was still, but her eyes laughed.

Then the laughter left her eyes and she said, "Matt, what's the point of all this, really?"

"God, Llona," I said, "if I waited for an answer to that, I'd never do anything."

"You can't bring Jim back. Or Jerry, either." She started scratching Spot's throat. While she did that, she must have had a long, silent conversation with herself, because at last she said, "Well, *I'm* alive." She looked up at me, as though she wanted confirmation of the fact.

She was alive, all right. Complex and beautiful and exciting and alive. I noted, for the record, that it had taken me until just now to link

Llona and Monica in the same thought; the thought was that maybe Llona was the girl who would help me get over Monica.

"I've got to go," I said, as I kissed her good-bye.

I was in the office, thinking things over at my desk, listening to the first sleet of autumn clicking against the brown-glass windows of the Tower. I couldn't decide which of Cobb's Commandos was going to get a tropical vacation at the Network's expense. After twenty minutes of agonizing, it finally occurred to my alleged brain to look at the files on these people. That made it easy. Cobb, Santiago, Arnstein, and Ragusa spoke Spanish. I wasn't about to leave New York with a killer running around my building. Jazz held the department together. Ragusa was still too inexperienced. I called Shirley at her apartment in Brooklyn, and asked her if she'd mind coming in.

You'd have thought I'd asked her if she'd mind if I gave her a mink coat. I never saw such a glutton for punishment.

I told Jazz to get busy making plane reservations, and contact the Network's Latin American news bureau to arrange for Shirley's accommodations. Then I put on the office TV and watched Bugs Bunny cartoons for a while.

Shirley showed up with a gleam in her eye and a packed bag in her hand. She was either a clairvoyant, or a sneak. Under intense grilling, she admitted she'd called back and found out from Jazz what was up. "I figured it would save time," she said.

"Right. I admire initiative. Remind me to put you in for a raise." Then, I told her why she was going to Costa Rica, and what I wanted to know. I didn't exactly tell her that if she was caught or killed, Jazz would disavow any knowledge of her actions, but I impressed on her the need to be careful.

After that, I returned like a tongue to an aching tooth, to Studio J. I wanted to see how the great Save "Sight, Sound, & Celebration" Scheme was coming along. If sheer activity counted for anything, it was coming along fine. The whole scene reminded me of one of those building-the-pyramids movies Hollywood used to turn out.

There were almost two hundred workers busily repairing the set. The carpenters were all but finished, and the electricians were busy wiring a new system of monitors, mikes, and lights; the set decorators were champing at the bit to lay the carpet and repaper the flats. It was going to be close.

Actually, just getting that army *there* was a remarkable achievement for Reigels, or Falzet, or whoever had done it. The workers had been flown in from Boston, D.C., Chicago, and L.A., all cities where the Network owns and operates TV stations. I found out later that the other three networks had offered to loan us men, but the International

Radio and Television Employees, the union here at the Network, nixed the idea.

You see, the only thing that irks the union more than management is another union. Millie Heywood tells a story about the time a visitor to the Network went to the men's room on the sixth floor, and had a heart attack while combing his hair. Somebody (probably another visitor) discovered him lying there, rushed out to call an ambulance, and, while he was at it, brought back a wooden chair for the victim to sit on while he waited.

After the patient was taken away, that stupid chair sat in that sixth-floor men's room for *eight months,* while the chair-moving union fought it out with the bathroom-cleaning union over who had the right to remove the chair. I repeat: this is a *true story*. The final compromise was this: a member of the chair-movers was allowed to take the chair out of the bathroom by belting it with a sledge hammer, while a member of the bathroom-cleaners followed him and picked up the splinters.

Naturally, then, no red-blooded son of IRATE would stand by and let infidels from some other union travel two blocks and invade their turf when fellow IRATE's could be brought in from hundreds of miles away.

In all fairness, I am constrained to admit that it didn't make much difference. "Sight, Sound, & Celebration" was now a guaranteed money-losing venture, through water-damage to equipment alone. It occurred to me, though, that the Network could have brought in all sorts of scab labor if it wanted to. With so many new faces in the room, who'd know the difference? There was too much work to do for someone to ask to see a union card every time you asked him to pass the hammer.

I was very surprised to see Ken Shelby and Lenny Green in Studio J, oiling the hinges of the Great Bomboni's magic cabinet, until I remembered that in another momentous jurisdictional decision, magicians had won the right to handle their own equipment. Green was a card-carrying magician; they probably both were.

"Hi, Matt," Green said. He moved away from the cabinet, and stepped on a little square rubber pedal on the floor that was connected to the cabinet by a tube. "Nothing," he said. He shook his head. "It's not gonna work."

Shelby showed him a hand, bidding his partner to be patient. "Let's oil the catch and try it again."

"Okay, but there's nothing wrong with the catch."

"What's the trouble?" I asked.

"Nothing really," Shelby told me, working the oilcan. "We're lucky —the main machinery for the thumps and rattles inside the cabinet is in good shape, but the compressed air gimmick that has the door swing magically open doesn't work."

"It's not the gimmick," Green said, "it's the wood. It swells up when it gets wet, you know? The door is too tight a fit in the doorway now to swing when the catch is released."

"Sure." I grinned. "Capillary action. I'm surprised at you, Ken. You directed 'Dr. Wonder.' You should know all about capillary action. It's the force that lifts tons of nutrients to the topmost leaves of a giant sequoia. It's the power that makes a wet sponge expand to twice its dry size—"

"Enough!" Shelby said, in mock torment. "What did I do to deserve the past coming back to haunt me like this?"

I snorted.

"What's that for?" Shelby wanted to know.

"You don't know the half of it yet."

"He knows enough." Lenny Green draped an arm around Shelby's shoulders. "Shelby and Green is as far back as I want my partner to go. Nobody needs him directing kids' shows."

Shelby put the oilcan down and said, "Right you are, Len. To hell with this door. We'll tell Melanie about it and ad lib around it during the show."

Green said, "Now you're talking." He turned to me. "Matt, is there a decent, stand-up saloon around here? If there is, I'm buying."

I shook my head. "I've drunk more since you guys got into town than I usually drink in a month." That was true, but it wasn't all their fault. The banquet had a lot to do with it.

"Hell," Green smiled, "you're not trying, Matt. Women love a drinking man."

"Cobb does all right," Shelby deadpanned. I felt a sick, guilty sensation. I hoped he was joking.

I was all set to go along with them but Colonel Coyle buttonholed me on the way out of the studio. *He* certainly didn't need a drink. He was already drunk, with power.

"I've got something to show you, Cobb," he said. "Come with me."

Shelby said they'd wait for me in his dressing room, and I went with Coyle. The colonel had taken over the J. V. Hewlen Kinescope Library as his seventh-floor command post. That way if anyone came to visit him, he could point to the empty spaces on the film rack and say that was what happened when you didn't listen to Security experts.

He'd picked Jerry de Loon's old work table as his desk. There was a scrapbook lying open on it. *My God,* I thought, *he's going to swap army stories with me.*

What he wanted to show me was a series of articles clipped from newspapers and magazines about the library project and about "Sight, Sound, & Celebration." He was angry over them.

"Look at this," he said, pointing a bony finger at a subhead that said, "Eighteen Months in Preparation." "Everything the enemy could want to know, right here! The layout, the schedule of events, even the list of all the personnel who would be here!"

The colonel's voice took on an ominous tone. "This is the doing of that Ritafio fellow."

It's lonely being sane.

"Of *course* it's the doing of that Ritafio fellow, Colonel. That's what he's supposed to do—get people to write articles about the Network."

"Well, it's dangerous," he blustered. "It's like the Pentagon publishing its plans."

"The Pentagon," I said, "doesn't have to worry about the Nielsens."

"I still say this publicity is dangerous. And I must say, I'm disappointed in you, Cobb. You face many of the same problems I do. I thought together we might formulate a plan to do something about the situation."

"Oh, is *that* all?" I said. It was useless to argue with him. "Why didn't you say so? There's only one thing you can do."

"What's that?"

"Write a memo."

He was not amused. "I know *that*," he began, but he was interrupted by a commotion in the corridor. I stuck my head out the door in time to see what looked like a gang rape of Melanie Marliss by five of the colonel's security guards. It took all five of them to hold her down—she was thrashing like a Great White Shark, and cursing like the fisherman who had just pulled him in. She had done some damage with her nails, too. At least three of them had parallel red scratches on their cheeks, like wet war paint.

I screwed my eyes shut, hoping it would go away. It occurred to me my life had gotten to be like a boxing match between a quadruple amputee and Muhammad Ali. A lot of bad things were happening, and there wasn't a whole lot I could do about it.

"What's going on, Cobb?" Coyle asked from his table.

I didn't want to talk to him. I opened my eyes. Things had changed, slightly. Melanie had cut down the odds with a well-placed knee. One of the guards was out of the fight, and might just possibly be singing a new part in the Network Christmas Choir.

I supposed I had to go rescue her, if only to save the rest of the baritone section. I dashed down the hall and yelled, *"What the hell is going on here?"*

One of the guards looked up to tell me, and Melanie bit a chunk out of his forearm. "Goddammit, get off her!" I yelled.

They sprang up as though Melanie were a bomb. "I'll have you all strung up by your balls!" she hissed.

"Go away," I told the guards.

"But—"

"Go. Or I'll turn her loose on you again."

They fled.

It was a ticklish situation. The bowling ball was going to be nothing compared to this. I couldn't stand it. I was debating whether to climb all the way to the roof to jump, or just smash a window and go from my office.

But Melanie was not angry. She was exhilarated. Mountain air couldn't have made her as refreshed. Her feminine radiance was at peak operation.

The question was unnecessary, but it was the only thing I had in my brain at the moment, so I said it. "Are you all right?"

"Ha!" Melanie said triumphantly. "And they used to say 'Harriet Gunner' wasn't true to life; that a woman couldn't fight that well. Ha!"

Take *that*, critics-of-the-past. At least the Network wouldn't have to worry about any future lawsuits. Melanie told me what was going on. She wanted to see Porter Reigels, but she didn't have a pass (the colonel was now issuing passes) so the guards stopped her.

"That wasn't so bad," she explained, "but when they said I was too old to be Melanie Marliss, I got mad, and decided to go through them. I would have, too, if you hadn't rescued me."

I shook my head. "Harriet Gunner was all right. *You're* the one who's unbelievable."

She kissed my forehead. "You're sweet. Do you know where Porter is? Lorenzo's around here somewhere . . ."

I told Melanie I couldn't help her, then left her and went to find her former employers. On the way, I reflected on the futility of trying to figure out anything. I mean, when you see one woman struggling with five men, it's only natural to assume *they* attacked *her,* right? I shook my head. The moral of the story was *"things are not always what they seem,"* and that didn't seem like much of a moral.

I made an interesting discovery when I told Ken Shelby and Lenny Green about Jim Bevic's possible talk with Ollie McHarg: Shelby and Green were a tragedy team as well as a comedy team. When they heard the news, Shelby's look of tight anxiety was a perfect complement to Green's expression of loose-jawed shock.

The choreography was there, too. Green slumped in the dressing room chair looking glum, and the taller Shelby paced rapidly, looking angry, rumpling his silver hair.

The lines were delivered with split-second timing, and read to elicit the maximum of their potential for gloom.

"McHarg," Lenny whispered, "that bastard. That *bastard*. He's behind this."

I told him we didn't know that, but he didn't hear me.

His partner didn't either. "He haunts me like a ghost! I—I can't stand it!"

"Me neither," the short man said.

Shelby glared at him. "*You* brought him into my life in the first place." Green took it without a word; he just lowered his head and looked at his hands.

"Look," I said, "I didn't come here to break you two up again, okay? I just want to know if it helps you remember anything. What could Bevic have found out from, or about, McHarg that he'd want to talk with one of you about?"

"Who says he wanted to talk to us?" Green protested.

"Who else connected with one, McHarg, and, two, Bevic, has had people trying to kill them recently?"

Shelby smacked the wall with an open palm and laughed so hard I worried for a moment he might be going into hysterics. "He's got a point, Len," he said, when he'd calmed down a little.

I nodded. "The only thing anyone could have been doing with that damned bowling ball was trying to kill you. Someone must think that Bevic made you dangerous in some way before he died. It's the only thing that comes close to making sense."

"What do you mean? Like he told us something? But he *didn't!*"

"*We* know that," Shelby told his partner. "And it could be even the killer knows it. But he's got as bad a one-track mind as you had when you wanted to get the act back together. You badgered me for twelve years, and it wasn't your life that was at stake. It seems as though the killer is determined to follow through on us, just to be complete."

"It's not only that," I said. Shelby and Green looked grim. "He doesn't want to take a chance that either or both of you is lying about having spoken to Bevic. If he kills you, he doesn't have to worry."

"Hey," Lenny Green said, suddenly excited. "Wait a minute. This means Alice is in trouble, too, doesn't it?" He grabbed his partner's wrist. "Ken, we'd better get over there, right away!" He reached for his jacket.

"Relax," I told him. "Coyle's got the building as secure as possible, and the New York Police Department is covering the hotel."

Shelby raised an eyebrow. "How long has this been going on?"

"Since the bowling ball fell," I said.

"Why weren't we told about it?"

"I don't know for certain, of course. My guess is that Lieutenant Martin doesn't want to tip off our boy."

"In other words," Shelby said with very precise enunciation, "we are bait."

I shrugged. "If you ask me, the only way you could be safer is to hole up in the Brant and forget about the show tomorrow night. Of course, if you do that, the killer will never be caught . . ."

Lenny Green's worried look seemed genuine. "Maybe we should, Ken. Stay in the hotel, I mean."

"No," Shelby said. I could have read the small print in a Network contract by the bright flashes coming from his eyes. "We're not going to let him do this to us, are we? In the old days, not even the censor could do that. No. The Reluctant Magician goes on tomorrow night, exactly as planned, and that's final!"

Green mumbled, "Whatever you say, partner," but he looked happy and relieved. I noticed that it hadn't taken Ken Shelby long to go back to making the decisions for the act.

I told them to think some more about Bevic and let me know if they remembered anything. I was beginning to remind myself of a broken record.

Just as I was about to leave, Ken Shelby reached into his pocket. "Wait a minute, Matt," he said, "I want you to be a witness to this." He turned to Lenny Green. "Your watch, partner. I lifted it when you grabbed my wrist a few minutes ago. You used to say I'd never be able to do it."

The little redhead laughed. "Son-of-a-bitch!" he said. "You finally got me!" Shelby smiled in return. "You taught me everything I know," he said.

I smiled, too. It was nice to think they were friends again. I said good-bye, and left the Tower. It wasn't very late, but the sun was down, and it promised to be a cold night.

I turned my collar up, stuck my hands in my pockets, and went home to Llona.

CHAPTER 21

*"Have you no decency left? At long last . . .
have you no decency left?"*

—JOSEPH N. WELCH, THE ARMY-MCCARTHY HEARINGS,
ABC AND THE DU MONT NETWORK

I'd already seen that Llona, so straight ahead and aggressive in the daytime, could be a different woman at night. By the time the sun rose on the morning of the Big Show, I was beginning to think she might be a different woman *every* night.

The Llona of Saturday night was an emotional basket case. She mumbled and jerked about spasmodically in her sleep. She'd wake up and look at me and cry, or not look at me and remain stonily silent. Then she'd turn suddenly and reach for me, demanding, insistent, even angry.

What she didn't want to do was talk. I finally asked her what was wrong, and that closed her down completely.

It couldn't stop me from figuring, though.

My best guess was that I had made as great an impact on Llona as she had on me. I decided that her determination to have no strings tied to her was colliding with an emotional attachment in the making. Now Llona was paying the price. You always pay for your hang-ups—I knew that from sad experience. It was nice to think I'd be the one to make Llona see the contradiction between her avowed philosophy and her True Self.

I had gotten up and was in the living room watching a retrospective on fifty years of the Network's sports programming when the phone rang. As usual, it rang at the worst conceivable moment—right in the middle of the film of Babe Ruth's famous home run in the 1932 World Series. I've studied that clip over and over, straining to see something, some little tipoff that would settle for me whether the Babe actually called his shot before the pitch came in, or if he was just stretching his back. I watched just as closely this time, but as the ball disappeared over the wall at Wrigley Field for maybe the thousandth time, the matter was still to be decided.

I picked up the phone.

"Matt?" Harris Brophy said.

"Yeah, hang on a minute, Harris." They had the homer in slow motion now, and I still couldn't decide. "To hell with it," I said. "What do you want, Harris?"

"You'd better come down to the shop, Matt," he said.

"I plan to, later."

"Uh, uh. You'd better tear yourself away from Llona and come down here now." There was a note of amusement in his voice. Harris found other people's sex lives amusing; it's not one of his more endearing traits.

"Why?" I asked. "Heard from Shirley?" That was a pleasant thought, though I knew it was too early for her to have accomplished anything in Costa Rica.

"No such luck," Harris told me. "We have heard from Wilma Bascombe. I've been briefed about her."

"What does she want?"

"She wants to talk to you, and she's very determined about it. She says you'll know why."

"She's wrong," I said. What now?

"Well, she says she'll wait for you. See you soon." I said sure.

Llona's peaceful sleep hadn't lasted long. She was sweated, and looked feverish. She'd taken hold of two tight fistfuls of bedding. It occurred to me that once in my life I should get involved with a normal, happy, well-adjusted girl, if only for the novelty of it.

I touched Llona gently on the shoulder and she jumped as though I'd poked her with an electric cattle prod.

"He-ey," I said softly, "it's all right. It's all right."

"Matt," she said.

"Who'd you expect, Spot?" I pushed some damp hair from her forehead. "Look, I have to go to the Tower for something."

"Why?" she said. She sounded suspicious.

"Duty," I said. "Why else? It wasn't *my* idea, believe me. Are you coming to work today?"

"Not to work," she said. "To watch. After the PR work I've done for this thing, they couldn't keep me away with vicious dogs."

"Speaking of vicious dogs, walk Spot, okay? He likes you."

"I like him, too." She turned on her side. "Matt, I—I want to talk to you later."

"Sure," I said. I bent to kiss her good-bye.

"Matt," she said. "Isn't this a rotten way to live? I mean, wouldn't it be nice if you could be in complete control of your own life?"

"Sure," I conceded. "It would be nice if Spot could tap dance and whistle 'Dixie,' too, but I don't spend a lot of time pining over it."

Llona's mouth turned up in a little smile, which I kissed. I told her I'd see her later.

Somebody called my name as I crossed the lobby of NetHQ. I turned around to see Murph, Wilma Bascombe's answer to Knucklehead Smiff. I stopped to talk to him. Maybe he knew what was eating his boss.

"I wanted to apologize about the other day," he said.

"Forget it," I said. "I was kind of worked up. How's Sammy's knee?"

Murph made a conciliatory gesture. "Don't worry about it. We were all worked up, too. Chauncey died the night before, you know."

"Chauncey?"

"Our dog. Sammy was pretty broken up about it." It didn't look as if Murph's eyes would be dry too long either.

"Oh," I said. "Where is Sammy, by the way?"

"He's home cooking." He did a funny little toss of his head, like a bashful kid, then said, "Well, I'm glad we got this straightened out, Mr. Cobb."

"Call me Matt," I said. What the hell, right? "Do you happen to know why Miss Bascombe is here today?"

"No, I don't, but it must be something drastic. She didn't say a word on the whole trip in from the estate. She's never done anything like this before."

"Hmm," I said. "Well, thanks anyway." What I was doing was about as intelligent as trying to guess who's calling when the phone rings. There's only one way to find out.

Harris met me in the outer office. He gave me some significant nods and knowing looks.

"Talk, for Christ's sake," I told him. "You look like your head's coming loose."

"It should," he said. "I've just been talking with Madame La Guillotine in there."

"What's she been saying?"

"Nothing much. It's chiefly her attitude and expression." Harris made a silent whistle. It took a lot to make an impression on Harris.

"All she *said* was that she wondered how much money you make," he went on.

"What did you tell her?"

"I said compared to the other vice-presidents around here, you hardly get anything, but that compared to the rest of us in the department, with the amount of work you do and the amount we do, you get about ten times what you deserve."

"Thanks, Harris," I said warmly.

"Any time," he replied. "Want me to go in and talk to her with you?"

"Not at all. I've got to catch up with the rest of you hard-working folks, don't I?"

Wilma Bascombe received me. It was my office, but there was the unmistakable feeling that I was waiting on her. She was smiling at me, not benevolently. I felt the need to have something solid between us, so I said nothing until I was safely behind my desk. I wished I could intimidate people through force of personality the way she could. She was wearing a simple suit in a deep purple that added to the effect of royalty.

"It's an honor to have you here, Miss Bascombe," I told her.

She huffed. "I didn't expect *hypocrisy* from you, Mr. Cobb. Please stop it. This is unpleasant enough." She opened her purse and took out a small mirror to look at her face. Apparently, what she saw satisfied her; all she did was touch the corner of a dark blue eye with her little finger, and pat once at her white hair. It was obvious she was giving me time to let her words sink in, but it wasn't doing much good, because I had no idea what she was talking about.

"I'm afraid you'll have to explain," I told her.

Wilma Bascombe was getting impatient with me. "I've come," she said, "to find out what your terms are."

"Terms?"

The former star started tapping her foot. "Don't pretend you had nothing to do with the telephone call I received early this morning, Mr. Cobb. I have studied and practiced deception in too many places for too many years to be taken in by something as clumsy as this."

I stood up, walked to the door, opened it. Wilma Bascombe looked quizzically over her shoulder at me.

"Good-bye, Miss Bascombe. I hope you have a pleasant trip back to the Island." I gave her my nicest smile. "Give my regards to Sammy."

"You'll regret this, Mr. Cobb," she said coldly. She rose. "I decided after you came to my house that I wasn't going to take it any more!"

"Mad as hell, huh?"

"What?"

"Never mind." I wasn't going to take any more, either. I wasn't mad, just tired. Overwhelmed by confusion after confusion. "If it matters," I went on, "you were about to tell me why I was going to regret this." As if I don't already, I thought.

"Ah, yes," she said. "Yes, I do want to tell you. I was ready to listen to your demands, if they were reasonable, but you choose to ignore that. Now let me tell you what *I* choose to do."

She was radiant, triumphant. At long last, the Empress was going to thwart all those who had used her, frustrated her, made a fool of her. I was the *de facto* representative of the Young Man from Washington and all the rest.

It was getting on my nerves. It was irritating to be considered contemptible by someone who had so thoroughly screwed up her own life. And through her own incredible gullibility, too. Furthermore, she was totally full of it in her accusations. I was going to tell her so.

But I couldn't. The look in her eyes, her bearing, the way she held every little part of that aging body was magnificent. Wilma Bascombe *was* a queen; a Hollywood queen, but born to that purple suit of hers nonetheless. She was—well, *special,* that's all. The words for what she had can't be found. Just say I could no more try to show Wilma Bascombe how silly and stupid she was than I would try to hamstring the last wild mustang.

Very humbly, I asked her what she planned to do.

She allowed herself a tiny bit of controlled, scornful mirth. "As soon as I leave here, I shall go directly to Lieutenant Martin of the police; then, I shall confess to these murders."

I slammed the door. The Empress jumped, put a hand to her breast in a feeble gesture of self-defense.

"You're going to *what?*"

"Confess," she said. "What else *can* I do?" And still, in her voice, there was an inexplicable tone of *that-ought-to-settle-your-hash-boy.* I decided this was a stupid dream; that I'd wake up next to Llona in a few minutes.

So, I decided if it was a dream, I might as well make the best of it. "Let me get this straight," I said. "Are you telling me you killed Jim Bevic? Jerry de Loon? Tried to get Shelby and Green?"

Wilma raised an eyebrow and looked at me with a detached, almost academic interest. "You really should have been an actor, Mr. Cobb. You're quite a convincing liar."

"Thank you," I said. "You should hear my Hamlet. But I would appreciate it if you would humor me and answer the question."

She shrugged. "All right, though I don't know why. You know as well as I that the only reason I plan to tell the police I killed those people is so that when *you* tell them I did, they won't believe you. Are you happy now, Mr. Cobb?"

CHAPTER 22

". . . Decide whether the celebrity is giving me a correct answer, or making one up. That's how they get the Squares."

—PETER MARSHALL, "HOLLYWOOD SQUARES," NBC

What it did was give me a headache.

I did not dare to ask this woman another question. I had a feeling that if I did, she'd give me an answer that would make all the convolutions in my brain smooth out.

"Come back in, Miss Bascombe," I told her. "Sit down. You won't have to go anywhere."

She came back and sat. I went to my desk and picked up the phone.

She asked what I was doing, but I wasn't about to go answering any questions, either. She found out soon enough when she heard me ask for Lieutenant Martin's office.

Wilma made a noise that was too dignified to be called a snarl. Then she took some loud breaths, and finally stood up and strode to the door.

I was going to tell her to stop, but that was the second the lieutenant picked up the phone. "What do you want, Matty?"

"More crank phone calls, Lieutenant," I said. Wilma stopped and looked back at me. I gave her my *I-told-you-so* look. "One crank call, anyway," I told the phone. "Wilma Bascombe this time, someone pretending to be me."

"Yeah? What does she say you told her?"

"She didn't say, but it must have been pretty awful. She expects me to tell you something that would get her arrested for murder."

Wilma was dazed; literally tottering in her tracks. I dashed around my desk to help her back to her chair. When I picked up the phone again, the lieutenant was saying, "Matty? Matty? What happened?"

"Nothing, forget it. Only I think we ought to get this straightened out, don't you? Should I bring Miss Bascombe downtown, or do you want to come up here?"

Lieutenant Martin sighed. "I'll come to you. Don't move. But, Matty, I want you to do one thing for me."

"What's that?"

"Next time you hear a little kid say he wants to grow up to be a cop, smack him in the mouth."

I told him I would and said good-bye. Now, it became impossible to get Wilma to *wait* to talk. She told me how humiliated she was, how I must forgive her, and the whole humble groveling number.

She was *still* gullible—my phone call to Headquarters could have been a blind. I didn't point it out to her—I wanted to hear about the mysterious threat, and the equally mysterious confession.

She told me about the confession first. "Why, because nobody *believes* me, don't you understand? If *I* tell the police I did something, all they'll do is look for evidence that I didn't. If I deny it, all they'll look for is evidence that I *did!*"

It made sense, sort of, especially if you grant the premise that people would always believe the opposite of what Wilma Bascombe said. It seemed a little drastic to me, though, especially considering what she told me about the threat.

Like Lorenzo Baker's secret admirer, Wilma's caller had spoken in whispers, making it impossible to tell if a man or a woman had been speaking. And like Lorenzo's friend, Wilma's caller hadn't paused for chitchat. Wilma couldn't remember the voice's exact words, but the gist of the whole thing was that Wilma had better get in touch with Matt Cobb, before Cobb and Shorty Stack turned up some "witnesses" who had seen her lurking around the grounds of the Shelby residence in Los Angeles the day Jim Bevic was killed.

"I was very frightened, Mr. Cobb," Wilma said gravely. "Everyone in show business knows the kind of things Shorty Stack can do. The kind of things he *has* done. When he was with Mammoth Studios back in the forties . . ."

"The caller didn't say anything else?" I wasn't especially eager to know about Shorty's sordid past; at least not right then. But I did note the fact that this man was *feared*. I'd have to keep an eye on him. It was likely he was so secure in his job because he had something to hold over the Network. I didn't want to ever be in a position where he had something heavy to wave over my head.

"No," Wilma Bascombe said, "that was all." She went on to explain, over my protest that it wasn't necessary, why she had assumed I, or an agent of mine, had made the call. "My number is unlisted, and I knew you had the facilities to find out what it was."

"It's not so hard to get someone's unlisted number," I said, but she ignored me.

". . . And besides, I know about this man Stack. I know that you're his superior. How could I assume you were any different than he is?"

That hurt. I was preparing a defense of my character when the lieutenant arrived, along with Detective Rivetz. Wilma went through the whole story again for their benefit. Rivetz took notes. When it was over, none of us was happy, with the exception of Wilma.

"It's nice to fear something terrible and not have it come true," she said.

Lieutenant Martin scratched his head. "I wish there was something we could do about this, but there really isn't."

"And that," Rivetz put in, "is a damn shame." He took a piece of paper from his breast pocket with one hand, while with the other, he performed the unprecedented action of taking off his hat.

"This is the receipt you got from Bevic," he said, handing Wilma the paper. "Cobb gave it to us to test. It checks out completely genuine." Wilma took it from him and thanked him. She raised a hand in a gesture of benediction, looked benignly at the three of us, and said she hadn't been so happy since 1950, when the man she loved had gone off to Korea.

"I think you really should tell your own story, Miss Bascombe," I said. "There's no disgrace in speaking out for yourself. Maybe others could learn from your life. And once it's all out in the open, you wouldn't have to be your own prisoner any more."

For the third time she rose to go. "Perhaps you're right, Mr. Cobb." She smiled, a warm smile this time. "Good-bye."

I promised to set up a meeting with a sympathetic editor at Austin, Stoddard & Trapp. She thanked me and the lieutenant and Rivetz again, and left.

The door closed behind her. I turned to congratulate Rivetz for trying niceness for a change, but he was laughing.

"She's up to something," he said joyfully. "How much you want to bet?"

"Shut up, Rivetz," the lieutenant said.

"Just talking," Rivetz said mildly. So much for *that* change of heart.

"Are you going to be back for the show?" I asked the lieutenant.

"Damn right. Anybody wants to try something tonight, they're going to have to do it right under my nose." Rivetz grunted his agreement, and they left.

I turned on the office TV to the Giants game on another network, and watched the game with one eye while I got a head start on Monday's work—okaying the work schedule for November, reading and approving Jazz's rendition of the monthly report to the Board, things like that. The Giants hung on teeth and toenails for a thrilling 9–6 win, so I left the post-game show on while I tried to call my apartment.

That there was no answer was a mild surprise, but I wasn't worried—I figured Llona was out walking Spot or something.

I did some more work, then tried again. Still no answer. After about two hours of this, I did start to get worried. I almost forgot, in fact, to switch on "Sight, Sound, & Celebration" at six o'clock.

I toyed with the idea of watching the show from someplace more immediate than in front of a TV screen, but I wasn't eager to hobnob with the various big shots who would be taking up those theater seats in the control room. Six hours was a long time to stand up in back of a set, which is what I'd have had to do if I went into the studio itself, so I decided to skip it.

Besides, I wasn't about to be inaccessible in an on-the-air studio at a time like this. With my luck, that would be the precise time Shirley called from Costa Rica with information that would make the world make sense. Until and unless I heard something from her tonight, Mr. M. and Colonel Coyle could have the responsibility for Studio J all to themselves. I wished them joy of it.

In the meantime, I leaned back to enjoy the show.

And it was one hell of a show. The first ten minutes were devoted exclusively to an introduction of talent. Name after name went by, each bigger than the last. Then the Anchorman came out. He always looked like everyone's rich uncle—tonight he looked like your rich uncle as a guest at your wedding—tuxedoed and as proud as if he were singlehandedly responsible for the success of not only the Network, but all of American television.

The show came back from a commercial to a monumental production number that used practically all of that huge, multileveled set. It was a salute to the Network's music, with the dancers wearing costumes from past Network hits, and dancing to the theme music that through sheer weekly repetition, is a part of every TV watcher's mental luggage forever. There was great camerawork, special video effects, and unbelievable color. It looked like Reigels had a winning show here. TV had come a long way from the blue-gray talking shadows that had flickered on a postage-stamp screen and captured little Matt Cobb's imagination so many years ago.

It occurred to me that little Matt Cobb had come a long way with it. I was on the inside, now, like a kind of electronic Alice. But TV was still magic to me. In spite of everything.

The Anchorman started to work his way around the hall. His first interview was with Hans Lafgar, age 100, who was the last survivor from the cast of *Die Walküre* that had started this whole craziness off.

That's when Llona came in. "Hi, Matt," she said. "What are you doing up here?" There was a note of something forced in her cheerfulness; she looked pretty well done in. Apparently, it had been even a rougher night than I had thought.

"Hello, stranger," I told her. "Where have *you* been all afternoon?"

"Oh, walking around the park with Spot. Then I went downtown to my apartment to change, and I lost track of time. How's the show?"

"Believe it or not, it's as good as you and Ritafio promised it was going to be."

"Impossible," she said. She sank into a chair. "This business can get to you," she said. I agreed. She looked at me quizzically. "Why aren't you downstairs?"

I told her about waiting for Shirley's call. Llona said, "Oh," kicked off her shoes, did that cute scissors trick with her legs, and sat back to watch the show. For a little while. Then she got up and started walking around the office with her arms folded across her breast. She went to the window and looked out at Manhattan, which is something to see, even on a Sunday night.

I didn't want to make a big thing of being worried about her—I waited until a commercial came on before I asked her what was on her mind.

She turned from the window and said, "I'm thinking about us, Matt."

So now it was official. There was an "us." "And?" I said.

"I don't know. I'm afraid."

"No need to be," I told her.

"Oh yes, there is. I'm not going to let you take me from myself, that's for sure."

"What is that supposed to mean?"

She leaned on her fists over my desk. Her face was stern, and her voice was tight. "It means I have plans and—and dreams that I'm *not* going to give up. Not even for you. *Especially* not for you."

I took her hands from the desk, held them in mine. "What have I asked you for, Llona?" No answer. "Well?"

"If you had . . ."

"I know, if I had it never would have gone this far, right?" The commercial was over, and the Anchorman was shouting from the screen about something. I turned the volume down. I went to Llona, took her by the shoulders, and pressed her into a chair.

"Look," I said, "I never told you 'I like you, *but* . . .' did I? I wouldn't ask you to give up a dream any more than I would ask you to cut off an ear. If you want to run for President of the United States, or run away to that island you're always talking about, go ahead. I'll be proud of you for it."

She bit her lip and looked at me. "You really mean that?"

"Want it in writing?"

"I think maybe I can take your word for it," she said. I bent and kissed her.

After that was finished, Llona said, "Matt, I think I ought—"

The phone rang, and I held up a hand for Llona to pause. "Matt Cobb," I told the phone. It was Harris from the outer office. Shirley was on the line.

"Put her through, Harris," I said. "This could be it," I told Llona. "Cross your fingers."

There was a click in the receiver, then live, from Costa Rica, it was Shirley Arnstein.

"Faster than usual, Ace," I told her. "What did you find out?"

Shirley sounded glum. "You'll have to tell me that, Matt. It looks like a fizzle to me."

"Where are you?" I asked. "Did you talk to McHarg yet?"

Shirley's answer was lost in a blare of fast, angry Spanish. Somebody said something about somebody's mother, then there was a crash.

"What was *that?*" I demanded.

"Oh, nothing. I'm calling from the police station—only phone in the village. They just arrested somebody for selling the chief a sterile rooster. Ignore it."

There was a noise like an elephant falling on a kettle drum. I ignored it. "Okay, what happened?"

"Well, he has a villa just north of here. I just mentioned around town that I heard he was interested in doing a book, and a jeep came by to pick me up in less than two hours. Matt, he looks like a *corpse*. Remember how jolly and confident he used to look on all the talk shows, before he took off with the money? Now, he's two inches from death. He keeps going to sleep while you talk to him."

There was a sound of glass breaking in the background. Either rooster fraud was a serious offense, or the suspect had objections about being booked.

"Okay," I told Shirley. "He's sick. Cheaters never prosper. What did he *say*, for Christ's sake?"

"He says he didn't tell Jim Bevic anything, once he found out that Bevic was planning his *own* book, and wasn't especially interested in working with McHarg. Called him a crook. It's important to McHarg that this caper stay notorious—'On top of history,' is how he puts it."

"Well, sure," I said. "He's hardly in a position to enjoy the money, is he?"

"I guess not. The amount he got is important to him, though. He— *mira, idiota!*"

"Are you all right?" I asked anxiously.

"Somebody spilled rum on me. Where was I? Oh, right, the money. He says he could have gotten more if he took more time to set it up, and made fewer promises to the investors. He says he scared off the smart ones.

"He told me, though, it was a real thrill for him to have met all those celebrities, and taken their money away from them." Shirley went on to list a few.

I interrupted her. "And, of course, your friends and mine, Ken Shelby and Lenny Green."

There was an enormous, roaring crash, then silence. I was afraid the phone had gone dead, but it was just the end of the fight. I wondered who won.

Shirley cleared her throat. "That's just it, Matt," she said.

"That's just what?"

"McHarg swears up and down that he never got a *nickel* from Shelby and Green, or anyone connected with them."

CHAPTER 23

"Do you think there's too much violence on television?"

—DAWS BUTLER, "BEANY AND CECIL," ABC

I must still have been able to speak, because I distinctly remember hearing Shirley answer questions. It seems to me, though, that I stood there screaming and stamping my feet on the floor. That was what I felt like doing.

The next thing I actually remember saying was, "Okay, Shirley. Good job, as usual. Come home as soon as you can."

"Right, Matt," she said. "Sorry." There was a click as she hung up the phone, but my line stayed open.

Harris Brophy's voice said, "Matt?"

"Harris? Were you listening to the whole conversation?"

"Sure," he said placidly.

I blew up at him. "Look, Brophy, any time you want this job, just say so—"

Harris laughed. "No way, José."

"—but until then, I'll tell you anything I want you to know. This line stays private. Is that clear? And another thing . . ."

The door opened, and Harris walked into the room. "I figured it was silly to get yelled at over the phone when I was only ten feet away," he explained. "I'm sorry, Matt, but it's at least partly your fault, you know."

"Yeah?"

"You run this outfit like the Three Musketeers. It's easy to forget who the boss is."

I shook my head at him. "What do you want me to do? Brand my initials in your hide?" From her chair, Llona laughed. Harris grinned, along with her.

I joined them. "Okay, Harris," I said. "What's on your mind?"

"Shirley's message. Do you think we ought to fill the police in on the ramifications?" He didn't spell out the ramifications—that was a compliment. My name has the honor to appear on the short list of people Harris Brophy doesn't consider stupid.

Llona wanted to know what Shirley had said.

I told her.

To judge from Llona's face, she was more upset to hear it than I had been. "What—what does that *mean?*" she asked. She seemed almost afraid of the answer.

I shrugged. "If he's lying, all it means is that he's managed to keep up with the news from the States in spite of isolation and creeping senility."

"Shirley *did* mention a stack of recent copies of the *Times* around Ollie's place," Harris pointed out. I had forgotten that—it had come during the mental spasm after Shirley sprang her surprise.

"That's probably it, then," I said. "Old Ollie wants to be remembered as everyone's favorite old scoundrel. He'd rather not be associated with nasty people like killers and murder victims.

"But if he's telling the truth . . ." I paused to think, chewing the inside of my cheek. "If he's telling the truth, that *certainly* explains Jim Bevic's trip to California. That's a statement that begs to be checked out."

"If he's telling the truth," Harris said, "the attempt on Shelby and Green makes no sense at all. I mean, McHarg's not getting the money makes it look like some funny business pulled by the two of them, right? So why try to kill them?"

I told him I couldn't believe he was asking *me*. All I could do was add this latest item to the theft of the bowling ball, and the kines; the crazy threats against Baker and Bascombe; and all other of the opium-dream details of this fiasco.

I sighed. "I suppose Lieutenant Martin ought to be told about this right away. Come down to the studio with me, Harris—he's probably not going to be easy to find."

Harris said, "I was just about to suggest it."

"Are you going to be waiting here, Llona?"

She'd been looking out the window again. "What?"

"I said, are you going to wait here?"

"Oh yes. Of course." She went back to the window.

I shook my head. If falling in love with someone was going to do *that* to her, maybe I should get out of her life right away.

I didn't have time to think about it at the moment. I touched her shoulder, then left with Harris.

We had to produce everything short of baptismal certificates to satisfy the guard at the door of Studio J we were who we said we were. Then we had to wait until a commercial came on before we could go in.

Once inside the big gray doors, we split up. I went around the back of the set to the right, where the door to the control room stairs was, and where the carpenter's bin had been. Harris went to the left.

About every twenty feet, I was stopped by guys in gray suits—either plainclothes cops or some of Colonel Coyle's men in mufti, I didn't bother to find out which.

There must have been a hundred people behind that set. There were IRATE's and security men of one kind or another, to say nothing of crew and celebrities. It made for slow progress, especially since any noise above a whisper would be a disaster—there were live mikes all over the set, for ambience noise. The audio men do that to keep the studio from sounding like a cave.

The Roger Nelson Dancers finished what they were doing, and another commercial came on.

I found Lieutenant Martin watching a perfume commercial on one of the monitors. He wasn't alone—one of the show's three floor directors (they're responsible for controlling traffic backstage) was watching it, too. The monitor was set up near the gap in the set where the Great Bomboni, his assistant, and his manager were to enter. A quick look at my watch showed me it was almost a quarter to twelve. "Sight, Sound, & Celebration" was practically over. I couldn't think of many people in this building who would be sorry to see it go.

By the time I joined Mr. M. at the monitor, the actress was through nuzzling the perfume, and Studio J was on the air again. It was as if someone had switched on the ozone-scented air in there as well as the cameras. There is something about live TV that really gets the adrenalin flowing.

The monitor showed the Anchorman in conversation with a country-singer-turned-actor. I pulled the lieutenant aside to whisper to him what Shirley had told me, and what I thought it might mean.

He listened, then responded. Considering that we had to talk in whispers, I was impressed at the vehemence Mr. M. was able to get in his swear words.

He cut off in mid-stream when Ken Shelby, Lenny Green, and Melanie Marliss emerged from the dressing room area, costumed and ready for the Reluctant Magician sketch.

"I want to talk to you later," the lieutenant hissed. Lenny Green gave him a nervous, crooked grin and said, "Jesus Christ, Lieutenant, we're on in fifteen seconds."

That, combined with a murderous look from the floor director, was enough to make Martin subside. We backed away from the monitor to give everyone plenty of room for entrances and exits.

Every performer has some last-minute nervous ritual. Lenny Green took deep breaths. Ken Shelby cracked his knuckles. Melanie made minute, unnecessary adjustments to her costume, reassuring herself that her seams were straight, and enough bosom was tucked in.

From offstage, the godlike voice of the announcer. "And now, the Great Bomboni!"

I gave in to a lifelong urge. "Break a leg," I whispered. Melanie showed me that multimillion dollar smile. I love those old show-biz movies.

"The Great Bomboni!" the announcer repeated, and Ken Shelby strode out onto the set. Lenny Green watched the monitor for his cue, and gave the line about the undersized outhouse. It said something about their comedy that the same professional audience that had laughed at the dress rehearsal was laughing just as hard now.

In fact, they were even better than they had been Friday afternoon. Shelby, as the Great Bomboni's manager, was even more determined to have the show go on. Green's substitute Bomboni was even more dubious about what he'd let himself in for. It was the magic of live TV.

The magic of the act—the stage magic—went along pretty much according to the script—Green had his pants ripped off, but kept going, running into Melanie on her way in with the turban. He decided to stay.

I noticed they left Green's cape striptease in. He was incredible. I hoped the folks at home were enjoying this as much as I was. Lieutenant Martin was being staunch and professional, scanning the area for potential evil-doers, but even he couldn't resist taking an occasional peek at the monitor. He was almost smiling.

They departed from what they'd done at Friday's rehearsal when they got to the part where the door of the magic cabinet was supposed to swing open. The way they handled the sticking door was to have Green, anxious to be locked in with Melanie, start trying to get inside while Shelby is still explaining the trick. There was a minute of hilarious pantomime while Green struggled with the stuck door. I remember thinking that a hundred-year-bath with a fire sprinkler couldn't have gotten the door that stuck.

Shelby finishes talking about trunks and cabinets and bolts and chains, and turns to see what's going on. There's a great reaction take. Finally, all three people onstage, pulling together (with Green pulling mostly on Marliss) manage to get it open.

More ad libs. Lenny says, "I'm disappearing from here, right?"

"That's right," Shelby replies.

Green looks up at him. "Good, because if I had to come through that stupid door, I'd *never* get out."

Melanie cracks up. Green says to her, "Okay, sweetheart, let's get in the box!"

He steps inside. Shelby slams the door behind him and shoots the bolt.

At that moment, my head tilted involuntarily upward, and I began looking for trouble on the catwalks. Talking to people later, I found out I wasn't the only one in Studio J who did that—practically everyone I spoke to did. Friday had made a big impression on us.

Sunday was about to make a bigger one.

I saw human forms up on the catwalks, but they all wore police uniforms and were armed to the teeth. Lieutenant Martin had that end sewn up very nicely.

Meanwhile, the show was going on, and I listened to it, even when my eyes were seeking reassurance above the lights. As soon as Ken Shelby had slammed the door of the magic cabinet, and even before he shot the bolt, Lenny had started with his yelling.

"Hey! Wha—what the hell!"

I wondered idly when they had found a chance to make a new tape —that wasn't what he'd said on Friday. Maybe Lenny was just ad libbing a little before he started the tape and the machinery going and left through the trap door. Or maybe it was something leading up to that surprise ending he'd been talking about.

Whatever it was, I decided, it must have been Lenny's work because the monitor showed a strange look on Ken Shelby's handsome face. He was too much a pro to let it throw him, though. The cabinet started thumping as it should have, and Shelby delivered his line over his partner's screaming.

"The Great Bomboni is calling on his friends in the spirit world to help him out of this worldly prison!"

The next line on tape was supposed to be "I'll call on my friends in the Police Department . . ." but that's not what we heard. With the greatest example of stark panic ever heard on television, Green's voice yelled, "No, I'm not! Ken, let me out of here. *Please!*"

Shades of Henny Youngman. The audience went wild.

The laughter went on, grew stronger. Green's voice said, "Let-me-*out! I can't breathe!"* It seemed as if the cabinet was going to shake itself apart. Great rasping coughs came from inside, followed by one long, rude, retching sound.

"Green's surprise ending," I said to Lieutenant Martin. The laughter was so strong it was no longer necessary to worry about talking aloud. "He made a new tape, and juiced up the shaking mechanism."

Mr. M. nodded. "Right, and now he lets his partner deal with it."

Ken Shelby seemed perfectly ready to deal with it. Drawing himself to his full height, and looking his most professorial and dignified, he raised his hand in a pacifying gesture and intoned, "Please! Ladies and gentlemen!"

The crowd quieted a little, though there was still laughter at what was now coming from the magic cabinet—it sounded like sobbing.

"Don't encourage him," Shelby said.

It brought down the house. The audio man testified later that his meters for every microphone hit maximum and that if it weren't for the built-in limiters they have these days, that single laugh might have blown out the Network's whole audio system.

The uproar continued. Ken took Melanie by the hand and began to stash her in the trunk. He paused when the laughter died.

There was no noise coming from the magic cabinet. Nothing.

The sixty-odd million people watching "Sight, Sound, & Celebration" joined those in the studio in the largest mass double take in history.

The monitor showed a close-up of Ken Shelby's face. We saw him gasp, then run right out of the picture. Up in the control room, Porter Reigels had him picked up in a long shot from the boom camera, camera twelve. It zoomed in to Shelby's hands struggling frantically with the bolt. Melanie came to help him. She looked as if she were about to cry.

When they finally yanked the bolt open, Shelby had to fight the water-swollen door. Meanwhile, camera twelve was zooming in closer and closer.

The door cracked loudly as it flew open, and camera twelve had a beautiful shot of the action as Lenny Green, in opera cape and green-and-yellow striped underpants, tumbled from the cabinet, and lay still on the floor of the set.

CHAPTER 24

"Rampart, we have a victim; male; approximately fifty years of age; approximately one hundred forty pounds. He appears to have inhaled some poisonous fumes . . ."

—RANDOLPH MANTOOTH, "EMERGENCY," NBC

I made my Network television debut one eighth of a second after Lieutenant Martin made his. As soon as Lenny Green thudded to the carpet, Mr. M. dashed in from the wings. I followed him. Everyone in the audience was still screaming and/or gasping.

The cameras left us almost instantaneously. Reigels switched to the Anchorman, who ad libbed some reassuring words, and The Show Went On.

Meanwhile, back at the catastrophe, I stiff-armed a hysterical Melanie Marliss out of the way, and pulled Ken Shelby away from his partner. I knelt beside Lenny, and undid the ribbon around his neck that held his cape. The bottom of the cape was wet with something that smelled bad.

Shelby kept saying, "I don't believe it! I don't believe it! Is he all right, Matt? Did he have another heart attack?" Melanie Marliss was babbling. By some kind of professional reflex, they had their hysterics in whispers—after all, there were live mikes in the studio.

I had something I wanted to ask the lieutenant—he was poking around inside the cabinet—but I was afraid to open my mouth for fear a scream would come out of it.

Harris Brophy and Detective Rivetz had worked their way around the back of the set and joined us. I said one word to Harris: "Ambulance." I was glad to find I didn't scream. The lieutenant said one word to Rivetz: "Headquarters." Our assistants left us again.

Lenny Green had no pulse; at least none that I could find. His skin was very cold. I found that the fumes of whatever liquid had soaked into his cape and socks and shoes were now making it hard for me to breathe.

"Mr. M.," I croaked, "what *is* this stuff?"

He was holding his handkerchief over his mouth and nose. He reached into the cabinet (which was practically awash with the liquid), and brought out a now-burst plastic bag. The tie band was still tight around its neck. The lieutenant took a little sniff at it. "Smells like chloroform," he said.

"We better get him some air, then," I said.

"Right, let's go. Where to?"

"Elevator. We have to take him out to the plaza."

"Can't we get him to a window?"

In the background, the orchestra started playing something soft, while the Anchorman did a talk-over.

"No windows are built to open in this building."

"Goddammit!" he spat. "I'm afraid for him, Matty."

"Then let's get going." I picked Lenny up with a fireman's carry. The orchestra got louder. I carried Lenny off the set as the Anchorman signed off.

". . . and we hope the Network can continue to be a part of your life, bringing you all of life's trials and triumphs, its fun, thrills, and excitement, for *another* fifty years of . . . Sight, Sound, & Celebration! Good night!"

Because of the gauntlet of curious stares we had to run, it seemed to take a lot longer to get to the ground floor than it actually did. By the time we made it, I practically sprinted for the bronze and glass door. I needed air myself.

It was cold outside, a clear, brittle, October cold, and the air felt good all the way down into my lungs. Anyone passing by on Sixth Avenue would have thought we were three drunks dragging ourselves from the Network Lounge.

I felt drunk. I was dizzy, I had a headache, and I was very glad dinner had been a long time ago.

I put Lenny Green down on the flagstones near the fountain. He looked bad. I started artificial respiration.

Lieutenant Martin was sitting on the low black-marble wall that ran around the perimeter of the plaza. He kept smacking his hand against the stone. "Dammit, Matty, right under my *nose!* Right under my goddam nose! That poor bastard is in there choking for air, and I stood around *laughing* at him. Ha, ha, very funny. I don't believe it! I ought to turn in my shield."

He went on and on, and as I listened to him, suddenly, I became Lenny Green, trapped inside the cabinet, breathing fumes instead of air, trying to get somebody, *one* person, out of the tens of millions who hear me, to help me. And getting laughs instead.

". . . *Laughing*, for Christ's sake," the lieutenant went on.

"Can it, Mr. M., all right?" I snapped. Lieutenant Martin stood up, wobbled, steadied himself, and looked up and down the street.

"And where the hell is that goddam ambulance?" he asked.

We never did see that ambulance. Since police cars cruise, the cops started arriving before an ambulance could. I don't know what Rivetz told them, but it brought them out in force. After a few seconds, the lieutenant got tired of waiting, and commandeered a blue-and-white to take us to the emergency room. Mr. M. and I both felt like we could stand a visit.

Lenny Green was dead by the time we got there. For all intents, he had been dead before the door of that cabinet was opened. The folks at the hospital (the same one Jerry de Loon had died in) ran a few tests, and found that he had died of carbon tetrachloride poisoning.

"Smelled like chloroform to me," the lieutenant said.

That was when we learned that carbon tetrachloride (CCl_4) *does* smell like chloroform. So now I knew what chloroform smelled like.

I had already known carbon tetrachloride was potent stuff. It dissolves grease, fat, certain rubbers, waxes, and resins, so they sell it for cleaning fluid. You may have some around the house. If you do, take a look at the label. You'll find you're not even supposed to open the *bottle* unless you've opened all the windows in your house first. And you're supposed to wear rubber gloves when you touch the stuff.

The lieutenant and I had both breathed and touched carbon tetrachloride, and since the hospital couldn't do anything further for Lenny, they concentrated on us. The first thing they did was condemn our clothes and wash us in soap and warm water. Then they gave us some mild stimulant and had us breathe oxygen from a tank.

The intern in charge of us was a studious-looking young man who had doubtless gotten an A in toxicology. He kept lecturing the lieutenant and me about carbon tetrachloride.

". . . the symptoms include," he went on, "dizziness, headache, nausea, subnormal temperature, feeble pulse, coma, fever, uremia, and . . . uh"—he adjusted his glasses—"uh, death."

I looked at him. He looked disturbingly like a teen-age kid dressed up like a doctor. "Death?" I said.

"Uh, yes."

"Death," I said. "Death. Listen, that strikes me as one hell of a symptom, Doctor." I wondered what they did—take a look at a corpse and say, "Aha, he's dead! Must be carbon tet!" He ignored me and went on with his lecture.

That was only fair. I was ignoring him, too. Instead, I was admiring the damnable cleverness of our killer. The Phantom of the Network. The bowling ball may have failed, but it got everyone involved expecting his next attempt to be an equally emphatic physical assault. As he knew we would.

So the bastard set a beautiful, yet simple booby trap instead. Sometime between the dress rehearsal and the show, he had gotten into Studio J (no great accomplishment), jammed the trap door under the magic cabinet somehow, and left that plastic bag of poison on the floor. With all the unfamiliar workmen running around, it would be easy—if anyone asked, he was working on the set, so what?

Now that I thought of it, I could narrow the time even more. Shelby and Green had checked out that cabinet Saturday afternoon, so the dirty work had to have been done after that.

Young Dr. Mouth had said at one point, ". . . when inhaled, a concentration of one thousand parts carbon tetrachloride vapor per million is sufficient to cause acute poisoning."

A little mental arithmetic was enough to show me that if only half the carbon tetrachloride that had been in the two-quart bag the lieutenant had found had turned to vapor, that magic cabinet could have held a *thousand quarts* of God's clean air, and Lenny still wouldn't have had a chance.

And of course, there was nothing like a thousand quarts of air in that cabinet. There was, though, a pool of *liquid* CCl_4, to slosh around, and splash on his shoes and socks, and on his bare legs as they hung from those ludicrous underpants, and poison him all the quicker.

I blew up. "Goddam it to *hell!*" I said. "I can't *stand* it!"

Everyone looked at me as though I were crazy, which I probably was. Lieutenant Martin said, "Now, Matty . . ."

"Now, Matty, nothing," I said. "Will you just look at this guy? Dropping bowling balls! Poisoning guys in their underwear on national TV!" I jumped off my table and started to pace, with my hospital gown flapping behind me.

"What next?" I wanted to know. "Is he going to fry somebody with a twenty-thousand-volt joy buzzer? Hit someone in the face with a vitriol custard pie? Jesus, I thought murder was supposed to be *serious!*"

"It's serious to me, Matty," the lieutenant said calmly. "No matter how they do it."

I shook a doctor off my shoulder. "You know what I mean," I told Mr. M. "But I promise you this: whoever this bastard is, he's going to be as sorry I got into this case as I am."

With that, I was all set to storm out of the hospital, but Mr. M. persuaded me to wait until we could send for some clothes.

"You guys look like hell," Rivetz informed us when we got back to Studio J. "Carbon tet is no fun, huh?"

I looked at him. My head still hurt. If I'd had any brains, I would have been lying down somewhere with a cool compress on my forehead instead of trading quips with Rivetz.

"No, Rivetz," I quipped, "it's not exactly a hint of mint."

Lieutenant Martin grumbled his agreement.

The seventh floor of NetHQ was about the same way it had been Friday afternoon, except that the set was in better shape, and the people lined up in the corridor were a lot quieter, a lot grimmer. A lot dryer, too. Cops and lab boys were there in even greater numbers. And making progress, apparently—they'd tabbed the poison for Rivetz.

"That's not all they've done," Rivetz said. "Lieutenant, you better see what they found in that cape you took off the body."

"Let me guess," he said bitterly. "Another bowling ball."

"That's not funny, Mr. M.," I told him. I rubbed my head. "Where's Brophy?" I asked.

Rivetz smiled. "Oh, I told him he could go with Gumple and watch our star players; the partner, the wife, the sex bomb, the taco chef—you know who I mean." He turned to the lieutenant. "That Brophy's a good man Cobb's got there. Doesn't go for bullshit. Could use him on the force." It hadn't occurred to me before, but Rivetz and Brophy *were* kindred spirits. They both thought the human race was totally worthless, and they both thought that was amusing.

"I hope you'll be very happy together," I said.

"What was in the cape, Rivetz?" the lieutenant asked.

"Follow me," the little detective said.

He led us to the back of the set, where, laid out on a sheet, were men's wallets. Forty-two of them, neatly arranged seven-by-six. A police expert was checking them one by one for fingerprints while happily humming "Old Dan Tucker" to himself.

Rivetz spoke to the fingerprint man. "Any change to the pattern?"

The expert managed to work in his "Nope," without missing a beat.

Rivetz explained. "Every one of these things has Green's fingerprints on them. His and somebody else's—different somebody else each time. Got to be the real owners, Lieutenant."

Mr. M. was scratching his head the same way he use to when he helped his son and me fix up a bicycle or something. "That much makes sense," he said. "I think it makes sense. I *hope* it makes sense. But will you tell me why in the name of Booker T. Washington this— this *comedian* would want to *steal forty-two wallets just before somebody bumps him off?*"

It took me exactly one point three seconds to figure it out. "Oh, for Christ's sake," I said in disgust.

"What is it, Matty?" the lieutenant asked.

I must have mumbled, because Mr. M. said, *"What?"*

"The Surprise Ending, dammit. Lenny Green's big surprise. The stars were supposed to mingle during the show, right? So Lenny mingled. And he picked pockets—if he could lift J. Edgar Hoover's wallet, he probably would have no trouble with this crowd. I bet the only reason he didn't pick *our* pockets as he was going out onstage was that his cape was full."

"So he picked pockets," Rivetz said. "Hot shit. What's the big surprise about that?"

"Look. Remember how the act was supposed to work? They run back onstage, with Green (who's disappeared during the act, remember), and they start to take their bows.

"So when they come back, Green yells to stop the orchestra, and says, 'Look what I found, while I was in touch with the infinite,' and takes out Orson Welles's wallet or something."

The fingerprint man was humming "Sweet Betsy from Pike" now. He left off long enough to say, "Second row, third from the right."

Rivetz was saying something about stupid, childish, crazy TV people, but I was talking to the fingerprint man. "You mean he actually *did* get Orson Welles's wallet?"

He nodded. "Second row, third from the right."

The lieutenant asked if it was okay to handle the wallets. The expert indicated the ones that were already done. Mr. M., Rivetz, and I started looking through them.

"Look at these *names*," I said. "Lenny Green wasn't stupid. He planned this back when he wanted to get Ken Shelby to get the act back together again. So with this, Shelby and Green are standing up there, and all these big stars get called up one at a time to get their wallets back. It would have been great. In fact, it was even greater for the re-formed act. It would have been a short cut to a return to equal footing with the very biggest in the business."

"Somebody had other ideas," Rivetz said.

"Yeah." I felt dizzy again. I closed my eyes, and all of a sudden I could hear Lenny thumping those walls again, yelling those oh-so-funny cries for help. I popped my eyes open, and shuddered.

The fingerprint man finished lifting and labeling the prints from all forty-two wallets, and stowed his gear away to the tune of "Haul Away, Joe." We checked through the rest of the wallets.

"My God," Rivetz said. "Bob Hope." A few seconds later, he said, "Who the hell is 'Kenton F. Schnellenbacher'?"

"Got me," I told him. "Let me see." He handed me a piece of folded black leather, undecorated, but one touch was enough to tell me its simplicity was understatement and not economy. There was some money in it—not enough to buy a motorcycle, but plenty for a down payment on one. "Carries a lot of cash," the lieutenant said.

Rivetz had unsnapped the card section, and the first thing I saw there was one of those gold-plated Social Security cards, the ones you can buy for a couple of bucks in any novelty store. The engraving on this one said, "KENTON F. SCHNELLENBACHER." The number was 446-59-0200. I have a good memory. The mystery was solved by a look at the next plastic window, though, since it held a picture of Alice Brockway. The wallet also held some cards that read "Shelby Realty," and a more recent Social Security card, in the name of Ken Shelby, with a different number.

"This is Ken Shelby's wallet," I told Rivetz. "Obviously, he changed his name before he got famous."

"Who can blame him?" Rivetz asked.

"True," the lieutenant said, "but—"

I interrupted him. "Of course Lenny Green would have to lift *this* wallet. This was for the *big* big finish. He hands his partner his *own* wallet back, Shelby does one of his patented reaction takes, and together they walk off happily into the sign-off."

"Yeah," the lieutenant said. "Well, Green signed off, all right. Goddammit, Matty, I have work to do. Harry?"

The fingerprint man stood up, brushed off his knees. "Yeah?"

"Get Gumple, print the rightful owners of these wallets, give them a quick check, and hand them back. All we need is to have forty-two big TV stars complaining to the press that the NYPD stole their wallets."

"Lieutenant," Rivetz said. "You sure you want Gumple for this? I mean, I don't want to talk about a fellow officer, but Gumple wouldn't know Sidney Poitier from Sidney Greenstreet."

"That's the idea—no favors. Now, Rivetz, I want to talk to Shelby, and Brockway, and Marliss, and Baker." He looked at me. "Anybody else?"

"Yeah," I said. "Porter Reigels."

"Why him?"

"Because he saw it happen from twelve angles instead of one. Granted, the box was gimmicked beforehand, but he might have seen *something*."

Mr. M. snorted. "Good luck." He turned around at a sudden thought. "Rivetz!"

"Yo!"

"I want you to get on the horn to Suffolk County and tell them to keep an eye on Wilma Bascombe!"

"All taken care of," Rivetz hollered back.

"Oh, good work then." To me, the lieutenant said, "Gonna be one long night, Matty."

"Mmm," I said. "How do you plan to handle the little meeting?"

"Well," he said, scratching at his white hair again, "I plan to act like we know what the hell we're doing around here."

I didn't say anything, but it seemed to me that would take one hell of a lot of acting.

CHAPTER 25

*"Sure you have a headache. You're tense,
irritable—but don't take it out on* them."
—ANACIN COMMERCIAL

As it turned out, I didn't have to do any acting in that particular scene
until later. Harris Brophy met me in the hall with a big smile on his
face. That always means bad news.

"Oh, Matt. Glad you're back. Falzet wants to see you."

"I'll bet he does," I said. The president would not be pleased, to put
it mildly, and a meeting with him now would be less than fun. "That's
another one I owe our friend the Phantom," I said.

Harris laughed. "Still, you have to admit there's a certain fiendish in-
genuity about the fellow that your average ax murderer can't match."

"You're starting to get on my nerves again, Harris," I said. "How are
the ex-partner and friends taking it?"

"Can you imagine zombies on amphetamines? It's like they're all not
saying or doing anything, and they're not doing it as fast as they can. I
can tell you this: nobody in that room is about to turn his back on anybody else."

Suddenly he dropped his smile from his handsome face and looked
at me. "Say, Matt? Are you feeling all right? You look awful."

"Only awful?" I felt worse. "Look, Harris, I want you to get in
touch with a few of your devoted secretary friends in the government.
As soon as you can. I want to know what the FCC is going to do about
this before they do."

"No problem," he said. "I'll get on it right away." I wanted to hug
him. You can forgive a lot in a man who says things like that, especially when he usually delivers on his promises.

Falzet must have been really eager to see me, because the guard at
the door to his office (no one was going to kill Tom Falzet, by God)
just waved me by.

The walk across that office is especially impressive at night. The president sits in front of the window, and lit-up Manhattan behind him

makes him look like he's throwing off multicolored sparks of pure power.

Falzet didn't rise to greet me (he never did) but he did wave me to a chair. He was writing something on the Class A memo pad—the one with the Network's logo embossed on it in gold. I snuck a peek before I sat down and found he was doodling sharks. It suited him.

"That was a catastrophe tonight, Cobb," he said. "I wanted to speak with you about it."

"Yes, sir," I said. "Are we waiting for Colonel Coyle?"

Falzet snapped his pencil. "No, we are not waiting for Colonel Coyle. I have already spoken with Colonel Coyle. Colonel Coyle has been *terminated*."

I was in no mood for Corporation Newspeak. "Terminated?" I made my eyes wide. "You mean you *killed* him?"

"No, goddammit, Cobb, I *fired* him!"

I smiled. I always get a perverse pleasure from irritating Falzet. It's a flaw in my character. "Oh," I said. "Now I understand. If you'll excuse me for saying so, sir, that really stinks."

He pushed his sharks away from him and drew himself up in his chair. "I didn't summon you to come here to hear your opinions on how I go about my duties."

I'd figured that much. "Why did you summon me?"

He slammed an open hand on the desk. "Dammit, Cobb, do you realize what this incident tonight means? What it's going to do to the Network?"

"Yes, sir," I said grimly. "I know. By tomorrow afternoon, six well-known child psychologists are going to say we destroyed the mind and morals of any child who happened to be watching when we callously allowed a man to be murdered on the air. They will call for censorship. Then six more equally eminent child psychologists will say that the only reason anybody is *ever* murdered is because we've been polluting minds and morals for years with violent TV. Somebody will ask that the FCC take away the Network's license. The FCC will announce hearings, and never mention the fact that networks don't *have* licenses, only local stations do. A congressman who has been justifiably unknown until now will call for hearings and a special prosecutor, and the Anchorman will interview him on the Evening News. I won't even talk about the day *after* tomorrow.

"But there is no way on God's green earth you can hold Coyle responsible for *any* of it!"

"Well, I do hold him responsible. And I hold you responsible as well!"

This was the ancient TV game of Find the Scapegoat. My policy is I won't play, and I especially won't be "it."

"Well, then," I said. "The answer is simple, isn't it? Terminate me, and hire God in my place. Because He's the only one who could have prevented it."

Falzet was steaming. It was better for him than a physical exam—if there had been anything wrong with him, holding that explosion of temper in the way he did would have killed him.

I admit I enjoyed it. He was afraid to fire me, because he knew that if he did, I could use my influence with Roxanne Schick as a lever and have him fired right back. I say he "knew" it because no other possibility would ever suggest itself to him. That's what *he* would do. My personal position is that I'd work as a taste tester in a poison factory before I resorted to something like that to keep one crumby job.

So he backed down. I assured him that Special Projects was already at work to lessen the ill effects of the murder, and told him that if it was all the same to him, I'd like to get back to work.

I was in worse shape than I thought—I fell asleep in the elevator on the way to the seventh floor. One second, I was feeling sorry for Coyle, trying to think of a way to get him his job back without anyone losing face, and the next thing I knew, the bell went off to announce my arrival on the seventh floor. It woke me up.

Various detectives were still at the interrogation assembly line, interviewing people who'd been in the studio. This, I reflected, was only the beginning of the fun. Since the booby trap had been set Saturday, cops would have to be sent to Boston, D.C., Chicago, and L.A., to talk to the extra help that had been flown in to replace the set, and ask them if *they'd* seen anything. Which they probably hadn't.

Detective Gumple had squinty eyes, bucked teeth, and slumped shoulders, which made him look like a gopher. He directed me to one of the conference rooms, where the lieutenant had gathered his audience, and handed me Ken Shelby's wallet. It checked out, Gumple informed me, because the fingerprint man had compared it with the prints he'd taken from Shelby after the bowling ball incident, but he, Gumple, hadn't had a chance to give the wallet back, and would I please do it, because I had an in with the lieutenant and he, Gumple, didn't want to go barging in on an important—

"I'll do it, I'll do it!" I said. "Give me the wallet."

The conference room was two doors down from the J. V. Hewlen Kinescope Library, and it looked as if the two rooms were about to have violence in common, as well as design and color scheme. The scene I walked in on would never be mistaken for a poster for National Brotherhood Week.

It had come out in conversation that Porter Reigels had been carrying a gun, and Lieutenant Martin had ordered him to give it up.

Reigels wasn't happy about the idea. He stood up to his full Texas height, and threw his hands violently over his head. He also knocked a fiberboard ceiling panel from its support and into the empty space above in the process.

Something like a quick bass note thumped in my brain. It was a feeling I'd had before, a maddening sensation that I ought to be thinking of something, or worse, that I *had* thought of something, but it had gone through my brain too fast for me to recognize what it was.

"*Shoot!*" Porter Reigels said. I almost ducked for cover, until I recognized the word for an expletive and not a command. "There's a maniac running around this place, Lieutenant," the director said, "and if I run into him, I don't aim to kiss him on the cheek if you know what I mean."

"No," I said, "you're going to call him out into Sixth Avenue at the stroke of high noon, right?" I was very sarcastic. I was irritated at not being able to pin down my inspiration.

It was the first anyone had noticed me. "Welcome to the party, Matty," the lieutenant said. He spoke to Reigels. "Look, we'll forget the law for now. Just give me the gun, and tomorrow you can see about getting a permit for it."

Reigels sighed, pulled out the little pistol, emptied it, and handed it along with the bullets to Lieutenant Martin. "Never mind about the permit," Reigels said. "I'm getting out as soon as I can, anyway."

Ken Shelby was draped over a black plastic chair. "Out of here? I'll go with you, Porter. Lieutenant, don't you think we've been here long enough?"

"You still haven't answered my question about what McHarg said, Mr. Shelby."

"What would you expect me to say? What do you expect *McHarg* to say? If *I* were a thief, I wouldn't want to be involved with this, either. And if other people McHarg had swindled were involved in some kind of mess, he would probably deny he ever had anything to do with them as well. That's what I say."

The lieutenant was forced to admit Shelby had a point.

Porter Reigels picked up where he'd left off. "I'm getting out of this room, out of this building, out of this city, out of show business *altogether.*"

Lorenzo Baker had been trying to keep a low profile, but he was having a hard time kicking his big-brother habit. "Come on, Porter," he said as he bent his mustache with a friendly grin, "it's not *that* bad."

"The heck it ain't! My career is through. Whoever this killer is, besides everything else he's done, he killed my show. He killed my career —not that it had much life left anyway."

"I don't believe you people!" Melanie swept an ashtray off the table. It clattered on the floor. She stood up and whirled on her audience.

Now that she had our attention, she used it. "Don't you realize that this person isn't *through?* That any one of us could be *next?* Mr. Martin, I *demand* to know what you're doing to protect me!"

"You mean 'us,'" I suggested.

She turned a puzzled look at me. "What?" People like that never notice when they begin talking about the good of the community and finish up talking about the good of their own selves.

"Never mind," I told her.

She turned her attention back to the police. "Well?" she demanded.

"We're doing all we can, Miss Marliss . . ." the lieutenant began.

"That's not enough!" she snapped. "That bowling ball almost hit me, you know."

Mr. M. holds his temper as well as anyone with a temper that size can be expected to, but enough was enough.

"You see here, young woman," he yelled. "Against my advice, the department has been ordered to bend over backward to accommodate the Network and all you famous guests. God forbid you should be inconvenienced over a little thing like murder. Two murders—no, three murders!

"Well that's over, for starters. And remember this. You said the killer might be after any of you. Keep in mind that he might also *be* any of you!"

Melanie and the rest were either shocked or intimidated into silence.

Lieutenant Martin dismissed the troops. "You can go now. One of my men will be around to speak to you tomorrow. Rivetz, I want you to go back to the hotel ahead of Mr. and Mrs. Shelby and check out their room before they go into it."

Shelby chuckled. "Why, Lieutenant?"

Mr. M. shrugged. "This might sound brutal, but now that Mr. Green is out of the way, he might decide to turn his attention back to you."

Shelby looked like a man who had just eaten a bad egg.

"Maybe you're right. Okay." To Rivetz, he said, "We're all yours. Lead the way back to the hotel."

Alice Brockway, who had spent the whole session looking at the toe of Rivetz's left wing-tip and saying nothing, showed a sign of life. She lifted her head to show everyone a surprised look.

Melanie and Lorenzo had left. Reigels was waiting in the doorway. "Coming, Ken? Alice?"

"Just a minute, Ken," I said. I was about to give Shelby his wallet, but I had to indulge my curiosity first.

"Yes, Matt?"

"When did you change your name?"

"My name?" He was good with his face. "What makes you think I changed my name?"

"Wait a minute, now," the lieutenant said.

"Well," I went on, "why do you carry a Social Security card in the name of Kenton F. Schnellenbacher?"

The curious look was replaced with a grin. "You've found me out," he said. "I *did* change my name. I carry that card—it's a facsimile, naturally—to remind myself of my first job, which was loading potatoes into every German restaurant in Yorkville, where I grew up. In Yorkville, *everyone* has a name like that. When I got a job outside the neighborhood, though, I found it was too cumbersome. It was long before I went into show business, even as a director. It's all legal, if that's what's bothering you."

"Then why lie about it?"

He was still grinning. "I didn't exactly lie, you know."

He was right. "Touché," I said. An English major shouldn't get fooled on things like that. "Okay, why did you duck the question?"

"Well, just because I occasionally like to remind myself of my humble origins, it doesn't necessarily mean I want to have to tell the potato story every time I'm interviewed. I mean, there are only so many hours in a day—"

"*You make me sick!*" The Alice Brockway of Wednesday was back; the harpy; the ungovernable fury. "You all make me so sick I could *die!* Everyone is worrying about his own problems, talking chitchat— *chitchat!*" She liked the word. People do that when they're angry, repeat a word over and over. "*Chitchat!* Laughing, telling stories. Damn you, *Lenny is dead!!*

"And nobody's doing anything . . . doing . . ." She started to cry.

Shelby put a sympathetic arm around her. "All right, Alice," he said soothingly. "This has been a shock to all of us. We'll go back to the hotel, you can lie down . . ."

"I'm going to Lenny! I'm not going to leave him lying somewhere all alone!"

"I don't think that would be a good idea, dear. No." Ken Shelby seemed very close to tears himself. "What good would it do anybody, Alice? He's dead. I—I can't go look at his body . . . God, Alice, he got me into show business . . . showed me the country. He brought us together. I don't know if I could take seeing him . . ."

"Oh, Ken," his wife began. "I—I—" She wanted to explain something, but couldn't. "I have to go to him. Please come." She had taken her husband's hands. She dropped them now, and ran past Reigels through the doorway of the conference room.

Ken Shelby shook his head, reached into his pocket, and handed Rivetz his hotel key. "Here you go. Check the room while we're gone. Where is he, Lieutenant?"

"The morgue by now, I suppose."

"Yes. That's where my wife and I will be if you need us." He followed her into the corridor of the Tower of Babble.

CHAPTER 26

"Shazam!"

—MICHAEL GRAY, "SHAZAM!" CBS

"What the hell good do you expect this to do, Cobb?" Millie Heywood asked. Her eyes behind her harlequin glasses were belligerent and suspicious.

"Expect?" I said. "I don't *expect* anything but a pain in the ass. And I was right. It's started already."

"Look, Miss Heywood," Lieutenant Martin began.

"Quiet!" Millie said. That nice little old-lady look Millie carried around with her always made her look out of place in the science-fiction surroundings of Network Master Control—as though you'd plunked your great aunt into the ready room of the Strategic Air Command. But those circuits and patchracks were her domain, and she made sure everyone knew it.

"I know," she said to the lieutenant, "that you can order me to run the goddam tapes for you now, instead of at some kind of respectable hour in the morning, but Cobb here put it as a favor, 'Do me a favor, Millie,' you heard him say it. So I want to know why. In the middle of the biggest case of mass panic around here since Oswald was shot, I got the Network put to bed, finally, but I've still got to take care of the kid, you know? So I'd like to know this is gonna be worth while."

The "kid" was Hildy, who was sleeping in a chair placed in front of a bunch of green lights. Millie had probably brought her along tonight for an inside look at the Exciting World of TV.

I tilted my head toward the young woman. "There's a tiny little chance something on one of those pieces of tape can point us toward the person who killed her man, Millie. The father of that bulge she's got her hands folded across. Let's wake Hildy up, and ask her if she wants us to wait."

Millie made a raspberry. "You would, too, you bastard."

"Besides," I said, suddenly impatient. "Nobody said *you* had to stay and punch the buttons, you know. You're not the only techy at the Network."

That did it. Millie stamped her little foot and thumbed her glasses to the top of her gray head, a sure sign she was mad. "Not the only one, you bastard, but the goddam best! All right, Cobb. Monitor D. You're gonna get instant replays until you get blisters on your eyeballs. Sit down!"

She stomped away to the VTR control bank while Mr. M. and I wheeled gray swivel chairs in front of Monitor D. Monitor D was engineered to give the best picture the art of electronics was capable of giving. It was usually used to match cameras for color before a show.

"Quite a way with women you have there, Matty," the lieutenant said with a tight smile as we sat down.

"Never fails," I told him.

"What order do you want to see these things in?" Millie asked.

"Whatever's easiest for you," the lieutenant answered.

"No problem, I put them on a playback disc while you were upstairs."

I never had gotten around to returning Ken Shelby's wallet, so just before Millie's brief tantrum, I'd gone up to my office and left it on my desk with a note for Jazz to get in touch with Shelby as soon as she got the chance tomorrow morning—later this morning actually. It was well into Monday already.

I turned to Lieutenant Martin. "Which one first?"

He blew a little gust of air through his nose. "Don't ask me, boy. You're the one that was so hot to do this. The New York Police Department could have waited till morning."

So it was up to me. "The bowling ball first, Millie," I called. "The one from Friday." I told myself it would be better to take things chronologically, but the real reason was I had to prepare myself before I could stand to watch Lenny Green tumble from that cabinet again.

Millie started the playback machine. The picture blinked a few times, then locked, and it was Friday again. Ken Shelby's comic temporizing; the bogus Bomboni; Melanie; the door swinging open; the magic; and so on, until the sprinklers cut loose over the fire in the trash bin, and the picture dissolved into oatmeal. We could see the shapes of the performers as they fled, and a dull red blur as the bowling ball came crashing down to the set.

"Hold it a second, Millie," I called. "Well, Mr. M., that do anything for you?"

He shook his head. "I'd just like to know who had the brass-bound guts to go up there with that bowling ball. I nearly wet my pants when you had me risking my life for a stupid piece of cardboard."

I let it pass. I drummed my fingers nervously on the console, watched the screen. "Roll it, Millie."

I was surprised to see just how similar the two abortive performances of the Reluctant Magician had been. The timing, the flow, were practically the same. Until, of course, the door bit, when the three stars had to work hard to pull the door open.

There was a pretty good shot of the inside of the cabinet, and I tried to see if I could spot the bag of carbon tetrachloride I knew was in there, but I couldn't. The insides of practically all magic apparatus are painted a dead black for the express purpose of keeping people from getting a good look at any gimmick that might be in there. Our friend the killer doubtlessly knew that.

I didn't even see Lenny Green step on the bag and break it, because his partner had closed the door behind him so fast. But I heard Lenny's cries for help, and I heard the laughter. All that cruel, stupid laughter. I had a silly notion that I could hear my own voice laughing as Lenny died.

The playback showed the rest of it, too, the truth slowly seeping through the studio; the laughter dying; and Lenny's body spilling to the set as the waterlogged door was finally wrenched open. I wondered how much the warping of the wood of that cabinet had contributed to Lenny's death.

"*It swells up when it gets wet,*" Lenny had said Saturday afternoon, "*that's all.*"

I felt that tight little bass note in the bottom of my brain again.

I jumped, as though I'd leaned up against a hot stove. "It swells up when it gets wet." What did I think I meant by that? All *kinds* of things swell up when they get wet.

"Run it again, Millie," I said. *Play it again, Sam,* I heard echo in my head. My mind was starting to race. I was weak and I needed sleep.

"Matty," Mr. M. began, but I insisted on seeing it again.

By the time the two segments were over this time, the bass note had drawn out into a low, rumbling pedal tone that was driving me crazy. I was about an inch away from *something*. I was about to call for Millie to show it again when Rivetz came in.

"Well?" the lieutenant asked him.

"No bogeyman in Shelby's room. Oh, the Brockway broad won't be staying at the Brant Hotel tonight. Guess the Network is out the money, eh, Cobb?"

"Ha, ha," I said. What *was* it?

"Why not, Rivetz?" the lieutenant wanted to know. "Where is she going to be?"

"Shelby and her had another tiff at the morgue," Rivetz explained. "I figured I better keep an eye on them, so I took them there myself. Brockway wanted to claim the body right away; Shelby said they ought to find out about Green's relatives at least. Which makes sense to me, but figure out a woman, right?

"Anyhow, it comes down to Brockway won't sleep under the same roof with such a callous bastard, so she's spending the night with Doreen somebody, actress on one of those stupid soap operas. Old friend or—what's so funny, Cobb?"

"Nothing," I said, but I went on laughing. Doreen had people crying on her shoulder in real life, now.

"Cuckoo," Rivetz said. "Anyway, I got the address and phone number, we can get her if we need her." He patted the notebook in his back pocket. "What now, Lieutenant?"

Lieutenant Martin looked at his watch, shook it, and said a swear word. "What the hell time is it?"

"About four-thirty," I said, without looking at my watch. "Four-twenty-seven," Rivetz said at the same time. It's a talent I have, completely useless, except as a constant reminder that I'm using up my life.

"Well," Mr. M. said with a sigh, "let's go talk to Wilma Bascombe. We'll make her place about sunup. Come on, Matty."

"No," I said.

The lieutenant was surpised. "No?"

"I'm close to something, dammit! I can feel it!"

"You're close to a breakdown, is what you're close to, Cobb," Rivetz said. "Go take a look at yourself in a mirror. You look like secondhand death."

"Shut up, Rivetz," the lieutenant told him. "What have you got, Matty?"

I shook my head, helplessly. "I—don't—*know!*" Rivetz made a noise. I ignored him. "Look. There's something on that tape, or something in my head, or both, that's important here. God*dam*, I wish I knew what it was."

"If you ask me," Rivetz said, "old Wilma Bascombe is our last stop on this case."

Mr. M. scratched his chin. "You think so, too, huh?"

I was disgusted. "Oh, come off it."

"Matty, she's the only one in this case that's had even the shadow of a motive against anybody. She was in L.A. when Bevic was killed. With her two sweet-boy friends, she's got built-in muscle for the theft of the ball and the films, and the catwalk business . . ."

The films, I thought. The theft of 1952. I grabbed my temples. Now *everything* was humming, not just my inadequate mind. The *air* was making noise.

". . . *And,*" the lieutenant continued, "she just *happened* to be in this building this morning, with that death-threat story. I bet they smelled that one over in Jersey, for Christ's sake."

"Besides," Rivetz put in. "You saw *one* of her boys in the lobby. Who's to say the other wasn't posing as a workman and planting the carbon tet in the magic cabinet? God knows it's easy enough to *get* the stuff."

"She's our best bet, Matty," the lieutenant concluded. "If you think about it, she's the only one who hasn't been threatened either physically or financially by what's been going on."

I closed my eyes. "You're probably right," I lied, to end the argument. "But I'm sorry, Mr. M., I'm just not up to a ride out on the Island. I think I'll go home and sleep on it."

He nodded and ruffled my hair, in a way he hadn't done since I was a kid. Then he smiled. "I always said you white boys needed more sleep. God knows it's a good idea. Well, let's go, Rivetz. Take care, Matty."

"Always do," I said. I waited until the policemen had left Master Control. Then I rubbed my eyes and sat up.

"Millie!" I yelled.

"What, what?" She must have dozed off for a few minutes.

"Let's see it again."

Millie rolled her disc. After a couple of times through, Llona showed up, looking for me.

"One of the guards told me you were here," she said. We kissed hello. I was glad to see her, but part of me was impatient with the interruption, anxious to get back to the monitor.

Llona was being motherly. "Honestly, Matt, don't you ever get enough?"

"My job, Llona." I rubbed my eyes, but they kept burning.

"Why don't you just stay home and stick needles in yourself? Matt," she said, suddenly very grave, "no job is this important. You have to look out for yourself too, you know. Come home."

"In a little while," I said. Something about that door . . .

"Now!" Llona stamped a foot. Now that I looked at her, she didn't look too great herself. She'd probably just finished handling the nation's ravenous newshounds. They'd sell a lot of papers with this story.

"I can't, Llona, honest. I—I'm close to something." That was a mistake—she wanted to know what it was.

"I'll tell you when I know myself," I said. I handed Llona my keys. "Look, I'll meet you later, I promise. We'll sleep the rest of the week."

"Mmm hmm," she said. She was skeptical, but she took the keys. She also agreed to put Hildy in a cab and get her safely to Millie's. We woke up the pregnant girl, and she left with Llona.

"Take care of Spot," I added as an afterthought. Some dog-sitter I was. I hadn't even thought of the poor little pooch for hours.

Millie ran the disc again. And again and again. It was just like Babe Ruth and that stupid home run, but grimmer.

There came a time when I knew I'd have to stop. I couldn't concentrate. My brain insisted on mixing its own images with what was on the tape.

So I saw Shelby and Green, and I saw the famous pants-down poster sequence. I saw Melanie Marliss, and I saw Lorenzo Baker and tacos and kung fu. I saw Lenny Green's pants get ripped off, and I saw him get blown up by his motel toilet bowl, and I saw him laughing about it. I saw the sprinkler cut in, and I saw myself as a kid, rushing home from school in the rain to get another sweet look at Alice Brockway. I saw Alice and me on that sofa in the Brant. I saw myself as a kid again, watching Saturday morning shows, and I saw Porter Reigels and Ken Shelby in primitive control rooms directing those same shows.

The audio got mixed up, too. In between the ad libs and the jokes from the monitor, I heard Porter Reigels say, "Real nice," and Llona say, "It's a *trap*." I heard Lenny screaming for help from inside the box —no, that was real, came right from the monitor. Get a grip on yourself, Cobb.

But the humming and buzzing got louder, and the voices went on. I watched Ken and Melanie struggling with the bolt, and again I heard Lenny. *"It swells up when it gets wet."*

Capillary action, I had said. *Makes a wet sponge expand to twice its dry size. Lifts tons of nutrients to the topmost leaves of a giant sequoia. I'm surprised at you . . .*

On the screen, Lenny Green's body fell for the fifteenth or twentieth time. I heard my own voice say to Porter Reigels, "Hey, I'm one of the good guys!"

The picture stopped. I sat there looking at the blank screen.

"How about it, Cobb?" Millie said through a yawn. "It's practically 6 A.M., for crying out loud."

The hum was gone. I was spent, drained, and disgusted with myself. *Congratulations, Cobb,* I mocked myself. What had I accomplished, I asked myself, aside from proving that that scene with Vivien Leigh hearing voices at the end of *Gone With the Wind* wasn't as stupid as I used to think it was?

And then, as though it were the most natural thing in the world, I answered myself. *You cracked the case, idiot.*

I closed my eyes and watched it all fall into place. Piece after piece. And the more of the picture I had, the easier the other pieces fit in.

The picture was ugly.

Before I even knew where I was going, I was out of Master Control and hurrying down the hallway. I stiff-armed the door to the men's room, found a stall, knelt, and was bitterly and violently sick.

I was wiping cold sweat from my face with a paper towel when I emerged. Millie was waiting outside the door.

"Jeez, Matt, are you all right? It sounded like you were coming up with your *soul* in there."

"Symptom of carbon tetrachloride poisoning," I told her. "Look it up." I grinned. I was weak, but I had to grin. Finally, someone besides the killer knew what the hell was going on around here. That part, at least, was a good feeling.

"Millie," I said, "are you all paid up and registered with the Projectionists Union?"

"Of course. Why?"

"Because," I said, "if I'm right, I'll be wanting you to run some kinescopes for me."

CHAPTER 27

"Patch me through to McGarrett."
—JAMES MAC ARTHUR, "HAWAII FIVE-O," CBS

I lost Millie momentarily in the hallway. She had short legs, and I was too pumped up to slow down for her. She ran a few steps, rounded the corner, and caught up with me.

"Cobb," she began. She managed to be breathless and menacing at the same time. "Cobb, this better *be* something. I mean, there better be some goddam point to this."

I stopped, looked down at her, and very gravely said, "Millie, the point is, 'Things are not always what they seem.'"

Millie thought it over for a second, then said, "Good!"

"Good?" I hadn't been expecting that.

"Yeah. Because you seem nuts!" She started walking again.

"No," I said, trying to catch up with her this time. "It's important that someone remember that; God knows I keep forgetting. I could have solved this case a week ago."

Something had suddenly occurred to me, a hole in my puzzle. *How did the fire get started?* Well, genius?

"We'll take the stairs," I said. "It's only three floors down." To hell with the fire, I thought. First things first. Let's see about those kines.

The seventh floor was deserted, except for a uniformed cop who told us Studio J was off limits until further notice.

Millie was all set to put up an argument. Nobody was going to keep the Chief Technician of Network Operations out of a Network studio while she was alive.

I spoiled her fun. While Millie was still flexing her lip, I smiled nicely at the policeman and told him our business didn't have anything to do with Studio J, which was a lie, but not a terrible one.

I took Millie's wrist, and pulled her instead to the J. V. Hewlen Kinescope Library. Very carefully, I closed the door behind us, and locked it. I walked over to the table Jerry de Loon had used for his work, rested my hands on the back of his chair.

I had a sore throat now, to go with my headache. I had to force the words out, and they came strained and a little hoarse.

"Sit down, Millie," I said. She sat, took off her glasses, and blinked at me as though it had suddenly occurred to her I might be dangerous.

"Before I do anything," I said, "I want you to know you may have to testify in court about what I'm going to do here, so pay attention."

"Uhh, right," she said, putting her glasses back on. "This is the stuff about things aren't what they seem?"

"That's exactly what this is!" I was suddenly furious with myself. I slammed a fist into the back of the chair. "I'm a goddam *idiot!*"

I saw I was scaring Millie, so, with an effort, I brought myself under control. "Look," I said. "You've heard about that incident with Melanie Marliss and the five security guards Saturday afternoon, right?" She nodded. "Well," I went on, "I remember thinking at the time that when you see a woman in a violent struggle with five men, you *automatically* assume they attacked her. It doesn't make sense any other way."

"Marliss never makes sense," Millie said sourly. "Never did."

"Neither has this case! That's the trouble! Another automatic assumption we made has messed us up from the beginning."

"What's that?"

"Well, let me ask you. Someone bursts into this room, assaults Jerry —injuring him fatally in the process, it turns out. When someone arrives to investigate, not only is the assailant gone, but Melanie's bowling ball is missing from the studio, and none of those kines from 1952 can be found in here. What's the natural assumption?"

"Wh—what do you mean?"

"I mean what did everybody automatically think?"

"That someone wanted that dumb ball and those dumb kines. Come on, Cobb, I'm a long time out of kindergarten."

I nodded and rubbed an eyebrow. "Okay, Millie, I'm sorry. But you've made my point. Everyone—the police, Coyle, and Matthew Cobb, boy genius, came to the conclusion that the criminal wanted to steal that stuff. And I'll bet fifteen Nielsen points that that's just where we went wrong."

Millie shook her head. "I'm sorry, Matt. You're too much for me. You trying to say he stole all that big heavy stuff without *wanting* to?"

"*No-oo!*" I laughed. "Do you see how insidious one of those damnable 'natural' assumptions is? No, he wanted to do what he did, all right. The point is, *he never stole anything!*"

"No, huh?" Millie's face said she wondered how she could get me to a doctor with the least possible trouble.

"No."

"Then where are the kines?"

"In this room. See if I'm not right. Can I move a chair without getting in trouble with the union?"

"What? Oh, sure, sure. Go ahead, Matt."

I pulled Jerry's chair a few feet from the table, and stood on the seat. I straightened up, put my hands against the fiberboard ceiling panel, and pushed. The panel gave, just as the one in the identical room down the hall had when Porter Reigels knocked it askew with his fist. Plenty of space up there. I should have thought of it days ago.

I stood on tiptoe and poked my nose into the darkness. I saw them, lying like flat gray beetles on the metal housings of the built-in fluorescent lights.

I could just reach one from where I stood. I stretched, got my fingers on the dusty can, and pulled it to me.

" 'Dandy Donny Daniels Show,' " I read from a hand-printed label on the can. " 'Kids show, Sat. Aft., 1952.' " The label had Jerry's initials on it.

"I'll be a spayed bitch in heat," Millie said. "You were right!"

"Yeah," I said. One day, I have to arrange to score a triumph under circumstances that will let me enjoy it. At that moment, I was too busy remembering what an idiot I'd been to enjoy anything. How many times had I wondered how the attacker had gotten away with the bowling ball and the heavy films? But of course, once it started to come to me, after the big stroke of inspiration up in Master Control, the answer to that came, too: He didn't carry them *anywhere*. It didn't matter *how* goddam heavy they were. True, it took the killer some time to get them distributed in the ceiling (couldn't have a telltale bulge in the fiberboard, after all), but he'd had plenty of time. He could have always given Jerry an additional clop on the head if the need arose.

I handed Millie the last reel of "Be Still My Heart." I looked around for anything else of interest that might be up there, but I didn't see anything. I stepped down. "Fourteen cans, Millie?" I asked.

She ran a stubby finger alongside them. "Yep, fourteen. That's all of them, right?" She shook her head. "He *hid* them, for God's sake. Why the hell would he kill poor Jerry just to hide them?"

"Mmmm," I said grimly. "Because he didn't want anyone to see what was on them!"

Millie eyed me suspiciously. "You know what's on them, don't you, you cagey bastard?"

"Let's just call Lieutenant Martin and watch the movies. Then we'll find out for sure, okay?" Millie shrugged and went to work setting up Jerry's old projector.

My part of the business was a little more difficult. It's very easy to call the police, but it's not so easy to call one particular policeman. All they'd tell me at Headquarters was that the lieutenant and Rivetz were out. I knew where they were—either still talking to Wilma Bascombe (a fool's errand, if my suspicions were correct) or trapped in the traditional Monday morning traffic jam on the inbound Long Island Expressway. God knew when they were going to be back. I couldn't even talk to Gumple—he was interrogating someone.

They said they had somebody just as good as Lieutenant Martin for me to talk to, but I doubted it. Nobody who hadn't been in on this from the beginning was going to be able to appreciate these films.

"Which one do you want to see first?" Millie demanded.

"'Dr. Wonder,'" I said. "How many are there?"

"Three cans. Six shows."

I made my lips tight and shook my head. Not good odds. Back in 1952, they produced thirty-nine episodes of a given series every year. Dr. Wonder, that kindly old gray-haired actor-scientist, used to do about four experiments a week. I would have called my case proved if these kines turned up any one of three—three that someone had turned to deadly use.

I got lucky, but it took a while.

It was in the fifth "Dr. Wonder" episode. Dr. Wonder had led his little friends from the fictitious TV neighborhood through the world of kites ("Bernoulli, Dr. Wonder? Was he Italian?" "Heh, heh, no, Bucky, he was Swiss."); light ("Pola . . . pola . . . pola . . . what?" "Heh, heh, *polarization*, Nancy."); and a dozen other topics.

I surprised even myself to find how incredibly well I remembered these shows. I don't mean just the format, or Dr. Wonder's indulgent little laugh, I mean specific episodes. Little Matt Cobb had paid closer attention to the talking shadows of his youth than even he was aware of. I could almost mouth the next stupid question Bucky or Nancy was scripted to ask.

And so when the teaser for the fifth episode came on, I knew I'd hit pay dirt.

"The Babe *always* knew he was going to hit that home run," I said.

"What?"

"Never mind, Millie. Watch the show."

We watched.

The doorbell rings. Dr. Wonder says come in, and Bucky skips in, crooked baseball cap and all. Dr. Wonder is sitting at a table, amusing himself by making matches burn underwater.

"Gee, whiz, Dr. Wonder," Bucky says. "How'd ya do *that?*"

"Oh," Dr. Wonder replies, "that's just one of the fascinating things we'll learn about today as we explore the world of . . . Fire and Water."

Five minutes into the show, Dr. Wonder made a volcano. He mixed iron filings, some sulphur, and some purple crystals of potassium permanganate in a coffee can, then buried the can down to the rim in a big wooden box of dirt he happened to have lying around the studio. He explained to Bucky how potassium permanganate is a powerful chemical doctors sometimes prescribe as a disinfectant, like boric acid, only stronger. Then he got a medicine dropper full of glycerin, and saying, "Now, don't you kids try this at home," he put two drops of glycerin into the mixture.

"That's how he did it," I whispered. The killer wouldn't have even needed the filings or the sulphur—they were just for sparks and "lava" to make the phony volcano seem more impressive. It was the glycerin and the permanganate that made the difference. It would have taken a couple of seconds at the outside to start that fire Friday afternoon. A paper spill of crystals in one pocket, and a medicine dropper with a tiny bit of glycerin in it in the other. They'd be harmless separately, but together they'd easily create enough heat to send the flammable stuff in the carpenter's bin up in flames. The potassium compound, in fact, would burn so completely, it is likely the police lab would never find a trace of it. And if the police noticed the traces of glycerin, well, they'd certainly find some obliging show-biz type like me to explain it away as makeup.

I remembered Lenny's telling me *he had to soak his infected foot.* I marveled how well the killer had used the people and things around him as essential parts of his plan. The Network's glycerin. Lenny's crystals. My stupidity. Especially that.

But Dr. Wonder was talking again.

". . . called *capillary action,* Bucky. That's how water tends to cling, and climb, and soak into things. It's the force that makes a sponge expand, and lifts tons of water and nutrients to the top of a giant sequoia . . ."

I pressed my knuckles into my temples. Dr. Wonder was long since a skeleton, and for all I knew, Bucky was a middle-aged science teacher at a junior high in the Bronx. But the Network had offered the doctor as my guru, and Bucky as my vicar, and I had accepted both so unconsciously and so thoroughly, I'd been quoting the old man all week, and had never even realized it.

"Really?" The ghost of Bucky's incredulous child-voice came tinnily from the speaker in the side of the projector.

"Absolutely," said Dr. Wonder with a grin. "Why, I can even make it lift *you!"*

Bucky didn't believe him, so Dr. Wonder had to prove it. Scientifically. Two coffee cans. Dr. Wonder loved coffee cans—coffee was a lot cheaper in those days. Cardboard, a large sheet of it, exactly the same kind, I noticed, that the Network carpenters used to label their stacks of lumber.

Bucky helped the doctor cut the cardboard into squares about four inches on a side. They stacked them in the coffee cans.

Dr. Wonder made the boy stand on the cans, one foot on each. Then he got a watering can and poured water into both cans. They laughed as Dr. Wonder accidentally poured some water on Bucky's sneaker.

Nothing happened for a moment. Then Bucky grinned and waved his arms in a circle. "I'm falling over!" he said.

"You're rising!" Dr. Wonder grinned back. Bucky regained his balance, and I watched with as much interest as I had when I was a child. The water swelled into the fibers of the cardboard and lifted Bucky two, three, almost four inches above the rims of the cans.

I remembered it. I remembered it in every corny, childish detail. And it had sat like a time bomb in my memory, waiting for something to set it off.

My memory, and the killer's.

There had been modifications, of course. Bucky weighed (at the time the show was done) maybe a hundred pounds. A standard bowling ball weighs sixteen. And there was no need to lift the bowling ball inches into the air—all that was needed was to lift it the fraction of an inch necessary to send it over the tiny lip at the edge of the floor of the catwalk. A small, folded wedge of cardboard, like the one we had found, would be ample.

And of course, the water hadn't come from a watering can, but from the Network's own fire safety system.

But, as Dr. Wonder used to point out with a twinkle in his eye—was in fact pointing out to me at that very moment from the screen—"The scientific principle doesn't change."

"No," I said, "only the human principle."

"Shut up, will ya, Matt?" Millie said uneasily. "You're making me nervous—talking to yourself that way."

"Okay, Millie, okay, that's it. Thanks a lot. Go on home; take care of Hildy and the cats."

"You ought to take your own advice."

I yawned wide. The yawn seemed to take on a life of its own, and I had to fight my mouth to close it. "Right as usual, Mildred, my dear . . ." Millie made a face. When I start doing Fields, I'm really on my last legs. "Sorry," I said. I looked at my watch and felt like yawning all over again. It was past nine, and most *normal* people would be just starting their day's work.

Including Jazz. A few words with my secretary, and I could go home, shave, wash the stink off me, and maybe even get a little sleep before Lieutenant Martin got back.

It turned out like most of my plans.

"My God, Matt," Jazz said when she saw me. "You look like you've been up all night."

"How about that," I said. "Look, Jazz . . ."

"There's a visitor in your office," she said, interrupting me.

"Who?"

"Take a look." She grinned. I wasn't really in the mood for games, but I was less in the mood to assert myself. I took the line of least resistance, and went into my office.

My visitor had white fur on his face, a little black nose, and pointy ears.

"Spot!" I said, "what are you doing here?" exactly as though I expected him to answer me.

"Woof!" he replied, which served me right. Spot was sitting on my swivel chair, shuffling papers around on my desk with his forepaws. He had precisely the right vacant smile on his face. Put a tie on him, and you could move him into my job tomorrow. Spot agreed to vacate my chair if I would scratch him behind his ears.

I resisted closing my eyes as I sat down, because I knew I'd go to sleep the second I did. And, I figured, as long as I had my eyes open, I might as well look at something with them. Spot was no help. He was making a contented, purring growl deep in his throat, and had no qualms about closing *his* eyes. He made me jealous. I tried looking out the window, but all I could see was the Brant, and I didn't want to worry about that place for a while. The walls of my office carry a lot of bad abstract art that I had wished on me by the official Network decorator. That left my desk.

Spot's pawing around had made my desk even messier than usual, so I noticed what was missing before I noticed what was there.

What was missing was Ken Shelby's wallet, which I'd left on my desk earlier that morning. I was moving things around, looking for it, when I found Llona's note.

"Dear Matt—Missed you. Looked here, looked in Master Control. They tell me you're off somewhere with Millie Heywood, looking at some kines, so I'll do some of your work for you, and return Ken's wallet. The Network can watch Spot for a couple of minutes—Love, Llona."

I reached for the intercom three times before I hit it. "Jazz," I said at last, "come in here right away!"

Jazz said, "Right," and appeared in the office two seconds later.

"How long ago was Llona Hall here, Jazz?"

She looked at her watch. "About twenty, twenty-five minutes ago. Right after I got to work, she came here looking for you. I told her what your note to me said, and she asked if she could go into your office to leave a note for you. I said okay. Did I do something wrong? You look mad."

"Not at you, Jazz," I assured her. "Did Llona say she was coming back for the dog?"

"Chure." It always amazed me how Jazz had conquered her Cuban accent on everything but that one word. "In fact," she went on, "I expected her back a lot sooner than this."

"Yeah," I said, biting my lip. There went my shower. "Okay, Jazz, back to work." I sat down at my desk again, and Spot closed his eyes, expecting the scratching to continue. I double-crossed him, by picking up the phone instead.

Things were no better at Police Headquarters. No, Lieutenant Martin was not yet back, though he was expected any minute. No, Detective Gumple was not yet finished interviewing the witness.

"Look," I said, "I *have* to talk to Martin. Can't you plug the phone into the radio?"

"Do *what,* Mr. Cott?" the voice asked.

"Cobb," I said. "Can't you patch the phone into the radio system? Christ, they used to do it on 'Police Woman' all the time. Call Martin on the radio, and plug my phone call in. Hell, just hold the microphone to the receiver, okay?"

"Oh," said the voice, suddenly enlightened. "One of *those.* Gee, I haven't done one of those in a long time. I'll get right on it."

"Thanks," I said sincerely. While I waited, I felt my face and debated if I shouldn't grow a beard, with such a good head start.

"Mr. Codd?"

"Cobb. Yes?"

"Sorry. Can't get him on the radio. He must be in a tunnel or something."

I looked at heaven. It occurred to me that one day, I was going to get a history-making stroke of luck. I was due for one.

"Okay," I said bitterly. "Thanks for trying. Take a message, okay? When you finally get through to the lieutenant, or when Gumple comes up for air, tell him to meet Matt Cobb, M-A-T-T C-O-B-B, as in corn-on-the, in room twelve-oh-three of the Brant Hotel. Got that?"

He read it back to me, and had it right.

"As soon as either of them can." I hung up the phone. "Damn!" I said. "Damn!"

I picked up Spot's leash. "Come on, boy," I said. "You don't want me to rescue Llona from the clutches of a killer all by myself, do you?"

Spot said, "Woof!"

CHAPTER 28

"Where everything doubles, and the scores could really change."

—ART FLEMING, "JEOPARDY," NBC

I've always thought October weather is the best weather of the year, and I offer that Monday morning as evidence. The air was pleasantly cool and sweet, even down on the street among the cars and buses, and the sky was so blue it vibrated at the edges of the buildings. It was as though the sky resented New York City for cutting it up into wedges, and partitioning it between skyscrapers.

It was the kind of day that would have made me feel glad to be alive, assuming I felt alive in the first place, and assuming I weren't already so worried about Llona that I had no room for any other kind of feeling.

A haughty doorman tried to tell me no pets were allowed in the Brant, and I called him a liar to his face.

It didn't faze him for a second. He brushed his lovely gray mustache into place with a white-gloved finger and said, "That has always been the Brant's policy, sir, I assure you."

I looked at him. We both knew the Brant's policy had nothing to do with pets, especially expensive pets like Spot. Now that the show was over, and the autograph seekers had mostly gone, the policy of the Brant was back to keeping the undesirables out; and smelly guys needing a shave, with feverish excitement in their eyes, definitely qualified as undesirables.

For some reason I can't recall, I had a fifty-dollar bill in my wallet. I gave it to him, and became desirable immediately.

Spot had no such problem; he was an aristocrat, and took the admiring glances he got from people in the lobby as nothing less than his due. He even deigned to let his fur be stroked occasionally. It made things easier for me—if anyone wondered about me now, I was just some schnook returning a rich guest's pet from his morning walk.

In a way, I was grateful for the delay, because outside of rescuing

Llona, if she needed any rescuing, I didn't have the slightest idea of what the hell I was going to do.

I decided, finally, to play it by ear—or rather by mouth. In the great tradition of American Entertainment, I was going to hold the fort until the cavalry arrived. All the way up in the elevator, I asked the fates to provide smooth roads and light traffic for the police.

On the twelfth floor, I scouted the layout before I did anything else. There was one strategic recess in the wall, where the door to the maid's closet was, that a person would have to pass to get to the stairs or the elevator. I told Spot to park his little carcass there, and told him to stay. He looked at me quizzically, but he obeyed. That little pooch was the closest thing I had to an ace in the hole, and if I had to play him, I wanted to know where he was.

Ken Shelby answered the door. I took a careful look at him. I dismissed it as too much imagination and too little sleep, but now that I knew he was a killer, he looked different to me. He seemed to be a different color around the edges, the way a sharp razor gleams more intensely than a dull one.

He showed me a little amused smile when he admitted me, which made him seem even more dangerous. I told my imagination to cut it out.

We exchanged good mornings, then he said, "Well, what can I do for you, Matt? You don't look so well. Haven't you been home yet?"

"Home?" I said. "I haven't even been to the bathroom. The Network has come up with a variation on the forty-hour week. They call it the forty-hour day."

He laughed, as though what I said had been funny. A mistake, I thought. A professional comedian should have been able to top that one without thinking twice. He did have things on his mind.

"I'm looking for Llona Hall," I said. "She's supposed to be bringing your wallet back." I looked around the sitting room. Llona wasn't there, and a sudden fear jumped into my chest and started crowding my lungs.

A voice from the patio fixed that. "Out here, Matt!" Llona sounded very happy to hear my voice. I was ecstatic to hear hers.

Shelby pointed and said, "After you," so I led the way through the open sliding glass door, past the curtain, and out on the balcony.

The Brant is famous for its views of the park, but I didn't want to see anything but Llona. She was safe, if a little worried. She was sitting on a wrought-iron chair at a round marble table, drinking coffee. Over the rim of her cup, she gave me a curious look. I couldn't tell if it was worry, relief, or something else.

Ken Shelby opened the curtain as he joined us on the balcony. "Might as well let some sunshine into the room, right? Have a seat,

Matt—no, not that one, I want to sit there. I like the fresh air, but I don't like looking out over the railing. It's a long way down."

I shrugged, and sat opposite Llona. Shelby made it a triangle by squeezing into the chair that was backed up against the balcony's low railing.

Shelby offered me some coffee; I refused. "The reason I'm here," I said, "is to bring Llona back to the Tower. Ritafio is crying real tears all over the PR department. Making the blotters soggy."

Shelby picked up his cup. "And they send a vice-president as an errand boy?" He turned to Llona. "You should be honored. What's the matter, Matt? Telephones all broken?"

"I was going on a coffee break. Why should two switchboard girls know Llona's playing hooky from her job to bring you a wallet?"

Llona should have said something. In a normal conversation, she would have made a remark about how taking care of celebrities was part of her job. Or something. This wasn't a normal conversation.

Ken poured himself some more coffee. "You wouldn't happen to be jealous, now, would you, Matt? Because if you are, I swear having coffee is the only proposition I've made."

"What makes you think I've got a right to be jealous?"

He smiled around the rim of his cup. "Never mind. None of my business, anyway. But I'd appreciate it if you'd let Llona stay. I want her help with a statement for the press about Lenny's death." He shook his head sadly. "Such a short comeback."

"Sorry," I said. "Ritafio's got first claim on her. Llona?" I wanted that woman out of there, preferably before the police arrived.

I was prepared to force the issue, but the issue got forced for me. Shelby put down his cup, pushed his saucer aside. Then he took his other hand from under the table, and put it down where the saucer had been. The hand had a gun in it.

A sarcastic voice somewhere in my head said, "Who was going to bullshit *whom*, Cobb?" I hated myself fully as much as the voice did, but I couldn't go on listening to it, because the man with the gun was speaking.

"Back away from the table, both of you. No, don't stand up, slide backward in your chairs. I want to see your hands, Matt. That's it. Now bring your chairs together side by side. Until your thighs touch. No reason this can't be a pleasant experience for all concerned, right?" Shelby's glasses gleamed above a very nasty smile.

The legs of the chairs Llona and I were sitting on were straddling the track of the sliding door to the suite. We formed a nice obstacle to anyone who might want to approach him, and by looking over our heads, he had a clear view of the front door. And twelve stories up from the street, no one was about to sneak up on him from behind. He'd taken a very strong strategic position.

"You called the police before you came here, didn't you, Matt?"

"Sure," I said. "I have four detectives and a deputy inspector in my vest pocket."

He scratched his gray hair, thinking about it. "Well," he said, "if they come, I'll still have you two to talk about with them, won't I?"

"They don't make concessions to people who hold hostages in this city, Ken. Besides, I didn't call anybody. Why should I?"

He ignored the question. "Well, it probably doesn't make any difference. The tickets will be here soon."

There was an airline ticket office down the street. "Going somewhere?" I asked.

"To the airport. You two can see me off, if you behave."

That, I knew, was a crock. Granted, the staff of the Brant might be obliging enough to get his ticket for him, even deliver it to his room, but he had no reason to think Llona and I would be obliging enough to let his plane fly out of U.S. airspace to some convenient country (Costa Rica, for example) with our little mouths tightly shut.

The way it looked from where I sat on the iron chair, if I was going to the airport at all, it would be as a corpse in the trunk of the car the hotel would probably also rent for him. The parking lots of the New York airports have replaced the Hudson River and the Jersey Swamp as the unmarked grave capital of the world. Hostage or not, I'd like my chances a lot better after the police arrived. I had to play for time until then.

I tried again. "How about answering this one, then? What happened this morning that prompted all this? The maid short-sheet your bed or something?"

He was enjoying this. I don't think anyone had ever seen Ken Shelby this relaxed, on screen or off. He shook his head, mockingly. "Nothing like that. Llona told me you found the kinescopes."

"So?"

He had to think about it for a minute. "I . . . reacted, and gave myself away to her. Unfortunate."

"And extreme." Even though I knew what time it was the effort it took not to look at my watch was sheer agony. Where were the cops? "So I found the kines. If it hadn't been me, it would have been a janitor, or an exterminator."

He adjusted his collar with his free hand. "Ah, but by then I would have been long gone.

"Don't try to make me underrate you, Matt. I've been watching you from the start, and I've been very impressed. Do you ever notice that, the way you tend to impress people? Melanie spoke very highly of you. So did poor Lenny. So did my wife."

Llona was distracting me. She wasn't crying, or trembling, or anything, but she was watching the interplay between Shelby and me in the same intent way a little girl watches the jump rope turn before she hops in. I could only hope she didn't do anything drastic.

"Your wife," I said to Shelby, "spoke very highly of you, too, you know."

"I'll bet. You were in bed with her at the time, of course?"

"No," I said. But I could almost feel Alice's kiss burning my lips again.

"No?" He seemed surprised. "Well, you missed a golden opportunity there, my boy. Alice is irrepressible in showing young men how much she admires them."

"And not-so-young men."

"What's that mean?"

"Your late partner. That's at least part of the reason you killed him, isn't it? Otherwise you could have left the country right after you killed Jim Bevic. Couldn't you?"

Shelby must have found that question a regular poser. He tilted his head back, and got such a dreamy look on his face, I thought he was going to give me a chance to jump him.

He didn't. He bit the tip of his tongue, looking for the right words. At last, he said, "Alice and I have had an understanding—a tacit understanding, but real all the same. Alice has always needed . . . ah . . . more than one man could give her."

"Or at least more than *you* could, right?"

That stung him. His face turned ugly and hot, and for the first time since I'd known him, he looked like a killer.

Shelby raised the gun. Llona gasped beside me.

The knuckle of Shelby's trigger finger whitened. *Where are the cops?* I wondered feverishly, stupidly. *Where in the name of God are the cops?*

I had resolved to face my last moments with my eyes open, so I had a great view of the storm passing from his face.

"I'll ignore that," he said quietly. "But another part of that tacit understanding was that it would be completely private. The men were to be made aware of that. No rumors. No stories. But now, one of her ruts has been turned into one of the classic laughs of show business."

"I don't follow you," I said.

"He even had the nerve to tell the story to *me*. As if I wouldn't know when my own wife had stopped using hair spray."

"Ah," I said. "So *Alice* is the woman in the toilet bowl story."

That was too much for Llona. "What toilet bowl story?"

"Quiet, Llona. Still, Ken, you ran a hell of a risk just to revenge a little joke."

He leaned forward in his chair, very earnest, eager to be understood. "Well, that isn't all of it, of course. I knew I was leaving the country, leaving Alice, my business, and especially show business forever. I wanted to give the public something to remember me by. I wanted to leave them . . . well, gasping. As I have." He sat back again, looking pleased with himself.

I nodded. "I should have realized that when I spoke with your wife." *Where are the cops?* "She told me everything I needed to know, really. How smart you are. How creative you are. How you like to be the unnoticed power behind the scenes—hell, it was all summed up for the world to see in that poster of the actor with his pants down, wasn't it? How you have a penchant—no, Alice said a *need*—to 'dazzle' people."

"Very perceptive, my Alice." He smiled as though he were proud of her. For all I knew, he was.

"And you're a great ad libber, too. That bit with the bolt while Lenny was suffocating was nothing short of genius. Not only do you build up the suspense for the folks at home, but you make sure the door on that magic cabinet doesn't get opened a second before you want it to. That way you could make sure the carbon tetrachloride had plenty of time to work. And that line was a classic. 'Don't encourage him.'

"Beautiful. So beautiful I had to throw up when I figured it out."

"You're too sensitive, Matt. Lenny fulfilled every comedian's dream— he left them laughing. He wouldn't have had it any other way."

Every second that went by was making it harder for me to suppress the desire to jump on Shelby and strangle him, gun or no gun.

"Jerry de Loon would have had it some other way," I said. "Jim Bevic, too." Far below, I could see a police car drive out of the park. I wanted to cry.

Shelby's gray eyes softened, and he nodded sadly. "I'm sorry about Jerry. He seemed to be a nice young man. In fact, he was responsible for the shape of my whole plan, in a way. Bevic I had to kill. I had no choice, though I must admit I was a fool to kill him in my own back yard and leave him there."

"Not necessarily," I said. *Goddam you, Mr. M., hurry up!* "Any number of people could have sneaked onto your property. You had no connection with Bevic that anybody knew about. If you tried to move him, you might have left traces of his presence in your car, and that wouldn't have done, would it? You were supposed to be in Arizona at the time, weren't you? And the police labs in this country are pretty thorough. No, once you had killed him, I think leaving him in your pool was probably the smartest thing you could have done."

"I never thought of it that way," he said. "You may be right, at that." He was pleased. I got the impression that he was enjoying our talk quite a bit. It's only natural for a performer to want to sit down and hash things over when the performance is done.

I wasn't enjoying it nearly as much. For one thing, my finale was yet to come, and I didn't have a glimmer of an idea of what it was going to be.

And I wasn't all I had to worry about. As if to remind me of that, Llona put one of her soft, warm hands in mine. I gave it a squeeze that was more reflex than reassurance.

I sighed inwardly, and decided to keep talking. It was our only hope. "You killed Bevic because he got to McHarg, right?"

"You tell me, Matt." He waved the gun, encouraging me. "Let's see just how good you are at figuring things out."

"Okay, correct me if I'm wrong. McHarg was telling the truth—still is. He never got a nickel from Shelby and Green. You took the money out of the joint account, and *kept it.*"

Shelby laughed. "You know, I wasn't going to use the money, at first. I was just going to keep it safe until McHarg took off, as I knew he would. Then I was going to bring it to Lenny and say, 'See, you little sawed-off dope, if I'd listened to you, we'd have lost that money.'

"But the more I thought about it, the more it seemed that Lenny deserved to lose it. God, he was stupid. A great comedian, but stupid.

"And if we did stay together, I could see what the future was going to be like. He was *already* harping about how I'd never been out of New York before I met him, and how he brought me into the business. As though I'd been an orphan in the streets, for God's sake. As though I hadn't been the one who made the act work, and booked us and watched the money.

"And there was always his unspoken attitude that he had *given* me Alice, as a gift."

I thought, privately, that that probably wasn't so far from the truth. Except it seemed that Lenny had given Ken only half of Alice. Witness her flight to Lenny's body last night.

Shelby was still talking. ". . . So I kept the money. I saved it from the garbage—it was mine. We'd made that bet, we split up the act. I just left, and used the money to set myself up in business. I didn't need him nearly as much as he needed me. Time has proved that."

"Uh huh," I nodded. "Now let's talk about the bowling ball trick."

"Wasn't that great?" He seemed very pleased with himself. "It came to me Wednesday afternoon, when Llona was showing us around the building—we dropped in on the room where the kid had been working on the kinescopes. He talked about having a bunch of 'Dr. Wonder' shows from 1952. That was my last season on that show—I formed the act with Lenny that year—so I remembered a lot of the things Wonder had done on the show. Especially the one we did about fire and water."

"I've seen it," I said dryly.

"Well, there you are. I was right to hide those kines. The kid—"

"His name was *Jerry!*" Llona exploded.

Shelby looked at her, surprised. Then he smiled. "Very good, Llona. *Jerry* told me he'd only seen enough of each show to identify it, but he might have gotten to that kine, and studied it fully, at any minute. I couldn't have that. I didn't mean to kill him, though. I guess I hit him too hard. I was really sorry about that."

"Oh," I said. "That makes it all right then."

He looked at me, suddenly the professor-character he played on stage. "I think you're forgetting who has the gun, Matt," he said, not unkindly.

"Ha, ha," I said. "Catch me forgetting someone is holding a gun on me." *Ha, ha, yourself, yutz,* I told myself. The fact was, I *had* almost forgotten about the goddam gun. *Where are the cops?*

Sometimes, when a show is running short, the stage director will give the performer a signal by pulling his hands apart slowly, as though he's pulling taffy. We call it a stretch. It means the performer has to ad lib, and fill in until the end of the show. Even the Anchorman, with his twenty-odd year tenure on the Evening News pales visibly when he gets a stretch sign. I never understood why until now.

I swallowed and stretched some more. "I suppose you set it all up Wednesday night, right? I mean put the bowling ball and the cardboard up on the catwalk. Weren't you afraid someone would find it?"

He shook his head. "People don't look up. Magicians learn that early. If you want to hide something, hang it over the audience's head. Besides, what if someone did find it? They'd only think I'd hid the bowling ball to confuse my reason for taking the kines."

I nodded grimly. Shelby's whole plan had been to confuse everyone; to make us juggle so many questions at once, it would be impossible to tell which was important. Or if any were.

"Those death threats against Lorenzo Baker and Wilma Bascombe were just so much hot air, right? You made those calls."

He nodded smugly.

"It kept the pot stirred up. Besides, Baker gets on my nerves, I thought I'd let the police get on his. As for Miss Bascombe, after what you told me about her I wasn't going to let her wander from Martin's attention for a second."

I sent Wilma a silent apology, then concentrated on opening my mouth again without screaming. I didn't need to. There was a knock on the door, and a voice said, "Room Service."

"Just a minute!" Shelby called. "Okay, Matt, Llona," he said calmly. "My tickets are here. Into the suite. Stay ahead of me, and go where I tell you."

He still had the gun, so we went. I happened to glance through the open doorway of the bedroom on the way. I remember thinking Llona's arrival must have interrupted his packing. Drawers and closets were open, and two half-full suitcases sat back to back on the bed, their lids touching to make a high, pointed arch.

"Stop," Shelby said. "Over there." He pointed with the gun to a place about eight feet to the right side of the doorway. "Stand there until I tell you to move. The gun will be on you, so don't get cute."

I had to move a heavy potted rubber plant in order to stand where he wanted us. Shelby didn't help. Out in the corridor, the bellboy was whistling "Nobody Knows de Trouble I've Seen." It struck me as a breach of decorum for the hotel, but it was a distressingly apt selection.

When Shelby was happy with our positions, he put his right hand (with the gun) in his pocket, and kept it there. He went to open the door. I wondered idly if he'd had the foresight to shift his change to the left side so he could tip the bellboy without letting go of the gun.

I didn't plan to wait and see. I'd just about given up on the police (they never *are* around when you need them, I thought grimly) but still had my hairy little ace in the hole, and this looked like my last chance to play him.

CHAPTER 29

"Missed by that much."

—DON ADAMS, "GET SMART!" NBC

Timing was going to be the most important part. I waited until Shelby lifted his hand to take the blue and white envelope, then yelled, *"Take him, Spot!"*

That wasn't the "kill" command—you can only expect so much from a dog, no matter how smart or well bred he is, and I didn't want Spot destroyed later because he'd butchered some helpless bellboy.

As it turned out, he didn't exactly butcher him, but it was a near thing. The command I'd given the savage Samoyed meant that he should latch on to the arm that had something in it, and as I'd feared, my timing was off. The bellboy still had the envelope when Spot arrived, so it was he who got those sharp teeth wrapped around his forearm.

It put a crimp in Shelby's composure, though, and that was all the edge I had any right to ask.

Shelby jumped away from the door—I'd counted on that. Let a snarling, ferocious beast start sprinting down a hotel corridor at you, and you'll jump back, too, even if you don't have three murders on your conscience.

I'd expected Spot's arrival to change the situation, but I hadn't expected him to do such a thorough job of it. All of a sudden, it was as if Mack Sennett had taken over as the director of an Alfred Hitchcock movie.

Of course, I couldn't appreciate this until later. When your life is at stake, there's hardly any difference at all between slapstick and suspense.

It started with Llona's walking right *toward* Shelby, with a puzzled look on her face, as though she'd decided she'd just take a peek and see what was going on in the hall. So the first thing I had to worry about was her. I danced over to her (expecting a bullet any second), grabbed her around the waist, and slung her to the floor alongside the brown sofa where Shelby's wife had nearly seduced me.

I should have left her alone. Shelby hadn't seemed especially eager to shoot Llona. Now she was out of the way, and I was standing there like the proverbial bug on a plate.

I ran. I circled to my left, his right, and he had to spin to keep me in view. Once, he thought he had a shot at me and fired the gun through the fabric of his pants.

The man who directed "Dr. Wonder," the man who had murdered people so scientifically, should have known better. Not only did he miss (the bullet broke a lamp) but the heat of the bullet set fire to his pants. If I'd had a brain cell or two to spare, it would have occurred to me that that might have happened. A bullet doesn't just leap out of a gun —it's pushed out by some rapidly expanding gases. And the reason they expand so rapidly is that they're extremely hot.

Shelby hadn't wasted any brain cells on the question, either, and he suffered for it now, yelling in pain, and slapping at his smoking trousers with his free hand. I figured it was a good chance to jump him.

Spot, meanwhile, was still worrying the bellboy's arm as if it were his favorite bone, backing up, all the while, to keep his prisoner off balance. Unfortunately, he backed directly through the doorway into the room, and I tripped over him as I made for Shelby.

I sprawled at Ken's feet, which gave him the opportunity to take the gun out of his pocket. His intention, no doubt, was to shoot me with it, but he was foiled when the bellboy, a kid who appeared to have more pimples than IQ points, finally decided he would be smarter to stop fighting Spot, and follow in the direction the dog wanted to take him, instead.

Naturally, since I was lying in his path, he tripped over *me,* landing with both knees on my back, cracking two of my ribs, and knocking the wind out of me.

That was the bad news. The good news was that in falling, his body had chopped down on Shelby's arm, and knocked the gun from his hand.

Llona had greeted each of these developments with a gasp, but she went into action now, running forward to pick up the gun, which neither Ken nor I could reach.

I was cursing at the bellboy to get the hell off me, but he had had a glimpse up Llona's skirt, and was now mesmerized. If I was going to get free, I was going to have to burrow out.

Spot had given the bellboy up as a bad job (and besides, as far as he knew, I had the malefactor in custody), and joined the fun on the floor. He loves to wrestle. He yipped happily, and bounced in and out of the pile.

I finally threw the bellboy away, and started to roll over. I nearly passed out from pain, and all I could see was bad news.

Llona was trying to fire the pistol. She had both hands on it, and her tongue was clamped between her lips in determination. Even if she did manage to fire, it was anybody's guess who or what she'd hit.

"Get rid of it!" I yelled. Shelby was starting to get up; he wanted that gun. He already had his hand out, as though he expected Llona just to *give* it to him. I whipped my legs around, and knocked Ken down again. I was discovering several new constellations every time I moved.

"Get rid of the gun!" I told Llona again. Shelby and I started to grapple.

"You'll regret this, Matt," he grunted.

I thought, Jesus, he talks during a fight, what does he think this is, a movie? But a second later, I told him, "Not as much as you will," and we fought some more. Get thee behind me, reality.

Now the bellboy re-entered the picture. "Gimme the gun, lady," he said. "I'll hold them while you get the police." There was no reason to believe he could make the gun go off any better than Llona could. I was glad to see Llona felt the same way. She ran away from him, out to the balcony. He chased her.

I kept wanting to tell Spot to rip out Shelby's throat, but whenever I tried to, I'd get punched in the stomach or the mouth, and not be able to speak for a moment. On top of everything else, I was irked that I wasn't able to handle the man better. After all, I had twenty years on him. Then I realized that he'd probably gotten *some* sleep in the last couple of days, that all his ribs were intact, and that he hadn't been a victim of poisoning by CCl_4, and I felt a little better, but not much.

To Spot, things were still fun, until he saw the bellboy, his responsibility, take off after Llona. He went after the bellboy again, caught him, and brought him down with a crash so loud that Ken and I both left off fighting for a split second to see what it was. We saw that he'd landed across the marble top of the table and knocked the coffeepot and everything else to the floor.

A combination of conflicting efforts tore Ken and me apart, and he decided to make one last try for that gun. I followed.

Llona saw us coming—saw Ken coming, rather, and she got a look on her face that was impossible to describe. All I could think was, that was the look she'd give her executioner.

She stood frozen for just a second, then glanced at me, turned, and dropped the gun over the balcony. I approved; I just hoped it wouldn't brain anyone below.

That act, the dropping of that pistol over that low, twelfth-floor railing, did something to Ken Shelby. Before he had been a desperate man. Now he was a desperate demon.

"You BITCH!!" he screamed, and sprang at Llona. He grabbed her by the throat, and bent her backward over the railing.

He was still yelling when I got there. I gave him a shot with the edge of my hand to the side of his neck. He felt it, let go of Llona, and spun his weight behind a fist aimed at my face.

I jerked my head back to dodge it, but when I did, I stepped in a puddle of coffee. On the tiles of the patio, it made a surface as slippery as Teflon.

I went down. This time, *I* landed on the poor bellboy, who was out for the count.

"*You*," Shelby said. He seemed to think it was enough of an insult all by itself. "You're going with me, Matt!" He picked up one of the heavy wrought-iron chairs, and raised it high over his head. The plan was obviously to deboss leafy designs into my skull, and the plan would have succeeded, except for teamwork.

There was only one thing I had time to do before he hit me—just as I had with Sammy, I pistoned back my leg and kicked him in the knee. It touched him, but I didn't know if it would have had much effect—he was farther away than Sammy had been.

At the same moment, though, Spot, seeing me in danger, or maybe just getting back into the fun, jumped up, and hit Shelby in the chest with his forepaws.

And while that was happening, Llona sideswiped his head with the empty coffeepot, making a noise like a warped gong.

Individually, probably none of these things would have had any effect. Collectively, they threw Ken Shelby off balance.

If he'd fallen down, he would have been okay, but he used the chair as a kind of crazy counterweight, and pulled himself into a sideways stagger. Even *that* might have been overcome, but his stumbling took him into another puddle of tepid coffee.

There's a movie where Charlie Chaplin tries to roller skate. Maybe you've seen it; if you haven't, you can imagine it. That's what Shelby reminded me of then, moving his feet in little chopping steps, but not getting anywhere, swinging the chair wildly around for balance . . .

He should have dropped the chair, but he just didn't think of it. He was fascinating to watch. It would have been great stuff for the comeback of Shelby and Green, but of course Lenny would have done it onstage. After all, Lenny was supposed to be the clown of the act.

Ken was so fascinating to watch that no one noticed how close he was to the railing until he raised the chair high, spun around, said, "Oh no!" and was pulled over the edge by the weight of the chair.

There was no scream, just a sound like a dropped watermelon a few seconds after Ken had disappeared.

And just like that, it was a tragedy again.

Without a word, I stood up and walked (carefully) with Llona to the balcony rail, and looked at the street below.

One look was enough. A crowd was already gathering down below. Some perceptive person was pointing up at Llona and me. The police would be here soon, at last.

We turned from the rail. Llona was crying, and shaking as though she would loosen her ligaments. "Hold me, Matt," she sobbed. "Hold me tight."

I put my arms around her and held her as tightly as I could. Maybe I could stop myself from shaking, too.

CHAPTER 30

"That's what they'd like you to believe."
—DICK MARTIN, "ROWAN AND MARTIN'S LAUGH-IN," NBC

In certain ways, television is far superior to real life. Take the matter of tying off loose ends. On "Barnaby Jones," they used to get everything explained in the three and a half minutes after the last commercial, and still have time for some scenes from next week.

After Ken Shelby died, the police and I spent something like eight hours getting the package together.

Of course, some things came easily enough, like the reason Martin and Rivetz didn't get there until the fun was almost over. They were cut off in Queens by a water main break.

"That's nice to hear," I had told them. "I was afraid you didn't love me any more."

Another thing that was nice to hear was the relative well-being of the bellboy. His space-cadet uniform was made of a heavy twill that cut the damage from Spot's mighty jaws to just a couple of U-shaped bruises.

After a brief detour to get my ribs taped, the next stop was Lieutenant Martin's office at Headquarters, where everyone, including me, heard for the first time Llona's version of what went on in Shelby's suite before I showed up. She said she'd brought the wallet back, and agreed to stop for a quick cup of coffee. She reminded the lieutenant that she hadn't gotten much sleep last night, either. She told us that Ken started acting strangely when she mentioned my finding the kinescopes, but that she still might have been okay if she hadn't taken a peek into the bedroom and seen he was packing. She'd known that the police had said that no one should leave town, so she got a little more persistent about the question of where Ken intended to go than he was willing to put up with. That's when she went from guest to prisoner.

"He wanted me to be there in case Matt showed up, or the police," she told the lieutenant.

I picked up the story from my arrival. When Mr. M. heard the story of Shelby's sleight of wallet with the million dollars, he got on the phone immediately. He woke Bob Matsuko in Los Angeles (it was still early in the morning out there) and told him he'd solved the Bevic murder for him.

There was a pause, and the lieutenant smiled. "Like *hell* I'm kidding," he told the phone. "We minority groups have to stick together. Here's what happened." He gave Matsuko a quick run-down of the case. I listened to what he said, and decided it was the craziest-sounding stuff I'd ever heard in my life. Then I remembered that I'd been the one who'd figured most of that out, and wondered what that implied about my mind.

Lieutenant Martin was still talking. "Of *course* it would be nice to have proof, even though he's dead. What I think . . . will you listen to me a second? I think you'll have to go over Shelby's books. The IRS will probably be glad to give you a hand, especially if Shelby or Green took that money as a tax loss when the theft was supposed to have occurred. Right. Okay. Somebody'll be here, we never close. Bye."

Mr. M. turned to me with a slightly troubled look on his face. "Now, Matty, I have to call the DA's office and see what they want to do about this."

The lieutenant started to pick up the phone again, but he put it down when Rivetz came in. The little detective had just come from the morgue; I imagined I could still smell death on him.

"Well," Rivetz said, taking his favorite seat on the window sill, "Shelby and Green are together again at last—about five lockers apart."

"What did you find out, Rivetz?" his superior asked.

"Well, at the hotel, that idiot bellhop is confused, but he's backing Cobb's version with everything he does remember. I got him downstairs giving a statement." That was nice of him, I thought.

"What about Shelby?" I asked. "You didn't happen to find a diagram of a killing bottle or something on him, did you?"

"I don't find anything on stiffs. Hate to touch them. What's a killing bottle?"

Aha, I thought. My brain did even stranger things when it was exhausted. It had me saying things before I even knew I knew anything about them.

I grinned. "Ken was very, very consistent, Rivetz. Dr. Wonder once did a show about collecting butterflies—Jerry didn't happen to have a copy of that one in the library, but I remember it. What you're supposed to do when you catch a butterfly is put it in a glass jar with a couple of drops of carbon tetrachloride on a piece of cotton. That way you can kill the butterfly without squashing it. You can add it to your collection without spoiling its looks. Ken turned Lenny's magic cabinet into a giant killing bottle."

"Oh," Rivetz said. "No, we didn't find nothing to make our job any easier. We hardly ever do. Something was missing from his belongings, though."

"What was that?" Mr. M. asked.

"That gold-plated Social Security card he had. You know, the one with his old name on it, whatever that was."

"Kenton F. Schnellenbacher," I said.

"Whatever. It wasn't in his wallet when the meat wagon boys took it off him. Wasn't in his suitcase upstairs. Boys searching the room haven't turned it up yet. Just the envelope with the two tickets to Brazil." Evidently Shelby hadn't thought Costa Rica big enough for both McHarg and him.

I scratched my head. "That's funny . . ."

The lieutenant shrugged it off. "Maybe he got rid of it. Maybe he lost it."

Rivetz had a suggestion. "It might have been jarred out of his wallet when he hit. I've seen some weird things happen with impact, and Shelby's body was busted open pretty good . . ."

"E—excuse me," Llona said in a choked voice, and left the lieutenant's office, trembling.

I looked at Rivetz. "Mr. Sensitivity," I said. He looked out the window and whistled. I turned to the lieutenant. "How about letting her get my dog from the desk sergeant and go home? The poor kid is beat."

Mr. M. thought it over for a second, then said okay. I wished I could go with her, but I knew it would be a while yet before I'd be going anywhere. I was a very key witness.

So I waited.

Lieutenant Martin made that call to the DA, I talked some more. Lieutenant Martin brought in reporters and had me talk to them. Then I was free for a while. That was a relief. I went to the candy machine and bought some Walnettos and a Butter Nut to celebrate.

Reports started to come in. A New York detective called from the Brant to say that cleaning fluid bottles in maids' closets on three floors of the hotel had been mysteriously emptied. So much for where the carbon tet had come from. A report came in from Los Angeles that hinted at big news from the IRS before too long.

I should have been happy, or at least relieved, but I wasn't. That made me mad at myself, and that made me even less happy. To pass the time, I ate my candy and tried to figure out what happened to the Social Security card. I should have skipped it. At first I couldn't come up with an answer; then I thought of one, but it didn't seem to make any sense.

Whoever had made that call from L.A. had a different definition for the phrase "before too long" from the one I had. The sun was sinking slowly toward the Hudson River by the time we heard from them again.

Lieutenant Martin picked up the phone, said "Uh huh" three times, whistled softly, then said "Uh huh" four more times.

He made a steeple of his fingers, reminding me of the lids of the suitcases I'd seen on Shelby's bed.

"Well, Matty," he said to me, "the Revenooers seem to think that embezzlement got to be a habit with your friend Shelby."

"Oh?"

"Guy on the phone tells me Ken has been systematically swindling his various real estate investors for years. If their accountants are undoctoring the books properly, there's evidence he's ripped off something close to two million bucks on this Arizona thing alone."

"He needs to dazzle people," I mumbled.

"What?"

"Never mind. This explains a lot. Can I use your phone?"

"Who are you calling?"

I left his grammar alone. "I'm calling the Wild Bull of the Pompous," I told him.

I dialed. The line clicked, and the phone rang at the Network switchboard. The operator picked it up, and I asked for Mr. Falzet's office. It was about time I earned some of my pay.

I told the president the case was closed, and the Network could breathe again. Falzet, naturally, wanted to know all about it, and I told him I'd report to him as soon as I could.

That turned out to be immediately. "There's no reason you have to hang around, Matty," the lieutenant said. "Go get some sleep." So I told Falzet to wait, I'd be at the Tower right away.

Falzet (or one of his secretaries) accomplished a lot while I was in transit. This wasn't just going to be a report, it was going to be a regular party. The big round table from the Thursday "production meeting" was back, as well as a lot of the cast: Falzet, Wilberforce, Ritafio, Reigels, the rest. There were a couple of additions (Melanie Marliss and Lorenzo Baker), and one notable absentee (Coyle).

The president was civil when he greeted me, practically cordial. From that I deduced that the ratings for "Sight, Sound, & Celebration" had been spectacular.

So I was businesslike. "Let me fill you in about what's been going on," I said, and started the damn story for what I hoped was the last time.

Everyone listened attentively. Ritafio took notes. Wilberforce polished his glasses absently and wore a mean little smile on his thin lips. Falzet cocked his head slightly, as though he were hard of hearing in one ear.

". . . And after Bevic talked to McHarg in Costa Rica," I was saying, when a draft around my ankles told me the door had been opened at the other end of the room, and Falzet said, "Ah, Miss Brockway. You've decided to join us after all?"

Alice was making determined, if wobbly progress across the big room. I turned in my chair to get a look at her. She was wearing a smart black dress, but what I noticed was her face. It had finally happened. Alice Brockway and Matt Cobb were finally the same age. She looked, and I felt, somewhere around a hundred and forty.

"What the hell is she doing here?" I asked quietly, hoping my voice wouldn't carry.

Wilberforce widened his grin three sixteenths of an inch. "I doubt she's collecting for the March of Dimes, Mr. Cobb."

And, of course, he was right. Alice wanted to join the party. "I have a right to be here," she insisted. "I—I have to know what's going on."

Melanie left the table and ran to the other woman. "Oh, Alice," she said. Alice didn't even appear to notice.

I shook my head. "You don't want to hear this now, Alice," I told her. I tried to sound kind.

"Why not?" Porter Reigels demanded. "She's got a right to hear it if any of us have."

Falzet was the boss. "Don't be a fool, Cobb. She's got to know eventually."

He was right. That hurt. And he'd put me down in perfect English, too. "Of course," I said. "Sit down, Alice." She sat between Melanie and Baker, and I had no choice but to go on with the story. I could hardly admit the real reason I hadn't wanted Alice to stay—after all these years, I didn't want to have to break the heart of the first girl I'd ever loved.

I sighed, and started again.

When I finished, the consensus was that I was either (a) crazy; (b) a liar; (c) a crazy liar. Alice Brockway was the only one who didn't start babbling as soon as I was through. Porter Reigels was the loudest, so he was the one I looked at when I said, "Any questions?"

"Yeah," he said. "Yeah. Kenny was a good friend of mine from a long way back, and I don't like thinking of him as a killer."

"It wasn't," I said quietly, "one of my major ambitions, either."

"Sure, *you* say. But you're standing there telling us the reason you know Ken is—was guilty was that he did the bowling ball thing. Wasn't that a heck of a risk? He knew it was coming down. If he's this big criminal mastermind and all, why'd he risk his own life like that?"

Wilberforce cleared his throat as though he intended to make a point. I could tell he knew the hole in Porter's logic. It was tempting to let him take over the dirty work, but this was my show, for better or (primarily) worse, and I'd do it myself. Builds character.

"Not a risk in the world, Porter," I told the Texan and the rest of the group. "The bowling ball couldn't fall until the sprinkler system had soaked the cardboard enough to push Melanie's ball over the rim. And it took the fire to set off the sprinklers.

"Not only did Ken start the fire—all he had to do was plant the crystals in the carpenter's bin beforehand, then put a drop or two of glycerin on it when he and Melanie came offstage before the bow—he could be *absolutely sure* nobody would be in the way when the ball fell."

I got puzzled looks from my audience. "Look," I said, "what would *you* do if you were out in the middle of a big open space, and water started falling from the ceiling? Melanie, you were right there, what *did* you do?"

She opened her mouth and raised her head as the dawn broke in her mind. "I ran for cover."

"Exactly," I said. "Toward the exits. *Away* from the center of the room. Don't you remember when we still believed in some Phantom lurking up on the catwalk? How we said how lucky it was the fire set off the sprinklers, and chased everyone away from the floor of Studio J?

"In fact, if I'm remembering correctly, Ken was the first one to suggest that. Wasn't he, Melanie?"

"You're right," she told me. She looked apologetically at the rest of the gathering. "He's right."

I nodded. "And I swallowed it whole." I gave a little rueful laugh. "Once everybody believed it, Ken ·had it easy. God, Lenny Green summed it all up before it even happened. He told me, 'It's not that the hand is quicker than the eye—it's that the mouth is mightier than the mind.' We saw what he wanted us to see."

Falzet was impatient. "But, Cobb, what I don't understand is why you're inferring to us that Shelby had a definite *reason* for the bowling ball incident."

Under some circumstances, I might have told him he meant "implying," not inferring, but not now. "He had a reason, all right. Ken may have been . . . ah . . . off the rails, but he wasn't naïve. I'm pretty certain the bowling ball incident was designed to neutralize Ollie McHarg. Because of Bevic, Ken knew we'd be looking for McHarg, or the police would, and he knew what Ollie would say if we found him before Ken had accomplished all he wanted to do. McHarg would tell us that he'd *never* taken any money from Shelby and Green.

"But with the ball-dropping, and all the other crazy things going on around here, we discounted McHarg's version as a self-serving attempt to disassociate himself from the murders. Because if we believed Old Uncle Ollie, *Ken* had to have stolen the act's money, and we could hardly believe that, could we? We had a video tape recording of Ken not-quite-being squashed by the Phantom. He was a potential *victim*, not a killer. All part of the same illusion."

Lorenzo Baker, speaking as a practical man and an experienced felon, brought the conversation back to basics. "Why didn't he just tell Bevic to go sell it somewhere else? The statute of limitations had to be up on the con job. He was home free. He didn't have to worry about what Bevic wrote."

"Yes he did," I said. "He wasn't worried about twelve years ago, he was worried about now. Swindles apparently were habit-forming for Ken."

Alice made a noise halfway between a whimper and a moan. "I knew it," she whispered. "I—some of my relatives are land developers; I know how that business is supposed to work. Ken was getting money at the wrong stages of the deal, in the wrong amounts. I didn't want to believe he was doing anything wrong . . ."

Melanie suddenly got all maternal, but Alice wasn't buying any. She pushed Melanie's hands away, and kept her eyes steadily on me. "Matt," she said, "how much did Ken . . . ?"

Maybe I didn't love Alice any more, but I was developing a kind of respect for her. She'd lost her man—both her men—in less than twenty-four hours, but she was facing it. A lot of people would be basket cases by now.

"He got at least a couple million, Alice. From what I heard before I left Headquarters, the guys going over the books figure it's been spent, or put in one of those anonymous banks in Switzerland, or maybe Panama."

"He didn't spend it." Alice sounded very sure.

I shrugged. "It doesn't matter. The important thing is that however much he got, and whatever he did with it, he was running out of ways to hide it. Look how fast the tax people were able to get onto it today.

"*That's* why Ken met with Bevic in secret, and why he panicked and killed him when Bevic revealed what Ollie McHarg had said. Ken couldn't afford *anyone's* being curious about his finances, and if a Pulitzer prizewinner like Bevic were to reveal that Ken Shelby had stolen money from his own partner years ago, people would start to get very curious."

There was silence for a few seconds while that sank in, then Falzet opened his mouth to say to the visitors how sorry the Network was about this tragedy, and if there was anything he could do, or that anyone in the Network could do, don't hesitate to ask, and similar bullshit.

I knew him. Inside, he was shouting with joy, because with all the pre-show publicity, "Sight, Sound, & Celebration" had come just a hair short of "Who shot J.R." in the overnights, to become the second-highest-rated show of all time; and because the Network had come through the scandal squeaky-clean.

He thought.

CHAPTER 31

". . . And you're special, just the way you are!"

—FRED ROGERS, "MISTEROGERS NEIGHBORHOOD," PBS

I went to my office to try to gather my dwindling resources before going home.

My secretary was lurking in ambush for me with a message. "The Brant has called three times, Matt. They want to know who's going to pay for two plane tickets to Brazil they got for one of the Network's guests."

"Jazz," I said, "I don't want to hear about those tickets, understand? Turn the whole thing over to Accounting, and forget you ever heard about it."

I had my feet up on my blotter, and my eyes closed, but sleep was miles away. I'd forgotten how. Instead, I let my mind wander, and as I knew it would, it took me through some rotten neighborhoods. After about ten minutes, I hit the intercom and asked Jazz to make a phone call for me. She asked me if I had the number; I said, "Look under 'United States Government.'"

She made the call, and a very polite female voice told me what I wanted to know. After that, there was nothing left to think about, so I set my jaw and headed home.

In costume and in action, Llona said she was glad to see me. She was wearing one of my shirts over panties, and was magnificent, but just barely decent. We embraced and kissed. The kiss was like a dream—fabulous, but unreal.

Spot was happy to see me, too. He ran around us, wagging his tail and yipping until the kiss was over and I stroked his head for him.

Llona smiled prettily and said, "I see you got through it okay, Matt."

I said, "Mmm," and went to sit in the green leather motorized recliner. I reclined, but left the motor off. "You seem fine, too, Llona."

"Thanks to you," she said. The Samoyed came over and rubbed his body against her bare leg the way a cat does. Llona laughed, and scratched his ear. "And you too, Spot. I wouldn't forget you. Something to drink, Matt?"

"Vanilla milk shake." I needed something sweet. "The stuff is in—"

"I know where it is. I've been prowling the kitchen all afternoon, looking for something to make you when you got home."

"I'll call for pizza," I said. She said it sounded like fun, and padded into the kitchen. Thanks to ridiculously expensive but very efficient electric appliances Rick and Jane Sloan had bought for the kitchen, it only took Llona a few dozen seconds to return with the milk shake. She made a good one. I sat sipping it, not looking at anything, trying not to think of anything.

Llona perched on the arm of my chair and started playing with my hair. "Penny for your thoughts?" she asked.

"Horace Walpole," I said.

"What?"

"Horace Walpole. Eighteenth-century British writer of gothic horror stories."

"What about him?"

"He said something profound once. At least once. I haven't read much of his stuff."

"And you have to be fair to the fellow, don't you?" She was teasing me, but she was right. "What did he say, Matt?"

"He said, *'This world is a comedy to those who think, and a tragedy to those who feel.'* "

She nodded and worked her mouth, as though she were tasting it. "That *is* profound, Matt. I guess the world doesn't change a whole lot, does it?"

"Hardly at all," I agreed.

"What is it to you? A comedy or a tragedy?"

I showed her a crooked grin. "Right now? A comedy. I'm too numb to feel. And people are always funny, if you're cynical enough. Take that crew I spoke to this afternoon. All kinds of questions about why Ken did this particular thing, or that particular thing, but not a word about why he became a thief and a murderer in the first place."

"Well, Matt, after all, they had a terrible shock—".

"Oh, I know that. I was just pointing it out. What do you think was wrong with Ken? Why didn't he just take off for Brazil right after he killed Bevic? His land frauds were going to be discovered sooner or later."

She kissed me on the forehead. "All a natural part of his character, Matt. You've been saying so yourself—Ken as the unseen power, making things happen in secret. He got a kick from it, didn't you tell me Alice said that? How is she by the way?"

"Stiff upper lip. Go on, Llona, I want to hear this."

"I'm a good student, huh?" She smiled and kissed my forehead again. "Well, he just gravitated into things that would help him feel that way."

The girl was very smart. She'd pegged it exactly, as far as I could see. A television director is an unseen power; a godlike, disembodied voice of command. And after Ken had been one of those, he'd become the hidden key to a magic act both on and off stage. From there, he'd found how nice it was to make money disappear with a few strokes of red or black ink. And from there, he'd tied it all together—protecting his frauds by using his experience and knowledge to commit a stage-magic murder.

"And not only that," Llona went on. "Ken was as big a ham as Lenny was, in his way. And he had a grudge against poor Lenny. And he was crazy. Just killing Jim and running away wouldn't have been . . . have been *artistic* enough for him. He'd have wanted to do something, well, spectacular for his finish."

Yeah, I thought crudely, *he was a real smash.*

I looked up at Llona. She was smiling; her eyes were bright. She looked as happy as I had ever seen her. I pulled her down to me and kissed her, hard, and for a long time, because I knew it was going to be the last time.

When our lips parted, I said, "Now let's talk about you, Llona."

She was shocked, or puzzled, I couldn't say which. "Me? What about me?"

I made a disgusted noise, and stood up. Llona was thrown off balance when the recliner straightened, and fell onto the seat of the chair.

"I didn't do this on purpose, you know," I told her, just for the record. "I'm willing to swear that only 20 per cent or less of my life happens on purpose. I didn't fall for you on purpose."

She sat up in a more dignified position, brushed her bangs out of her eyes. "Matt . . ."

"Tell me about the tickets, Llona."

"Tickets?"

"The airline tickets. The ones the bellboy brought."

"What about them?"

"Do you notice you're starting to say that a lot?" She was good with her face. I could almost believe she was afraid I was cracking up. "Never mind," I told her. "*Two* tickets, Llona. *Two* of them. That doesn't jibe with what he told us about his plan, does it? He said he'd keep us with him until he boarded the plane, right? What did he need another ticket for? He wasn't planning to travel with a bass fiddle or anything."

"I . . . he . . . Matt, you're exhausted, you're not yourself. You should go lie down . . ."

She was right. Fatigue had brought with it a kind of counterfeit peace, a strange detachment, as though the real Matt Cobb were somewhere else watching, and Llona and I were just two more talking shadows on the tube.

"Why two tickets, Llona?" I said. I sat on the couch, across from her, and looked into her eyes.

The eyes said she was humoring me. "He was lying to us, Matt, that's all. He wasn't going to leave us at the airport, he was going to take one of us along as a hostage. That way the one of us he left behind couldn't tell the authorities."

I nodded. "That's a possibility," I conceded. "It has some pretty big flaws, but it's one possibility."

"What do you mean, Matt?" All the concern in her face was tender concern, concern for me.

"You know how tight security is at Kennedy, at all the New York airports. There was no way he was going to get that gun on the plane. And it would have been pretty difficult for him to hold one of us hostage without a gun, wouldn't it?

"See if this doesn't make more sense. Shelby kills me, and the gun and I *both* wind up in the trunk of a rented car in the airport parking lot, and he flies off to Brazil arm in arm with you. Then he doesn't have to worry a *damn* about the one left behind's calling the authorities. A much smarter plan. Worthy of the Phantom of the Network, wouldn't you say?"

Llona was close to tears. "Matt, please, don't hurt me like this, how can you even *think*—"

"Because I notice things," I told her. "It's my curse. I don't always have time to think, because I'm busy being afraid for my life, or maybe I'm even thinking about something important. But I always notice. I can't help it."

"But to think I'd want to help someone *kill* you!"

"Oh, *I* wasn't the one that was supposed to be killed, necessarily. It was better for you if I neutralized Ken—caught him or killed him. You showed your preference when you dropped the gun off the balcony.

"But Shelby wanted me dead, and *he* thought you agreed with him. I wondered why he acted so strangely. Like when he congratulated you when you threw in that touching piece of business about Jerry de Loon. Very clever, Llona. Brilliant, in fact. Ken thought you were stringing me along for him, while all the time, you were stringing him along for *you.* I thought you were a spunky damsel in distress, and he was sure you were his dedicated accomplice. Smooth work. You were even smarter than Ken. You manipulated the manipulator."

She lowered her eyes and looked at her lap. "I thought you . . . felt something for me, Matt."

"Don't, Llona," I warned. "You *know* what I feel for you, goddammit. You left that note. You knew what was on the kines, so you calmly walked across the street and bet my life on a showdown with Shelby. *You* couldn't lose however it turned out.

"You know, even while the fight was going on, I wondered why Shelby always acted as though he expected you to give him the gun; why he didn't shoot you when you were wide open at point blank range. Why he ignored me and went for you when you dropped the gun over the railing. Why did you do that, Llona? Did you figure I'd be easier for you to handle than he would?"

"It's not true, Matt, none of it is true, I swear." She was out of the chair, hands spread, pleading.

"Enough lies, Llona, all right? Hell, even the suitcases call you a liar. Did you see the suitcases? Back to back on the bed, both open, lids forming a pointed arch? Did you ever *pack* two suitcases at once? The only reason to do it is to sort things as you take them out of the drawer, maybe heavy fabrics in one bag, light in the other, or whatever.

"But if that's what you're doing, putting the bags on the bed back to back is just *stupid*—you'd have to walk around the whole bed every time you wanted to put something in the far bag. It makes a whole lot more sense to put both bags side by side.

"But there's one way back-to-back bags make sense—when *two* people are packing. Both those suitcases had clothes in them, Llona. You lied to Lieutenant Martin when you said you came in and found Shelby packing. He started packing when you got there, *and you helped him!*"

"*No!*" Llona blurted. There was real fear in her face now.

"No?" I said it as coldly as I could.

"*Yes!*" she said. "I did help him, but not at first! I mean, I found him packing, and after he pulled his gun, he—he had to hold it on me, so he made me take over!" Her voice carried an undertone of "How can people be so *dense?*"

It didn't work; she was slipping. "Right. He made you take over the job, so you started in on a new suitcase. Sorry. Besides, why wasn't any of this in your story to the lieutenant?"

No answer. Instead, she caught my eyes, and put an infinity of pain in hers. "Matt, Matt, what *made* you like this?"

I found it amusing, in a sick sort of way, that I had legitimate answers to all her rhetorical questions.

"Rivetz couldn't find a Social Security card," I told her. "And it bothered me. He thought it might have been jarred out of Ken's wallet when he splattered, but that seemed pretty unlikely. I had time to kill, so I thought about it.

"The card was in the wallet when I put it in my office. It wasn't in the wallet when they took it from Ken's body in the morgue. Who had the wallet in the meantime? You. Only you.

"That struck me as odd. I didn't believe it for a second, but I still had time to kill, so I speculated on why you might want that Social Security card. I thought of what I knew about the card. It was in the name of 'Kenton F. Schnellenbacher.' Ken told us he kept the replica in memory of his tough life before he changed his name. The number was"—I closed my eyes to think—"446-59-0200; that's close, if it isn't it.

"And then *that* struck me as odd. Because if what I knew about Social Security was right, the payments you get when you retire are based on the total amount you paid in during your working life. In that case, they wouldn't give you a new number when you change your name, they'd just adjust your current records to reflect the new name.

"I called Social Security a little while ago, and they told me I was right. And they told me something else I'd wondered about.

"Social Security numbers are assigned *geographically*. For instance, everyone in my family has a number that starts with zero. Everyone, in fact, who has *ever* gotten a number on a card issued by the New York office has had a number that begins with a zero, or with a one. Period.

"Now, a big part of the Legend of Shelby and Green is the fact that Ken had never traveled from the metropolitan area until he teamed up with Lenny Green. Yet the card he said he carried as a keepsake, the card he said he was issued when he was very young, begins *four-four-six*.

"*Four-four-six,* Llona. That comes under the range of numbers issued by the *Kansas City* Social Security office. And *that* means either Ken got lost on his way to the Federal Building downtown years ago, or *that card is a fake.*"

Llona was back in the chair, curled up. Her lovely legs dangled over the side, and her hands covered her face.

"It's not going to change because you're not looking at me," I informed her. She shook her head, but still wouldn't give me her eyes.

I couldn't think of anything to do but go on. Sometimes telling the truth is like draining a sore. "The next thing I had to do was figure out a reason for Ken to have a faked Social Security card. Lieutenant Martin gave me the answer as a gift when he passed on the information about the phone call from the Coast. Ken's embezzlement, and how the IRS thought the money was probably in a Swiss or Panamanian bank.

"The banks in Switzerland and Panama have one thing in common with Social Security cards—numbers. If—and it was still 'if' at the time —you *had* taken the card, or if Shelby had given it to you, you just might have had the key to his box of stolen goodies.

"I told myself I was an idiot, and tried to forget it. But all afternoon, all these other things came infiltrating my brain like the V.C. used to infiltrate Saigon. And they were about just as welcome. But they were there. Maybe Ken didn't trust his memory. Maybe he needed someone to travel for him while he stayed in a safe country.

"Where's that card, Llona?"

She took her hands away from her face. Her expression was very cold. She looked as disgusted with me as I was with her, which seemed a little hard to believe.

"No one will ever find it," she said defiantly. "I kept bending it until it broke, and I did it over and over until it was just pieces, and I threw each piece down a different sewer."

"You trust your memory, huh?"

"Yes, I do," she said.

"Yeah, you have a lot of confidence in yourself. You proved that this morning." I walked over to my own window, to my own view of the park. With my back to Llona I said, "When did you do these things, Llona? When did you find out about Shelby? When did you come to an understanding with him?"

No answer.

"Want me to guess? All right, I'll guess. You found out Saturday morning, when we made that sentimental journey to your home town. Jim Bevic *did* write a letter to his brother, didn't he? You found it and read it when you went to Alex's house, and found out all about Ollie McHarg's story and the missing money. Maybe there was more than that. Maybe Jim had dug up some evidence about Ken's shady land deals. Maybe Jim told Alex he had an appointment to meet secretly with Shelby at Shelby's place.

"I like that last one. That would have dumped it right in your lap. Not only would it have saved you the trouble of figuring anything out, it would have been evidence you could control Shelby with. Was that it, Llona?"

I tried to read Llona's face as she played with her lovely dark hair. She may have been thinking of killing me, but it didn't show.

"I like to think you worried about it," I told Llona. "Saturday night, with all your crying, and whimpering in your sleep, and the way you clung to me after we made love; I like to think your conscience didn't die without a struggle. I like to think that it at least *occurred* to you that that letter was evidence that would lead to more evidence that would have let us put Shelby away.

"And by God, I hope you have some appreciation of the fact that if you *had* given me that letter, instead of what?—hiding it? destroying it? —Lenny Green would still be alive."

"I wanted to tell you. Lots of times." Llona was still looking off into space. "Saturday. Sunday evening in your office."

"But your better judgment won out." I picked up what was left of my milk shake and finished it with a loud slurp.

"I didn't know he was going to kill Lenny!" Llona was intense, earnest. "You have to *believe* that, Matt. I didn't speak to Ken about—about the letter until late Sunday morning, when you were busy with Wilma Bascombe."

"So there was a letter."

She closed her eyes. "I *knew* you would be like this." She sounded impatient. "Yes, there was a letter, just like you said. But Ken told me it was *over*—that the bowling ball trick was the end of it. I didn't even know how he worked that."

"To hell with the bowling ball trick!" I snapped. "What fascinates me is the fact that Ken went ahead and killed Lenny, and you *still* didn't say anything. He must have had a lot of faith in you. Or did he just know that if you talked, he'd turn you up for your little blackmailing escapade? He was a remarkable judge of character. But it's funny how it was really Lenny who caught him. Lenny stole the wallet. Ken should have seen something like that coming."

Llona met my eyes for the first time in a long time. She wasn't crying, but her eyes were shiny and wet. "I did it for you, you know."

Every compartment of my mind had a response to that, and they raced for my throat to find expression. Incredulity won.

"You *what?*" I squeaked.

"I did it for us."

I exploded. "*Four men are dead, Llona!* Four human beings! And two of them died because of *you!*

"There is nothing, Woman, *nothing* you could do for me that could make me wink at a pile of corpses. Have I made myself clear?"

Llona whispered, "Five million dollars, Matt. Maybe. At least two million. Jim Bevic said in the letter he thought it might be seven, or eight. In a numbered account in . . . somewhere."

I had the number. Llona didn't want to make it too easy to find the bank. I had to smile.

Llona read the smile to be something it wasn't. She stood up and approached me; put a hand on my chest.

"Come with me, Matt. Really, that's why I did everything, really. So we could be free. Don't you know why we came together so quickly? Because we both hate our lives like this, doing trivial things, having to cater to stupid people. We were cut out for something better."

As deeply as I looked into her eyes, I couldn't penetrate to a place where she didn't seem to mean it. I shook my head. "Even if I did hate my life, I'd still want to be able to like *me*. I won't live off a corpse. No matter what the wages."

"Oh, Matt," she said, as if trying to make a point to a mentally impaired child, "we can't change the past. Nothing we do can bring any one of them back."

That's a wonderful rationale. The Llonas of the world will tell you it's futile to talk about any wrong they may have done, any harm they may have caused, because "You can't change the past." The fallacy of that is, when they did what they did, *it wasn't the past.* And an evil in the past won't stay there—it has a way of trickling down into the present and poisoning the future.

I didn't bother to tell Llona this. I had a feeling she wouldn't even understand it.

"Come with me, Matt," she said again. "We'll be rich. We'll be free." A special light came into her eyes. "We can buy that island, our own island. We'll lie in the sun all day, and make love all night. It will be beautiful. We can be happy."

And looking at her face, I could almost believe she would be. I hated her, pitied her, loved her, and wanted to kill her, all at once.

She rested her head against me. "We deserve it, Matt."

I grabbed her by the shoulders, pulled her off me, and held her at arm's length. My ribs hurt.

"Why?" I snarled. Maybe I would kill her.

She looked scared and bewildered.

"Why do we deserve this stolen money? Does Jerry de Loon deserve to be dead? Does poor little Hildy deserve to bring up her baby alone and broke? Does Wilma Bascombe deserve to have to live in terror her whole life because once she trusted someone who didn't deserve it? Did Jim Bevic's parents deserve to lose their son?

"What's so great about *us,* Llona? Why do you deserve to move into a murder case and exploit it to your own profit? Why do I deserve a share in the loot?"

I'd been shaking her pretty hard. Spot was barking at me, and Llona was screaming. I got hold of myself and let her go. Llona was crying angry tears, and had both hands clutched in her hair.

"Don't do this to me! You can't do this to me! *I love you!* I love you, Matt, *don't hurt me!*"

I was breathing hard and trembling, working diligently to get myself under control. My ribs ached from the exertion. Sometimes I get scared at how close I come to the edge.

When I was in command again, I said. "Love is a trap, Llona. It's a relationship where you can be used and thrown away after."

She stopped crying when she recognized her own words.

"*God damn you,*" she said with a fierce intensity. "*God damn you to hell.* Who do you think you are, to lecture morals to me? Who?" If she loved me a minute ago, she hated me now.

"All my life," she started, then choked on her own emotion and started again. "All my life, I've made my own way, and I promised myself I'd be *free;* and when the chance came, I took it, and *I don't care,* Matt Cobb, who's dead or what your altar-boy code makes you think!

"My God, how could I ever have wanted you at all? I've just realized you *like* it! You like being nothing and having nothing. You live with a borrowed dog in a borrowed house, and you eat by picking over the Network's garbage. And you like it!"

"The top two buttons of my shirt are open. If you're going to wear it, wear it right." She had seemed to want me to say something, and I obliged.

The *non sequitur* made her furious. "What's the matter, little boy? Afraid you'll go to hell for sleeping with me? Afraid I contaminated you?" She tried to button the buttons, but her fingers wouldn't work properly.

She gave up in fury and disgust. "Why don't you just call the police and have them take me away? Jail will be better than this."

I smiled. I didn't want to, but I could feel it taking over my face, and I couldn't stop it. Llona asked what was so funny.

"You were right, you know," I told her, "about my having nothing. And one of the many things I don't have is evidence."

Emotion, animation, and intelligence all drained from her face. She looked idiotic, practically comatose. It took her five seconds to say, "What?"

"I mean, aside from firing you from the Network, there's not a single goddam thing I can do to you, Llona. You destroyed the evidence, and there's no way now to prove it ever existed. You attempted blackmail, but Shelby's the only one who could testify to that, and he's dead. You conspired to help a murderer escape, but we'd need Shelby's testimony for that, too, because all the rest is memories and inferences inside my head, and the courts don't accept that sort of thing.

"So congratulations, Llona, you're free at last. Whatever you do now is up to you."

"You don't have a tape recording of this? You—you haven't been to the police?"

"*No evidence.* An admission isn't enough. That's not to say you couldn't go to the police yourself."

I might never have said that, for all the attention Llona paid to it. "Then all this was just a *joke?* What has all this been about, for God's sake?"

"No joke, Llona," I said seriously. "I just wanted you to know. I have played the sap for you," I said with bitter irony, "and I want you to know I realize the full extent of my stupidity. And even though all I could accomplish by denouncing you would be to make myself and the

Network look stupid, I wanted you to know that in spite of what I felt, what I wanted, and what I hoped, I finally saw the truth."

"What does that mean?"

I wasn't sure what it meant—maybe it meant something I didn't have the words for. But I said, "It means I'm not the only one with eyes. Shelby stole that money from *somebody,* and that somebody might be angry. So you'd better be careful."

Llona looked solemn and nodded.

"And now, I think you'd better get the hell out of here."

"Yes," she said.

"And I don't want to see you again around the Network."

Llona never moved from the living room—she just stripped off my shirt, and dressed, unhurried and unashamed. I watched her in silence because she wanted me to say something or look away. God, she was beautiful.

When she was dressed, she looked as cool and sweet as she ever had. She gave me a look it was impossible to interpret, and said, simply, "Good-bye, Matt."

"Good-bye, Llona." I watched her walk to the door. I felt anger over my powerlessness to stop her, and I felt guilty over a not-quite-crushed desire to go with her, in spite of everything. But I stayed where I was. Virtue triumphant. Hooray for me.

When Llona got to the door, Spot ran to her, panting happily and wagging his tail. He thought we were going for a walk, and kept looking back at me to see what was keeping me.

I said, "Come, Spot," and though the Samoyed was torn, he dutifully scampered back to me.

Llona looked over her shoulder at us, opened her mouth, closed it, and left.

Spot protested when he heard the door close. He cocked his head at me, looking puzzled.

I held up the tennis ball for a game of fetch, but he wasn't in the mood.

"You loved her too, didn't you, Spot?"

"Woof!" he said soulfully.

I laughed. "We sure can pick them, can't we?"

CHAPTER 32

"Like a bolt out of the blue . . ."
—CLIFF EDWARDS "UKULELE IKE," "DISNEYLAND," ABC

A lot of interesting things have happened since Llona walked through that door, the most important from a personal point of view being that I got over it, more or less. She was gone from New York in less than a day. She told Sal Ritafio and the super at her building that she just wasn't interested in the kind of life she had any more. That must be a pretty common feeling—her departure raised barely a ripple.

I kept my mouth firmly shut about the real reason she left, and waited for my ribs to heal.

A lot of the other people involved in the Network's troubles over its fiftieth anniversary have been pretty busy, too. Colonel Coyle got a job at another network, and announced he was beginning work on his autobiography. This caused our own fearless leader to come down with an acute attack of paranoia, and order Special Projects to prevent publication of that book, he didn't care how. We're working on it. We're going to fail, but Falzet doesn't know that yet. I'm looking forward to what the colonel has to say.

I'm looking forward to another book, too. In a couple of months, Austin, Stoddard & Trapp will bring out *Abandoned Empress*, the autobiography of Wilma Bascombe. It'll make a fortune. The grapevine already brings news of movie rights sales.

Alice Brockway will be back in the movies, too. After she got her two men safely buried, she went into hiding somewhere, then emerged after a few weeks to announce that she had been offered a part in Melanie Marliss's new picture.

The movie, by the way, is *not* going to be produced by Lorenzo Baker. Lorenzo and Melanie had a Falling Out in the middle of a concert in the Santa Monica Civic Auditorium. Nobody has said anything about drugs, at least not in public, but Shorty Stack and I have our opinions.

Shorty also tells me ("This is the gospel, Matt, baby,") that not only is Porter Reigels Melanie's new producer and director, but he's soon to be her third husband as well. The Hollywood press drools at the prospect.

Hildy had the baby on Thanksgiving day—Gerald Matthew Millard de Loon. The "Millard" is as close as Hildy could come to "Millie" in a boy's name. Millie Heywood has taken to referring to herself as the kid's grandma, and woe betide anyone so foolish as to bring up such unnecessary topics as biology and genetics. She and I are pulling strings and lobbying to find a job for Hildy when she decides she wants to go to work.

Nothing much new in Special Projects, except Harris and Shirley asked for their vacations to be at the same time, and I'm considering it.

And a few weeks ago, I was visited by a lawyer. He came to my office. His name was Wesley J. Smythe, but what he looked like was Butch Q. McGurk. His face had been blasted from red sandstone, and his body looked like a barrel made of very hard wood. His voice, though, went with the name. It was disconcerting.

He had a proposition for me, but he took his time getting around to it. We sat there for fifteen minutes, with him waffling, and me nodding my head and wondering how he'd managed an appointment.

". . . now, Mr. Cobb," he said, "I have a client . . ."

"Glad to hear it," I said. I tend to forget my manners when I'm bored.

It didn't bother him at all. ". . . who has instructed me to make a proposition to you that is quite irregular."

I sighed. "Irregular propositions are nothing new to this office, Mr. Smythe. Let's hear it. It's only fair to warn you, though, that I have a lot of friends in the police department."

"Heh, heh, heh." His jowls shook with amusement. "It's irregular, but I can find nothing in the law to prohibit it. And this is really personal business, Mr. Cobb.

"You see, my client wishes to establish a trust fund, and for certain reasons, which frankly, my client refuses to explain, you and I are to be the trustees."

"I don't know much about the law, Mr. Smythe, but that doesn't seem irregular to me. Surprising, yes, but not irregular. Who's your client?"

"That is the . . . er . . . that is the irregular part. I am not permitted to say. I *am* to tell you, as I must, that the beneficiary of the trust is Gerald Matthew de Loon, and—"

I had a feeling I knew where the conversation was heading, and I didn't like it. "You left out Millard," I interrupted.

Smythe raised a bushy eyebrow. "Beg pardon?"

"It's Gerald Matthew *Millard* de Loon. Do you want to upset his grandmother?"

"Heh heh. No, of course not. The trust is intended to provide for the needs of the child and his mother—and quite handsomely, if I may say so—until he attains the age of twenty-one, or until he completes his studies."

I was trying to figure out how I was supposed to feel. "You can't tell me anything about your client's identity?"

"I have the strictest instructions on that point. However, I am empowered to give you this."

He handed me a note. Envelope and stationery were both pure white. Written inside with a fountain pen were four lines:

> *It was six million dollars.*
> *The sun shines every day and the water is warm.*
> *No one should have to bring up a child alone and broke.*
> *Don't hate me.*

No signature. I wondered what she had in her mind when she wrote it. A plea for forgiveness? Or was she just rubbing my nose in it?

All I knew was, before I opened that envelope, I wasn't going to be Smythe's co-trustee, but after I read it, I was. Maybe that was what she had in mind.

I told Smythe, and he smiled beneficently, and said I could come to his office to sign the necessary papers at my convenience. Which I did.

I still have that note. Sometimes I take it out and look at it, and I think about my six-million-dollar woman; this other Phantom of the Network; this talking shadow I'd held and kissed but never come close to understanding.

And I try again to decide how I'm supposed to feel.

William L. DeAndrea is the author of three previous mystery novels. His first, *Killed in the Ratings*, won the Edgar Award for the best first novel of 1978 from the Mystery Writers of America; his second, *The Hog Murders*, won the Edgar for best paperback mystery novel in the very next year. He is also the author of *The Lunatic Fringe*, a historical mystery set in 1896, when Theodore Roosevelt was police commissioner of New York City. *Killed in the Act*, the author's first novel for the Crime Club, continues the adventures of Matt Cobb, the trouble-shooting Network vice-president who was introduced in *Killed in the Ratings*. Mr. DeAndrea holds a degree in broadcasting from Syracuse University, and now makes his home in New York City.